HOT SPOT

NOVELS BY MICHAEL CRAFT

Rehearsing

The Mark Manning Series

Flight Dreams
Eye Contact
Body Language
Name Games
Boy Toy
Hot Spot

The Claire Gray Series

Desert Autumn

www.michaelcraft.com

HOT SPOT

Michael Craft

ST. MARTIN'S MINOTAUR
NEW YORK

www.minotaurbooks.com

Library of Congress Cataloging-in-Publication Data

Craft, Michael.
    Hot spot / Michael Craft.—1st ed.
       p.   cm.—(The Mark Manning series)
    ISBN 0-312-28900-6
      1. Manning, Mark (Fictitious character)—Fiction. 2. Politicians—Fiction.   3. Wisconsin—Fiction. 4. Weddings—Fiction. 5. Gay men—Fiction. I. Title.
PS3553.R215 H68 2002
813'.54—dc21

2002017102

First Edition: July 2002

10 9 8 7 6 5 4 3 2 1

*Mon huitième roman,
c'est aussi pour Léon.*

Acknowledgments

The author wishes to thank Philip Burgess and Michael Held for their generous assistance with various plot details. Notes of gratitude are offered to Mitchell Waters, Teresa Theophano, and Keith Kahla for their professionalism and enthusiasm.

Contents

PART ONE

Masters of Spin

NORTHERN NUPTIALS

Candidate for Illinois lieutenant governor to be wed in Dumont

By GLEE SAVAGE

Trends Editor, Dumont Daily Register

Sep. 7, DUMONT WI—Carl Creighton, Democratic candidate for Illinois lieutenant governor, will wed Roxanne Exner, a Chicago attorney, in a private ceremony this afternoon at the home of *Dumont Daily Register* publisher Mark Manning.

The groom, Mr. Creighton, is an Illinois deputy attorney general and running mate of Lowell Sagehorn in the gubernatorial race. The bride, Miss Exner, is a partner in the Chicago law firm Kendall Yoshihara Exner and a graduate of Marquette Law School in Milwaukee. Her mentor there, the Honorable Stanton Uhrig, now a Wisconsin supreme court justice, will preside at this afternoon's ceremony.

Miss Exner is a longtime friend of Mr. Manning, who was a reporter for the *Chicago Journal* before moving to Dumont three years ago. Mr. Manning and his life partner, Dumont architect Neil Waite, will stand as witnesses to the civil ceremony.

Distinguished guests include Gale Exner of Minneapolis, mother of the bride; Lauren Creighton of Denver, daughter of the groom by a previous marriage; Betty Gifford Ashton of Dumont, philanthropic matriarch of a local paper-mill empire; and Blain Gifford of Chicago, Mrs. Ashton's nephew and escort.

Mrs. Ashton happens to be a cousin of Raymond Gifford, the Republican candidate for Illinois governor; her nephew Blain Gifford serves as campaign manager. Chick Butterly, Democratic campaign manager and assistant to Mr. Creighton, will also attend today's nuptials, leading some commentators to label Dumont, Wisconsin, a political hot spot in the closely contested Illinois race.

After the private indoor ceremony, a large reception will be held on the lawn of the Manning-Waite home on Prairie Street. The newlyweds will then depart for a brief Hawaiian honeymoon before returning to Illinois and the campaign for this November's election. ❑

O ur friend Roxanne has never been the sort of woman who dreamed of a big church wedding, one with all the trimmings. Candles, bridesmaids, lacy white veil, thundering organ—she wanted none of that. In fact, her prolonged foot-dragging in deciding to commit to the M-word, even after several years of courtship by a perfect soul mate, qualifies her as one of the wariest brides on record. So it's ironic, almost fitting, that Roxanne's special day—her divine union, her dignified nuptial celebration—unraveled before the eyes of her guests and degenerated into the definitive wedding from hell.

That Saturday, though hectic, began agreeably enough. Roxanne had driven up to Dumont from Chicago on Wednesday; she and Neil, the man in my life, had been friends since college and had now spent the last few days on final preparations for the wedding at the house on Prairie Street. Carl, Roxanne's groom, who was running for lieutenant governor of Illinois, had arrived in town with his campaign manager late Friday night, having spoken at a political fund-raising dinner before heading north on the four-hour drive.

Saturday morning at seven, Carl was still in bed, but Roxanne was wide-awake—looking a bit wired, in fact—when Neil and I returned from an early run in the park and found her sitting in the kitchen with Barb Bilsten, our housekeeper. On the table was a platter of doughnuts and bagels, which the ladies grazed upon, and a wide-open copy of the *Dumont Daily Register*, the newspaper I own and publish.

"We're in luck," said Neil, closing the door behind us. "It's a beautiful day for the reception, but I think it'll get hot." September in central Wisconsin could go either way.

"So long as it doesn't rain," Barb told him, pouring more Diet Coke for herself. Though she was our paid domestic help, she dressed and acted more like family than a maid. That morning, she wore an outfit resembling a glammed-up sweat suit. "You guys ready for coffee?"

I shook my head. "Just water, thanks." Still winded from our run, I stepped to the sink, filled a glass, and drank.

Neil followed. I filled another glass for him and watched as he downed it. At thirty-six, he was the youngest in the room, looking barely a day older than when I'd met him five years earlier. Shirtless and sweating, no one on earth looked better in a pair of nylon running shorts—not to my eyes. Eight years his senior, I still found it amazing that this fascination was mutual.

Setting down the glass, he stepped behind me and massaged a kink from my shoulder, asking Barb, "Is the tent crew coming back before the caterers arrive?"

With one hand, she raised a finger, signaling that she couldn't speak before swallowing a gob of bagel, heavy with cream cheese; with the other hand, she riffled through the pages of a notebook, checking. She nodded. "Tip Top Tent and Awning will finish up before ten; that's when the folks from A Moveable Feast are scheduled to arrive."

"Then," mused Neil, forgoing my shoulder to muss my damp hair, "wedding guests at noon, ceremony at one, reception at two."

"God help me," muttered Roxanne, the first words I'd heard her speak that day. She slumped within her long, silky robe, looking beautiful as ever in spite of her pout and the early hour.

I crossed to the table. "What's the matter—cold feet?" I grabbed an old gray T-shirt that I'd draped over one of the chairs before leaving the house.

She didn't look at me, but thought aloud, "I suppose it's too late to back out . . ."

Slipping the shirt over my head, I agreed, "Very poor form."

"*And*," said Neil, breezing over to the table and sitting next to Roxanne, "very bad press. It wouldn't look good for the would-be lieutenant governor to be dumped by his would-be wife within mere hours of the nuptials. What a loser. Who'd vote for a guy like that?"

Roxanne smirked. "I would never 'dump' Carl. It's just that, well . . . I've always had these . . . commitment issues."

"*Tell* me," I snorted, sitting with the others.

"Now look," said Barb, having listened to this exchange with weary patience (she'd heard it before), "no one's backing out of *anything* today. Everything's set. Besides, Roxanne, you'd be nuts to let go of Carl. If you do"—she laughed, picking up a butter knife and cutting another slab of cream cheese—"I just might snag him myself."

"And I'd want you to have first dibs on him," Roxanne assured Barb. They were an intriguing pair, if *pair* could be used to describe them.

There were ready similarities. Roxanne's thirty-nine years closely trailed Barb's forty-one. Neither had ever married (not just yet, that is); both were assertively independent and decidedly straight. They each knew the meaning of a high-pressure career: Roxanne was a big-gun lawyer, while Barb had been a money manager working in Wall Street securities, a profession she had chucked two years earlier before coming to work for us.

There were differences as well, most obviously Roxanne's Waspish cynicism, compared to Barb's Jewish verve.

Barb gave Roxanne a get-real stare. "He's *made* for you. He's smart, ambitious, moneyed—"

"—and," I interjected, "heterosexual." Roxanne still bore the scars of some previous psychological battles. She'd kicked a self-abusive booze habit five years earlier, largely in response to the emotional fallout she suffered after introducing Neil and me. She'd made the mistake of setting her sights, romantically, on both of us; then Neil and I found love together, leaving her feeling abandoned and spiteful, a perilous combination for a woman prone to binge. She sank so low, she finally resolved to swear off alcohol—her career, her life, depended on her will to change. Through this painful self-renewal, she'd also learned a tough lesson about the pitfalls of her yen for gay men, though this was a taste she was slower to quell.

She turned to me, peeved. "You just can't *wait* to get me out of circulation, can you?"

Neil told her, "Mark and I have already had a good, long talk with Carl about that. He plans to keep you under lock and key."

We'd had no such conversation, of course, and Neil's transparent canard was nothing more than good-natured goading. Still, he'd hit dangerously close to the issue that had been vexing Roxanne for some three years, since she and Carl had first gotten involved, back when they worked at the same law firm. Now here she was, on the morning of her wedding, wondering whether one man's love and commitment was worth the price of her own independence.

For the sake of accuracy, I should point out that I merely suspected Roxanne of harboring these qualms; she didn't voice them. Instead, she leaned over the table, tapping a finger on the newspaper, open to the society column about the wedding. She asked, "How did what's-her-name—Betty Gifford Ashton—get in on this?"

"La-di-da." Barb raised a pinkie.

Neil shrugged. "Sorry, Rox. You told us to 'invite whoever should be there.' Betty's about as A-list as they get. We didn't know about her political connections."

I clarified, "We didn't know she's related to Carl's opponent in the governor's race, but we did know that she goes *way* back with the Uhrig family."

Roxanne nodded. "Ah . . ."

"Who?" asked Barb, looking bewildered.

Roxanne explained, "Stanton Uhrig, Wisconsin supreme court justice. I knew him back at Marquette. He's a brilliant mind—and a wonderful man. When I wrote to ask if he'd consider officiating at the wedding, he consented at once."

I picked up the story: "Justice Uhrig phoned me at the *Register* a few weeks ago, wondering about Betty Gifford Ashton. Both the Uhrigs and the Ashtons are old-money families in Wisconsin. They ran in the same circles, but Stanton hadn't seen Betty in years. He inquired about her health and asked if she'd be coming to the ceremony."

Neil told Roxanne, "The invitation went out that afternoon."

"Little did we know," I added, "that the Gifford side of Betty's family hails from Illinois and that her cousin Raymond Gifford is the Republican candidate for governor there. As luck would have it, she asked her favorite nephew, Blain Gifford, the Republican campaign manager, to escort her to today's ceremony."

"Isn't it wonderful," Roxanne mused dryly, "how weddings have a way of bringing people together?" She closed the newspaper.

The back door cracked open. "Any coffee left?"

"Come on in, Doug."

Sheriff Douglas Pierce strode into the kitchen, shower-fresh from his morning workout, carrying a bagged kringle. He set the large, horseshoe-shaped Danish—a local specialty—on the table, leaning to give Roxanne a kiss. "Well, today's the big day."

She eyed him coyly. "That's one way of putting it."

Slipping off his handsome, tweedy green sport coat and hanging it on the back of a chair, Pierce asked, "How do you manage to look so relaxed and seductive—at the crack of dawn on your wedding day?"

We all laughed. Roxanne, we knew, was anything but relaxed, but her tone had indeed turned seductive. She made no secret of her attraction to Pierce, which he took in stride. Even though our sheriff, at forty-seven, was comfortably aware of his rugged good looks, he was off-limits to Roxanne—not because she was betrothed, but because he was gay.

Barb got up, stepped to the counter, and poured a mug of coffee for Pierce. Returning to the table with it, she insisted that he take her chair. "I shouldn't be sitting around this morning anyway. There's *more* than enough to keep me busy—and I still need to practice."

"Aww," Roxanne cooed, "it's so *sweet* of you, Barb, to play at the ceremony."

"My pleasure"—she faked a clumsy curtsy—"but I'm just one lowly clarinet. Our quintet's been looking forward to today. It's a nice change of pace from orchestra rehearsals." Barb served the Dumont Symphony Orchestra in two capacities, as principal clarinetist (she was astoundingly good, considering that music was her hobby, not her calling) and as treasurer of the orchestra's board of directors.

Neil told her, "I'm glad Whitney suggested having the quintet play at the reception—a classy touch." He was referring to Mr. Whitney Greer, executive director, or manager, of both the community orchestra and the local theater group.

"Whitney's been great," said Barb. "We need amplification for today's outdoor performance, and he volunteered to set everything up for us. He'll roll up his sleeves and be working right alongside the tent crew and the caterers."

"And the florist," added Neil, "and the landscapers, the photographer, bartender, deejay—"

"Lord," said Roxanne, rising, running a hand through her hair, "I had no idea this would turn into such a production—I just wanted to keep it simple. The last thing I meant to do was bring mayhem to your household. We really should have had the wedding in Chicago." She crossed to the refrigerator, took out two big bottles of Perrier, and set them on the counter.

Pierce wrinkled his brow. "Why *aren't* you getting married in Illinois? I mean, you're both *from* there. Why have the wedding in Dumont?"

She might have answered that her reticence to marry had prompted the decision to hold the wedding in faraway Smalltown, Wisconsin—as if the distance would allow her to slip into matrimony unnoticed, without fanfare. Or she could have explained that since this was Carl's second marriage, the first having ended in a messy divorce, they simply wanted a low-key ceremony on neutral turf, nowhere near his ex or the social circle that he had once shared and had abandoned. Or she could have invoked the desire for privacy, since the wedding, planned a year earlier, now fell in the midst of a high-profile political campaign; a Chicago wedding would precipitate a media circus and hyped-up publicity. Or she could have probed deeper, confessing that she'd never quite given up on either Neil or me, that by marrying under our roof, by having us stand as her witnesses, she was, by some stretch of imagination, wedding us as well as Carl.

Instead, Roxanne simply told Pierce, "Because Dumont sort of feels like home now." She took a third bottle of water from the fridge and began loading them in a shopping bag.

Neil told her, "If Carl wins, *Springfield* will come to feel like home—and that's almost four hundred miles south of here."

She shrugged. "Carl would maintain an office in Chicago as well as Springfield. We'd spend time in both cities."

"Sounds hectic," I said. I didn't mention that it would leave little time for her Wisconsin visits, which we'd all come to expect and enjoy.

As if reading my mind, she stopped fussing with her stash of bottled water and gently reassured me, "Let's not worry about crossing that bridge till we have to. It looks as if this election will be one of the tightest on record, so I may end up spending *less* time in Springfield, not more. Meanwhile, we need to focus on getting today behind us."

"Now, now," said Neil, "let's show a little enthusiasm."

She flashed him a plastic smile.

Barb carried her glass and a few dishes to the sink. "I'll be upstairs if anyone needs me. What time is your mother coming over, Roxanne?"

"Not till eleven. She insisted on helping me dress, but it's no big deal."

Neil shook his head. "But it *is* a big deal. Gale wants to be a part of it."

"I meant," said Roxanne, crossing her arms, "the *dress* is no big deal. It doesn't quite qualify as a gown with a train—it's not even white."

Barb approved. "Such brutal honesty—I admire that." She turned to Neil with a nod—so there—then left the kitchen, heading for the front hall.

Pierce broke into laughter. All heads turned to him. "Oops," he mumbled, then lifted his coffee mug to cover his grin.

I told Roxanne, "Sorry I had to miss dinner with your mother last night, but when there's a last-minute crisis at the paper—"

"It's *not* a problem," she said with a flick of her hand. "I don't expect my friends to put their world on hold just because the kinfolk are gathering to witness my ritual yoking."

"Stop that," said Neil. "Your mom is happy for you."

Under her breath, Roxanne rejoined, "Exactly. Too happy."

Roxanne's mother, Gale Exner, had arrived from Minneapolis the previous evening. Neil knew her from his college days with Roxanne, but I had yet to meet her. I knew little of Roxanne's family: she had no siblings, her father had died some years ago, and her mother, according to Neil, was "a spitfire." Like mother, like daughter, apparently.

"Morning, Thad!" said Pierce with a broad smile, looking up from his coffee.

"Hi, Sheriff. Hi, Roxanne—today's the big day."

"So I've heard." Though Roxanne delivered the comment dryly, she punctuated it with a wink, lucently charmed by the kid.

Who wouldn't be? At eighteen, Thad was now a man—a young man in his prime, gracious and self-assured. My nephew (more precisely, my second cousin) had grown into a happy, intelligent, well-adjusted human being, which came as something of a surprise to me. I'd had my doubts.

Less than three years earlier, when I'd first moved to Dumont, Thad Quatrain was orphaned asudden and was left in my care. He was then at an awkward and rebellious stage of adolescence—homophobic too—so the prospects of his adapting to life with Neil and me, his "two dads," seemed chancy at best. Somehow, though, we managed to pull together, the three of us. Neil got him interested in school theater, which gave him a sense of direction and drive. And now, with his high school days recently ended, he was preparing to fly the nest—for California—to begin college, where he would study theater with the illustrious Claire Gray. He would leave on Thursday, five days from now. For months, his impending departure had weighed far more heavily upon me than the minutiae and hoo-ha of Roxanne's nuptials—to each his own priorities.

Padding barefoot into the kitchen that morning, Thad wore an oversize T-shirt and a pair of baggy flannel shorts. Stepping up behind Neil's chair, he gave his "other dad" a shoulder hug.

Neil looked up at him. "You're up kind of early, aren't you?" When not in school, Thad could easily sleep past noon.

He explained, with a tone of understatement, "I still have a few boxes to pack." We were sending most of his things out West ahead of him. "Morning, Mark"—he moved around the table and gave me a quick hug from behind.

I patted his hand on my shoulder. "You could at least *pretend* you're sorry to be leaving. It's called 'acting.' "

He didn't answer; we both knew only too well that his emotions were mixed. Cuffing the side of my head, he paused, fingering my sweat-damp hair. "God, Mark, you could use a shower."

I laughed. "You're right."

Neil slid his chair back and stood. Ominously, he reminded everyone, "Less than five hours." Leaning toward Roxanne, he stage-whispered, "Wedding bells."

She groaned. Then she hefted the shopping bag and stepped to the back door. "I'd better get that bar stocked with something I *can* drink. Otherwise, I just might be tempted . . ." Without finishing the thought, she stepped outdoors in her slinky silk bathrobe.

The house on Prairie Street had been built by my uncle Edwin Quatrain, Thad's grandfather, some fifty years prior. The architect was a student of Frank Lloyd Wright's from Taliesin, the mastermind's school in Spring Green, Wisconsin. The three-story structure, brick and bold, foursquare and masculine, was a textbook example of the earlier Prairie School style, with high rows of leaded, horizontal windows, a shallow roof that appeared flat from the street, and deep, overhanging eaves. A single feature of the design, however, set the Quatrain home apart from others within its stylistic idiom. A huge half-round window, or lunette, topped the facade, peeking out from under the roof like a droopy eye. This idiosyncracy, which made the house more appealing, not less, to many architecture buffs, was the exterior manifestation of an interior oddity that had captivated my imagination since an early childhood visit to Dumont.

Upstairs, on the third floor, a wonderful, lofty studio space, or great room—a glorified attic—stretched the entire width of the house and most of its depth. Overhead, from the vaulted ceiling, hung an iron chandelier. At the back of the room, a brick wall was pierced by a massive fireplace that a boy could stand in. The front wall was dominated by the wide, arched window, affording a panoramic view that skimmed over a nearby park and reached beyond the roofs and treetops of the town to distant, hazy countryside.

On that Saturday in early September, the view from the semicircular window was largely green. But any week, any night, the season's first frost might sag from the clear but black skies, blushing the trees with crimson, spangling them with gold.

It wasn't sweater weather yet though. In fact, as Neil had predicted at breakfast, the day had turned hot. Arriving guests were relieved to discover that the grand old home had been invisibly modernized with central air-conditioning. The forty or so who gathered in the towery, festooned great room would be able to witness Roxanne's yoking in dry, cool comfort; the hundred others who would later join us for the lawn party would need to find their comfort at the bar.

"Mark *Manning?*" asked a woman in pink, rushing toward me ahead of Neil. "At long last—such a pleasure." She thrust her hand forward to shake mine, then leaned in close to kiss my cheek. "Roxanne has spoken of you for *years.*"

"Mark," said Neil, moving up to us through the mingling crowd, "I'd like you to meet Gale Exner, Rox's mother."

The introduction merely confirmed my hunch; it was easy to discern Roxanne's features in the woman. Though doubtless in her early sixties, Gale looked more like fifty, and indeed, she could have passed for a pretty and sophisticated older sister of Roxanne's. She had spoken merely a dozen words or so, but in them I could detect Roxanne's cadences and, just below the surface, that nascent note of irony that always colored Roxanne's speech. I gave her a hug. "It's a pleasure, Gale. And how nice to meet you under such happy circumstances."

Grinning, she rolled her eyes—I'd seen Roxanne make the same wordless comment a thousand times.

Picking up on this, Neil asked her, "You're *happy* for Rox, aren't you?"

Gale smiled. "Of course, honey." She tugged Neil's shoulder and mine, huddling close to us. She whispered, "It's just so long overdue!"

Neil shrugged, assuring Gale, "Roxanne took her time, that's all. She's highly discriminating—and deserves to be. Carl was well worth the wait."

Gale breathed a contented sigh. "And it was *so* good of you two to host the ceremony here in your home. Everything's *gorgeous*, Neil. I assume you had a hand in the decorating."

She assumed correctly. Neil had draped some hundred yards of white theatrical gauze from the chandelier to the corners of the room, where it spilled down the walls and puddled opulently on the floor. At the front of the room, he'd constructed a pair of fantasy trees flanking the arched window, creating a sort of arbor where the yoking proper would occur. The trees were hung with crystal prisms and woven with full-blown roses in a palette of pastels, along with fragrant, white Casablanca lilies and massive, pink ginger stalks. The middle of the room had been cleared of its furniture, replaced by rows of white, wooden caterer's chairs, divided by a center aisle that would allow Roxanne's grand entrance.

"Yup," I answered for Neil, "he's the one with the eye."

Brushing aside this flattery, he tapped his brow, telling Gale, "If my eye can be trusted, your suit is Vera Wang. It's stunning, Gale. And coral is definitely *your* color."

I laughed lamely. "I thought it was pink."

Gale patted my arm. "Roxanne says it's red—as if I'd wear a red dress to my own daughter's wedding." Harrumph. Then she eyed Neil approvingly. "If *my* eye can be trusted, we're wearing Armani this afternoon."

He was indeed—an elegant new Armani suit, slate gray. Big, clunky black shoes, Prada. By far the more fashion-forward of us two, Neil had set the style for our ritual march down the aisle with Roxanne. Though my clothes mimicked his, they lacked the Italian pedigree.

As we pattered on in this vein, guests continued to arrive in the great room, greeted by the gracious strains of Barb's woodwind quintet. She played the first-clarinet part, carrying the melody of something lively and lovely from the eighteenth century, probably Mozart, possibly Haydn.

"There she is—the mother of the bride." Carl Creighton broke through the little crowd with Justice Uhrig in tow (I'd yet to meet the judge in person, only by phone, but his pleated, black robe was a no-brainer).

Turning at the sound of Carl's voice, Gale rejoined, "There he is— the candidate."

"Not *today*." He raised a finger in amiable admonition. "Today, my only role is that of the groom." As an afterthought, he added, "And of course, your future son-in-law."

"*Please*, Carl—let's not go there!" Her low chortle sounded more like a grunt.

I could understand her reluctance to be cast in any role maternal to the groom. Gale looked younger than her sixty-some years; Carl on the other hand, was twelve years Roxanne's senior, fifty-one, and due to his distinguished crop of prematurely white hair, he looked older still. The net effect was that Gale and Carl looked nothing like mother and son, by marriage or otherwise. In fact, they could have passed as a nicely matched couple.

They continued to exchange playful comments, both in a festive mood. While I noted that Gale's words found their humor in subtle, benign sarcasm (like mother, like daughter), Carl's words conveyed only genuine happiness. Three years earlier, after his divorce, when he'd stunned Roxanne with his suggestion of courtship, he'd already set his sights on this day. Roxanne had needed slow, persistent wooing, which Carl patiently delivered. Now here he was, eager to commit his remaining years to her. He had dressed for the occasion in a dark blue suit of conservative cut—typical of many in his lawyerly wardrobe—forgoing the usual maroon necktie of his political campaign, opting instead for tone-on-tone silvery stripes that echoed the luster of his hair.

Dropping his sportive manner, he cleared his throat and told Gale,

"Allow me to introduce Stanton Uhrig, associate justice of the Wisconsin supreme court." The man in black stepped into our circle of conversation. Carl told him, "This is Gale Exner, Roxanne's mother."

Gale bobbed her head and offered her hand. "Such a pleasure, Mr. Justice Uhrig." I suppressed a grin—she'd consulted Emily Post for this moment.

The judge took her hand. "The honor is entirely mine, Mrs. Exner. I've had only the highest expectations for Roxanne since her law-school days at Marquette. I wish her all the best with Mr. Creighton. I also wish"—he winked—"that you'd simply call me Stanton. This is, after all, a family affair."

Gale blushed, which seemed as unnatural to her as it would to Roxanne. The old guy had charmed the pants off her—so to speak.

I introduced myself and Neil, and we were soon gabbing on a first-name basis.

"Mark?"

"Yes, Stanton."

"I really can't tell you how proud we are here in Wisconsin that you've returned to your native turf."

I reminded him, "I was born in Illinois."

"Yes, yes, yes." He wagged a hand, dismissing this detail. "But your roots are here. Your mother was a Quatrain, and your uncle Edwin founded Quatro Press right here in Dumont. Now, to have you living here, practicing your extraordinary journalistic talents, it's rather like coming full circle, isn't it?"

Was it? I simply said, "Thank you, Stanton."

"It's wonderful, having so many of the state's grand old families represented under the same roof this afternoon—the Quatrains, the Uhrigs, the Ashtons. You did say that Betty Gifford Ashton would be attending today, didn't you? I haven't seen the woman in years."

Neil answered for me, "I spoke to Betty myself after you phoned Mark about her. She was delighted to hear that you'd be in town today; she accepted our invitation on the spot. In fact"—Neil craned his neck, looking through the crowd—"I think she's just arrived."

We all turned in time to see Betty Gifford Ashton enter the room like royalty. The word *matronly* sprang to mind, a succinct description

15

of her appearance and bearing. She was eighty years old, healthy, alert, pleasingly plump, dressed in a blue print dress and squat, off-white, open-toed pumps, greeting everyone she passed with a queenly nod, a cheery smile, and a twinkle in her bright, clear eyes.

She was also matronly in the sense that she was independently wealthy—as widowed matriarch of two industrious families, the Giffords of Illinois and the Ashtons of Wisconsin, she reigned over an empire of investments, securities, and most significantly, a handful of central-Wisconsin paper mills. A benevolent monarch, she had doled these riches to her extended family in the form of trusts, stock transfers, and outright gifts. She was no less generous to the Dumont community at large, where she was always ready to write a fat check for any worthy cause. She lent her name to any board, foundation, or committee that asked, and in fact, I'd gotten to know her at meetings of the Quatro Press board of directors, on which we both served.

The sprightly widow was not the type to stay at home and complain of the ravages of her advancing years. To the contrary, she was a model of positive attitude and loved little more than an invitation to cocktails at the club or, better yet, dinner at the home of friends. Needless to say, her attendance was de rigueur at any gathering of social importance; if Stanton Uhrig had not suggested inviting her to today's festivities, Neil and I would eventually have plucked up the moxie to do so on our own.

"Betty!" called Stanton to the lady as she approached our group. "My God, you look marvelous, Betty. The years have been good to you." He folded his robes around her, giving her a hug.

Without speaking, she stood back from him, holding his hands, taking a moment to give him a slow once-over. With a little laugh, she said, "You're looking very, uh . . . *judicious*, Stanton. The lofty position becomes you."

"Nah"—he fingered his robe's velvet trim, as if he'd never noticed it—"just part of the act."

She laughed again, truly amused, exuding genteel, old-money bonhomie. "Oh!" she said, catching her breath midtitter. "I don't believe any of you have met my sweet nephew. Blain, dear?"

Though her reference to Blain Gifford conjured the image of a prep-school boy in knee pants, the man who appeared from behind her was well into his forties, possibly fifty. He was clean-cut and handsome in a cool, military way, dressed impeccably but without flair. His look and attitude was all business, no nonsense.

"In fact, Mrs. Ashton," said Carl, "your nephew and I are already nodding acquaintances—from opposite sides of the campaign trail." Proving this assertion, Carl and Blain nodded an antiseptic greeting.

"Ah," she said, recalling a paltry detail, twirling a hand, "this . . . governor's business." With a bubble of laughter, she added, "You boys *will* behave today, won't you?"

"Of course, Aunt Betty," said Blain with a suck-up simper; his aunt was a heavy contributor to the Republican campaign, which he managed. Blain then leaned to remind Betty, "I'm forty-nine now. I'll behave."

Carl told them both, "I'm honored that you're here today, and I'm certain Roxanne will be pleased to meet you as well." Smiling and relaxed, he added, "I, for one, am *grateful* for a breather from the politicking." As he said this, Chick Butterly nosed up behind him.

Chick was the Democratic campaign manager, who had driven to Dumont with Carl the night before. Though he was staying at the house with us, he'd arrived late and slept late, so I'd barely met the man.

"Ah, Chick," said Carl, noticing him, "you know Blain Gifford, of course. This is his aunt, Betty Gifford Ashton. And this is Justice Stanton Uhrig, who's known Roxanne since . . ."

The introductions continued, with a copious exchange of handshakes and good wishes. I noticed, though, that Chick appeared to be as discomfited by the presence of the Gifford-Ashton clan as did Blain by his own unlikely presence at the wedding of a political foe. Chick was younger than his Republican counterpart, perhaps forty or so, and his style was less buttoned-down, but otherwise, he and Blain seemed cut from the same cloth. Both were attractive, single, energetic, committed to their candidates, and prone to swagger. Political differences aside, I couldn't help entertaining a fleeting vision (shame on me) of the two rival spinmeisters tangled in bed—they'd make a hot middle-aged couple.

Neil checked his watch, telling me, "We'd better start seating people. If we linger too long, Rox might bolt." He was only half-joking.

"Good idea."

On either side of the aisle, we had reserved the front row of chairs for special guests. One of the aisle seats was for Roxanne's mother; the seat across from her was for Lauren Creighton, Carl's adult daughter from Denver. As I'd yet to meet the woman and wouldn't recognize her, I nabbed Carl and asked, "Has Lauren arrived yet?"

He glanced about the room, then frowned. "Sorry, don't see her."

"We can hold back a few minutes. It would be a shame to start without her."

With a doughy smile, Carl explained, "Lauren has been, well . . . less than supportive of this marriage. She agreed to come, but it wouldn't surprise me if she backed out. Let's proceed; she may still show up."

"Of course she will." My assurance, while obliging, was grounded in nothing more substantial than wishful thinking.

So we saved the aisle seat for Lauren, assigning other prime spaces to Betty Gifford Ashton; her Republican nephew Blain Gifford; his Democratic counterpart, Chick Butterly (on the other side of the aisle, of course); Sheriff Pierce; my nephew Thad, who was looking manly and handsome in a new, tan summer-weight suit bought with an eye toward California; and his theater friend Kwynn Wyman, lovely in lavender. Thad and Kwynn had become best of friends over the last two years, had recently graduated together from Dumont Central High, and would soon be parting ways with the start of college. Roxanne had come to know both kids well during her frequent visits and had asked me to seat them in front.

The other rows were filled with an assortment of friends—Roxanne's, Carl's, and ours—from Chicago and Dumont. There were an inordinate number of lawyers, as both the bride and the groom hailed from that field. Owing to Carl's spot on the Illinois gubernatorial ticket, there was considerable public interest in the ceremony, but members of the press had been neither invited nor allowed to attend. That is, save three—me, of course, and two of my staffers from the *Dumont Daily Register*. We'd have an enviable exclusive on that afternoon's proceedings, and our coverage would doubtless be picked up and spread by wire service.

Glee Savage, our features editor, was there to follow up on that morning's society column. Her able pen would surely depict the gathering in my attic as a veritable who's who of Midwestern gentry. A career journalist in her fifties, Glee was our local fashion-and-culture maven. Relishing this role, she never failed to dress for the part. That afternoon, she wore a smart linen suit of brightest mustard yellow, as well as one of her trademark wide-brimmed hats, this one of tightly woven straw, glossy black. She carried, as usual, an enormous flat purse.

Lucille Haring, the *Register*'s managing editor, was also in attendance. A computer wiz and a crack researcher, she'd followed me to Dumont from the *Chicago Journal*. What she lacked in people skills was more than compensated for by her technical expertise, her analytical mind, and her probing nature. Thirty-something, with short-cropped red hair, Lucy shared not a jot of Glee's fashion sense. At that afternoon's festive assemblage, she wore, as usual, an olive-drab pantsuit that made her look more like a Texaco attendant than a wedding guest. She was at the nuptials to gauge the general scope of the story and to assist me in planning the *Register*'s treatment of it. More to the point, Lucy was there because she'd long carried a torch for Roxanne and now needed to witness, with her own unbelieving eyes, the ritual that would place the object of her unrequited affection forever off-limits.

When Neil and I had seated all of the guests, we nodded to Carl and Stanton. Carl nodded back, and with a smile, he gestured for the judge to accompany him to the front of the room, where they stood before the arched window, between the fanciful, flowered trees, facing the assembled guests.

According to plan, Neil and I then retreated to the back of the room, where we would meet Roxanne. Having lost her father, having bristled at the notion of being "given away" by *anyone*, and having always enjoyed flouting convention, Roxanne had simply asked us, her two closest friends, to escort her down the aisle. As Neil and I neared the back of the room, I glanced amid the wind quintet at

Barb, who glanced back at me while playing; she understood that they should pause at the next convenient break in the music.

The third-story great room had a back hall and stairs—for servants' use in yesteryear—leading down to the bedrooms on the second floor and to the kitchen on the first. Roxanne, primping in a guest room, was to keep an eye on the clock, proceed to the back hall, then wait for us in the stairwell till she heard the music pause.

When the music did pause, the crowd instinctively hushed. Neil and I were at the top of the stairs but didn't see Roxanne. "Pssst," Neil signaled down the stairwell with a look of mild panic.

"If they play 'Ave Maria,' " said Roxanne, appearing at the foot of the stairs, "I'll gag." Hitching her skirt, she climbed the stairs toward us.

"C'mon," said Neil, offering his hand and a smile, "this won't hurt a bit." When Roxanne arrived at the top and stood with us in the service hall (we were out of view of the guests), Neil said, "You're gorgeous, Rox. You've never been more beautiful."

He was right; I was speechless. I knew from earlier countless, and seemingly interminable, discussions that Roxanne's dress was Karl Lagerfeld, Paris couture. It was silk, of course, in a pale, muted color more gray than beige (Neil had called it "oyster"). The skirt dropped to midcalf (Neil had called it "tea-length"). The top was gauzy, giving a tasteful glimpse of Roxanne's cleavage (Neil had called it "a semi-sheer bodice"). She carried a small bouquet of frilly white flowers (Neil had called them "freesia") and a couple of red roses (I knew a rose when I saw one). She wore no hat or any suggestion of a veil, but her hair, I noticed, had been fussed up, looking poufier than usual (I had no idea how Neil might describe it).

The silence was broken by Barb's clarinet as she sounded the opening measure of an elegant, serene little march—French, I thought, probably from a ballet. Another clarinet joined in, with a flute playing above, an oboe below. For a long moment, time stood still. The music swelled with a confectionary quality, an aural counterpart to the sweetness of the blooms that fragranced the raftered great room.

"Gentlemen?" said Roxanne with a grin uncharacteristically sheepish. "Shall we?" Flowers in hand, she offered her elbows. Standing on either side of her, Neil and I touched our fingers to her forearms, and the three of us started down the aisle together, perfectly in step.

The moment we strode into view, the guests, whose heads had turned in anticipation, rose. We were greeted by a chorus of quiet, approving gasps—Roxanne's appearance was that stunning—not only her dress, not only her inherent beauty, but her luminous, palpable happiness. I dare add that Neil and I looked pretty good ourselves and must have framed her nicely. Cameras clicked and flashed as we passed; friends beamed; those on the aisle whispered well-wishes.

As we neared the front of the room, I heard a muffled whimper that crested with a single, gulped sob. Glancing over my shoulder, I expected to see Roxanne's mother contentedly mourning the loss of her baby's maidenhood. Instead, I saw that the emotion behind the sound had been true grief, having erupted not from Gale Exner, but from my normally staid and stoic managing editor, Lucille Haring. With her eyes redder than her coppery brush cut, Lucy swiped a tear from her cheek with the back of her hand.

Standing next to Lucy, Glee Savage snapped open her enormous purse and plucked out a dainty pastel handkerchief, offering it to her butch coworker. Lucy accepted it with hangdog resignation; the discreet honk of her nose was effectively masked by the nasal strains of a brief solo oboe passage.

Glancing over my other shoulder, I noticed that the chair on the aisle was still vacant—Lauren Creighton had failed to appear at her father's wedding.

When Roxanne, Neil, and I arrived at the arched window, facing Carl and the judge, Roxanne paused, plucking one of the red roses from her bouquet—a departure from the plan of the ceremony. She handed the flower to Neil and kissed his cheek near the corner of his mouth. Then she removed the other rose, gave it to me, and kissed me as well. It was a touching gesture; the little crowd ate it up. But I knew that its significance ran far deeper than friendship, ritual, or courtesy. Earlier that morning, I had wondered whether Roxanne imagined wedding us as well as Carl that day, and now I knew she did. Just as Lucy was mourning her loss of Roxanne to Carl, Roxanne was mourning, beneath a convincing show of happiness, her loss of

Neil and me—in her mind, I was sure, we were still "the two that got away."

Carl stepped forward and joined Roxanne, taking her hand, facing Justice Uhrig in the center of the window. Neil and I stepped aside, near each of the flowered trees, to perform our mute duties as witnesses. Barb's clarinet played the final cadence of the graceful little march. Then, for a moment, there was silence.

The judge cleared his throat. "My friends, on this happy occasion I'm honored beyond measure to unite in marriage two good and loving people, members of the bar. The bride I have known some two decades since her law-school days at Marquette, where I was privileged to teach and advise her; she was among the most apt students of jurisprudence I have ever encountered. The groom I have met only today, but his reputation precedes him as a brilliant barrister, an able public servant, and now, a seeker of the second-highest office in Illinois; we all join, of course, in wishing him success and fortuity in his worthy quest." Stanton paused, then peered compunctiously into the front row. "Sorry, Betty."

The assembly joined the wealthy Republican matriarch in laughter.

As Stanton rambled eloquently onward about the dignity of public service and the sanctity of marriage, I pondered the scenario that had led Carl Creighton and Betty Gifford Ashton to meet that day on opposite sides of the political fence. Ironically, they had far more in common than their party labels would suggest.

Not to question Carl's principles or dedication, but he was the definitive country-club liberal if ever there was one. By breeding, education, and lifestyle, he was a blue-blooded member of the social elite. Though fiscally conservative, he had also come to espouse the tenets of enlightened social liberalism, due largely to rubbing elbows with the likes of Neil and me. So Carl felt partly at home on either side of the political spectrum.

Back during his days at the Chicago law firm where he'd worked with Roxanne, he had avoided political issues, feeling that any form of controversy was bad for business, period. This worked to his credit when, three years ago, his appointment to the post of deputy attorney general was based solely on his impeccable credentials. Then, when it became apparent that the next governor's election would be a wide-open race, Carl's name popped up within *both* parties as a possible number two. Roxanne (too feminist to find any use for Republicans) was persuasive, so the Democrats got Carl, but in truth, he could have served on either ticket with equal commitment and aplomb.

At the sound of Carl's voice, I blinked, returning to the moment. He'd begun his prepared vows—which sounded, in truth, a bit like a stump speech. His words, if not quite poetic, were intelligent and sincere; his delivery was that of a well-practiced orator. I'd attended too many self-scripted weddings where both bride and groom had mumbled nervously through their mawkish testimonials. Carl's tribute to Roxanne was far more articulate, arising from his precise, legalistic thinking, polished by his years of experience arguing in court. And here he was once more, standing before a judge—except that now he was not pleading a case, but pledging his troth. He referred to his love of Roxanne, which was based in friendship, and his respect for her, which arose in response to "her whole person."

As his words sank in, I realized that his sentiments were carefully weighed and perfectly expressed—he was telling Roxanne what she needed to hear, and he meant every fervid phrase. Mulling this, I didn't notice his concluding remarks; it was the pause that caught my attention. The next voice I heard was Roxanne's.

With everyone else present, I turned my head toward her, not only to listen, but to watch. Instantly, I could read in her face that any issues she'd harbored with regard to Neil and me had been resolved—the impromptu ritual of the roses had apparently done the trick and exorcised her demons of past longing.

Her features were light and easy. Her eyes focused on Carl without distraction. Her voice was clear, her tone decisive. Her words, like Carl's, were well polished, and though she lacked his vocal strength, her delivery bested Carl's in its flair. Their rhetorical skills were complementary, just as their attraction was mutual.

As she spoke of their enduring friendship—a friendship that not only had survived intimacy, she said, but had been nurtured by it—

I glanced at Neil, standing opposite me at the window. He was beaming a smile at Roxanne, content in her contentment, mentally nudging her toward Carl and commitment.

I didn't notice when Roxanne had stopped speaking. Now it was the judge whose voice commanded attention: "Well, then, repeat after me." And with no particular fanfare, he ran Carl through the formula, then Roxanne. The couple exchanged rings, then kissed. Slam, bam—man and wife. A moment later, Justice Uhrig was introducing Mr. and Mrs. Carl Creighton to the assembled guests, who had risen to their feet, breaking into applause.

Roxanne's mother was sniffling now; Glee Savage shed a tear as well; Lucille Haring bawled like a baby. On the other side of the aisle, Betty Gifford Ashton and her nephew Blain clapped politely, adding their unaffected smiles to the general air of festivity. Neil and I stepped together to share a hug—we'd *done* it, we'd yoked Roxanne— then we shook the judge's hand before wrapping Roxanne and Carl in a group embrace, replete with sloppy kisses.

Justice Uhrig raised his hands, quelling the merriment. "Marriage," he told everyone, "is many things, but in essence, it is a contract. In the eyes of friends and family, Carl and Roxanne have now entered a binding agreement. In the eyes of the state, however"—he chortled—"we still have some paperwork to tend to. Therefore, on behalf of our hosts, Mr. Manning and Mr. Waite, I'd like to invite everyone to enjoy refreshments outdoors in the garden. The bride, groom, witnesses, and I will adjourn briefly to execute the marriage contract itself."

Barb and her quintet launched into a lively transcription of Mendelssohn's wedding march. Then—tailed by Neil, the judge, and me— Roxanne and Carl whisked their way up the aisle.

Saturday, September 7, midday

S o far, so good. The ceremony had gone like clockwork. Nothing hellish had yet materialized to darken Roxanne's nuptials.

Gathered in the den around my uncle Edwin's massive mahogany partners desk, we had just finished with the contracts. Justice Uhrig stood. Stepping away from my usual chair, he unfastened the collar of his robe. "Hope you don't mind," he said with a note of modesty, as if undressing in our presence, "but the day has grown a touch warm for black."

We chorused our permission through lighthearted laughter, urging him to get comfortable for the lawn party. "Let me hang that for you, Stanton," offered Neil, who took the folded robe from the judge's arm, hooked it on a coat tree near the door, and returned with the judge's suit jacket, helping him slip into it.

Carl took Roxanne's hand, telling Neil and me, "Guys, we can't thank you enough for opening your home for us today. Everything has been perfect—low-key, yet elegant and dignified."

"Amen," Roxanne seconded without a trace of sarcasm.

Neil shrugged. "We're just happy to be a part of your special day. I'm sure you'd do the same for us."

"We *would*," said Roxanne. "And someday, if this country's moth-eaten laws ever change, we will." She was referring, of course, to the issue of gay marriage.

The judge chuckled. "Ah, there's the Miss Exner I came to know at Marquette—still that edge of the renegade, I'm delighted to observe."

Slyly, I noted, "The justice has raised an interesting point. Is it now Miss Exner, Mrs. Creighton, or some hyphenated fusion of your own invention?" Both Neil and I had been wondering how Roxanne would handle this, but owing to her fierce independence, we assumed the issue of Carl's "naming rights" was touchy at best, so neither of us had had the nerve to ask about it.

Carl turned to her, grinning—did this signal that they'd had lengthy discussions of this very topic, or did it mean that Carl himself had not yet had the mettle to broach it?

With unexpected easiness, Roxanne told us, "Technically, of course, I *am* Mrs. Carl Creighton. For my law practice, I'll probably continue to use Exner—I've built my own reputation, and why tinker with the name of the firm? Socially, however, and *politically*, I have no problem being known as Carl's wife."

Neil and I glanced at each other, both with arched brows—this was *not* the Roxanne we'd known, loved, and tussled with for years. Had the ring on her finger somehow pinched off the blood to her brain?

Then Neil's confused visage was transformed by a knowing smile. "I get it," he said with a hint of accusation. "Milady Exner-Creighton already has her eye on the governor's mansion." Laughing, he blurted, "Rox has hitched her wagon to a star."

Surely, I thought, Roxanne would counter Neil's gibe with some snappy retort.

Hardly. With no trace of umbrage, she quipped (at least I presumed she was quipping), "Why do you think I persuaded Carl to join the Democratic ticket? Lowell Sagehorn is a widower—he'll need a woman of bearing, intelligence, and style to serve as hostess at puffy, stuffy state functions." For the sake of precision, she added comically, "That would be me, Mrs. Carl Creighton, wife of the lieutenant governor."

Carl squeezed her shoulder, telling us, "And I won't mind sharing her a bit." Still hanging in the air, though, was the unstated but implied extension of Roxanne's thought.

In a sense, she had already leapfrogged through the pecking order of Illinois society, envisioning her future role not as second lady of the land, but as first. What's more, Lowell Sagehorn, if elected at a grandfatherly seventy-two, might very well vacate his office on a catafalque, changing Roxanne's status from de facto to official. The frailty of Sagehorn's years was not mentioned, though, doubtless in deference to Stanton Uhrig, who'd already seen his fair share of birthdays.

Dismissing this topic, Neil said, "Let's join the party. It ought to be in full swing by now."

Our business was done, our guests were waiting, and we all needed a drink (especially Roxanne, though she knew better than to touch anything stronger than Perrier), so without further discussion, we left the den. The most direct route to the festivities was through the kitchen, which led to the backyard, but Neil observed, "There's something sort of lowbrow about a wedding couple making the grand entrance to their reception through the back door. Let's walk around the house." So we left the house through the front hall, stepping from the porch to the side yard to the driveway.

Cars were parked up and down the street, and the happy din of the party could be heard from the rear of the property, beyond the garage. It was a bright September afternoon as the five of us walked along the edge of the driveway—hot too. I'd been outdoors barely a minute, and I already wondered how long I'd need to wait before I could gracefully remove the jacket of my dark gray suit.

Near the garage, a couple of service trucks were parked in the driveway, trapped there by cars that had brought the first of the guests. One of the trucks, a large beat-up van, was from Tip Top Tent and Awning. Another, newer and tidier, was from A Moveable Feast, the catering company. We squeezed past the trucks single file, emerging into the crowded backyard.

"Hey," the call went up as Roxanne and Carl appeared, "they're here!"

Barb and her woodwind quintet cut their stylish cocktail music midmeasure and struck up a regal-sounding fanfare (it would have sounded more authentic and rousing if played by trumpets instead of reeds, but it was stirring nonetheless, due largely to several thousand watts of amplification). The guests, well over a hundred in all, turned to us, greeting the bride and groom with applause, hailing them with best wishes.

Some of the guests had video recorders, which swung toward us to document the moment. Other guests had brought their children, and some of the younger ones rushed forward, swarming around the bride. Roxanne lapped up the tykes' adulation, giving her a benevolent, maternal glow—a Lagerfeld Madonna, as it were.

Roxanne and Carl stood serenely together as the fanfare continued, and the whole gathering seemed in suspended animation (except, of course, for the buzz and skirr of the kids). During this lull, I got a good look at the setting—and I was instantly in awe of Neil's handiwork, the organizational and aesthetic skills he'd channeled in transforming our workaday backyard into a fanciful, matrimonial garden of delights.

The festive scene was dominated by tents—there was a large one for dining, another for dancing, smaller ones concealing preparation areas. Various food stations would soon be laden with thematic buffets keyed to huge ice sculptures that glistened and dripped in the sun. A multitiered wedding cake (the mere sight of it made my teeth tingle) was enshrined in a little tent of its own, which in turn was topped with merry pennants lolling on a languid breeze. At the far corner of the lawn, a long, jaunty canopy covered the bar. In another corner was an ornate little stage, like a Sousa-era bandstand, where the quintet played; the chamber musicians would later be replaced by a lone deejay with his arsenal of recorded dance music. Temporary wiring powered all of this, swooping prettily from tent to tent. Swaying beneath the wires were glass wind chimes and colorful paper lanterns.

It could have been a scene snipped from a movie of some lavish Gatsby-style shindig. Everything was perfect—except for the heat. One of the ice sculptures, which was meant to depict a sea horse, already looked more like a drooping, malformed question mark.

When the fanfare finished, the party's babble swelled again. Guests mingled, waiting their turn to greet Roxanne and Carl as the couple began moving into the crowd. Carl, I noticed, was shaking hands with his campaign manager, Chick Butterly, as Thad moved toward Neil and me with his friend Kwynn. "Hey," said Thad, stepping between us, "you guys looked pretty good up there. You nearly stole the show."

"Thanks," said Neil, playfully cuffing our kid on the chin, "but please, save the compliments for Roxanne—today is hers."

Kwynn stepped into our conversation, looking bubbly. "Everything was so *beautiful*," she gushed. "You certainly know how to throw a party, Mr. Manning."

"That's kind of you, Kwynn, but the credit goes entirely to Neil."

"Aw, shucks," he said with feigned modesty, stubbing the ground with the squarish toe of his big black shoe.

"Mark! Neil! Thank you *so* much for inviting us," said Kwynn's mom, Lisa Wyman, crossing a patch of lawn toward us with her husband, Lee. Though Kwynn had had a front-row seat at the ceremony with Thad, her parents were among the larger number of guests invited only to the reception.

"Delighted you could attend," we told them. "Thanks for coming."

We gabbed a few niceties; then Lee Wyman said through a wistful chuckle, "Well now—not long before we're *all* empty-nesters."

"Oh, Lee," his wife moaned, "don't even bring it up. I can't bear to think about it." Her tone was touched with humorous exaggeration, but her words were genuine. She was suffering every bit as much as Neil and I were. None of us relished the prospect of losing a child to college.

Kwynn said reassuringly, "I don't leave till next week," as if it were years away.

Lisa shook her head in bemused disbelief. Her baby was leaving home.

Lee leaned close to me, saying, "Thanks again, Mark, for all your help—the internship, the recommendation letter to Northwestern. Lisa and I are forever grateful."

I shook his hand. "I'm just glad it all worked out." This was an understatement.

A year earlier, Kwynn and Thad had been equally enthused about theater, and they'd talked about heading off to drama school together. I'd always liked Kwynn, but I was afraid that perhaps she and Thad were getting too involved, too young; I'd preferred that they concentrate more on the future than on each other. This may have bothered Kwynn's parents as well, but their overriding concern had been their daughter's intention to devote a costly college education to a pursuit that, realistically, offered so little promise of ultimate success. Fortunately (at least from the perspective of us four fretting parents), Kwynn had also developed a strong interest in journalism, so when she began her senior year at Central High, I offered her an afternoon internship in the *Register*'s newsroom, which she snapped up. Before long, she was weighing college journalism programs, and my written support of her application to Northwestern University—which had one of the best j-schools around—cinched her acceptance.

Her father told me, "Hard to believe they're starting life on their own."

I nodded silently. There was nothing else to add.

Lisa tugged her husband's sleeve. "The crowd is thinning. Let's go introduce ourselves to the happy couple." And they ambled over to Roxanne and Carl.

Thad asked Kwynn, "Thirsty?"

"Yeah!"

They weren't the only ones—I needed a drink.

"Let's get something," he told her. Then, turning to Neil and me, he offered, "Can we bring you anything?"

"No, thanks," I said. "We'll take care of it." The bartender wouldn't likely give them what I wanted.

As they turned from us and headed toward the bar, Kwynn called to a man who passed them, "Hi, Uncle Dale. Everything looks great."

Having no idea whom she was speaking to, I reminded myself that even though I'd moved to Dumont nearly three years earlier, even though my family had deep roots here, I was still something of an outsider. In smaller towns, it seemed, everyone was related; chances are, every Dumonter at the party that day had some shirttail connection to the others.

The man in question approached us. "Well, Neil," he asked through an apprehensive grin, "what do you think?"

Neil echoed Kwynn's appraisal: "Everything looks great, Dale."

Dale was visibly relieved. Though I didn't know what, exactly, was being appraised, I assumed he'd had something to do with the setup of the party. He wore a faded denim shirt and olive-colored work pants.

As if reading my uncertainty, Neil explained, "This is Dale Turner, owner of Tip Top Tent and Awning. Dale, this is my partner, Mark Manning."

"Hey, Mark, it's a pleasure," said Dale, shaking my hand. His tradesman's calluses felt oddly comforting against my typist's fingers. "I really appreciate the opportunity to work an event like this. It's a cut above the usual."

A rugged sort, he was clearly no stranger to physical work. I judged him to be a few years younger than me, in his mid to late thirties. I also found him handsome (reasonably so) and congenial (surprisingly so—I still found it disarming when a blue-collar type could interact so easily with Neil and me, an openly gay couple—perhaps the times were truly changing). Holding up a video camera that was strapped to one of his palms, he told me, "I'm really proud of this job and want to make sure it's well documented."

"Hope it brings you many more." I added my compliments to Neil's, and as we chatted, I learned that Dale was also an electrician, so he'd been responsible for the wiring as well as the tents. His conversation was animated and enthusiastic, and it was plain to me that he paid attention to detail and took pride in a job well done.

"Pops! *There* you are!"

We turned to see a young woman hailing Carl as she moved through the crowd toward him. "Uh-oh," said Neil under his breath, "must be the wayward daughter of the groom."

Neil and I asked Dale to excuse us, then made our way toward Roxanne and Carl, arriving just as Miss Creighton did.

"God, Pops," she said, engulfing him in a dramatic hug, "I'm *sorry*

I'm so late. I made a wrong turn driving from the airport; then I couldn't find the bed-and-breakfast, and there was no time to freshen up. I'm a fright. I apologize. And to think I missed the main event—"

As she yammered on in this vein, her jaunty manner struck me as far less contrite than her words. I knew she lived in Denver, where, following in her father's footsteps, she'd recently begun practicing law. I reasoned she was twenty-six or so. Despite the apologies for her appearance, she looked just fine—hardly "a fright," as stated. In fact, most men would describe her as beautiful, though in a hard-edged, professional sort of way. She wore her hair in a severe, stylish, expensive cut. She dressed in basic, urban black, which doubtless functioned nicely in taking her from office to courtroom to cocktails. Though her dark attire was certainly proper for today's dressy cele-bration, I couldn't help thinking that it seemed better suited for eve-nings than for an afternoon lawn party under a hot sun.

Carl held his daughter's hands at arm's length. "Let me look at you," he said with a wistful shake of his head. "God, Lauren, you're truly a woman now."

"And a lovely one at that," said Roxanne, standing at Carl's side, still carrying her wedding bouquet.

Lauren glanced at her as if affronted by a stranger—as if Roxanne had thrust herself into a private conversation.

This interplay seemed to escape Carl, who beamed proudly, sighed contentedly, then cleared his throat. "Lauren, honey, it's time. It's my very great honor to introduce you to the woman who's changed my life—*this* is Roxanne Exner."

"Also known as Mrs. Carl Creighton," said Roxanne, extending her hand to her new stepdaughter. "I'm so pleased to meet you, Lau-ren." A benign smile concealed Roxanne's thoughts.

Lauren read this greeting (accurately, I believe) as something of a challenge. She extended her own hand and pumped Roxanne's once, curtly, lawyer to lawyer, as if preparing to do combat before the bench. She thought for a moment before speaking. "You're everything Pops said you were, Roxanne. Too bad Beryl isn't here today—you could compare notes." She was referring to her mother, Carl's ex.

Roxanne grinned prettily. "From everything *I've* heard, Beryl and I don't have much in common." Meow.

Emerging from his blissful fog, Carl could not mistake the ugly tension between the two women. Rescuing the moment, he spun his daughter toward Neil and me, saying, "Lauren, honey, you must meet our two closest friends, Mark Manning and Neil Waite."

She smiled, then shook hands with both of us. "It's a pleasure, gentlemen. I've heard so much about you. I know how much Pops appreciates all you've done, especially . . ." She gabbed onward, sounding sincere, with no hint of subterfuge in her remarks. She seemed, well . . . *nice*. With her back to Roxanne, it was as if the new bride, the wicked stepmother, had vanished, and with her, the implied defamation of Lauren's mother. Lauren was now pleasant as pie; it even crossed my mind that it might be fun to socialize with her sometime, a notion that I instantly dismissed out of loyalty to Roxanne.

Neil small-talked, "Where are you staying?"

Lauren whirled a hand in the air, trying to remember. "It's like this . . . *mansion*. But they call it a bed-and-breakfast."

Neil said, "Must be the Manor House, over on La Salle, near the park. Best in town." With a chuckle, he added, "It was, in fact, a mansion."

"Ah!" said Roxanne, piping in from behind. "That's where my mother is staying. It *is* charming, isn't it?"

Lauren slowly turned. With her lips pinched in a steely smirk, she underwent a sudden transformation to her nail-spitting mode. I held my breath, wondering how she would reply.

"Uh, Mr. Waite?"

We all swung our heads, grateful for the interruption.

A woman with a long white apron, presumably from the catering company, stepped forward. Wiping her hands on the apron, looking frazzled, she told Neil, "Sorry to intrude, but I'm having a bit of trouble with the béarnaise—I think it's the humidity. Perhaps I could try another sauce. Would a bordelaise be all right?" She lifted the apron and dabbed sweat from her forehead.

Neil stepped over and hugged her shoulder. "Not to fret, Alanna. It's no disaster."

She sighed, relieved. "Thank you, Neil. I just hate to throw last-minute changes at you. Everything has been so beautifully planned."

"No one will be the wiser," he assured her. "Whatever you come up with will be wonderful, I'm sure."

"Everything *smells* wonderful," said another voice.

We turned. Chick Butterly, Carl's campaign manager, had entered our circle of conversation. I hadn't been aware of his presence until he spoke, and I was left with the unlikely impression that he had followed the cateress across the lawn. As I pondered this, he said to the woman, "Sorry. I don't believe I've had the pleasure. I'm Chick Butterly."

Neil caught my eye, and I could tell that he shared my confusion. Then he introduced the woman to all of us. "This is Alanna Scott, proprietor of A Moveable Feast, which is catering the reception. She's a rare culinary talent."

As we greeted her in turn, she smiled modestly, itching, I was sure, to return to her makeshift kitchen. Right now, she was dealing with a sauce crisis and had scant interest in socializing with the guests. I judged her to be in her late thirties, hardworking, and (despite her sweaty brow and food-stained uniform) good-looking. She appeared to be as baffled as I was by Chick's interest in her.

"I could *really* use some help," said another voice.

We all turned. The man who had voiced the testy comment wore a uniform embroidered with the logo of A Moveable Feast. He looked every bit as haggard as Alanna and a few years older, about my age. Though his apron bore no food stains, it was drenching wet.

Alanna crossed her arms, asking with strained patience, "What's wrong, Wes?"

He tossed his hands. "It's hotter than hell, and we have about a hundred and fifty thirsty guests—that's what's wrong. I'm good, babe, but not that good."

"I suggested hiring a backup bartender, but *you* wouldn't hear of it."

"I don't *need* some clueless kid behind the bar who wouldn't know his ass from absinthe. I *need* a few servers to run drinks. The guests are three deep at the bar now." Then, salvaging some shred of manners, he told us all, "Sorry, folks. This event sort of . . . got away from us. We're trying to do our best, but we're a little overwhelmed."

Again, Neil played mediator, telling us, "This is Wesley Scott, Alanna's husband and co-owner of A Moveable Feast. He's doing a fine job with the bar."

With an apologetic shrug, Wes explained, "I'm booze, she's food."

Chick watched this exchange without expression. Was he disappointed to learn that Alanna had a husband? Or was he encouraged by their public sparring?

Alanna stepped near her husband. "Okay, look," she said, trying to remain calm, trying to fix the problem and get the job done, "I can make do without some of the kitchen help for a little while. I'll get them trays and fresh aprons and send them out to take drink orders. That should relieve some of the pressure."

"Great," he said, "that's all I ask." Then, trying to inject a lighter note, he added, "Say, you folks look *thirsty.* It's *hot* out here. Come on over to the bar; I'll take care of you."

I was tempted to hightail it to the bar with Wes, but just then I noticed the matronly Betty Gifford Ashton pecking her way through the crowd toward us, so I decided to stay put.

Lauren Creighton looked parboiled in her black dress, so she raised a finger and told Wesley, "Wait up." Then she followed him toward the bar, disappearing into the crowd.

Neil told Alanna, "Thanks for patching that up. Meanwhile, your sauce. I had a thought—is Nancy Sanderson here?" He was referring to the owner of First Avenue Grill, our favorite local restaurant.

Alanna nodded. "She's here. We said hello."

"Are you two on . . . friendly terms?" He must have been wondering if they saw each other as competitors.

"Very friendly," Alanna assured him. "Nancy's been wonderful to me. If it weren't for her, I wouldn't even be in the food business."

Neil grinned. "I know this is your show, Alanna, but if anyone can rescue a finicky béarnaise, it's Nancy. I'll bet she'd be flattered if we asked."

Also grinning, but warily, Alanna wondered, "Can *you* ask her?"

"Let's go." And they disappeared into the crowd.

Chick turned to Carl. "When you have a minute, let's phone Lowell"—he patted a lump in his jacket pocket, presumably a cell phone. "The candidate asked me for frequent updates, and I'm sure he'll want to congratulate his newly married running mate."

Roxanne elbowed her husband, telling him under her breath (but loudly enough for Chick to hear, which was the point), "Don't let the geezer talk you out of our honeymoon. I'm sure he'd much prefer to have you back in Illinois, helping him prep for Wednesday's debate."

Blain Gifford stepped into earshot with his aunt Betty on his arm. With arched brows, he asked, "Campaign strategy on your wedding day? I must say, I admire your sense of focus." The Republican campaign manager chortled.

Carl smiled, patted Roxanne's hand, and was about to respond. But before he could speak, Chick said, "Timing *is* everything, isn't it, Blain?" His tone was congenial enough, but I had no doubt he meant to needle his foe.

"Indeed," Blain told his Democratic counterpart, "especially in politics."

Betty tittered. "Now, boys, *stop* that. The election will wait." She struck her nephew's arm with her fingertips.

"Certainly, Aunt Betty," said Blain.

"Of course, Mrs. Ashton," said Chick with a deferential bob of his head.

Betty had referred to the two politicos as "boys," and at the moment, they were acting like chastised, obedient children. They were grown men, of course, both in their forties, but from the perspective of Betty's advanced years, it was easy to understand how she viewed them as mere pups. What's more, due to their respective positions, these pups were mutual antagonists, and I half expected to catch them exchanging low growls while Betty wasn't looking. This restrained combativeness only heightened the appeal of the fantasy I could not shake—Blain and Chick tussling in bed together.

"I do wish," said Betty, "that someone would introduce me to the bride." Her head wobbled as she smiled expectantly.

Everyone scraped and bowed, muttering apologies for their clumsiness. I took charge. "Betty," I said, taking her arm and inching her forward, "I'd like for you to meet my dear friend, the former Roxanne Exner, now Mrs. Carl Creighton." Turning to Roxanne, I told her, "And this is Betty Gifford Ashton, one of Dumont's leading citizens and a generous benefactor to our community." As a needless afterthought, I explained through a chuckle, "Betty also happens to be a cousin of Raymond Gifford, who'd like to be governor of Illinois."

Roxanne gave me a quick smirk—"I *know* that, Mark." Then she turned her attention to Betty. With a gracious smile, she extended her hand, saying, "It's an honor, Mrs. Ashton. I'm delighted you could share this day with Carl and me."

Betty beamed, wiggling Roxanne's hand. "My, aren't you lovely, dear? It's a pleasure—and such an irony—meeting you after all these years."

I had no idea what Betty meant by her comment, which implied that she knew of Roxanne from the past, a prospect that struck me as highly unlikely.

The comment slid past Chick, who seemed to have things on his mind weightier than the ladies' chitchat. Blain, though, had heard his aunt's words clearly and appeared to be as bewildered by them as I was. Carl's features registered cautious surprise, as if wary of whatever Betty was driving at. As for Roxanne, well, her face fell. Her smile disappeared as though she'd been slapped.

Betty seemed oblivious to the sundry effects of her words. She prattled on, saying, "Do tell us about the honeymoon, dear. Didn't I read in the paper that you're going to Hawaii? It should be lovely this time of year—well, I guess it's *always* lovely there, isn't it?"

"Uh"—Roxanne was at a loss for words—"yes, Hawaii."

As Roxanne was clearly ill at ease, Carl jumped in, telling Betty, "The trip is all too brief, I'm afraid. We're leaving later today, after dinner. We'll spend Sunday through Tuesday on the island, then return to Chicago overnight so I can be present for Wednesday's debate between Lowell Sagehorn and your cousin."

"Ah," said Betty, nodding, following along. Then she frowned.

"That *is* a terribly brief trip, considering the distance, isn't it? I should think you'd stay longer. The debate isn't all *that* important, is it?"

Her nephew Blain coughed, covering a laugh. "Truth is, the Wednesday-night debate is *very* important. In a race this close, that one televised encounter could make all the difference, giving either side the momentum it needs to coast toward November."

"Ah." Betty nodded vacantly, not caring a fig for these details.

Blain continued, talking more to himself than to his aunt, "I still need to tighten up a few of our positions with Raymond. I hope to God I brought those latest polling figures. I'll have to check my briefcase back at the Manor House."

"Oh?" Carl said brightly. "The Manor House? That's where my daughter, Lauren, is staying."

Absentmindedly, Roxanne added, "My mother too."

Through an awkward smile, Blain said, "Can't say I've met them yet. By the end of the day, I'm sure we'll all be best of friends." His words were polite but empty; his mind was busy crunching numbers and tweaking his candidate's opening statement.

Chick was surely running a few calculations of his own, but he couldn't resist dropping, "The Manor House? I hear it's very nice. But I'm staying right here." One-upping Blain, he gestured at the house that backdropped the lawn party.

Thad popped out of the crowd and whisked up to me. "Neil said to tell you the mob at the bar is thinning out." Thad carried a tall, icy glass of lemonade, half-empty. Noticing my eyes on it, he offered, "Want some?"

I did, but it would have been rude to indulge in front of the others, who were all thirsty. "Nah"—I smiled. "We'll get our own. But thanks for the update."

He shrugged. "Enjoy the party," he told us, then melted back into the crowd, doubtless in search of Kwynn.

Carl noticed my smile, which hadn't faded. "He's a great kid."

"He is. We're going to miss him."

Blain Gifford seemed mystified by this exchange.

I explained, "Thad's leaving for college next week. Neil and I still haven't adjusted to the idea. The house is going to seem awfully empty, I'm afraid."

"You mean," asked Blain, sounding dense, "the boy is . . . *yours?*" I expected him to add, But you're *gay.*

"Thad is my nephew, but Neil and I have stepped into the role of parents."

"You've . . . *adopted* him?" His tone carried the ring of incredulity—and a dash of disgust.

"I'm his legal guardian, as stipulated in his mother's will. Since Thad was sixteen, already approaching maturity, when our lives merged, the rigmarole of adoption, to say nothing of the name change, didn't seem to make sense. But sure, Neil and I have given it serious consideration. We'd gladly call Thad our son."

"Is that *legal?*" asked Blain. "I mean, adoption." Specifically, he was inquiring about adoption by gays, but *gay* was a word he seemed to have difficulty saying.

With a humorless laugh, I assured him, "Yes, it's legal—at least the last time I checked—at least in Wisconsin."

"Roxanne?" said Carl, interrupting Blain's insipid questions. "Are you all right? You're looking pale."

As he said this, I noticed with dismay that Roxanne did not look well at all. What's more, she'd barely said a word since being introduced to Betty. Even her bouquet now looked limp.

"It's just the heat," she assured us all. "I'm fine. Thirsty—but I'll live." She mustered a laugh, brightening some.

I told her, "Wes apparently has the situation at the bar under control. Can I get you something?"

She shook her head decisively. "No, thanks. I'll take care of it myself. Betty? It's been a pleasure to meet you." She patted the old lady's hand before excusing herself and heading off alone toward the bar.

Chick said to Carl, "This might be a good time to put in that call to Lowell. He's expecting to hear from us." I couldn't decide whether Chick's suggestion was made because he was eager to make the phone call or because he was eager to impress Blain Gifford with his attention to the minutiae of running a campaign he intended to win.

"Good idea," said Carl. "Let's find somewhere quiet." Then he turned to the rest of us. "Betty, Blain, Mark—if you'll excuse us, please—" And he wandered off with Chick, away from the crowd.

"Such a nice man," said Betty, watching Carl leave. "What a shame he's a Democrat."

Under his breath, Blain told her, "In name only, Aunt Betty."

I asked her, "Would you care for a drink? *I* would." I removed my suit coat and draped it over my arm.

Betty raised a finger, preparing to answer my question, presumably in the affirmative, when she stopped short, peering at my face. I wondered if I'd broken out in hives. She stepped within inches of me, gazing even closer, as if mesmerized. "Has anyone ever told you that you have the most remarkably green eyes?"

"Once or twice," I allowed.

"Blain, dear," she said, tugging her nephew near my face, "have you ever seen such handsome green eyes?"

Overcoming some initial reluctance, he looked straight into my eyes.

Enjoying myself, I arched my brows as if to ask him, Well? *Have* you? Have you ever seen such handsome green eyes?

He sputtered, "Uh, no, Aunt Betty, I've never seen eyes so green." Through a cough, he added quietly, "Most handsome, yes."

With utter ease, I told them, "Thank you, both." I flashed Blain a wide smile, wondering if he might compliment my teeth as well, but he said nothing, backing off a step.

Admittedly, it was an awkward moment for him, forced by a doting aunt (one with long purse strings, at that) to play googly-eyes with an out-loud homosexual. Blain was, after all, a Republican—not just any Republican, but a Republican *campaign manager*, a master of spin—not at all the sort to be gushing over the color of other men's eyes. I almost pitied his innocent little predicament, except that I did enjoy watching him squirm.

What's more, I couldn't help thinking that perhaps—just maybe— I hadn't been too far off the mark in my fantasy of Blain bedding Chick Butterly. Was Blain's aunt more tuned in to her nephew than

40

he himself was? Was Blain the Republican in fact a closeted—and conflicted—*gay Republican?* Why, it was enough to make one's mind reel, was it not? I scolded myself for even thinking such blasphemy.

"Betty! Betty, love!"

We turned. Betty blinked. "Whitney!" she bubbled. "What a nice surprise."

Mr. Whitney Greer whisked into our presence. This was the man who served as executive director of both the Dumont Symphony Orchestra and the Dumont Players Guild. It was he who had recruited our housekeeper, Barb, for the orchestra board; he'd also assisted in assembling the chamber group of musicians for the wedding. On that hot afternoon, he wore a perky blue-and-white-striped seersucker suit, buff-colored bucks, and enormous Jackie-style sunglasses with almost purple lenses. His most distinctive feature, however, was the lavish crop of tightly curled, radiantly blond hair; both the curls and the color, Barb had assured me, were natural. Fifty and single—and unflinchingly flamboyant—Whitney was widely assumed to be gay, but in truth, I had no specific knowledge of his sexual history. I had not even heard reliable gossip in this regard. In any event, Whitney Greer made Blain Gifford nervous, as evidenced by a right-wing squint that was both cautious and curious.

"Whitney, dearest," said Betty, "what are *you* doing here?"

"Why, it's *the* social event of the season," he gabbed comically, flicking a wrist. "Every now and then, they trot me out to mingle with the elite."

"Nonsense"—she laughed, reaching to pat his arm—"you're elite as they come."

Dropping the camp, he explained, "I had to help with setting up the performance area for the musicians. Amplifying a woodwind quintet can be a tad tricky, especially outdoors. They're sounding good though"—he cupped a hand behind one ear, pausing to listen to Barb's group—just checking. "With my duties done, I thought, hell, join the party."

I interjected, "We'd have invited you regardless, Whitney. You're always welcome at our home." This was true enough—we'd come to know Whitney well during the past year, due to Barb's involvement with the orchestra and Thad's involvement with the theater—but my comment was meant mainly for Blain's ears. I hoped he might be further disquieted by the whole "gay thing." If he was, I couldn't tell, as he'd begun flipping through the pages of a small notebook he'd removed from his pocket, pretending not to listen.

Betty noticed this as well and apparently judged her nephew's disinterest to be ungentlemanly. "Don't be rude, Blain, dear. You remember Whitney, don't you?"

Blain looked up from his notes, gave his aunt a flimsy smile, then glanced briefly at Whitney with a nod of recognition and a flat greeting: "Whitney."

The greeting was echoed in kind: "Blain."

Then Blain returned his attention to his notes and Whitney returned his attention to Betty. What, I wondered, was that all about? Clearly, they knew each other. Presumably, Blain Gifford had paid previous visits to his aunt in Dumont and had, at some point, met Whitney Greer. When, though, and under what circumstances? And why were both of them now so standoffish? Blain's cold manner didn't surprise me much, but Whitney's did.

Whitney was telling Betty, "In all seriousness, love, we simply can't thank you enough." He turned to me. "I know you're well aware of it, Mark, but it bears constant repeating: Betty Gifford Ashton's profound generosity to the arts has made the difference between culture and . . . well, *wilderness* here in Dumont. Without her benevolence, we'd all have reverted to buckskins and jug bands *ages* ago. She is, in every sense, a true angel. No, better yet, a goddess."

"Oh, tut now," said Betty, dismissing the tribute. "I merely write a check now and then. You're the one, Whitney, who rolls up his sleeves and gets his hands dirty."

He raised one brow. "Not if I can help it." And he threw back his head to heave a wild laugh that momentarily drowned out the party babble and the amplified music.

Betty tittered, pulling out a lace hankie to dab her brow.

Blain had had enough of Whitney. He shut his notebook, slipped it into a pocket, and removed a cell phone from another. "I really need to check in with Raymond," he told us curtly. "Excuse me, please." And with that, he leaned to kiss his aunt's cheek and walked away.

Whitney caught my eye and, unseen by Betty, pressed his index finger to his tongue—Blain was enough to make him gag. I telegraphed my agreement through a poker face.

"Betty, love," said Whitney, taking both of her hands into his, "have a *wonderful* time this afternoon. I'll try to catch up with you later, after dinner, and if you have a moment, maybe we could sip a few drinks."

"That would be lovely." Clutching her handkerchief, she wiggled a happy nod.

"Mark," Whitney continued, "*fabulous* party. Thanks so much for including me." He offered a quick, limp handshake, waved another farewell to Betty, and skittered into the crowd.

I smiled at Betty. "I don't know about you, but I can't wait till after dinner for a drink. Shall we get something?"

Laughing, she fanned herself with the hankie. "I thought you'd never ask."

So I offered my arm and began escorting her through the crowd toward the bar.

It was slow going. The lawn was bustling with guests, and Betty took her time, even with my support, walking through the lumpy grass. Along the way, we were repeatedly stopped by friends who exchanged idle pleasantries with both of us. At last, though, the brightly striped awning of the bar was within sight, and I noticed that the clog there had indeed cleared—everyone, it seemed, except Betty and me already had a drink in hand.

Then I noticed Roxanne, just nearing the bar, also empty-handed. As the central figure of this event, she'd encountered nonstop well-wishing as she'd attempted to move through the crowd. Somewhere along the way, she'd abandoned her bouquet. She was nodding and gabbing, extricating herself from another knot of guests, within a few yards of her goal. The bar was momentarily empty. Wes stood behind it, ready to serve.

Betty and I both had the same idea. We instinctively quickened our pace, hoping to take advantage of the lull.

Off to the side of the bar stood a long galvanized tub, bobbing with bottles—beer and wine chilling in water and cracked ice. Several sweaty little kids milled nearby, and when Wes turned his back, they huddled around the tub, reaching in for ice, giggling, splashing the cold water on themselves and the grass at their feet, which was already soggy. Wes turned with a frown, shooed them away, and reached into the tub, rearranging some bottles. Then he flicked the frigid water from his hands, set up a fresh row of glasses on the bar, and dunked several of them into the tub for ice, awaiting his next order for cocktails.

"Hey, Mark."

I turned. Doug Pierce had walked up behind me, looking cool with a tall lemonade in one hand, handsome as ever in his summery green sport coat. "Hi, Doug," I told him. "You know Betty Gifford Ashton, don't you?"

"Of course." He smiled at her. "Hello, Betty."

"Afternoon, Sheriff. Lovely affair, isn't it?"

As they exchanged bits of small talk, I listened politely, feigning interest, trying to nudge the three of us toward the bar. We had nearly arrived when Roxanne at last stepped away from her little crowd, joining us within a few feet of the bar.

Betty was babbling something at Pierce. Roxanne grinned, grabbed my shoulder, and said into my ear, "Christ, I need a drink."

"Now, now," I lectured under my breath. "Watch the booze."

She tisked. "Believe me, alcohol is the *last* thing I need today. Perrier will be just fine, thanks. But I need it quick—I'm ready to drop."

With a laugh, I told her, "Betty too. Let's get you gals fixed up." So I ushered Roxanne up to the bar, then turned and guided Betty up next to her. They nodded hello, making some reference to the heat.

Stepping back, I joined Pierce, waiting a few feet behind the ladies.

He said, "I have to hand it to you guys. You and Neil really have a flair for making a party an 'event.' Dumont's never seen anything like this."

"Maybe so." I patted his back in thanks for the compliment. "But the festive mood is far from unanimous. For starters, the rival campaign managers, Chick and Blain, seemed ready to lunge at each other, and—"

Pierce laughed. "The morning paper was right: Dumont, Wisconsin, of all places, has become a political hot spot."

"If you saw it in the *Register*, it must be true."

As we continued in this vein, I kept an ear on the ladies' prattle at the bar.

"Just Perrier, please," Roxanne told Wes. "I stocked you up this morning—top shelf, over at the end."

The bartender glanced over his shoulder at the green bottles. "I wondered where those came from. Right away, ma'am." He dumped melting ice from one of the glasses back into the galvanized tub and scooped up some larger cubes from the water. Drying his hands on his apron, he turned to Betty, asking, "And you, ma'am—lemonade? I also have a nice mango-flavored iced tea."

Betty hesitated. "I don't suppose you have a nice bottle of bourbon?"

Wes laughed. "Indeed I do."

"Straight up. Rocks, please."

"Coming right up, ma'am." Wes freshened another glass of ice, then squatted beneath the bar to rummage for a full bottle of bourbon, twisting open its seal with a distinct snap.

While he worked, Betty dabbed and fanned her face with the lace handkerchief, telling Roxanne, "I can't remember a September as hot as this one—and I've seen quite a few."

Roxanne suggested, "Why don't you dip your hankie in the ice water? I'll bet you'd find it cool and refreshing."

Betty eyed the vat. "Thank you, dear, what a splendid idea." As Wes turned and reached to retrieve a bottle of Roxanne's Perrier from the shelf, Betty stepped over to the tub, her open-toed pumps squishing the soggy turf. Then she dipped her delicate hankie into the cold water.

Pierce said something to me, and as I turned to listen, we both noticed something go haywire with the sound system. The music fizzled and grew staticky; the volume dropped by half. Curious, I stood on my toes to glimpse across the lawn toward the bandstand. Then, from behind me at the bar, I heard Roxanne gasp. I turned.

Roxanne had one hand raised to her mouth. Her other hand, trembling, pointed toward Betty.

My head swung in time to see Betty standing at the vat, as if frozen there, with her hand still in the water. Her wide eyes stared wildly into space. Her mouth sagged, as if trying to speak. Her entire body shuddered, as if with fear, as if possessed. Before I could comprehend what I was seeing, let alone react to it—*pow*—a loud crack sounded from behind one of the tents, the music stopped dead silent, and Betty Gifford Ashton dropped to the ground. I gazed in disbelief at the hot spot beneath her feet where the wet grass steamed.

"Good God," said Pierce, rushing past me and kneeling next to her. Regaining my senses, I joined him, rolling my jacket and propping it under Betty's head. Pierce reached into a pocket and tossed me his cell phone. "Call for help," he told me without emotion, searching for a pulse. Then he straightened Betty's legs, bent over her, and began to attempt CPR.

I punched in the number to report what had happened. Bewildered conversation, then horrified gasps, erupted from the crowd as the tragedy became apparent. While speaking to the dispatcher on the phone, I saw Dale Turner, the tent guy, rush forward in a panic; then he dashed behind the scenes to try to determine what had gone wrong with the wiring. The dispatcher informed me that help was on its way. Pierce's face had grown bright red as he struggled, undaunted, to revive Betty.

It was obvious, though, that these efforts would be for naught. I had no doubt that our town's benevolent matriarch was dead.

On the icy surface of the galvanized tub, her little lace hankie floated serenely among the bobbing bottles of beer.

Police and ambulance crews arrived within a few short minutes. Paramedics relieved Pierce of his exhausting efforts to restore Betty's heartbeat, but even with the aid of their lifesaving gadgetry, they were no more successful than Pierce had been. Betty was declared dead at the scene.

Pierce stood, smearing mud from the knees of his slacks with paper napkins from the bar. "God," he said, "what a way to go. At least it was quick."

A team of deputies began taking statements from witnesses while circulating among the crowd of onlookers, who were held at bay by yellow police tape that was already strung around the bar area.

"Sheriff?" said another of the deputies. "Look at this." Standing at the far end of the vat, behind the bar, he used a stick to pull from the icy water the head of an orange, heavy-duty extension cord. Its other end was overhead somewhere in the rigging of the tent. The deputy held the stick at arm's length, as if the cord drooping over it were a venomous snake.

Pierce shook his head, telling the deputy, "There's no danger now, Jim. All the circuits blew." Though the faltering sound amplification had first harbingered serious electrical problems, moments later, the surge that killed Betty was sufficient to shut down the entire electrical supply for the lawn party.

"Sweet Jesus!" said Blain Gifford, running through the crowd toward us, arriving at the police tape just in time to see the paramedics hoist his aunt's body onto a gurney, covering her—face and all—with a blanket. *"What happened?"*

Pierce lifted the tape for him, but restrained him from approaching the body. "Mr. Gifford," he said solemnly, "I'm sorry. All of Dumont shares your loss. A most regrettable accident has killed your dear aunt."

He looked bug-eyed, unbelieving, at the plump, shrouded figure on the gurney. A pair of muddied off-white pumps peeped from one end of the blanket. "But . . . how?"

"She was apparently electrocuted by a live extension cord that somehow found its way into that tub of ice water near the bar. When she reached into the water to dampen her handkerchief, the current passed through her to the ground—the turf was soggy under her open-toed shoes. At her age, I imagine, she went into instant cardiac arrest. Dr. Formhals should have no problem issuing a quick, complete report." Pierce was referring to Vernon Formhals, the county coroner and medical examiner. Pierce reiterated, "I'm sorry, Mr. Gifford."

Blain stood motionless, trying to comprehend the freakish mishap that had taken his aunt's life.

Roxanne was propped at the bar—she hadn't moved since witnessing the gruesome incident—slugging down a sweat-streaked glass of Perrier. Neil was with her by now. I stepped over to them and wrapped Roxanne in a hug. There was really nothing to say. Still, she managed to mumble into my ear, "Upstaged at my own damn wedding."

"It's awful," I sympathized, "seeing something like this happen."

Neil told her, "I'm just thankful it wasn't you. *Anyone* could have stuck their hands in that water."

Roxanne's brow wrinkled. Slipping out of my hug, she noted, "The bartender *did* have his hands in the water, frequently. So did that pack of kids. Why, then, did *Betty* get zapped?"

I shrugged. "Lousy timing, I guess. Timing is everything." As I said it, I recalled hearing the same words only minutes earlier, during the testy tête-à-tête between Chick Butterly and Blain Gifford. Timing, they had said, was everything in politics.

As if responding to my thoughts, Chick now moved into view, following Carl Creighton through the crowd. Pierce waved them inside the police tape, and they beelined toward Roxanne and me. Carl put his arms around Roxanne, saying nothing. Chick asked me, "Is it true—Mrs. Ashton is dead?"

"Yes"—I nodded toward the gurney—"I'm afraid that's Betty. She was electrocuted before our very eyes."

Carl stared at the shrouded corpse. "How dreadful. I just can't believe it." Then he noticed the bereaved Blain Gifford standing a few feet away, head bowed. "Blain," said Carl, approaching the opposing campaign manager, laying an arm across his shoulders, "I'm astonished. And terribly sorry. I know how close you and your aunt were."

Blain raised his head and looked at Carl. He was clearly distraught and grieving, but no tears—stiff upper lip. He told Carl, "A woman of her age—well, I knew we'd face this one day. No one lives forever. But I never could have *dreamed* she'd go like this . . ." He shook his head numbly.

"It was an accident," Carl told him. "Your aunt was loved by all who knew her. You can take great comfort in that."

"Uh, Sheriff Pierce?"

We all turned as Dale Turner walked slowly into our midst from behind one of the tents. His denim work shirt was stained dark with sagging circles of perspiration. Soot blackened his hands and smudged his face where he'd wiped away sweat.

"Yes, Dale." Pierce rushed over to him; the rest of us gathered around. "What *happened* back there?"

He started to explain, "I checked the temporary fuse box—"

"*This* man is responsible?" demanded Blain, sounding more indignant than bereaved.

Pierce raised a hand, speaking flatly, patiently. "Now hold on, Mr. Gifford. We're trying to get to the bottom of this, and Mr. Turner is trying to help. This is Dale Turner, owner of the tent company that set up the event. Dale was also responsible for wiring the tents and supplying power; he's a certified electrician. I've known Dale's work for some years, and he's always been conscientious and thorough. As an additional safeguard, city inspectors must approve every temporary installation before the final permit is issued, which they did here late yesterday; I'm sure everything was up to code. If we determine, ultimately, that someone's negligence *was* responsible for this accident—"

"If everything was up to code," snapped Blain, "an accident like this could never happen."

Dale raised a sooty finger. "Uh, Sheriff Pierce? What I was trying to say was, I've got a sorta queer feeling that what happened *wasn't* an accident."

During a long, suspended moment, Dale's circle of listeners registered a spectrum of surprise ranging from speechlessness to muttered oaths of incredulity. I, however, did not share this reaction. Since mulling the maxim that timing is everything—especially in politics— I myself had been left with a sorta queer feeling that Betty's demise could not be dismissed as the lamentable but random result of some capricious twist of fate.

"Okay, Dale," said Pierce, "we're listening. What did you find?"

"First," he said, pointing to a bundle of cables looped through the awning over the bar, "you need to understand that the power serving the bar tent runs on its own circuit—precisely because of the dangers associated with water. If anything shorts, we want this circuit to shut down at once. That's why we have circuit breakers or, in this case, a fuse box."

Stepping to the galvanized tub, he continued, "I have no idea how a live extension cord got into the water, but it did. That alone should have shorted the circuit and shut it down, but it didn't. So when the unfortunate old lady stuck her hand in the water, grounding it through her feet, she allowed a tremendous voltage surge, which lasted a few seconds. Eventually, the draw was so great, the entire power supply shut down." Grimly, he added, "It toasted every circuit in the box."

Pierce was taking notes. "Back up, Dale. You said that when the cord fell into the water, it should have shorted, breaking that particular circuit. Why didn't it?"

"That's the whole point, Sheriff." Dale sighed heavily. "I hate to say it, but someone had rigged the fuse box so that the bar circuit *couldn't* blow."

Chick looked baffled. "How do you rig a fuse box?"

Roxanne's cynical edge did not serve her well at that moment. "Don't tell me," she said, hand to hip, rolling her eyes sarcastically. "Not the old penny trick?"

I flashed her a stern look.

Blain tisked, asking anyone, "What on *earth* is she talking about?"

"She's right!" said Dale, winking his approval of her smarts. "The lovely bride is absolutely right on the money."

She turned to me, twisting her lips in a smirk—so there.

I winced, chagrined that she, a lawyer, did not yet understand the implication others might draw from her ability to name, on the spot, the far-fetched means that had apparently been used to trigger Betty Gifford Ashton's outlandish demise.

Dale explained to everyone, "Back when most people had fuse boxes instead of switchable circuit breakers, there was an old, and dangerous, trick of bypassing a blown fuse by inserting a penny in the socket beneath the fuse. That's exactly what was done here." He opened one of his hands, and there in his sooty palm was a charred penny. "When the cord dropped into the water and shorted, the fuse on that circuit couldn't do its job, so the surge just passed through the penny, causing a brief brownout—when the music sounded funny—until that poor lady grounded the surge and blew the whole system." He handed the penny to Pierce.

"Had any of the other fuses been pennied?" asked Pierce.

"Nope. Just the bar circuit."

We all gathered around the sheriff, staring at the penny that had already blackened his fingers. I told him, "Too bad Dale handled it," meaning that Dale had probably contaminated the evidence with his fingerprints.

"Nah," said Pierce, pausing in thought, "I doubt that it matters. Anyone devious enough to plan such a crime would have sense enough to clean his fingerprints from the penny first."

Blain cleared his throat, looking sidelong at Roxanne. "Don't you mean his *or her* fingerprints, Sheriff?"

"For Christ's sake," snapped Chick the Democrat at Blain the Republican, "what the hell do you mean by *that?*"

Blain didn't answer.

Neil's jaw dropped.

Roxanne looked at me stone-faced, suddenly aware of the connotations of her smart-mouthing.

Carl ran a hand through his silvery hair, looking perplexed. "Douglas," he said to the sheriff, "if I'm not mistaken, you just now referred to this tragedy as a 'crime,' correct?"

He showed us the penny in one hand, his notes in the other. "It sure doesn't look like an accident. I'll be investigating the electrocution of Betty Gifford Ashton as a probable homicide."

Blain asked, in a tone sounding more like a command, "May I assume you'll treat this case as your top priority, Sheriff?"

"Of course, Mr. Gifford. The lethal wrongdoing against your aunt is an assault upon our entire community."

Blain gave a single, brusque nod.

Carl stepped Roxanne away from the group and spoke quietly to her.

She listened, then responded briefly, matter-of-factly.

Carl told Pierce, "Roxanne and I had planned to leave for Hawaii this afternoon. We understand, though, that you may need us here, and frankly, it might just 'look bad' for the two of us to leave town so quickly in light of these regrettable circumstances."

Roxanne asked Neil and me, "Do you mind, guys, if we intrude for another night? We should be out of your hair tomorrow."

"No problem at all," we assured her. "You're always welcome."

Her tone was collected and businesslike when she told Pierce, "We'll help any way we can, Doug."

"Thanks, Roxanne. Sorry this had to darken your special day."

I caught her rolling her eyes again.

Pierce continued, "I'll need to question *all* of you, naturally. So please, don't wander too far."

We turned our heads toward a ratcheting sound as the paramedics raised the gurney. Deputies then cleared a path, and Betty's corpse was wheeled out to the street.

N eedless to say, the party was over.

Originally, the wedding reception was intended to linger toward a late-afternoon dinner, with the reveling to continue into the evening. Now, however, the festive celebration of Roxanne and Carl's new life together had been overshadowed by the grim circumstances of Betty's sudden death. Out of respect for the Gifford and Ashton families, Carl announced to the guests that all were welcome to stay for dinner, which would now be served as soon as possible, but the bar would close immediately afterward, and there would be no music or dancing. The message was clear: eat and get out.

Doug Pierce could not stay for dinner, of course—he had to do whatever cops do as immediate follow-up to a crime—but he phoned me later in the afternoon, asking if he could return to the house that evening and gather the principals for a review of the day's events. He stressed that this was not to be a formal interrogation, merely an airing of facts and thoughts from witnesses and family. He definitely wanted to question Carl, Roxanne, and the two rival campaign managers, Chick and Blain, as they were all out-of-towners who would be difficult to reach later. Beyond that, I was to include anyone I deemed relevant.

I included myself, naturally; I'd been an eyewitness to Betty's electrocution. I wanted Neil with me (so I wouldn't have to repeat everything later) and also Lucille Haring (so we could later compare notes for the *Register*'s coverage of the story—a big one, by our standards). Roxanne wanted her mother, Gale Exner, with her that evening, and Carl wanted to be with his daughter, Lauren Creighton. All were informed, and those staying at the Manor House agreed to return to my home on Prairie Street at seven.

It also made sense, I thought, for the catering couple, Alanna and Wesley Scott, to attend the meeting, as well as the tent guy, Dale Turner. But they would be outdoors all evening with their crews, dismantling the lawn party under the watchful eye of our housekeeper, Barb Bilsten. No problem, I reasoned—these were all locals, and Doug could easily follow up with them later.

One person I did not want at the meeting, or even around the house that evening, was Thad. With his looming departure for college, he had enough on his mind already. So when he announced his intention to visit friends that night with Kwynn, I wished him a good time and suggested he take my car.

Pierce arrived a few minutes before seven. His habit was simply to pop in through the back door, but as the backyard was a shambles and the driveway was clogged with trucks, he rang the front bell, underscoring the official nature of his visit.

"Hi, Doug," I told him, opening the door and admitting him to the front hall. Lamely, I observed, "This day hasn't gone exactly as planned."

He offered a weak smile. "I know. Sorry. How's Roxanne dealing with it?"

With a shrug, I answered obliquely, "You know Roxanne . . ."

"Did she attend the dinner?"

"Oh, sure. She and Carl mingled and table-hopped, just like a normal wedding—no clanging of glasses though. Then they went upstairs for a nap."

Pierce sighed at the irony. "And this was to be their wedding night. They were supposed to be on a plane for Hawaii by now."

"They don't seem to mind waiting till tomorrow." Under my breath, I added, "It's not as if they've never slept together."

Pierce responded with a feeble laugh, then asked, "Where shall we do this?" He looked about; the formal entry hall led to several rooms.

"By my count, there are ten of us. My den is the perfect setting for a serious discussion, but it's too small, and the dining room is full of gifts and whatnot. So let's use the living room."

"Fine." Pierce followed me across the hall to the big, elegant parlor, a room we rarely used.

Once before, on a Christmas Day shortly after my move to Dumont, Sheriff Pierce had gathered a group of us in this same room to question us about a different mishap. My cousin Suzanne Quatrain, Thad's mother, had been killed that afternoon as we all prepared to have Christmas dinner as a reunited family. On that cold day in December, nearly three years past, fireplaces had blazed throughout the house, including the one in the living room, where Pierce had stood framed by the ornate mantel as he questioned our stricken family.

Now, on a warm September evening, the fireplace was dark, cold, and lifeless, but it would once again provide a backdrop for Pierce as he queried us about the circumstances of an unexpected death. Working together, he and I moved some of the furniture—a sofa, a love seat, and several chairs—so that the group of us could face him in a loose, comfortable semicircle.

While arranging the room, I asked, "Do you mind if I take notes tonight?"

"Not at all. Please do. I'm starting from square one, without a clue where this is headed. I'm open to any theories you can offer."

"I've asked Lucy to sit in as well."

He shrugged. "It's your house, Mark."

We had just finished with the furniture when I heard Neil arrive, entering through the front door. He'd offered to drive over to the Manor House and pick up the three wedding guests who were staying there—Gale Exner, Lauren Creighton, and Blain Gifford—a prickly trio if ever there was one. "I think we're meeting in the living room," he told them from the hall, then led them in.

Gale had changed from her coral-colored, mother-of-the-bride silk dress to a darker, less festive linen suit. Carl's daughter still wore urban black, but it was a different outfit entirely; while the color was appropriate to the occasion, I got the impression that it signaled not mourning, but the monochromatic palette of Lauren's wardrobe. Blain, the victim's nephew, had not changed from the dark business suit he'd worn to the wedding; he'd been dealing with issues and emotions far too weighty to allow attention to his appearance, as evidenced not only by his mussed clothes, but also by his five-o'clock shadow, which made him look uncharacteristically butch, less slick.

By now, the three had become acquainted. None had met prior to the wedding, but they had doubtless been introduced at the reception or afterward at the Manor House, if not during their car ride together with Neil. They wandered into the room slowly, as if wary of whatever awaited. Gale browsed a bookshelf. Lauren made some approving comment to Neil regarding the decorating. Blain simply sat down, choosing the love seat.

Neil asked, "Would anyone like a drink?" The others gave a smattering of vague, indifferent answers, which Neil interpreted as affirmative, so he excused himself briefly to set up a cart for drinks.

As he stepped out to the hall, I heard Chick Butterly, who was staying in one of the guest rooms, descend the last few stairs from the second floor, asking Neil, "Have Carl and Roxanne come down yet?"

"Haven't seen them. Would you mind rapping on their door?"

Hearing no further discussion, I assumed that Chick had gone back upstairs and that Neil had proceeded to the kitchen.

Moments later, the doorbell rang, so I left the living room to answer it. As expected, Lucille Haring was waiting on the front porch. "Evening, Lucy," I told her, swinging the door open. "Thanks for coming back."

"When duty calls . . ." She waved a folder she carried, having already done some digging in the *Register*'s morgue.

I asked, "Background on the victim?"

She nodded her crop of spiky red hair. "There's not much—a few snippets of social reporting, recognitions of Mrs. Ashton's philanthropy, but not a whiff of anything that might explain what happened today."

"I'm not surprised. Families like the Ashtons are generally press-shy. Where there's wealth, there are often secrets."

Lucy grinned. "May I quote that?"

"You'd *better* not," I told her with feigned menace.

As I led her toward the living room, three sets of legs turned the landing and descended the stairs to the hall. Two of them wore pants. The third set was bare below the knee, looking good on a pair of smart, black heels. Lucy paused to take a long look, and I now understood why she had so readily assented to a dreary Saturday evening of research and note-taking—"when duty calls," indeed.

"Hello, Roxanne," Lucy said brightly, ignoring Carl and Chick. Through a smile, she added, "Sorry the day worked out the way it did." Her inflection carried no hint of sorrow. If my guess was correct, Lucy had actually taken a measure of solace in the day's events, thinking they might portend a doomed marriage for Roxanne. If they did—and if Lucy had her druthers—Roxanne would be back in circulation pronto.

"Thank you, Lucille," Roxanne told her dryly.

"You're looking wonderful this evening."

Roxanne allowed, "Amazing what a nap can do."

Though inwardly chuckling at this interplay, I realized that Lucy's observation was dead-on. Roxanne certainly did look wonderful that evening, which came as something of a surprise. After all, she'd had a harrowing day—not only the anxieties of the wedding, but the shock of the apparent murder and the disappointment of a postponed honeymoon. Now here she was, spiffed and radiant, looking well rested from a sound, fitless nap, primped for a soirée with friends. Fine, I thought, except that this evening's planned amusement would not be charades or canasta, but a murder investigation.

Neil trundled into the hall from the kitchen with a fully stocked cocktail cart. Chick looked it over, raising his brows. Suppressing a laugh, he commented, "And here *I* thought we'd been summoned for a police questioning."

"No reason we can't be civilized about it," said Neil, rolling past us and into the living room. We followed him.

"Good," said Pierce, rising from the sofa, where he'd been talking with Roxanne's mother, "everyone's here."

In subdued tones, Roxanne greeted her mother and Carl greeted his daughter. Chick the Democrat mumbled polite condolences to Blain the Republican.

Neil and I offered drinks to all and served those who wanted them. Roxanne had her requisite Perrier, her mother took some white wine, and a few others opted for hard stuff. Neil had his usual evening cocktail—Japanese vodka on ice with a twist of orange peel—while Pierce and I went dry.

When all were served, I prompted everyone to sit. Blain had not moved from the love seat. Roxanne joined her mother on the sofa; then Carl joined Roxanne, and Lauren joined Carl—one big, happy family, knee to knee, all four in a row. I took a chair near an end table, where I could write a few notes. My pad was already open, and I removed from my breast pocket my pet fountain pen, an antique Montblanc. Neil chose a chair near mine, and Lucy sat in the remaining chair, near another end table, where she could open her folder and spread out her notes. Pierce intended to stand, which left only Chick Butterly to be seated.

As logistics would have it, the only seat remaining was on the love seat, next to his rival, the bereaved Blain Gifford. Without comment, Chick sat, mustering a show of ease as he did so. Instinctively, Blain crossed his legs and his arms, as if compacting himself to maximize the distance between the two men. Once again, I noted their similar appearance, their equivalent but opposing roles in the election, their bare ring fingers. Once again, I could not help but fantasize that their public, mutual aversion hid private, mutual lust.

In my mind's eye, Blain, the older of the two by several years, shifted his weight on the love seat and, without hesitating, wrapped an arm around his counterpart's shoulders. Blain's other hand reached around Chick's face and cradled his neck. Then Blain brought his face to Chick's and, with closed eyes, kissed the younger man deeply. Chick groaned, flopping his head back, parting his legs. A moment later, he seemed buried by Blain as the two of them groped in a frenzied embrace, rolling to the floor with a loud thump, crashing into the cold andirons on the hearth.

"We're here tonight," said Pierce, strolling in front of the fireplace, "due to the untimely death of Betty Gifford Ashton and the perplexing circumstances surrounding it."

Snapping my attention back to reality, I unscrewed the cap of my Montblanc.

"Thank you," Pierce continued, "for agreeing to meet with me this evening. I truly appreciate everyone's cooperation."

I jotted a few ink loops to get my pen started.

Chick and Blain got up from the floor, brushed themselves off, and sat again on the love seat, legs primly crossed.

"Doug?" said Neil. "A few of our guests haven't met you."

Pierce straightened his tie, not vainly, but appearing slightly self-conscious. He told the room, "My name is Douglas Pierce, and I'm proud to serve as sheriff of Dumont County, an office that voters have entrusted to me twice. In this capacity, I'm the community's chief law-enforcement officer. Most of my day-to-day duties are purely administrative, but I sometimes take active charge of an investigation when circumstances of the case point to homicide."

Roxanne stage-whispered to her mother, "Doug's been a busy man since *Mark* moved to town."

Gale arched her brows, as if to ask, Really?

Carl shushed his bride with one hand. With the other, he swirled the ice in a glass of Scotch.

Chick slid over on the love seat and stuck his tongue in Blain's ear.

Shaking the image from my head, I tried to focus on Pierce. "Unfortunately," he continued, "the circumstances of Mrs. Ashton's death are indeed suspicious, warranting the department's full and immediate attention. That's why I've asked all of you to meet me here tonight."

Roxanne cracked, "Reminds me of the drawing-room scene from some Agatha Christie whodunit."

"Roxie, dear," said Carl, "this really isn't a joking matter."

"Sorry," she said, trying to look contrite.

Her facetious manner had me baffled. Not only was it inappropriate, but it left me with the disturbing impression that she found nothing to mourn in Betty's gruesome extinction.

"Oooh . . . ," Blain groaned softly, enjoying the loud squish of Chick's tongue in his ear. "Yeah, deeper."

Pierce said, "Mr. Gifford, I want to give you my personal assurance of a speedy resolution to the mystery of your aunt's death."

Blain looked up from his end of the love seat, still dazed by the day's events. "Thank you, Sheriff. I spoke with Raymond Gifford, Betty's cousin, not a half hour ago. He asked me to extend his gratitude for your efforts, while exhorting you to resolve the matter expeditiously."

From the other end of the love seat, Chick turned, caught Carl's eye, and mumbled, "Spoken like a true politician."

"Chick, please," Carl mumbled back, "there's no need for insinuations."

Blain sniffed. "And there's no cure for offensive behavior. I'd expect little else from Mr. Butterly."

Chick crossed his arms with a derisive snort.

Roxanne's mother couldn't suppress a quiet gasp. "Really, gentlemen, this sniping is uncalled-for."

Lauren, Carl's daughter, piped in, "You're a fine one to talk—Mrs. Buttinsky."

"I beg your pardon?"

"Don't play stupid with me. You're obviously well practiced in the fine art of intrusion. You couldn't wait to intrude your daughter into the Creighton family."

Gale sputtered, "But I . . . I never even met . . ."

"Lauren," snapped Carl, "that's enough."

Roxanne laughed airily, leaning from the sofa to tell Neil, "I do apologize for my stepdaughter's behavior. Isn't she horrid?"

"Roxanne," said Gale, wagging a finger, "don't dignify her conduct by sinking all the lower."

Carl nodded his agreement to Gale, then turned to Lauren, telling her firmly, flatly, "Not one more word."

Lauren tossed her head, folded her arms, and twined her legs. Her corkscrewed, black-garbed body looked like a five-foot string of licorice slouched at the end of the couch.

Pierce lolled at the fireplace, elbow on the mantel, waiting for the volley of insults to play itself out. When an uneasy silence at last reigned, he told everyone, "Tensions, I know, have a way of flaring when people are faced with shocking events, but—"

"'Shocking events'?" interrupted Roxanne, smirking. "Is that a play on words, Doug, or was it just a subliminal slip?"

Doug looked as aghast as I felt in reaction to her insensitive remark. Before Doug could say anything, Blain rose, trembling with a fury that he struggled to control. Facing Roxanne, he demanded, "How dare you! How dare you make light of my aunt's woeful death? Does the new Mrs. Creighton truly find humor in an old lady's electrocution?"

All heads turned to Roxanne.

Staring at Blain with pale, sagging features, she now realized how profoundly unsettling we'd found her glib attitude. With quiet sincerity, she assured Blain, "I do apologize. Forgive me." Her head dropped. "I don't know what got into me."

Glad that she'd come to her senses, I told her, "As Doug was saying, we're all on edge—that's all."

"Oh?" said Blain, speaking to me but still fuming at Roxanne. "You think it's that simple? You think Mrs. Creighton's behavior can be dismissed as . . . *edginess?* I certainly don't. I have a better theory."

"Like what?" said Chick, looking up at him from the love seat.

Blain paused for effect. "Am I the only one present to recall how readily Mrs. Creighton 'guessed' the so-called penny trick that killed my aunt?" Insinuation hung in the air like the heavy, noxious smoke of burning tires. Straightening his lapels, Blain sat again.

Chick stared bug-eyed at his foe. "For God's sake, Blain, you don't seriously mean to suggest—"

Smugly, Blain told him, "If the shoe fits, my friend."

"I can't believe that you'd stoop to politicizing your own aunt's death—talk about a master of spin."

"Look who's talking," said Blain. "Who's spinning whom?"

I caught Lucy's eye and could tell from her expression—and from her frenzied note-taking—that she found this exchange as deliciously newsworthy as I did. Whether any of it would see print, however, was entirely another matter.

"Gentlemen," said Pierce, having heard enough of their sparring, "this early in the investigation, vague finger-pointing and name-calling serves no useful purpose. Let us, instead, focus on what we do know, which can in turn lead us to understand what specific questions need to be asked."

Carl said, "Thank you, Sheriff. Please proceed. And I suggest that the rest of us do more listening and considerably less talking." He rattled the ice in his glass, then took a sip of the Scotch.

Pierce nodded his thanks. "First, the simplest, most direct answer to what happened and who was responsible might rest with an eye-witness—someone who saw it might be able to explain it. We've already taken statements from everyone who was in the vicinity when Mrs. Ashton was killed. Unfortunately, it transpired so fast, and everyone was so stunned, no one could make sense of it. I myself was standing within a mere ten feet of Betty when she stuck her hand in the water, and I saw nothing that could explain the deadly chain of events.

"Lacking a substantive firsthand account, we noticed that a number of wedding guests were shooting home videos at the reception, and we asked to borrow those tapes. My deputies and I have already scanned some five or six of these videos, and I'm sorry to report that none of them show the scene at the bar at the time of the incident. We'll view them again more carefully, but it's a long shot that these tapes, lacking the critical scene, will provide meaningful clues as to exactly what happened.

"All we know is that a live extension cord ended up in the water immediately before Betty was killed. Other people—the bartender, for example—had their hands in the water earlier, with no adverse effects, so the timing of these events is critical."

Timing is everything, I recalled, especially in politics.

Pierce continued, "Since no one directly observed any suspicious behavior behind or near the galvanized tub at that moment, we're left with a single, crucial question: How did the cord get into the water?" He paused, inviting a response.

Thoughtfully—helpfully—Roxanne suggested, "Either someone put it there, or it fell there. If someone *put* the cord in the water, that clearly shows criminal intent. But if the cord somehow *fell* into the water, it may have been the result of accident or negligence."

"*Criminal* negligence," stressed Blain.

"Fair enough," said Pierce. "When we determine how the cord got into the water, we'll be in a position to determine where, and with whom, the responsibility rests. Right now, I'm working on the assumption that we're faced not with an accident and not with mere negligence, but with murder."

Murder. The word had not till this point been spoken, and the effect on Pierce's nine listeners was chilling. In the near silence of the living room, I heard Lucy underline the word on her pad. I knew what she was doing because I had just done the same.

"Murder always has a motive," Pierce reminded us. "Why, then, would anyone want to see Betty Gifford Ashton dead?"

"But that's nonsense," said Blain. "My aunt was the sweetest person alive. She had no enemies—none. Her generosity was legendary. I find it inconceivable that anyone was hell-bent on her destruction."

Carl told Pierce, "I admit, it seems most unlikely."

Pierce looked to me, guessing I was one step ahead of the discussion.

So I told everyone, "Murder isn't always the result of revenge or passion. Sometimes it springs from cold, unemotional greed. Yes, Betty's generosity was legendary; so was her wealth."

Pierce agreed, "When a wealthy person dies unexpectedly, under suspicious circumstances, it's a reasonable assumption—at least for starters—that someone had something to gain."

Chick glanced at Blain while telling Pierce suggestively, "Probate should prove interesting . . ."

Predictably, Blain bristled. Though I expected a comeback, I was surprised by the tack he took. Looking Chick in the eye, Blain told all of us, "I would resent the innuendo lurking in that comment if it weren't so patently ludicrous. I have nothing whatever to gain from my aunt's death, and in fact, I fear there may be a great deal to lose." His words ended with a tantalizing pause.

Pierce asked, "What loss are you referring to, Mr. Gifford?"

"Have you forgotten? Betty's cousin, Raymond Gifford, is running for governor of Illinois. Trust me: Betty has been the single largest financial backer of Raymond's campaign. Now that she's gone, I have no reason to hope that her funding will continue—unless, by some chance, she had the foresight to look after Raymond in her estate planning."

"She never discussed it?" asked Pierce.

Blain shook his head. "I don't even know who her lawyer is. So the bottom line is this: without Betty's support, Raymond Gifford's campaign may now be in serious jeopardy."

Chick looked over his shoulder to Carl. Presumably, Blain's words were music to Chick's ears—the Democratic ticket had just gotten an unexpected boost. But Carl's face showed no hint of joy in this news. To the contrary, he already understood its implications.

Blain spelled it out. "If I'm not mistaken, Sheriff, you just told us it was reasonable to assume that my aunt Betty died because someone had something to gain from it. Without question, the Sagehorn-Creighton ticket stands to gain a great deal from my aunt's death. To my way of thinking, this casts suspicion on anyone within the Democratic campaign—my counterpart Chick Butterly, for instance, or the esteemed Mr. Creighton, or even his *charming* bride." Blain looked squarely at Roxanne, concluding, "Betty Gifford Ashton's killer may be no further than this room."

As these words registered with all of us, Chick sputtered in the silence, searching for the opening phrase of an emphatic rebuttal. Before he found it, though, there was a rapping at the doorway to the hall. We turned.

" 'Scuse me," said Barb, our housekeeper, "hope I'm not interrupting anything important."

Under his breath, Blain muttered, "Nothing important at all—just trifling chitchat."

I asked, "What is it, Barb?"

She stepped into the room. In the hall behind her was Dale Turner, owner of Tip Top Tent and Awning. She explained, "The crew has finished dismantling the party tents, and Dale just discovered something that he thinks might be useful."

" 'Useful'?" asked Pierce, intrigued. He waved Dale into the room.

The man in work clothes stepped hesitantly into our midst, doubt-less feeling out of place. In one hand was his camcorder, in the other a videocassette. "I didn't realize it earlier," he told us, "but I think I got the whole thing on tape."

Pierce's face seemed both brightened and confused. "How? Why didn't you say something before?"

Dale shuffled apologetically, explaining, "I brought my camcorder this morning and took a few shots. I was really proud to be working on such an important party. You know—good for future business. This afternoon, after the guests arrived, I shot some more tape. At some point, I needed to give Wes and Alanna, the caterers, a hand with something, so I set the camera on a table and then forgot that I left it there. I thought I'd shut it off.

"A few minutes ago, I remembered the camera and went looking for it, hoping someone didn't walk off with it. But there it was, right where I left it. And get this: I had *not* turned the camera off, so it shot some two hours of tape, which ran out. Scanning back through the viewfinder, I discovered that the camera was aimed directly at the bar—well, the camera was resting sideways on the table, but the bar was dead ahead. I'm pretty sure the tape must have caught what happened to Mrs. Ashton." He extended his arm, tape in hand. "Would you like to have it, Sheriff?"

Pierce strolled forward, grinning, taking the tape—as if Dale even needed to ask.

"Can I get it back, I mean eventually?"

"Sure, Dale. It'll be in good hands. Thanks for bringing this to our attention."

"You're, uh, welcome." Dale backed out of the room and returned to his duties outdoors.

Barb sauntered over to me, glanced at my notes, and nudged my shoulder with her elbow. "Sorry to interrupt," she said through a haughty smirk, then left the room.

Pierce exhaled loudly, sounding pleased. "With any luck," he told us, rattling the plastic cassette, "this could tell us everything we need to know."

"Which," said Chick, standing to face Blain, "should put an end to some scurrilous allegations."

"I hope so." Then Pierce told all of us, "After calling everyone together, I'm sorry to dismiss you so quickly, but I need to study this tape. It may tell us far more than our collective recollections of the incident. Besides, it's been a rough day on everyone. Get some rest. Depending upon what I find on the tape, I may need to meet with some of you again tomorrow, so I'd appreciate it if no one left town too early in the morning."

We assured him that the day had been far too exhausting to permit anyone's hasty exodus. Sunday morning, we hoped, would be a lazy one.

"Good," said Pierce, patting his pocket for keys. "Can I give anyone a lift back to the Manor House? I'm headed downtown."

Gale Exner and Blain Gifford accepted his offer.

But Lauren Creighton hesitated.

"No, thanks," she told him. "I think I'd rather walk."

PART TWO

Whiffs of Scandal

'OUR FALLEN ANGEL'

Betty Gifford Ashton, benevolent paper-mill heiress, is dead at 80

By CHARLES OAKLAND
Staff Reporter, Dumont Daily Register

Sep. 8, DUMONT WI—Betty Gifford Ashton, widow of the late Archibald Ashton and matriarch of the local paper-mill dynasty that bears his name, died Saturday afternoon when she was electrocuted at a wedding reception for Mr. and Mrs. Carl Creighton of Illinois. Mrs. Ashton was 80 years old.

The tragedy occurred at the home of *Register* publisher Mark Manning during a lawn party celebrating the nuptials. Seeking relief from the day's heat, Mrs. Ashton was killed when she dunked a handkerchief into a vat of ice water, where a live extension cord may have fallen from the tent rigging. Attempts to revive her proved futile; she was declared dead at the scene shortly before 3:00 P.M.

Dumont County coroner Vernon Formhals explained, "Mrs. Ashton grounded the shorted circuit through her feet, with the current passing through her body from her hand. Her heart, in the pathway of the alternating current, suffered ventricular fibrillation that produced a fatal cardiac arrhythmia. There were no external signs of injury, and the victim was an otherwise healthy octogenarian."

Sheriff Douglas Pierce, who witnessed Mrs. Ashton's death, told the *Register*, "Circumstances and timing of the tragedy are highly suspicious. Our initial investigation will treat this death as a possible homicide." He added that there are presently no suspects in the case. The motive for foul play remains a mystery.

Betty Gifford Ashton leaves a legacy of philanthropy and community service. "She was without question Dumont's greatest patron of the arts," said Whitney Greer, executive director of local orchestra and theater groups. "Betty was truly an angel. Sadly, she is now our fallen angel."

Mrs. Ashton had no children. She is survived by several nephews, nieces, and cousins on the Gifford side of the family, all from Illinois. Funeral plans are still pending. ❏

Sunday, September 8

I n the dark netherworld of a wee-houred Sunday, my dozing brain played host to a docket of fitful phantasms that scratched at my subconscious between slim intervals of rest. Whether my sleep was colored that night by sheer exhaustion (induced by Saturday's truculent turn of events) or by keyed-up anxiety (induced by the same), I cannot be certain. Both fatigue and jitters were doubtless the cause, the dual roots, of my dreams.

Most of these visions were disjointed and grotesque, menaced by a cast of nightmarish standbys—deep foreboding, sudden death, and slow decay. Especially bothersome was a rambling, extended mindblower featuring a serpentine bolt of electricity—a hostile, hissing personification of life-zapping energy that bore an uncanny resemblance to Roxanne. The bride of Carl Creighton who skittered through the night looked more like a twitchy Elsa Lanchester, replete with high-voltage zigzags streaking her shocked-erect hairdo.

Not all of my reveries, however, were so discomfiting. In fact, the last of my dreams, which seemed to play out during my final minutes of early-morning slumber, was decidedly pleasurable.

I am in a space that resembles the living room of the house on Prairie Street. I recognize the fireplace against the far wall; the mantel is familiar, but the andirons are strange and intricate, made of pierced and hammered brass. In the grate, a fire burns green, spitting tiny, pinkish sparks. In front of the fireplace is a long sofa of lavish Victorian design—all velvet, tassels, and fringe, with a curlicued back and enormous rolled arms—not at all like any of the furniture in the real room. The sofa, I notice, is the *only* furniture in this room. Spread before it is a Turkish rug, brightly patterned with arabesques in a palette of deep jewel tones. The air is heavy with the spice and tang of incense, conjuring the woozy atmosphere of a harem.

A figure moves. There are two of them. Then I understand that this place cannot be a harem; there are no women.

The two men are clothed, wearing business suits. Silhouetted by the fire, they sit side by side on the sofa, each with legs politely crossed, as if waiting for a bus—except that one of them has just wrapped an arm around the other's shoulders. Their faces are lost in shadow, but I can tell they do not see me. I watch them as if from behind a curtain, peeking like a voyeur through the slit.

The one who has been caressed leans toward his suitor, rolls his head on the other man's shoulder, and whispers, "Blain." Then he slowly slides his tongue into the other man's ear.

"Oooh . . . ," Blain groans softly, enjoying the loud squish of his partner's tongue. "Yeah, deeper."

Aware that I am dreaming, I recall that I imagined a scene much like this only a few hours earlier, downstairs in the living room, watching Blain Gifford and Chick Butterly on the love seat. Just now, I heard Blain's name spoken. Is the other man, the one tonguing him, Chick?

Blain rolls his head against his partner's mouth; the protruding tongue scrapes the stubble of Blain's beard. Their lips meet, and both begin heaving a deep exchange of breath. Their lungs go through the motion of breathing, but their shared oxygen is quickly spent, and they grow light-headed. Needing air, Blain backs off for a moment. As their mouths disengage, a strand of spittle sags from their lips, backlit by the fire.

Blain holds the other face in front of his own, gazing into features I cannot discern. "Your eyes," he says. "I've never seen eyes so brown. Most handsome, yes."

And they're at it again, mouth to mouth, struggling to embrace each other, to loosen their Windsor-knotted neckties, to unbutton each other's shirt, to squirm out of their suit coats as they ball themselves together, panting and tangling on the sofa before the fire.

Quite a show. I begin to feel the warmth of arousal. Still, I find it difficult to focus on the foreplay, intrigued by Blain's words about the other's eyes. I recall that Blain used these same words—nearly—at the wedding reception when his aunt Betty asked his opinion of my eyes. His reply was the same, except that my eyes are green, not brown.

Which again leads me to wonder about the identity of the other man on the sofa. He could be almost anyone—anyone but me. Brown is the most common of eye colors, a color you barely notice. I try to recall if Chick Butterly's eyes are brown, but I cannot; this detail has escaped me. Even if he does have brown eyes, I remind myself, so do most other men. The man on the sofa with Blain might be Chick, or it might be any of a billion others.

Pondering this, I watch through the slit of the curtains as Blain and his brown-eyed amorist grow ever more fevered in their horny delirium. They've managed to kick free of their clothes by now, at least most of them. The fire glows with an oily sheen along the contours of their flesh—firm flesh, I note. Blain isn't bad, not bad at all, for a man in his late forties.

Neither is Mr. Brown Eyes. Since I can't see his face, it's impossible to tell if he's in his twenties or his fifties. In terms of sheer stamina, he's not the least bit lacking. Nor is he lacking between his legs. My eyes bug at the sight of his endowment, which Blain is enjoying with abandon, lucky guy.

Caught in their frenzy, just watching it, I feel the tingle of orgasm begin to mount within me.

They tangle on the sofa, groaning as Blain's back arches over the hips of the other. The one on the bottom slaps Blain's buttocks with a resounding thwack. Both howl their pleasure, tangling all the tighter, losing their equilibrium, finally crashing to the floor with a loud, reverberant thud that sprays a shower of pink sparks from the crackling green fire.

"Good God," said Neil, peering wide-eyed over the edge of the bed at me, "are you all right, Mark?"

From the floor, I blinked at the bedroom ceiling, disoriented by the light of dawn. Bound in a sheet, which I'd snapped from the bed like an overwound window shade, I began to laugh—in spite of my embarrassment, in spite of the pain that already warmed the hip that had taken the brunt of my unceremonious landing. Sitting up, I sputtered, "Hope I . . . hope I didn't wake you."

"You scared the shit out of me." Neil flopped sideways on the bed. With his elbow in the mattress, he propped his head in his hand, watching, amused, as I used the sheet to clumsily dab the glutinous drizzle of semen from my inner thigh. Seeing me wince, he asked through a cautious grin, "You *are* all right, aren't you?"

Before answering, I tried standing for a moment, then sat on the bed, nesting my rump against Neil's belly. "Yeah, no damage." The absurdity of the situation again washed over me, and I raised a hand to my mouth to stifle laughter. "Hope I didn't . . . didn't wake the others."

Dryly, Neil assured me, "Our houseguests have heard worse."

Lifting my feet from the floor, I stretched out next to him, face-to-face, flinging a leg over his hips. I felt his penis bob against mine. "Hmm. *Someone's* ready."

"I'll say. Too bad you're running on empty."

"Don't kid yourself."

End of discussion.

It was the "morning after"—after the wedding, and after the murder. Despite my pleasant dream, despite the sensual diversions Neil and I enjoyed before rising, I greeted the day with impatience and a measure of disappointment. This was not to be the quiet Sunday morning we'd looked forward to.

We didn't even entertain the notion of taking an early-morning run together, our way of "relaxing." Our three guests had spent an extra night, and Barb was surely whipped from her dawn-till-dusk duties at Saturday's wedding, so Neil and I decided to take charge in the kitchen and attempt to get breakfast together for the household. It was shortly after seven o'clock.

I had showered for the day and dressed to spend a few hours at the office—khakis, polo shirt, and loafers. Neil had thrown on a rumpled pair of shorts and a T-shirt—he looked spectacular in anything. His bare feet squeaked on the kitchen floor as he squatted to rummage in a cabinet. "So tell me," he said, looking up over his shoulder, "what were you dreaming?"

I had just finished loading the coffeemaker. Switching it on, I hesitated before answering, "You wouldn't believe it."

He laughed. "I presume it wasn't a nightmare." He pulled out a box of cereal and peered inside. Finding it nearly empty, he crushed it in his hands and trashed it. A tired little cloud of sugary corn dust rose from the garbage, then vanished.

Leaning back against the edge of the counter, I explained, "I *did* have nightmares—the stress of the day, I guess—but the dream that knocked me out of bed wasn't the least bit ghoulish. In fact"—I paused for effect—"it was agreeably tawdry."

"I figured." He closed the cabinet, stood, opened a cupboard, and continued to forage. His grin said, I'm waiting . . .

So I told him about my dream, how the setting was and wasn't our living room, how I'd watched two men in business suits heat up for some steamy sex on a tasseled Victorian couch.

"But that's absurd," he interrupted. I was about to agree when he continued, "*Victorian?* Not in *our* living room." Neil was kidding (sort of), but I appreciated his discerning taste. The man had standards, and he stuck to them.

I agreed. "It *was* absurd—not just the setting, the clothes, and the sex, but the identity of the parties involved."

"Anyone I know?" Neil opened a bag of pastries and bagels left over from Saturday's breakfast. Jabbing a doughnut with his finger, he judged it fresh enough to serve again and emptied the bag onto a platter. The bagels, obligingly, didn't need to be tested, there being no way to distinguish stale specimens from fresh.

"Truth is, I couldn't see either of their faces, but one of the men addressed the other as—get this—Blain."

Neil turned, arching his brows. "The Republican? How delicious." Since Blain Gifford and Chick Butterly had similar looks, jobs, and temperaments, we'd begun referring to the spinmeisters simply as the Republican and the Democrat—behind their backs, naturally. "Who was the other guy?"

"I'm not sure, but I have a theory." Then I told Neil about the bizarre, similar scene I'd imagined in the living room the previous night while Pierce was questioning the group of out-of-towners. "There was no mystery whatever about the identity of the other man on the love seat with Blain. He had his tongue in Blain's ear. It was Chick."

Neil flopped a palm to his chest in mock horror. "The *Democrat?*"

I shrugged. "They're both sort of hot—in a buttoned-down, middle-aged kind of way. Don't try to tell me you haven't noticed."

Neil didn't respond—he'd noticed. During this lull in our conversation, the coffeemaker dripped and gurgled. The kitchen began to fill with the brew's hearty, cheery smell.

I continued, "So it's reasonable to assume that Blain's partner in the dream was also Chick—he stuck his tongue into Blain's ear again."

"But Blain didn't say the guy's name, and you couldn't see his face, right?"

"Right." Then I recalled, "Blain did make some reference to the other guy's handsome brown eyes."

Neil closed the cupboard door. "That doesn't tell us much. He could be *anyone.*" As an example of this assertion, Neil fanned his hands and framed his face—à la Judy Garland—batting the silky lashes of his brown, cowy eyes.

"Hey," I said with feigned enlightenment, "maybe it *was* you."

Deadpan, Neil assured me, "I have *never* stuck my tongue in a Republican's ear." As previously noted, the man had standards.

I picked up the platter of pastry and carried it to the table, setting it next to a copy of that morning's *Register*. Neil had beat me downstairs by a few minutes, so I assumed he had brought the paper in from the front porch. My thoughts returned to the enigma of the brown eyes. "Oh, well. It seems we'll never know the identity of the man of Blain's dreams."

"It was *your* dream"—Neil chortled—"not Blain's."

"True enough." My tone turned serious as I asked, "Do you think it's . . . possible? I mean, God knows, I'm not 'into' dreams, but I get these persistent vibes. Do you think it's possible that Blain is gay? Or Chick? Or both of them?"

"I doubt it—not likely in politics. In any event, their time's not long in Dumont. Chances are, we'll never know."

"So many mysteries . . ." Even as I said the words, which were nothing more than idle banter, the newspaper caught my eye. Its headline reminded me that another mystery—a real, bona fide, deadly mystery—loomed over our lives that morning.

"That's pathetic." Neil had stepped up beside me, gazing at the sad excuse for a Sunday breakfast that sat on our table. "We can't serve that to guests."

I frowned; Neil was right. "Maybe Doug is on his way over with a kringle."

"Hope so. But we'd better not leave it to chance. I'll run out." Neil crossed to the refrigerator and opened the door, checking inside. "We have plenty of milk and orange—" He stopped short. "Oh, wow! Pay dirt!"

I laughed. "What'd you find? Don't tell me—a big, cheesy breakfast soufflé, with a note from Barb. 'Just pop it in the oven.' "

"Better." He reached inside with both arms and carefully removed a large box. "Leftover wedding cake."

My mouth instantly watered. "Leave the door open. I'll get the milk."

And we set to it.

We had barely finished devouring the two oversize wedges of chilled, buttery cake—I could already feel the buzz—when Barb rattled the back door open and appeared in the kitchen. With a snort, she observed, "Didn't take you guys long to get into *that*."

I dabbed my lips with a napkin. "And a pleasant good-morning to you, Barb."

She closed the door with her hip and lugged a full shopping bag to the counter. "I'm surprised you're up already."

Neil countered, "I'm surprised *you're* up. We thought you were still in your room, sacked out."

"I should be, but we can't expect *guests* to eat wedding cake for breakfast." She began unloading an assortment of "appropriate" breakfast items from the bag—eggs, fruit, yogurt, juice, muffins, and a new heap of bagels.

"Actually," said Neil, scraping his plate with his fork, "it wasn't bad."

"I know," Barb mumbled. "Already had mine." She deposited some of her bounty in the refrigerator, thumping it shut. Then she flung open a row of cupboards and began setting stacks of dishes on the counter.

Neil laughed. "It's no big production, Barb."

She turned, hand to hip. "Look who's talkin'." Her point was valid—Neil didn't know the meaning of "casual dining" if guests were involved.

I told them both, "That's why I insist on going out for Thad's going-away party. You've both worked like drudges on this wedding. Wednesday evening will come all too quickly."

"Don't remind me," Barb moaned. Thad would travel to California on Thursday, and we weren't dealing with it well.

Trying to sound upbeat, Neil asked, "Everything's set with Nancy?"

He was speaking of Nancy Sanderson, owner of First Avenue Grill, the lady who'd helped rescue our béarnaise at the reception. I'd booked her entire dining room for our farewell party. "All set."

With the prospect of Thad's departure hanging over us, our conversation lapsed. I helped myself to another slice of cake—just a sliver this time, half a sliver—while Neil got up and began helping Barb with something. They rattled about, saying nothing.

"Oh," Barb finally said, "that was nice, Mark, quoting Whitney Greer in your story this morning. He's so sincere—even if he is kinda flighty." Apparently Barb, not Neil, had brought in the newspaper.

I glanced at the *Register* on the table. Though the page-one story carried Charles Oakland's byline, I had written it. I'd taken to using a pen name when reporting, so as not to confuse our readership with my editorial persona. I told Barb, "Whitney was a natural as an interview for this story. His credentials in arts management are first-rate—he's a Peabody graduate. And he gave me some good quotes—I loved that 'fallen angel' bit. Made a great headline."

Neil squinted. "Not to split hairs, but isn't a fallen angel a devil?"

I hadn't thought of that. "The context makes his meaning clear."

"Sure," said Barb matter-of-factly. "Whitney worshiped that old gal. She kept the orchestra afloat."

"The theater too." Neil shook his head, concerned, no doubt, about the future finances of these two performing-arts groups. The full impact of Betty Gifford Ashton's death was not yet wholly known.

As if reading my thoughts, Barb said, "Whitney will pick up the pieces. Say what you will about him, he's the kind of guy who 'makes it happen.' In fact . . ." She hesitated, as if tempted to tell us something. Then, with a flip of her hands, she concluded, "Never mind. Not now."

Neil and I glanced at each other—what did *that* mean? We knew better, though, than to try coaxing information from Barb. If we confirmed that she had tantalized us, we would only strengthen her resolve to stay mute.

As an offhand addendum, she told us, "Just a little project I've been working on," tantalizing us all the more.

"Morning, gang."

We turned at the sound of Roxanne's voice. She had just entered the kitchen from the front hall with Carl. She was in her satiny robe, looking far more relaxed than on the previous morning. Carl wore fresh, dressy pajamas that looked as though they'd never been slept in.

"Mr. and Mrs. Creighton," I hailed them. "Good morning."

Neil told them, "You're up and about awfully early."

Carl confirmed, "Bright-eyed and bushy-tailed."

Roxanne volleyed back some crack about the bushiness of someone's tail, but I wasn't quite listening, focused instead on Carl's reference to eyes. He was indeed bright-eyed that morning, and I noted that his bright eyes were deep brown.

"We were up even earlier," said Roxanne, "on the phone, trying to straighten out our travel plans to Hawaii. The only direct flight we can get is from Chicago this afternoon, so we'll need to get on the road by ten or so."

"Plenty of time," said Carl, undaunted by the prospect of a four-hour drive—and a nine-hour flight.

Neil tried to tidy up the table, setting the newspaper squarely in one corner. "It's a shame you have to be back on Wednesday for the debate. If your return flight is Tuesday evening, that gives you only two nights on the island."

"I *know.*" Roxanne's tone made it plain that these logistics had already been discussed from every angle. Turning to Carl, she said, "Honest, I wouldn't mind in the least if we postponed the trip until after the election."

"Nope," said Carl with good-natured finality. "I'm taking my bride to paradise."

Barb piped in, "Hold on to *that* one, Roxanne."

"I intend to." Roxanne gripped Carl's upper arm with an exaggerated display of possessiveness, as if sinking her claws into him. So far, at least, marriage seemed to agree with her—a transformation that I found both gratifying and surprising.

Another transformation, equally surprising, was Roxanne's mood shift since the night before. By the end of our group meeting with Pierce, she had become somber and withdrawn, paying penance for the glib attitude and injudicious remarks that had cast her in an unflattering—and possibly suspicious—light. This morning, though, she was her wisecracking self again, freshly risen from her marriage bed, bubbling vacuously about spas and restaurants in Honolulu, as if Betty's electrocution had been merely a technical glitch, a downer now best forgotten.

"Oooh, yummy," Roxanne squealed, "wedding cake!" She'd glimpsed the box on the counter and the smears of white frosting on my plate.

"Any left?" asked Carl, practically licking his lips.

"Plenty," said Barb through a half laugh, "but I thought I'd serve you guys a *real* breakfast. Can't I fix you some eggs?"

Roxanne made an icky-poo face. "Eggs? I've been *dreaming* of that cake."

I was tempted to share a dream or two of my own, but resisted. Roxanne would not appreciate knowing that she'd traipsed through my night in the guise of Mrs. Frankenstein. And Carl would doubtless be dismayed to learn that someone resembling his campaign manager had triggered (as my eighth-grade nun had sternly termed it) a nocturnal emission.

Before long, the five of us were crowded around the table, gobbling cake. I had a mere *quarter* sliver this time, practically nothing. When the milk ran out, we switched to coffee. The hot, robust, acidic flavor provided a pleasant counterpoint to all the sugar.

We spoke of the wedding, the honeymoon, the election, Thad's college plans—anything to avoid *the* topic, the glitch, the downer. Betty's beatific mug shot gazed mutely up at us from the corner of the table.

Eventually, when our conversation hit a lull and the silence lasted a moment too long for comfort, Neil told Roxanne, "It was great to see your mom again."

Roxanne nodded, raising a finger while swallowing a forkload that contained more frosting than cake. She closed her eyes in momentary rapture as the creamy gob slid from her tongue to her throat. "I think Gale was looking forward to yesterday more than I was. Too bad the festivities . . . uh, soured. Anyway, she enjoyed seeing you again, Neil. And, Mark"—Roxanne turned to me—"she *adored* meeting you, at long last."

"The pleasure was entirely mine. Your mom's a wonderful person, and meeting her explained a lot."

Roxanne blinked. "Like what?" She whisked a stray lock of hair from her face.

I shrugged. "Oh, you know, general stuff, roots. Like mother, like daughter."

Roxanne rolled her eyes—classically beautiful blue eyes—glamorous, movie-star eyes, except that she'd smeared buttercream frosting on one of her brows while fussing with her hair.

Neil told her, "Sorry there was no room for her to stay here at the house."

Roxanne brushed off the apology. "You guys aren't running a *hotel*, and there's only so much room. Carl and I felt that it just made more sense, logistically, to give the extra bedroom to Chick." With a laugh, she patted Carl's arm, telling us, "They have the damnedest conversations at *all* hours."

Carl smiled at her, explaining vaguely, "The rigors of a campaign . . ."

"Besides," Roxanne told Neil, "Mom has never enjoyed being a houseguest. We tried it, *once*, at my place for a weekend, and she's stayed at hotels ever since. Trust me, she's much better off at the Manor House."

I wagged my head, musing softly, "I'd love to be a fly on the wall at breakfast in *that* dining room. Picture this—table for three—Gale Exner, Lauren Creighton, and Blain Gifford."

Neil grinned but dared not laugh.

Carl sighed, setting down his fork. "It does seem like a roguish conspiracy of fate, doesn't it?" Demonstrating that he too saw the humor in the situation, he added, "I hope they don't have adjoining rooms—or share the same bath." His brown eyes returned to his white cake.

"It's entirely possible," Neil warned us, still grinning. "The Manor House was built as a home, not a guesthouse. Our unlikely threesome may be learning a lesson in togetherness."

Barb listened to us silently, pouring herself another glassful of diet cola. She'd not been present for the testy fireworks that had erupted at Pierce's meeting in the living room, so she now glanced from face to face, trying to piece it together.

Roxanne assured us, "Even if they *are* in close quarters, Gale can handle it."

I was skeptical. While Gale Exner did indeed strike me as the most mature and diplomatic of our three guests at the Manor House, I'd seen her spunky edge as well. Not only was there a goodly bit of her in Roxanne (and vice versa), but Gale had nearly lost control last night when Carl's daughter had referred to her as Mrs. Buttinsky.

Tuning in to these thoughts, Carl told everyone, "I really must apologize to everyone—once again—for Lauren's unconscionable behavior yesterday. She's simply not 'dealing with' my marriage to a woman other than her mother. That's no excuse, I grant you—"

"—but it *is* an extenuating circumstance," Roxanne finished the thought with lawyerly objectivity. Humbly, she added, "I was in rare form myself last night. Sure, we were all on edge, but that hardly justifies the things I said. I owe a round of apologies—to all of you, of course, but specifically to Lauren and Blain."

Carl sighed. He hadn't paid much attention to Roxanne's words; he was still fretting over his daughter. "Lauren's always shown signs of that disagreeable streak. I wish I'd tried correcting it when she was younger, while I was still around for her."

With a smug grin, Roxanne reminded him, "Beryl has been 'around' for Lauren, consistently. Pardon my saying so, but the little lady in black *still* blossomed into a princess."

Carl couldn't deny this unflattering assertion, adding to it, "A *spoiled* princess. I'm hoping, now that she's off on her own, in Denver, building a career, she may learn a few lessons in life and acquire some much needed maturity. Good God, she's twenty-six now—time to grow up."

"My, my, my," Roxanne mimicked a crone of a wife, fingering the lapels of her robe as if it were a tattered, drool-stained shawl. Seemingly toothless, she added, "Our thweet little Lauren, all growed up."

Carl laughed. "Well, in fairness, she *has* shown some progress. For instance, earlier this year, she bought a house."

Neil admitted, "A sure sign of maturity."

"Not only that," added Carl, "but it's an *old* house in one of Denver's historic districts. She's begun a complete rehab, and believe it or not, she's now taking an active role in the whole process, tinkering with plumbing and all manner of menial tasks. Lord knows where she picked *that* up—certainly not from me."

I told him, "There now. She *is* maturing, building her own life."

"I hope you're right, Mark. Unfortunately, she still leaves plenty of room for improvement with regard to that *attitude.*"

Roxanne told him, "Even so, I was way out of line, and both

Lauren and Blain need to hear mea culpas from *these* very lips." With a napkin, she dabbed the labial organs that had committed the offense. "I'll try to patch things up before we head out of town."

With unspoken gratitude, Carl patted her hand.

Neil told Roxanne, "Good idea. Take the high road. But don't be *too* hard on yourself. After all, Blain Gifford all but accused you of murdering his aunt."

There. Neil had raised *the* topic, the glitch, the downer.

"Huh?" blurted Barb, looking wide-eyed at us over her glass of pop. Suppressing a belch, she asked, "That Blain creep thinks Rox killed the old lady?"

We paused, unsure who should answer. Carl took charge. "No, Barb, I'm sure Mr. Gifford merely got carried away by the tensions of the day."

"But why would he even *think* such a thing, let alone say it?"

I explained, "Roxanne happened to be standing near Betty at the bar, and she suggested—helpfully and innocently—that Betty might find it refreshing to dip her handkerchief into the vat of ice water."

"Then," Neil picked up the story, "after Betty was electrocuted, Rox theorized that the fuse box had been rigged with a penny, which turned out to be exactly what had happened."

"Just a lucky guess," said Roxanne with a crooked smile. "So to speak."

"What the hell's the matter with that Republican?" asked Barb, indignant. (I noticed that she'd arrived, as Neil and I had, at the obvious means of distinguishing between the two campaign managers.) "You don't go around accusing people of *murder* on the basis of half-assed circumstances."

"Exactly," said Neil. "Doug saw Blain's empty ranting for what it was worth—nothing. He reminded all of us that murder always has a motive. Clearly, Rox had no motive whatever to harm Betty Gifford Ashton." With a snort of laughter, Neil rejected any such suspicions as ludicrous.

Barb seconded Neil's snort.

Was it my imagination, or did Roxanne and Carl steal a shared glance just then? It may have meant nothing, but I couldn't help feeling that the look in their eyes conveyed apprehension. This interplay was discreet and private, as if . . . well, as if they were guarding a secret. What's more, Roxanne's visage seemed momentarily drained and lifeless. I'd seen that look just yesterday—at the reception, when Betty had spoken of the irony of meeting Roxanne "after all these years." What in God's name, I wondered, was going on?

"Roxanne?" asked Barb. "What did you think of the music yesterday?"

Neil interjected, "You're fishing, Barb."

Roxanne didn't hesitate to supply the sought compliments, embellishing her tribute with profuse thanks for the extra dimension Barb's quintet had added to the day's festivities. The spark and color had returned to Roxanne's face, and I gladly dismissed her mysterious mini-funk as a passing reaction to *the* topic, the glitch, the downer.

We prattled on in this vein, eating day-old wedding cake, avoiding unpleasant issues, speaking again of the wedding, the honeymoon, and the election. Neil began razzing Roxanne about her sudden interest in politics and accused her of harboring unbridled ambitions to become "the first lady of the Land of Lincoln." While laughing this off, Roxanne repeated the phrase, clearly loving the ring of it.

The ring of the telephone nipped our conversation, sounding especially intrusive on a Sunday morning. I sat nearest the counter where the phone jangled a second time, so I rose to answer it.

"Hello?"

"Morning, Mark." It was Sheriff Pierce; we knew each other's voice so well, we rarely bothered identifying ourselves on the phone. "Hope I'm not calling too early."

It was around eight o'clock. "Of course not. By this hour, you've usually strolled through the back door. We've missed you, Doug."

"Yeah, sorry. I meant to bring over a kringle."

"We could have used it," I lied. In truth, I was feeling sort of sick from so much cake. The others in the kitchen had not resumed talking; they wondered, as did I, why the sheriff had phoned. "What's up?"

"I had a late night—didn't even make it to the gym this morning."

"Hence, no kringle."

"Very perceptive"—he laughed. "I was busy last night reviewing videos of the wedding reception. Of most interest was the tape that Dale Turner shot inadvertently."

"Dale said that the tape might have captured the moment of Betty's electrocution. Did you find anything?" The others in the kitchen were by now turned in their chairs, necks stretched, openly eavesdropping.

Pierce paused. "Yes, we have indeed found something."

"Can you tell me about it?"

"I'd prefer to show it to you. Could we meet at your office?"

"Sure. I have a VCR there, and I'd planned to meet with Lucille Haring this morning anyway—this is a big story for us. When would you like to come over?"

"I need to clean up. How about an hour? Nine o'clock."

"I'll be there."

"And, uh, Mark, is Roxanne around?"

Catching her eye, I told Pierce, "Yeah, she's right here."

"Ask if she'd mind coming with you. What I've found, well . . . it relates to her."

I lowered the receiver from my ear and turned toward the table, where a foursome of curious faces looked up at me, hungry for information. "Roxanne," I began uncertainly, "Doug Pierce is meeting me at my office in an hour to review part of Dale Turner's tape. He wonders if you could join us."

Predictably, my words were met with quiet, cautious surprise. Roxanne turned to Carl, who arched his brows, then nodded.

Roxanne told me, "Sure, Mark, tell Doug I'll be there. Carl and I would like to be on the road by ten or so, but we should have plenty of time."

"Mark," said Carl, "if Douglas wouldn't mind, I'd like to be there as well. It's not clear to me where this is heading, but . . ." He trailed off, sounding concerned.

I lifted the receiver again. "Doug—"

"I heard, Mark. Fine, no problem if Carl wants to come too."

"Then we'll see you at nine."

Doug and I said good-bye, then hung up.

"*Whew,*" said Barb, rising from the table. "That was ominous."

"No, it wasn't," I told everyone, forcing a soft laugh (in truth, I'd found Doug's request highly ominous). "Doug simply said he'd 'found something' on the tape, and I imagine he wants Roxanne to see it because she was standing right there when everything happened."

"That's reasonable," said Neil, also rising. He helped Barb clear some cake debris from the table.

Roxanne and Carl stood. Carrying a few cups to the sink, she said, "We'd better get cleaned up and packed. We can leave town directly from Mark's office."

Carl agreed, suggesting, "We should stop at the Manor House and say good-bye to Lauren and your mother, then—"

"Hey, where's the fire?"

We turned toward the voice in the front hall.

Chick Butterly laughed, entering the kitchen. "Don't tell me it's too late for breakfast already—it's barely past eight." He wore running shoes, nylon shorts with a pager clipped to the waistband, and a loose jersey singlet.

Neil's eyes popped; I'm sure mine did as well. We'd never seen Chick in anything other than stuffy business clothes, and his running gear gave him an altogether different charisma. He was more than good-looking; he was built, ripped, hot, you name it. What's more, he had deep, gorgeous, limpid brown eyes.

Barb said, "Just tidying up, Chick, but sure, I can fix you some breakfast. How do you like your eggs?"

He winced. "Uh, maybe later. Right now, I just need some coffee. Thought I'd go out for a run. I saw a park nearby, right?"

I told him, "Just down the street. Neil and I run there all the time."

"Great. Join me?"

I was tempted. And how. "Uh, I'm already cleaned up for the office. But, Neil, if you'd like to go, don't mind me."

Neil eyed me askance. With a grin, he asked, "You're sure?"

I smiled. "Sure I'm sure. Show our guest the secret route."

Chick quipped, "This is sounding better and better."

While Barb poured a cup of coffee for Chick, Carl explained that he and Roxanne would be going to the office with me for a while.

"We need to be on the road by ten in order to catch that flight to Hawaii, so be ready."

"No problem." Chick checked his watch, slurped his coffee.

Neil jerked his head, signaling for me to follow him to the hall. When we were out of earshot of the kitchen, he asked, "You're really okay with this?"

"Well, *sure*. Besides, you're on a mission."

He crossed his arms. "And what might that be?"

"When you're out there in the park, just the two of you, running side by side, switch on the gaydar. I want to know: Is he or isn't he?"

Carl and Roxanne packed their things and loaded their car, leaving it at the house on Prairie Street so Chick Butterly could load his bags while we were at our meeting. I drove Carl and Roxanne downtown to the *Register*'s offices, arriving at a minute or two past nine. Doug Pierce's unmarked, tan, county-issued sedan was already at the curb as I turned my black Bavarian V-8 into the driveway and parked in my reserved spot.

I opened the street door with my key, and we entered the quiet lobby—it was dark behind the glass cage where Connie, our weekday receptionist, normally answered the phone, watched the door, and logged staffers' ins and outs. Leading Roxanne and Carl upstairs to the second-floor newsroom, I told them, "These offices are typically dead on Sunday, but I asked Lucy to put some extra staff on duty today. There's just no telling how this story might evolve."

Both Roxanne and Carl nodded, but neither spoke. They seemed absorbed in their thoughts, particularly Roxanne, who appeared downright somber.

As we arrived at the top of the stairs and began our slalom through the maze of desks, the reporter in the city slot told me, "Sheriff Pierce arrived a few minutes ago. He and Lucille are in your office."

My office suite was at the far end of the newsroom, behind a wall of glass. An outer office, originally intended for a secretary, now served as a small conference room. My working office was within, and I could see Doug and Lucy huddled near my desk, fussing with something—doubtless the VCR that shared space with a television and sound system in a cabinet along the side wall.

"Morning, all," I told them, sounding a chipper note as I entered the outer office with the Creightons in tow.

"Hi, Mark," they answered. "Good morning." Their tone didn't mimic mine. In fact, they both sounded preoccupied, barely turning to acknowledge our arrival. Pierce moved stiffly, and his shoulders looked crooked, as if he'd pinched a nerve in his neck. He held a remote control in one hand; a rewinding videotape produced a flickering, garbled image on the screen.

As Carl and Roxanne squeezed into my office, Pierce and Lucy greeted them, but there was no chitchat about the wedding or joshing about their "first night" together. Even Lucy, who normally went ditsy at the sight of Roxanne, seemed as restrained and sober as her drab-colored pantsuit.

I took the chair behind my desk, offering the two guest chairs to Roxanne and Carl, who sat without speaking. Pierce and Lucy remained standing near the television. The cassette clicked inside the machine, and the screen went black.

"Well," I asked, "what did you find, Doug?"

He gave the obvious answer: "A section of tape." Rubbing his neck, he added, "It speaks best for itself." He pushed the button, and an image flopped to life on the screen.

As the picture came into view, I saw Lucy steal a glance toward Roxanne, and I found it disconcerting that Lucy's lower lip was pinched between her teeth. Clearly, she'd already seen the tape, and for the first time, I considered the possibility that the video might spell real trouble.

Concerned as I was for Roxanne, I was watching her, not the television, as the tape began to play. What reaction, I wondered, would she have to what she saw on the screen? I could imagine any of a range of emotions, but I was baffled when her head began to sag sideways. When her ear touched her shoulder, her hair flopped over her face. As she brushed it aside with one hand, I noticed, to my astonishment, that Carl had aped this bizarre posture.

Turning toward the television, I saw both Pierce and Lucy doing the same. Then my eyes went to the screen.

"Dale's camcorder," Pierce reminded us, "was left running on a table near the bar. Unfortunately, the camera was lying on its side, but it captured exactly what we need to see."

This explained everyone's odd viewing position, which I too adopted. It also explained the crick in Pierce's neck—he'd studied this tape for hours.

"The sound is worthless, just party babble near the camera"— Pierce muted it—"but the video gives us a good look at the scene near the bar when Betty was killed."

"Do tell," said Carl. "What a lucky coincidence."

"Yes," Pierce agreed, "lucky for the investigation. Here we go."

We all watched silently as the action transpired sideways on the screen.

I am in the foreground with Betty Gifford Ashton; Roxanne is a few feet beyond, extricating herself from a clump of well-wishers; the bar is dead ahead, with kids milling about, stealing ice from the vat. Wesley Scott, the bartender, banishes the youngsters, rearranges bottles in the tub, and sets up a row of glasses, dunking them into the tub for ice. Pierce catches up with me, chatting; then Roxanne slips away from her friends, joining us. A few moments later, I usher Roxanne and Betty to the bar for drinks. Pierce steps up as well, and I stand next to him, waiting a few feet behind the ladies. The angle of the camera affords a clear view of everyone's actions, including those of Wes the bartender.

Instinctively, at this point, everyone in my office leaned an inch or so closer to the screen.

Roxanne is seen ordering her Perrier from Wes, pointing to the green bottles on a shelf behind him. Wes nods, dunking deep for another glassful of ice. Then he exchanges some banter with Betty, freshens another glass of ice, and leans beneath the bar to look for a bottle of bourbon. Roxanne and Betty are chatting as the older woman dabs and fans her face with a handkerchief. Roxanne points to the vat, saying something. Betty turns, eyes the vat, and nods. Wes gets up with the bottle of bourbon and turns toward the back shelf, reaching for a bottle of Perrier. Betty has stepped to the tub. Now she dips her lace hankie into the water.

Knowing what would happen, I blinked, unwilling yet eager to witness the deadly moment, feeling as dirty, perverse, sickened, and guilty as if I'd been caught trafficking in snuff porn. Across the desk from me, Roxanne gasped. Carl mumbled, "Dear Lord." Though I tried to look away, I couldn't keep my eyes off the screen.

Betty's hand is in the water, and she seems to have frozen there. In the video, I turn, looking off toward the bandstand, wondering what has happened to the music. Roxanne is trembling, speechless, pointing, trying to get my attention. Then I turn to see Betty. Her eyes stare wildly, blindly into space. Her mouth sags. Her entire body shudders, then drops. The grass at her feet steams. Pierce and I rush toward her—

The action stops, catching both of us midstride.

"There," said Pierce with a click of the remote, "what did you see?" The tape began to rewind.

Carl straightened his neck and took a deep breath. "It was awful. We saw the final, agonizing moments of that dear lady's life."

"Yup. What else?"

Though the tape was inarguably disturbing, Roxanne must have concluded that her apprehensions had been unwarranted. With re-newed spunk, she ventured, "We saw what can happen when you wear open-toed pumps." Grinning, she crossed her legs, displaying nice calves and spike heels, but no toes.

Dryly, Pierce agreed, "I suppose so, yes. What else did we see?"

Frustrated by my own lack of insight, I answered, "Nothing. We saw nothing more than what we saw yesterday afternoon. You and I, Doug, were both eyewitnesses—so was Roxanne. We clearly saw what happened, both in reality and now on the tape, but I can't begin to make sense of it. What are you driving at?" I rolled my head, soothing my neck.

Pierce paused, turning to my managing editor. "What did *you* see, Lucille?"

Lucy looked at Pierce for a moment, then at Roxanne. Turning to me, she ran a hand through her close-cropped red hair. "I've seen the tape more than once now, Mark. Before you arrived, I saw it in slow motion. Your focus sort of changes when you have time to see what's going on."

"Exactly," said Pierce, "it's all a matter of focus. When a woman is being electrocuted, it's only natural—you look at the woman."

At that moment, however, I was looking at Pierce's eyes. I'd just noticed—his, like so many others', were a deep, masculine brown.

He continued, "Now that we've all witnessed the more sensational aspects of Betty's passing, let's take another look. If we focus not on the victim, but elsewhere in the scene, the sequence of events begins to make sense. And Lucille is correct—it helps to slow down the tape." Pierce fiddled with the controls, replaying the tape from the moment when Roxanne and Betty step up to the bar and order drinks.

At half speed, Roxanne points to the green bottles of Perrier on the shelf behind Wes. Betty asks for bourbon, and Wes stoops to find it. Betty fans herself with her hankie, and Roxanne gestures toward the tub of ice water. Betty turns to the tub.

"Now," said Pierce, "let's watch what happens frame by frame." He further slowed the tape, which now showed jerky images in half-second bursts. He added, "Don't watch Betty. Watch the Perrier."

Uh-oh. I had no idea what significance the Perrier could have, but I knew only too well that the bottled water was linked to Roxanne. Pierce knew this also; he'd been in the kitchen with us on Saturday morning as Roxanne removed the bottles from the refrigerator, explaining her intention to stock the bar.

Glancing at Roxanne, I noted that her smug puss had turned wary as she leaned her head sideways to watch the flickering screen. I assumed the same position and watched as well.

Moving at a stop-and-go snail's pace, Wes rises from behind the bar with the bourbon, sets it down, turns to the back shelf, and steps toward it. He begins reaching toward the end of the shelf, where three matching green bottles are clearly visible—the bottles placed there by Roxanne. Betty has stepped toward the vat of ice water, arriving as Wes places his hand on the bottle at the end of the shelf. Betty reaches to dunk her hankie in the water as Wes tilts the bottle to pull it from the shelf.

"There," said Pierce, freezing the action on the screen.

"What?" asked Carl.

"Oh, my God," mumbled Roxanne.

"What?" Carl repeated.

Now I saw it.

Lucy tapped a fingernail on the screen. "Look at that—on the shelf, wedged behind the bottle—it's the head of the orange extension cord."

"Oh, no . . . ," someone mumbled (it may have been I).

Pierce advanced the tape by a single frame. "As the bottle leaves the shelf"—click—"the head of the cord begins to slide"—click—"and then the rest of the orange extension cord can be seen"—click—"as it swings in an arc from the tent rigging"—click—"and drops into the rear of the vat." Freeze.

We knew what happened next. None of us needed to see Betty's hand plunge into the water. None of us wanted to watch the onset of her cardiac arrhythmia.

Pierce turned off the television. "Where does this leave us?"

No one wanted to state what seemed suddenly apparent.

So Roxanne herself said it: "I'm a murder suspect."

"Roxie, dear"—Carl turned in his chair, wrapping an arm around his wife—"that's surely an overstatement. Granted, it does appear that the cord that fell had been wedged behind the Perrier, and it's common knowledge that you had put the Perrier on the shelf. But it's a leap of logic for anyone to conclude that you were responsible for rigging the cord. It could have been anyone. For that matter, it could have been entirely inadvertent, an accident."

Roxanne shook her head softly. "Thanks, Carl. But you're forgetting something. The fuse box had been rigged so that the circuit wouldn't blow when the cord hit the water. That was no accident." She didn't need to add how quickly, openly, and blithely she'd guessed the penny trick that had accomplished the sabotage.

"Correct," said Pierce. "I have no doubt that it was foul play that led to Betty's death. I have many doubts, however, about the implications of this tape."

"Sheriff," said Carl, a touch of panic coloring his voice, "you can't seriously believe that Roxanne had some connection to yesterday's tragedy. It simply doesn't add up."

"Except"—Roxanne heaved a sigh—"my actions on the tape seem to put me in control of both the timing and the sequence of events. Consider: I stepped up to the bar with Betty, ordered a glass of Perrier, showed the bartender where to get it, then suggested that Betty stick her hand in the water." She put a palm to her forehead. "Christ."

I hadn't even thought of that twist. Such an interpretation of the tape could lead some to conclude not only that Roxanne was responsible for what had happened, but that the results had been devilishly calculated and premeditated.

"Roxie, dear"—Carl patted her hand—"it might be best if you refrained from voicing such speculation."

"Look." Pierce cleared his throat. "I have a murder investigation on my hands. We're all friends here, but I'm a cop first and have to remain objective about the facts of the case. On the surface, yes, the tape could easily be construed to implicate Roxanne—sorry. At the same time, knowing her as I do, I'm only too eager to lay those suspicions to rest. So help me here. Right up front, is there anything that negates the possibility of Roxanne's complicity?"

"Motive," I said without hesitation. "As you yourself said last night, Doug, murder always has a motive. What conceivable motive could Roxanne have had to want Betty Gifford Ashton dead? She didn't even know the woman."

I looked to Roxanne, assuming she would affirm my assertion, but at that moment, her head was turned, sharing a tight-lipped glance with Carl. Once again, I recalled Betty's comment to Roxanne at the reception about the irony of meeting "after all these years," forcing me to wonder if my words just now had sprung from wishful thinking instead of firm knowledge. Had the two women in fact known each other in some prior context?

Lucy, of course, was not privy to my doubts, and she rushed to Roxanne's defense. "Mark's right—Roxanne simply had no reason to harm Betty. And even if by some stretch of imagination she *did,* Roxanne wouldn't stoop to electrocuting an old lady, and she certainly wouldn't do it on her wedding day, not at the height of her husband's political campaign." With a crisp nod, Lucy added, "Roxanne is far smarter than that."

Roxanne thanked Lucy with a wan smile. Lucy, I'm certain, was reeling inside. Yes, she assured herself, I still have a chance, I still have reason to hope . . .

"Well spoken, Miss Haring," said Carl, sounding every inch the candidate. "Sheriff Pierce," he added, sounding more like a lawyer, "both Mark and his editor have raised valid, helpful points as to why Roxanne should not be considered a suspect in this presumed crime. I'd now like to add a further observation, a point of unassailable logic that negates any possibility of Roxanne's complicity."

Needless to say, Carl had captured our attention. Three years earlier, when he'd been appointed a deputy attorney general, he was at the top of his legal craft. Now we were being treated to a taste of the jurisprudential skills that had earned him such a lofty reputation.

Carl stood, making my cramped office feel even smaller. "The point I wish to raise is a simple one, an ironclad issue of timing."

Timing is everything, I recalled. Especially in politics.

"Even if it could be proven that Roxanne had harbored some motive to wish harm upon Betty Gifford Ashton—which she did not, of course—and even if one were to postulate that Roxanne would be willing to visit disaster upon her own wedding reception in fulfilling this morbid wish—a ridiculous postulation—there remains the issue of timing, which would not have allowed her to act upon such intentions."

I wondered where Carl was headed with this. If timing were the issue, the scene on the videotape had made it appear that Roxanne was not hampered by, but in control of, the timing of events that killed Betty. Roxanne herself had voiced this observation—in detail—only moments earlier.

"The timing in question," explained Carl, "relates to *what* Roxanne knew and *when* she knew it."

Roxanne grinned, telling her husband, "Get to the point, counsel."

He asked her, "Who, Mrs. Creighton, was responsible for drawing up the guest list for yesterday's nuptials?"

"I was, in part, and so were you. Most of the local guests, however, were invited by Mark and Neil."

Carl turned to me. Winking, he asked, "Is that true, Mr. Manning?"

"Indeed it is. The former Miss Exner asked Neil and me to 'invite whoever should be there,' or words to that effect. At the prompting of Justice Uhrig, we decided that Betty Gifford Ashton should be there." Sensing the direction of Carl's logic, I added, "No, Roxanne never reviewed the final guest list."

Carl turned to Pierce. Sitting, resting his case (as well as his rump), he said, "You see, Sheriff? Roxanne had no idea that Betty would be at the wedding. I myself didn't know this until the ceremony, when I first met Betty. She and Roxanne met later still, at the reception—I was there when Mark introduced them."

"That's right." I nodded, recalling the incident.

"Which means simply this: by the time Roxanne and Betty met, Roxanne had already stocked the bar with her Perrier, hours earlier. After meeting Betty, Roxanne mingled with the crowd until encountering Betty again at the bar. In short, Roxanne had no *opportunity* to rig either the extension cord or the fuse box during those few minutes after she became aware of Betty's presence. Timing is everything." He smiled, concluding, "Case closed."

A wave of sighs and light laughter swept through my office. Carl's listeners had understood his logic and accepted his conclusion. Pierce thanked Carl for dispatching the matter so neatly. Lucy seemed giddy with relief, scribbling notes that she added to a folder. Roxanne sat quietly, eyeing me. Did she already know that something was troubling me? Could she read it in my face?

Pierce was saying, "Dale Turner's videotape has given the investigation a promising start, but thanks to Carl, we now know that initial assumptions can prove groundless. I've got my work cut out for me."

Roxanne leaned to Carl, whispering something. They shared a few sentences. I hoped she was telling him what I now found so bothersome.

But no.

"Doug," said Roxanne, emerging from her huddle, "Carl and I think it might be best to cancel our honeymoon."

Lucy could barely conceal the pleasure she gleaned from this unexpected news. "Oh, Roxanne," she said with a forced frown, trying
to muster a tone of concern, "are you sure?"

Carl answered, "We're both aware that the circumstances captured
on the tape will, in some people's eyes, cast Roxanne in a dubious
light. We *know* better, of course, but frankly, we're concerned that
even the slightest whiff of scandal could jeopardize the gubernatorial
race, which is exceedingly tight. It might appear insensitive or even
clandestine for us to whisk off to Hawaii just now, so we'll simply
postpone the trip until after the election. We want to make ourselves
fully available to the investigation until the matter is sufficiently resolved to put Roxanne firmly above suspicion."

Pierce asked, "Will you be staying here in town?"

As Lucy waited to hear the answer, her nonchalant air was con-
tradicted by the blanched knuckles that gripped a ballpoint pen.

"Not unless you think we should," said Roxanne. "Chick Butterly
needs to get back to Chicago today. You can reach us there on a
moment's notice."

Thank God, I thought. Neil and I wanted our house back.

"Fine," said Pierce. "I appreciate your sensitivity to the case."

Carl checked his watch. "It's past nine-thirty. Chick expects to
leave by ten."

Roxanne reminded him, "We no longer have a plane to catch, so
it won't matter if we run late. I think we need to spend a few minutes
at the Manor House. My mother deserves to hear about the honeymoon face-to-face, and I assume you'll want to say good-bye to
Lauren."

Carl nodded.

I offered, "I can drive you there right now," and we all stood.

Pierce and Lucy said their farewells to Roxanne and Carl. I
thanked Lucy for putting in the extra hours on a Sunday, and I told
Pierce I'd phone him that afternoon—perhaps we could later put our
heads together and compare notes. He gladly welcomed my thoughts
on the case, and I knew that I'd secured, once again, an inside news
source for an important, evolving story.

But in the whirl and mishmash of taking our leave, I was unable to concentrate on our random scraps of discussion, unable to focus on the details and logistics that were bandied about. I was still stuck on one tiny but crucial aspect of Carl's articulate, logical argument about the timing of Saturday's chain of events. Because Roxanne had not drawn up the guest list and because she did not meet Betty until the afternoon reception was under way, Carl had reasoned that Roxanne would have had no opportunity to rig either the extension cord or the fuse box.

I well recalled, however, that it was early Saturday morning when Roxanne had learned that Betty would attend the wedding. The news had been spelled out in Glee Savage's society column in that morning's paper, and Roxanne had asked me about it, with a measure of dismay, while we sat around the kitchen table.

Carl had slept late on Saturday and never did appear for breakfast. What's more, Sheriff Pierce did not arrive from his workout that morning until after Roxanne had asked about Betty. So neither Carl nor Pierce now understood that Carl's logic was flawed to its core. While I still had no reason to suspect that Roxanne had harbored any *motive* to harm Betty, she'd had abundant *opportunity* to do so—during the final hours of setup for the lawn party, while stocking the bar with her Perrier.

As we left my office, Roxanne was uncharacteristically mute. Catching my eye, she read my face and understood that I'd found the chink in Carl's logic.

I, in turn, understood her fragile expression.

Her eyes silently pleaded, Don't say a word.

I phoned the Manor House from the car to let Gale Exner know that we were on our way, telling her only that Roxanne wanted to bring her up-to-date on "a few matters" before leaving town.

With a soft laugh, Gale noted, "That's terribly cryptic-sounding, Mark." She was correct.

As a writer, a reporter, and a rationalist, I have trained myself to be a ruthless defender of clarity, whether in thought or in word—to eschew obfuscation, as a tweedy-vested rhetoric professor had preached and hammered during my freshman year of college. The principle has served me well, and I recommend unswerving adherence to it. That morning in the car, however, I was disinclined to tell Gale that her daughter was suspected of murder and that the honeymoon, therefore, was off. So I obfuscated.

(Professor Precision would doubtless interject here that I have erred in using *obfuscate* intransitively. But he is now dead, and the stewardship of usage has fallen to the likes of me.)

Intrigued, Gale told me she'd be waiting for us in the mansion's front parlor.

We tried to reach Lauren Creighton as well, but she wasn't in her room and the proprietor wasn't sure of her whereabouts, so our only option was to hope we could locate her after we arrived.

We arrived within minutes and parked at the curb in the deep shade of an ancient red maple. The tree was so old and its trunk so massive, the sidewalk swooped around it. Another walk, lined with red brick, led straight from the street to the front terrace of the Manor House, built as a home by some forgotten industrialist, now a lavish bed-and-breakfast with some six or eight guest rooms, all of them updated with minibars and fax machines, some with Jacuzzis. The style of the brick building was a pretentious Georgian/Gothic hybrid, sporting heavily carved limestone trim—the word *stately* sprang to mind.

Carl, Roxanne, and I got out of the car and started up the walk. The lazy Sunday morning surrounded us with its clear sky and warm September breeze. Finches chirped, robins trilled, cardinals sang. Smells of sausage and syrup drifted from the flung-wide French doors of the dining room. The facade that rose before us was whimsically opulent, as picture-perfect as a movie set. I almost forgot that our visit had somber overtones, and I hadn't a clue that the situation would grow even bleaker before our departure.

As we climbed the front stairs, the screen door opened before us, seemingly of its own will. Blinded by sunlight, I couldn't see the figure who stood masked by the shadows within, arm outstretched against the door's long, taut spring. "Good morning, Mr. Manning. Always a pleasure to welcome you to the Manor House."

"Good morning, Milton." I recognized the voice of the proprietor,

Milton Tallent, an accommodating man in his sixties, a widower who had retired from a banking career several years earlier and then, as something of a lark, had taken on the role of an exclusive hotelier. Stepping into the foyer with the Creightons, I introduced Carl to Milton; Roxanne had already met him, on Friday evening after her mother's arrival.

"I'm so sorry," Milton told Roxanne, "that the festivities of your special day took such a dreadful turn. I do hope you're not the suspicious sort."

"I beg your pardon?" she asked quietly, with blank amazement. She doubtless wondered, Do I appear suspicious even to this man I barely know?

"I suppose the word I meant to use is *superstitious*. I hope you find no ill omen in this calamity—with regard to the future happiness of your marriage."

"Ohhh," she said with a lilting laugh, a flick of the hand, and exaggerated relief, "of *course* not."

Milton was taken aback by this response—literally, he stepped backward a pace, as if wary of Roxanne, wondering what was wrong with the woman. He squinted at her with pinched brown eyes.

Carl chortled, explaining, "My dear wife has been under a bit of strain, Mr. Tallent—the pressures of the wedding, you know, and the nasty turn of events."

"So I see. Yes. Of course." Milton didn't budge an inch nearer.

"Rox-aa-anne," warbled a voice, Gale's, "is that you, honey?"

Roxanne looked about the foyer, down the hall, up the main staircase. She called, "Hi, Mom. Where are you?"

"Right here." Gale appeared in the doorway to the walnut-paneled parlor, just across the hall from the library. "Now—what, may I ask, is the nature of this mysterious visit?" She gave us all a friendly scowl, adding, "Not that I don't appreciate seeing my daughter, even under the most *trying* of circumstances."

Roxanne stepped to her mother, greeting her with a kiss. Carl and I followed, offering hugs. After a brief exchange of small talk there in the hall, followed by an awkward silence, Roxanne said, "Let's sit down." And the four of us entered the parlor.

Neil and I had attended several social functions at the Manor House (the place was *perfect* for Christmas parties), and upon first seeing the interior, Neil had judged it "stylistically confused." Indeed, Milton Tallent had approached his renovation of the grand old home more as a hobbyist than as a purist, and with considerably more money than subtlety. So the various public rooms tended toward the thematic, each a modern caricature of a different stylistic period—the Tudor library, the Louis Quinze dining room, the art deco powder room, and (need I say it?) the Victorian parlor.

There, against the back wall of the parlor, facing a velvet-swagged conservatory window, stood a fanciful and eerily familiar sofa. With rolled and tasseled arms, curlicued back, and hideous clawed feet, it was the very settee upon which Blain Gifford and his brown-eyed yum-yum had lolled and frolicked in my dream.

Carl entered the room with mild astonishment, arching his brows; though he was by no means an aficionado of interior design, his privileged upbringing told him at once that the room's decorating was over-the-top. Roxanne and Gale showed no reaction to the gaudy setting, having already seen it; besides, each of the ladies had other things on her mind. I too had a great deal on my mind that morning, and I too had seen the room before, but I was suddenly preoccupied with that god-awful sofa. How had it slipped into my dream? Why had it seemingly landed in my own living room? And most baffling, why had it become a stage for the sex rumpus of two opposing political-campaign managers?

Carl was telling Gale, "We just came from a meeting with Sheriff Pierce at Mark's office. There have been some developments with regard to the death of Mrs. Ashton." He sat on the sofa, taking the center cushion.

Roxanne and her mother chose a pair of gnarled armchairs, separated by a round, spindly mahogany table that bore a chimney lamp, grotesque and bulbous, painted with huge pink rhododendrons and festooned with ruby-glass prisms. I remained standing.

"Mom," said Roxanne, "the videotape that the tent guy gave to Sheriff Pierce last night did indeed capture the scene at the bar when Mrs. Ashton was killed."

"Thank goodness," said Gale. "What a lucky coincidence."

Carl told her, "Those were my exact words when the sheriff told us what he'd found. Then we saw the tape. It was, well . . . somewhat disturbing." Carl too was obfuscating.

Gale nodded. "I'm sure it was. However enlightening the tape may have been, it *must* have been disturbing to watch an old lady die of electrocution."

Roxanne reminded her mother, "I saw it happen in the first place, so viewing the tape was like reliving the horrible moment."

Carl breathed a sigh. "But it doesn't end there, Gale. You see, the events depicted on the tape might be construed as having implications that we *know* are beyond the realm of possibility."

Enough obfuscation. "Gale," I said, "at first blush, the tape suggests that Roxanne could be connected to Betty's death."

Gale responded to my words with speechless bewilderment, falling back against the black horsehair cushion of her chair.

Roxanne took charge, objectively relating to her mother what we'd seen on the video, explaining how her actions seemed to put her in control of the timing and the sequence of events that killed Betty.

Gale stammered, "The sheriff doesn't think . . . he can't actually believe . . ."

"No," Carl assured her. "Douglas made a point of affirming his friendship to Roxanne. He asked for our help, up front, in disproving any possibility of her involvement." Carl paused, then smiled. "Fortunately, I had my thinking cap on." He proceeded to detail his reasoning that Roxanne could have had no opportunity to rig the electrocution—based on his belief that Roxanne had had no knowledge of Betty's presence at the wedding until mere minutes before Betty was killed.

Roxanne's eyes slid toward mine as her husband raised this point in her defense. I hoped that she would now correct his mistaken notion. But she did not. In fact, when my eyes met hers, she flashed an unconvincing smile, as if to tell me, There now. Neat and tidy. Everything's under control.

Still speaking to Gale, Carl concluded, "Roxanne's lack of *opportunity* to commit the crime, coupled with the more obvious assumption that she had no *motive* to harm Betty, sufficiently convinced the sheriff that Roxanne could be held above suspicion."

"Thank God," muttered Gale, resting a hand over her heart.

Roxanne cracked, "Good thing I married a lawyer."

Carl added, "Douglas was clearly pleased to have such firm, logical evidence of Roxanne's noncomplicity. Unfortunately, from the standpoint of the investigation, he's back at square one. If you ask me— based on what we saw on that tape—the bartender should be at the top of the suspect list."

"That's what I was thinking," I told everyone, happy to focus on something other than Roxanne's lie of omission. "Wesley Scott's actions on the tape can easily be interpreted as controlling both the timing and the chain of events that killed Betty. What's more, he was the one who was *there* all the time, at the bar, even during setup for the party. He had *many* opportunities to rig both the fuse box and the extension cord."

"Exactly," agreed Carl.

Gale turned to her daughter. "Which means you're, uh . . . off the hook?"

Roxanne laughed. "Yes, Mother. Even so, Carl and I have talked it over, and under the circumstances, we think it makes sense to postpone the honeymoon. So we're not going to Hawaii today. We've decided to wait until after the election."

"Oh, honey"—Gale's face fell—"that's seems so drastic. But why?"

Carl answered, "It was Roxanne's decision entirely, Gale. She's worried that it might look bad, politically speaking, for us to traipse off to paradise in the wake of a murder at our wedding. She has a point. The Illinois governor's race will be perilously close, and any minor wrinkle, even the slightest whiff of scandal, could throw the election to our esteemed opponent, Raymond Gifford."

Roxanne added, "And we wouldn't want *that*, now, would we?"

Gale smirked. "Of course not, dear. But I find it difficult to imagine—"

"Did I hear correctly?" a woman's voice interrupted from the hall. "The honeymoon's *off?*"

We all turned toward the doorway. There stood Lauren Creighton, hand to hip, looking more amused than surprised by this news. She wore a laid-back Sunday-morning ensemble of jeans and sweatshirt, both emblazoned with designer labels.

Carl rose (the Exner ladies remained seated). "Lauren, honey," he said through a cautious smile, "we called ahead but couldn't reach you. Where have you been?"

She ambled a few paces into the parlor. "In the library—across the hall. I've been reading the papers for *hours.*" This seemed a reasonable assertion, as her feet were bare; she hadn't been outdoors.

It also seemed reasonable to assume that she'd heard every word of our conversation, that she'd been aware of our presence since the moment of our arrival. I had no doubt: after we'd greeted Gale and settled into the parlor, Lauren had forsaken her newspapers, padded across the hall, and lurked outside the doorway, soaking up every delicious detail of Roxanne's potential plight.

Lauren repeated, "The honeymoon's *off?*" With a smug nod, she added, "Good idea, Pops. I approve."

Fooling no one, Carl pretended to believe that his daughter had not been eavesdropping. Obligingly, he summarized the morning's events, concluding, "No, then, the honeymoon is most definitely not 'off.' We've merely postponed it—due to the political realities of a tight election."

"Hmmm." Lauren sauntered farther into the room, approaching Roxanne. With a bent smile, she observed, "It's looks as if things are getting sticky for my new stepmom."

Roxanne glared at the younger woman.

Gale gripped the arms of her chair so tightly, her hands looked more bony and ferocious than the sofa's clawed feet.

"Now, Lauren . . . ," Carl began.

With wide, innocent eyes, she asked, "Have you told Beryl about these disturbing developments?" Lauren knew very well that her father had not recently spoken to her mother, certainly not in regard to his honeymoon.

Silence magnified the tension in the room. Then the silence was broken by the slap of the front door, pulled shut by its spring. All of us, even unflappable Lauren, started, as if roused from napping by a gunshot.

Footfalls approached from the front of the hall. Blain Gifford then passed the parlor doorway as he rushed toward the staircase at the rear of the house, presumably on his way to his room. But a moment after he passed, his footsteps stopped. A few seconds later, he appeared in the doorway again. Standing with feet spread and arms crossed, he observed the scene in the parlor, telling us, "Well now, isn't this handy—finding all of you here together."

I had no idea why he would find our assembly "handy," but at the moment, I was more intrigued by his appearance than by his words. Until now, I had seen the Republican wearing only dark, proper business attire. This morning, though, he sported starched, well-pressed, heavy khakis and a soft, cuddly powder-blue knit shirt; oxblood loafers, with matching belt and watchband; a neat, trim haircut, brushed and parted, with fetching dashes of silver creeping back from the temples. All in all, he looked ... well, he looked a lot like *me*. Granted, he was four or five years older, and his eyes weren't green (they were blue, the color of his shirt), but he was about my height and build, and I couldn't help gaping at my sartorial clone. He and I could easily have passed for a well-heeled, middle-aged, suburban gay couple on our way out for Sunday brunch.

These observations only heightened my curiosity: Was he or wasn't he? If Blain Gifford was gay, how could he reconcile his sexual identity with the hostile attitudes of the political party he worked for? Why had he appeared in my dream—on the exact sofa that now sat within a few feet of both of us? Who, in my dream, was Blain's brown-eyed lover? Was it his younger, hunkier Democratic counterpart, Chick Butterly? And what, if anything, had Neil learned about Chick during their run together in the park that morning?

Carl was saying, "Again, Blain, on behalf of Lowell Sagehorn and the entire Democratic campaign, I want to extend sympathies on your dear aunt's passing." Carl, I noted, was now obfuscating death.

Blain nodded a silent acknowledgment of the condolences. Then, with a steely expression, he told Carl, "I've had a rather busy morning, sorting through some of Aunt Betty's affairs."

Gale sighed. "It helps to keep busy. Sometimes, after a loss, it can be oddly comforting to lose oneself in the minutiae of settling the loved one's estate." She doubtless expected Blain to thank her for these sentiments. When he reacted, instead, with a look of perturbation, Gale elaborated, "Closing the book, so to speak."

"Mrs. Exner," he said flatly, "I'm certain there are those who are only too eager to 'close the book' on my aunt's death. Unfortunately for *them*, I do not share their urgent desire to bury the past."

"Them?" asked Gale through a squint of confusion. "Who?"

Blain ambled a few paces into the parlor, exactly as Lauren had done, projecting the same smug attitude. Speaking to Gale, he told everyone, "You see, Mrs. Exner, while going through some of my aunt's files, I discovered something that will be of interest to all present."

Roxanne looked up at Carl from where she sat. Carl returned her gaze without expression.

Noting this, Blain said, "Unless I'm mistaken, Mr. and Mrs. Creighton are highly eager to bury the past."

Carl closed his eyes.

Roxanne froze motionless.

Gale looked at her daughter with dismay.

Lauren, sensing trouble for both Carl (whom she loved) and Roxanne (whom she loathed), was uncertain whether to react to Blain's statement with umbrage or with glee. Seeking clarification, she asked Blain, "Huh?"

At the moment, I was equally confused and could not myself have phrased the query with greater eloquence.

Blain stepped forward and began, "This goes back some five years."

The time frame apparently had meaning for Carl, who sat on the sofa again, eyeing his knees.

Blain continued, "I should have picked up on this yesterday, at the wedding reception, but it just didn't click. It clicked for Aunt Betty, though, and she alluded to it. I had no idea what she meant when, meeting the new Mrs. Creighton, Betty said, 'It's a pleasure—and such an irony—meeting you after all these years.' "

I could recall the incident vividly, and I remembered being as confused as Blain had been by the meaning of his aunt's words.

"Then," said Blain, "this morning, I went over to Betty's home and began sorting through her files, as suggested by the family's local attorney. It was all rather tedious—until I ran across the records of an incident I'd forgotten. Not quite five years ago, just after Thanksgiving, the Illinois branch of the family was involved in an important stock transaction, a merger that required a filing with the Securities and Exchange Commission. The SEC filing was botched, however, by a Chicago lawyer who missed a crucial court date after a long weekend bender."

Uh-oh. When Blain had first mentioned the five-year time frame, Carl had identified the incident. Now that Blain had spoken of a bender following the Thanksgiving weekend, I had no trouble connecting the dots.

I recalled that Roxanne had introduced Neil and me five years ago, come October. He and I would ultimately find love together, which had *not* been Roxanne's plan, so she cut off communication with both of us and took solace in the bottle. Later, after Christmas, we had a rapprochement, and she explained that she had, with great difficulty, kicked her self-destructive habit. I could still remember the watershed moment, back at my loft in Chicago, when Roxanne had told me, "I binged on Thanksgiving and screwed up royally with a client after the long weekend. That's when I knew I had to stop."

Blain Gifford now explained (needlessly, from my perspective), "The venerable law firm handling that transaction was Kendall Creighton Yoshihara of Chicago. The boozing lawyer who botched the filing was none other than Miss Roxanne Exner."

"Oh, God . . . ," Roxanne moaned, dropping her face into her hands.

I stepped over to her chair and put a hand on her shoulder.

Gale reached from her chair and patted her daughter's hand. I assumed that Gale had known of Roxanne's earlier problem and the general incident that had prompted the reform, but I doubted if Gale had known there was a specific connection to the Gifford and Ashton families. It had never been apparent to me; even Roxanne, Carl, and Blain had seemingly pieced it together just this weekend.

Lauren stood stone still, watching all this interplay with wide, smiling eyes, like a cat sizing up an unsuspecting mouse. The mouse, of course, was Lauren's new stepmother.

Blain concluded his revelations, "With the missed opportunity for the merger, a fortune was lost. On top of which, the fines for noncompliance with the filing were staggering. Needless to say, the family sued the law firm for malpractice."

Carl stood again, looking a tad wobbly. He told Blain, "The entire incident was indeed unfortunate. I was still with the firm back then—my name was on the door—and to this day I don't know why it took me so long to discover that Roxanne was in trouble with liquor. She needed help, understanding, and mentoring—not the denial of her coworkers."

Roxanne looked up at Carl lovingly. "Don't blame yourself. The problem was me, me, me."

Carl insisted, "Other than that one grievous lapse, you have *never* discredited the firm. To the contrary, your contributions have been exemplary. Your expertise was attested to two years after the incident, three years ago, when you were named a senior partner in the firm. You've succeeded in putting your addiction behind you, Roxanne—you have nothing whatever to apologize for."

Blain stamped his tasseled loafer. "I *beg* your pardon? Miss Exner's little 'lapse,' as you so euphemistically phrase it, cost my family not only a great deal of money, but a considerable dollop of embarrassment as well."

"Mr. Gifford"—Carl squared his shoulders—"let me remind you that your family and our firm settled the malpractice claim, and quickly, out of court. The Giffords recovered their monetary losses."

Blain stamped his other loafer. "Hah! The settlement covered only a *fraction* of the potential profits that were lost."

"Why, then," Carl asked calmly, "did your family settle for our offer?"

With strained patience, Blain explained, "Though I myself was not involved in the proceedings, I assume the Gifford family had no taste for wrangling in court, which would have required a full, public airing of our financial dealings."

Gale piped in, "So? Were the Giffords hiding something?"

Roxanne turned her head slightly and flashed her mother a grin. "Certainly *not*." Sniff. "My family protects and values its privacy. It's that simple."

"Fine," said Carl, "but everything has its price, and the price of the Giffords' privacy was a settlement. We'd have gladly met the family in court, but they backed down."

Blain sputtered, struggling to respond, but words escaped him.

Lauren strolled into the circle of conversation. "Now, now, Mr. Gifford. There's no point in arguing with *lawyers*, is there?" The irony escaped no one that she herself was a lawyer.

Carl cleared his throat. "Lauren, honey? Maybe you should stay out of this. It really doesn't concern you. Besides, what's done is done." With a shrug, he added, "Why dredge this up at all?"

As if on cue, Blain Gifford and Lauren Creighton turned to look at each other. As their eyes met, they shared a smile.

Lauren paused for effect, then told Blain, "If I'm not mistaken, the point of dredging up this past unpleasantness is to shed light on a more recent debacle. Last night, during our group meeting with Sheriff Pierce, you voiced your suspicion that my father's new bride had been involved in your aunt's death—in part because she'd 'guessed' the so-called penny trick that caused the electrocution. Last night, your suspicion may have seemed far-fetched. Now, in light of these past conflicts, it seems that Miss Exner did indeed have a motive to silence your aunt."

Roxanne stood. "That's ridiculous, Lauren."

"Really? Is it?"

"Yes, really. The five-year-old conflict—*settled* conflict—between the Gifford family and my law firm is distressing, certainly. I'm not proud of what happened, but why on earth would I try to 'silence' Betty Gifford Ashton for remembering it?"

"Because," Lauren quoted her father's exact words (confirming that she'd eavesdropped on our entire conversation), " 'the Illinois governor's race will be perilously close, and any minor wrinkle, even the slightest whiff of scandal, could throw the election to Raymond Gifford.' " Lauren smirked, and with good reason—she'd also heard us discussing how guilty Roxanne had looked on the videotape we'd seen that morning.

"Well, I *never* . . . ," said Gale from where she sat.

"Lauren, honey," Carl began, "I really must insist that—"

But Lauren forged ahead. "So here's where we're at: several whiffs of scandal have been raised. The new wife of the Democratic candidate for lieutenant governor of Illinois is an alcoholic who once brought considerable financial harm to the family of the Republican gubernatorial candidate. A benevolent old lady has now died as the result of a grisly, mysterious mishap, which the local sheriff has declared a homicide. Meanwhile, the alcoholic wife has been entertaining the notion of moving into the governor's mansion one day, so she had a highly plausible motive for silencing the old lady who recalled her sordid past. What's more, the alcoholic wife not only 'guessed' the penny trick at the scene of the crime, but just this morning, she was shown a videotape in which her actions seemed suspiciously in control of the timing of the events that caused the electrocution. I believe any prosecutor would conclude that the alcoholic wife had the means as well as the motive to kill the benevolent widow."

"Lauren," said Carl, trying to control his anger, trying to lecture his daughter as objectively as she had lectured us, "you know very well that you can't build a case on *motive* and *means* alone. A viable suspect must also have had the *opportunity* to commit the crime. Since you seem to have heard everything that's been said this morning, you already know that Roxanne learned of Mrs. Ashton's presence at the wedding only minutes before the tragedy. Roxanne couldn't possibly act that quickly—not in the presence of more than a hundred would-be witnesses—not that she'd even consider anything so heinous in the first place."

Carl stepped to Roxanne, opened his arms, and embraced her, patting her back. Confident that he'd once again nailed the crucial point of her innocence, he rested his head against hers, whispering words of assurance through her hair. With passing moments, the Victorian parlor became eerily quiet as everyone in the room weighed the significance of that morning's revelations.

Clearly, Roxanne was in trouble.

And so far, Sheriff Pierce had yet to investigate a single other suspect.

The investigation proper would not begin until Monday morning. The remainder of Sunday was consumed by a hectic string of meetings, conversations, and improvised planning sessions.

The plot was thickening, so Roxanne and Carl not only canceled their flight to Hawaii; they also canceled their plans to return to Chicago that day. Chick Butterly checked with Lowell Sagehorn, his party's standard-bearer, and the two decided that Chick should remain in Dumont as well. Sagehorn was wary of the developments concerning his running mate's new bride and wanted Chick on the scene to keep an eye on the situation and to report back.

The bottom line, as far as Neil and I were concerned, was that we would not be losing our houseguests for at least another day or two. We yearned to claim back our home, to focus on Thad and his departure for college. But Roxanne was an old friend, and as her dilemma deepened, we understood that she needed our support—as well as our guest room.

Around noon, I found myself alone with Neil in the kitchen on Prairie Street. Roxanne and Carl had gone upstairs to unpack. Chick was in his room, on the phone. Barb was also upstairs, helping Thad pack more cartons. Though I knew the corrugated boxes contained mostly clothing and books, I couldn't help feeling that they contained Thad's very boyhood. His youth was being sealed tight with thick, clear packing tape, soon to be shipped away.

Neil turned to me from the refrigerator. "There's more cake."

I groaned.

"I suppose I could fake some sort of sandwich."

"That would be great. Oh, by the way, I love you."

Neil strolled over to the table, where I was sitting. "It's *only* a sandwich." He sat next to me.

"Pardon the non sequitur; I wasn't talking about lunch. I was talking about 'us.' What we have—it's so stable, so committed, so normal."

Neil laughed. "Don't tell Blain Gifford that. He thinks we're a perversion, an abomination."

I qualified, "A faction of his political party thinks that way. We don't know what *he* believes."

"He's a campaign manager. He tows the party line."

"I suppose." I recalled Blain at the reception on Saturday, questioning me, aghast, about the legal status of Thad's relationship to Neil and me. I also recalled Blain entering the Manor House parlor that very morning, looking like a suburban gay clone. "Unless . . ."

"Yeah, yeah"—Neil mussed my hair—"unless your dream revealed deep, dark secrets. Trust me though. You were at least half-wrong."

"Oh?" In light of that morning's developments, I'd forgotten about Neil's run with Chick. "Any vibes?"

"Definitely. Chick Butterly is straight, period. There we were, alone together, running through the idyllic setting of the park, and all he did was talk about—get this—Alanna Scott."

I quipped, "Were you expecting him to make a pass at you?"

Neil grinned. "If Chick were gay, it might have happened."

I couldn't argue that point, so I mused, "Alanna Scott, the cateress. Hmm. At the reception yesterday, I thought I sensed some interest on Chick's part."

"He's interested, all right—he wondered how long Alanna and Wes have been married, wondered if they had kids, wondered why their relationship looked so shaky."

"I noticed that too. Both Wes and Alanna did seem on edge, but I assumed they were just stressed-out by the reception."

Neil shrugged. "Chick has his own theory. But even if he's right, what's in it for him? I mean, he's from Chicago and Alanna is up here."

"For a while, *everyone's* up here in Dumont. Besides our three houseguests, the crowd at the Manor House is staying in town as well. Blain Gifford needs to look after his aunt Betty's estate, and neither Roxanne's mom nor Carl's daughter is ready to leave."

"Sounds cozy over there. I bet there'll be some icy stares in the hallway after this morning's revelations and accusations."

I had, of course, filled Neil in on everything that had transpired that morning. There was one minor point, however, that I had not shared with him. He knew only that Carl had raised a vigorous defense of Roxanne, "proving" that she'd had no opportunity to commit the crime. Sheriff Pierce had accepted Carl's logic, which was all Neil had wanted to know—he hadn't pressed me for details of Carl's rationale. Had he done so, I'd have explained that Carl's reasoning had been flawed, that there had indeed been ample opportunity for Roxanne to rig the fuse box and the extension cord. And Neil would instantly have known that I was correct because he himself had been present in the kitchen early on Saturday morning when Roxanne had asked us about Betty.

For now, though, I was more comfortable keeping this knowledge between Roxanne and me. Our shared, secret truth raised some weighty questions that I needed to discuss with her, but as a friend, I felt that I owed her my confidence—at least for a short while.

The afternoon provided no opportunity for me to have a private conversation with Roxanne, so I tended to other matters.

Immediately after lunch, needing to phone Sheriff Pierce, I went to the den. My sanctuary, originally my uncle Edwin Quatrain's home office, occupied a front corner of the house, just off the main hall. To one side of the door was a tufted leather seating group, which faced a fireplace, now screened and dark in September. The other side of the room had windows to the front porch, and before the windows sat my uncle's massive partners desk. In all probability, it had never been moved since the house was built, more than fifty years earlier.

Sitting in my usual chair and reaching for the phone, I dialed (more accurately, I punched buttons—though the desk was vintage, the phone was not). As it was a Sunday and I had used Pierce's direct number, he answered the call himself.

After some greetings and rhetorical throat-clearing, I said, "Doug, when I drove Roxanne and Carl over to the Manor House this morning, we had an unusual confrontation with Carl's daughter and—more significantly—with Blain Gifford. Some background has come to light, and you need to know about it. On the surface, it paints Roxanne in a bad light, but I think—"

"Mark," he interrupted, "I appreciate that you're bringing this to my attention, but I already know the whole story. After you left the Manor House, Blain wasted no time tracking me down. He told me about the botched SEC filing, the malpractice suit, and his aunt Betty's recognition of Roxanne at the reception. He's trying to make the case that this constitutes a motive for Roxanne to kill Betty—a deadly cover-up meant to protect Carl's chances of being elected lieutenant governor. This only reinforces his previous theory that Roxanne had the means to commit the crime—knowledge of the penny trick."

"Christ, he's turning into a loose cannon."

"He is. After speaking to me, he phoned to set up a meeting with Harley."

"No." (Not Harley Kaiser, not the Dumont County district attorney, not the local prosecutor whom Roxanne had once branded a "hot dog," not the officious homophobe whose disdain for me was topped only by his outright contempt for a certain sassy Chicago she-lawyer.)

"Yes."

"Look, Doug, I'm starting to sense real trouble here. Kaiser will latch onto this like a dog with a bone."

"A hot dog with a bone?" quipped Pierce. Roxanne's slur had stuck.

"God, don't remind me."

"To tell the truth, I'm concerned too, Mark. I have a difficult, high-profile investigation ahead of me. Not only has one of Dumont's most prominent and beloved citizens died under mysterious circumstances, but her death has implications for both sides of an important out-of-state political contest. Now the local DA is about to enter the fray, and you know as well as I that if Roxanne is in the picture, his objectivity is out the window. No question, Harley will go gunning for her, and he'll expect *me* to bring her in. I know Roxanne, and I know she had no complicity in this, but it'll be difficult to conduct an impartial investigation with Harley Kaiser hell-bent on nailing one particular suspect."

Pierce had opened the door, so I stepped right in. "Need some help?"

He hesitated—briefly. "I do, in fact. You've helped me think through some difficult cases before. Could we get together and do some 'unofficial' brainstorming? I'd be happy to come over to your place."

I readily agreed.

Later that afternoon, Pierce arrived at the house.

We settled into the den, facing each other in comfortable leather chairs near the hearth of the cold fireplace. I set my open steno pad on the wide arm of the chair, uncapped my pen, and scribbled some loops to get the ink running.

"I've already heard from Harley," said Pierce. Blain Gifford had indeed met with the DA, and the DA, as predicted, had lapped up Blain's speculative scenario featuring a nefarious Roxanne. Pierce concluded, "Harley wants action."

"You've told him, I assume, that you've already questioned Roxanne and Carl, finding no reason to deem Roxanne suspicious—correct?"

"Correct."

"What's next?"

"A methodical questioning of other witnesses and possible suspects."

"Wesley Scott?"

"Top of my list. In Dale Turner's video, either Wes the bartender or Roxanne could be seen as controlling the sequence of events that killed Betty. It's possible, of course, that the timing of their actions was sheer coincidence. In any event, it's time to talk to Wes. Care to come along?"

Silly question. "What time?"

"Nine tomorrow. I already phoned the catering shop and caught Wes. I didn't mention the video—just said I needed to do some routine questioning, which is true enough. He was perfectly agreeable."

"Will Alanna be there as well?" Though I had no reason to suspect her of murder, I was intrigued by the notion that her marriage was rocky—and I was further intrigued by Chick Butterly's apparent interest in the woman.

"I assume so. We need to talk to her—she might have seen something."

I started writing notes. "Who else?"

"Next, we ought to visit Dale Turner."

I nodded. "The tent guy who shot the video."

"More to the point, he's the electrician who wired the party."

I finished the thought: "And Betty was killed by a faulty fuse box and a stray extension cord. Do you suspect him?"

Pierce shrugged. "No reason to—I know of no connection between Dale and the Ashton or Gifford families. Besides, the electrocution reflects poorly on Dale, to say the least. I phoned him a few minutes ago. He's as eager as anyone to get this wrapped up."

Among those *most* eager to wrap it up were Pierce and I. Though we sought the same solution, our reasons for seeking it differed greatly.

For Pierce, crime-solving was the job he'd been elected to perform. His professional integrity and competence were at stake, and his judgment was now being second-guessed by a myopic prosecutor.

As for me, I'd suddenly taken an active role in an evolving news story, a hot one, the sort of story that sells newspapers, lots of them. What's more, this was a story in which I had an intense personal interest. In the eyes of some, Roxanne was now considered a murder suspect, so I felt fully motivated to bring my own investigative talents to the fore in hopes of exonerating her.

Both Pierce and I sensed, though, that the questions surrounding the mystery of Betty's death would not be answered easily. I doubted that our two interviews on Monday morning would point the way to a quick resolution, but they would get us rolling—part of the tedious grunt work of mounting a thorough investigation—a necessary component of both police work and journalism.

I had plenty to ponder, so it's little wonder that later, after Pierce had left the house and the day had drawn to a close, I spent a restless night. Though dreams didn't plague me, my thoughts did.

There was Roxanne's dilemma, naturally. I'd known her for years, our friendship had survived even the pangs of misguided passion, and she'd introduced me to the man with whom I'd built a life. Now Roxanne was in a bind, and I wanted to help her.

Equally disconcerting (and sleep-robbing) were the ethical issues raised by Roxanne's acquiescing in Carl's mistaken belief that she'd had no opportunity to kill Betty. Roxanne knew better, as did I, and we'd both committed a lie of omission in letting everyone think otherwise. We'd deceived, most notably, Doug Pierce—along with Carl, Lauren, Blain, Neil, and everyone else involved. The ethics and mandates of jurisprudence, journalism, and friendship swirled in a conflict that I found impossible to sort out in the darkness of a troubled night.

Most troubling, however, was a question I was loath to voice, even to myself, even in words that had no more substance than the ephemeral stuff of thoughts. But the question kept scratching at my conscience, quietly yet boisterously.

What if Blain Gifford and Lauren Creighton were right? They'd demonstrated that Roxanne had had a plausible motive and a plausible means to murder Betty Gifford Ashton, and their theory was held at bay only by Carl's argument that Roxanne had lacked the opportunity to commit the deed. But I knew otherwise.

Staring blankly at the ceiling, I wondered the unthinkable:

Did Roxanne in fact kill Betty?

Monday, September 9

T hough it seemed I had not slept at all overnight, I knew that I had. My fretful thoughts had felt like a single, uninterrupted, nightlong monologue, but surely I had dozed between these recurring bouts of introspection. Having confronted an unsavory possibility, I had apparently defanged it because, when I woke to the new week, I was oddly refreshed.

Neil and I went for an early run that morning, and it felt good to be a couple again, just us, distanced from the wedding, the murder, and questions of Roxanne's role in it. The morning was cool, nudging toward autumn, so we took our time in the park before returning to the house, showering, and dressing for the day.

It was well after eight o'clock when we appeared in the kitchen. Pierce had already arrived with his kringle (maple-flavored, not my favorite), and Barb was busy gabbing, cracking eggs, and slurping diet cola. The three Chicagoans were still upstairs, and it was safe to assume that Thad would sleep for hours yet.

Pierce and I were on a mission that morning—our schedule of interviews was set—but we spoke little of it in the kitchen. Instead, Neil told us about an architectural project that had gotten his creative juices flowing, a new headquarters for an office-furniture manufacturer to be located in an industrial park near the edge of town. Barb yammered about the opening concert of the community orchestra's next season, now less than two weeks away. One of the works on the first program featured a prominent clarinet solo, which, as principal, she would play. Her rambling discourse included frequent references to Whitney Greer, the orchestra manager. Was it just my imagination, or had that name been popping from her mouth with unusual regularity of late?

Shortly before nine, Pierce, Neil, and I left the house through the back door, leaving Barb to her domestic duties and her clarinet practice. Out in the driveway, Neil and I kissed; then he got into his car and headed downtown to his office on First Avenue. It was a workaday routine that could never bore me, a comforting ritual that underscored the permanence of our shared life. However, that morning differed from most other Mondays in that I would not follow Neil downtown to my own office. Rather, I would accompany the sheriff to two interviews, the opening salvo of a murder investigation.

We agreed to ride together in my car, as the first of our appointments would take us to the other side of town. The catering company was located in an older neighborhood where small businesses mingled with houses and apartment buildings. At a minute or two after nine, I pulled to the curb in front of A Moveable Feast.

The tidy building, painted white, appeared to be a former shop, perhaps a shoe store. Plate-glass display windows symmetrically flanked the front door, displaying not wedding cakes or flowery table settings, but simply the office within. I saw a counter, a round conference table, and a bank of glass-doored, restaurant-style refrigerators along one wall. I followed Pierce as he stepped beneath the sign, opened the door, and entered.

We were greeted by the smells of spice and dough and garlic and meat—a confused but delightful olfactory hodgepodge. The sound of someone chopping something crisp, perhaps celery, drifted from the kitchen behind the office. A radio played softly. An unseen man spoke on the phone; his cadences signaled the wrap-up of a conversation. All of this was underlaid by the sleepy drone of the refrigerators.

When the talking on the phone ended, Pierce called, "Anybody home?"

A moment later, a man of about my age stepped into the office from the back room. I recognized him at once as Saturday's bartender, Wesley Scott; his shirt bore the logo of A Moveable Feast. Seeing us, he said, "Oh. Sorry, Sheriff. Didn't hear you come in. I was busy with some bookkeeping."

As Wes moved around the counter to shake hands, Pierce said, "You know Mark Manning, don't you?"

"Sure thing—hosted Saturday's party." Wes turned to me. "Sorry how things turned out."

I nodded, shaking his hand. "Yeah, what a shame. But it wasn't your fault—the party itself was flawless." I was being polite. For all I knew, the party's catastrophic ending may indeed have been his fault.

Pierce gestured toward the round table. "Mind if we sit down?"

"Not at all. My time is your time. Happy to help—if I can."

He was certainly accommodating. I recalled his testiness at the reception, complaining to his wife about needing help at the bar. I wondered if Wes was naturally pleasant and had merely been stressed on Saturday, or if he was naturally sour and was merely acting gracious now.

Sitting, I looked toward the back room, toward the chopping. "Should Alanna join us?"

"Sorry"—Wes tossed his hands—"Alanna isn't here. That's, well, to tell the truth, I forget her name; we have a lot of part-time help. I think Alanna is out shopping, or meeting with a prospective client, not sure. Anyway, when you called, Sheriff, it wasn't clear that you wanted to talk to both of us. Hope this isn't a problem for you."

"Not at all. We'll catch up with Alanna later." Pierce sat, motioning for Wes to do likewise.

Once seated, Wes wasted no breath on chitchat. "What *happened,* Sheriff? At the party, I mean. How did the extension cord get into the water? Poor Mrs. Ashton—God, that could've been *me.*"

Pierce had his notebook out (so did I). "That's what we're trying to figure out, Wes, and we hope you can help. After all, you were right there when disaster struck, and you were on hand prior to the party as well, during setup. Did you observe anything suspicious leading up to the accident?" Pierce, I noted, who'd been the first to declare Betty's electrocution a homicide, was now referring to it as an accident. I assumed this was a ploy, meant to sanitize the situation and put Wes more at ease.

The strategy worked. Wes shook his head, brow pinched in thought. "Anything suspicious? Like what?"

Pierce reviewed, "Well, we all know that the bar fuse had been defeated with a penny so it wouldn't blow when it was shorted—that was discovered at the scene. And we all know that a live extension cord found its way from the tent rigging into the vat of ice water immediately before Betty dipped her handkerchief into it. Did you observe any suspicious activity with regard to the fuse box, the extension cord, or the wiring in general?"

Wes shrugged. "No. I mean, there was a lot of activity, especially during setup, especially with the wiring. But that's not unusual—it's a big job."

I asked, "Did a lot of people work on the wiring."

"Just Dale Turner. He has a crew for erecting the tents, but as far as I know, he always handles the electrical himself. That's his thing."

Pierce asked, "So if anyone else had been monkeying with wires, you'd have found that suspicious, right?"

"Right. Oh, yeah, there was that one guy. He's kind of—I'm not sure how to put this—effeminate? He did a lot of fiddling with cords for the stage, and I pointed him out to Dale, but Dale said he was a sound tech or something."

I suppressed a grin. "That would be Whitney Greer. Yes, he handled the amplification for the woodwind quintet."

Pierce made a note of this, asking Wes, "Anyone else?"

Wes paused in thought. "Not that I can remember."

"If you don't recall *seeing* anything suspicious, perhaps you *heard* something. Was anything menacing or disparaging said with regard to Mrs. Ashton?"

"Sheriff"—Wes gave Pierce a get-real stare—"I have never heard *anyone* say an unkind word about Mrs. Ashton, before the accident or since."

With a half laugh, I added, "She doesn't strike me as the type to have enemies lurking in dark corners."

"True . . ." Pierce added something to his notes. "Wes, are you aware that my department has been reviewing a number of home videos that were shot at the reception?"

"Sure. I saw your deputies collecting them. And later, word got around that Dale Turner gave you a tape. Were any of them useful?"

"Yes, one was. Dale's tape gave us a good look at exactly what went on at the bar when Betty was electrocuted. Let me walk you through what we saw." And Pierce described the sequence of events captured on the tape.

Wes listened, nodding. "That sounds about right—I can't say I recall the exact timing of every detail, but if it's on the tape, that's that."

I looked up from my notes, asking Wes, "When you reached for the bottle of Perrier and took it off the shelf, did you, uh . . . *notice* anything?"

"No"—he slowly shook his head—"I just remember thinking that your friend, the bride, had shown a lot of foresight in stocking the bar with her own Perrier. We wouldn't have had it; this is La Croix country. She seems to be a thorough planner."

This last remark was doubtless intended as a compliment to Roxanne, but it could also suggest scheming and premeditation on Roxanne's part—if one were willing to consider that she may have had a hand in Betty's undoing.

Pierce took a deep breath. "Wes, on the videotape, when you took the bottle off the shelf, we *did* notice something. It happened so fast, I needed several viewings, in slow motion, to catch it."

Wes watched the sheriff with an expression that was both quizzical and wary. "Well," he asked, forcing a smile, "what did you notice?"

"The head of the orange extension cord that ended up in the water had been wedged behind the bottle of Perrier at the end of the shelf, the one you pulled. As you lifted the bottle, the cord was released and slid into the water just moments before Betty dipped her hand-kerchief."

With widened eyes (brown eyes, I noted), Wes said flatly, "You've got to be kidding."

Pierce shook his head. "That's how it happened."

"Good God," said Wes, starting to piece together the implications, "then it *must* have been deliberate; Betty *must* have been murdered."

"Yes," agreed Pierce, "Betty's death was no accident. Someone was very clever."

"Fiendishly clever," I added.

Pierce said, "One of the things we need to establish is, where was that extension cord *supposed* to be?"

"I don't follow," said Wes.

Pierce elaborated, "The cord was wedged behind the Perrier, so it wasn't supplying power to anything. It seems unlikely that there would be an extra, live cord hanging around, unless it was specifically intended for its deadly purpose. But if the cord did have some legitimate purpose, wouldn't the lack of power be noticed?"

"I can't imagine . . . ," began Wes. Then he snapped his fingers. "The blender. I'll bet that cord was meant for the blender."

"Well," I asked the logical question, "did the blender work?"

"I never got around to using it. The party was a big one, and I knew I'd be busy, so I didn't want to be bothered fussing with blender drinks. While setting up the bar, I hid the blender under the counter so the guests wouldn't get ideas."

"Was it plugged in when you moved it?"

"No, its cord was still wrapped around it."

"Was the orange extension cord nearby?"

Wes closed his eyes, thinking hard, then opened them with a sigh. "Sorry. I don't remember seeing the cord at all. But that doesn't mean it wasn't there. I had plenty *else* on my mind."

As Wes yammered on about his frazzled state on Saturday, I weighed the significance of the fatal extension cord's intended purpose. If it was meant to power the blender, then set aside, it could have been wedged behind the Perrier bottle by anyone, but most likely Wes, sometime after the reception began. On the other hand, if the cord's sole purpose was murder, it would doubtless have been rigged before the reception began, anytime after Roxanne had stocked the bar with her Perrier. Roxanne herself could have done this—while pennying the fuse, in fact—but how would she have come up with a spare extension cord on the spot like that?

Wes was telling Pierce, "Whoever wanted Betty dead went to a lot of trouble to make sure that everything went like clockwork, unless—" He stopped short, recognizing where his thoughts were headed. Looking intently at Pierce, he asked, "You don't think . . . you don't think that I . . . ," but he couldn't bring himself to voice the words.

Pierce wagged his hands gently, a consoling gesture. "I'm glad you appreciate that the tape could be read in such a way that you appear to be controlling the events that led to Betty's death. And because you had complete access to the bar area before and during the party, it's *plausible* that you rigged both the bottle with the cord and the fuse box with the penny. In other words, we might say that you had the means and the opportunity to commit this crime. What I must find out, Wes, is this: Did you have a motive? Did you have any conceivable reason to harm Betty Gifford Ashton?"

Far from consoled by these words, Wes sputtered, "My God, you *do* think I'm responsible."

I told him, "Being purely objective, we recognize that some of these circumstances point to you. But every murderer has a motive. Did *you* have one?"

He blurted, "Of *course* not."

"Mr. Scott? Excuse me?" said a woman's voice.

We turned toward the back of the office, where a woman in an apron had just entered from the kitchen. The chopping had stopped; the radio no longer played.

Wes replied, "Yes, uh . . . Susan?"

"It's Sandra, sir." She untied her apron. "I've finished with the list your wife left for me. Is there anything else?"

"No, not this morning, thank you. Why don't you phone back this afternoon and talk to Alanna—she may have some projects that I don't know about."

Sandra folded the apron she'd taken off. "Right, happy to. Have a good day, gentlemen." And she bowed out. We heard her footfalls as she retreated through the kitchen and left through a back door.

Save for the squeaky murmur of the refrigerators, the office where we sat had grown dead silent.

Wes now rested both hands flat on the table, calmly telling Pierce, "I had no motive whatever to harm Betty Gifford Ashton. I didn't even know the woman. Sure, I'd seen her several times at parties we'd catered, and I knew her picture from the paper—who in Dumont wouldn't? But we were never introduced. I mean, come on, we didn't exactly move in the same circles."

Pierce asked, "And you weren't acquainted with any other members of either the Gifford or the Ashton families?"

"Not at all."

Mulling the most obvious of possible motives, inheritance, I asked, "And you're not in any way related, by blood or marriage, to either family?"

"I wish! No, Mr. Manning, I have no connection to the Gifford-Ashtons—social, marital, or otherwise."

"Wes," said Pierce, "we're not trying to badger you, believe me. It's just that I want to place you above suspicion and move on to the next phase of my investigation. So let me ask you outright: If it came down to it and I were to subpoena bank records, store accounts, e-mails, the works, would I find anything connecting you to the victim or her family?"

Wes brought his hands together on the table, folding one over the other, looking perfectly at ease. "No, Sheriff, you'd find nothing at all." He laughed, adding, "Maybe a bad check or a sloppy balance here and there. Come to think of it, I could *use* a little help. Care to take the ledgers with you this morning?"

Pierce echoed his laugh. "No, thanks, Wes. I'll let you know if we need anything, but I doubt it'll come to that." The sheriff's light-hearted tone signaled that his official inquiry was complete. He closed his notebook.

Mine was still open, and I glanced back through my notes.

Wes pushed his chair back. "Can I get you guys something?"

Pierce shook his head. "Thanks, but we just came from breakfast."

A note caught my eye—something I'd scribbled earlier about Chick Butterly and his apparent interest in Alanna Scott, Wes's wife. "As long as you're offering, Wes, I *am* a bit thirsty. Some water would be great."

He stood. "Sorry, no Perrier."

"No problem—tap, La Croix, whatever."

Pierce said, sure, he'd have some too, so Wes gathered glasses from a shelf and three bottles from one of the refrigerators, setting everything before us on the table.

After we'd poured, toasted a speedy resolution to the mystery, and sipped, I said to Wes, "I'll bet you're glad to have the weekend behind you. I know *I* am. The wedding and all—it was a lot of pressure on everyone involved."

Wes nodded knowingly. "Weddings always are. For most people, a wedding is the biggest party they'll ever throw. People get so edgy, I wonder why they bother."

Pierce reminded him, "You'd be out of business if they didn't."

"*That's* for sure."

With a grin, I told Wes, "You had a few edgy moments of your own on Saturday." I raised a brow.

Wes dropped his head. "Yeah, sorry about that. It was hot, and everyone seemed to arrive at once, so things got away from us at the bar. I do apologize—I shouldn't have shot off my mouth like that."

I accepted the apology with a shrug. "Alanna seemed to deal with it."

"She would. She always does—she's used to it."

I flashed Pierce a meaningful glance, letting him know that I deemed this small talk significant.

Picking up on my cue, he said, "Uh, Wes, I don't mean to intrude, but is everything all right between you and Alanna?"

Wes looked at the ceiling. "You're not intruding. Heck, it's obvious to everyone—things have been better between us."

Swirling the carbonated water in my glass, I asked idly, "Business issues?" Granted, it was an audacious question, but considerably less ballsy than the question I really wanted to ask: Sex problems?

Wes took no offense at my curiosity. In fact, he seemed grateful for our concern. "It started out as a business issue, but it runs deeper than that now."

Pierce prompted him, "Mark and I are good listeners."

"Thanks, Sheriff. This isn't the usual kind of 'guy talk.'"

I couldn't resist noting, "So? Doug and I aren't the usual kind of guys."

We laughed. It helped. Pierce and I no longer felt that we were prodding, and Wes felt more inclined to open up.

"Alanna and I love each other," Wes assured us, "but our marriage is less than perfect. Who am I kidding? It's on the rocks. And the root of the problem is . . . well, in a word . . . children."

That wasn't the root I'd expected. "I thought you were dealing with business issues."

"Originally, yes. And the business issue was children."

Stupidly, I asked, "You have kids?"

He smiled. "No. That's the point. We got married about ten years ago, sort of late for both of us; I'm forty-three now, Alanna's thirty-nine. We opened A Moveable Feast during our first year together. Things are really good now, businesswise, but it's been a struggle. Getting established was rough.

"Like most couples, we wanted kids. Back then, Alanna was nearly thirty, so I was nervous about waiting too long. But she felt we needed to focus on the business for a while and get our feet on the ground financially before starting a family. Sound reasoning—can't argue with that.

"But now we have that footing. A Moveable Feast is prospering. We've been secure for several years, and time is slipping away fast if we still intend to have kids—which I've always wanted. Alanna, though, just isn't interested. She says it's *already* too late. She's still fertile, but she's afraid pregnancy is too risky at her age.

"It's frustrating. I mean, she's the one who wanted to wait in the first place, so she must have weighed the risks back then and decided they were worth taking. I thought we had an understanding, an agreement, a deal. And now she's backed out of it." Wes stopped talking; his story was finished. Staring at nothing across the table, he rubbed a finger around the rim of his glass.

Capping my pen, I asked him, "So you feel . . . cheated?"

"I do. And I know it sounds sort of nuts—it's usually the husband who leaves the wife in the lurch, feeling unfulfilled—but it's the other way around with us. Yes, I do feel cheated. I guess I'm bitter, and sometimes it shows."

From my very first encounter with Wesley Scott, that bitterness had shown. His snit at the reception about needing backup help at the bar had been an inauspicious introduction to the man who would, only a few minutes later, move the bottle that released the cord that fell into the water that carried the current that stopped the heart of a wealthy old woman.

I wondered about the implications of Wes's conflict with his wife. There was no reason to doubt his story, even though he himself had said that the conflict seemed backward, which it did. What's more, there was something slightly emasculating in his confession—to two other men he barely knew, but knew to be gay—that a woman was thwarting his own child-rearing instincts.

Did this make Wes more sympathetic in my eyes? Or less so? Tapping the butt of my fountain pen on the cover of my steno pad, I couldn't decide.

No question, Wes had something of a churlish edge. Did this signal that he was a grump to the core? Or was he simply unhappy about his marital circumstances? More important, I asked myself, was he capable of murder? With no apparent connection to the victim or her family, it seemed that Wes had no motive to harm Betty. However, he'd had both the means and the opportunity to do so, as suggested by the videotape.

Was there something I was missing? I hoped so, as I was still focused on Roxanne—who'd had not only the plausible motive of silencing Betty, but also the means and the opportunity to act on that motive. Very quickly, I feared, I might need to prove Roxanne's innocence.

And the only sure way to do that was to prove someone else's guilt.

———

Pierce got into my car and pulled his door closed. As I turned the key in the ignition, he told me, "Next stop: Tip Top Tent and Awning."

I needed directions. Dale Turner's tent company was located nearer downtown, in an industrial district served by rail. In earlier years, it had been a flourishing area of enterprise anchored by Quatro Press, Dumont's largest industry, but when my uncle's printing company later moved to more modern quarters, served by its own rail spur, the old neighborhood entered an era of decline, with many of its buildings relegated to use as warehouses. One of these hulking brick structures was now home to Tip Top Tent and Awning.

I pulled to the curb behind one of Tip Top's battered trucks that was parked in front of the building. I saw another of the trucks backed up to a loading dock in an alley alongside the building. In striking contrast to this general state of dilapidation, a cheery awning stretched across the grimy windows of the facade. Alternating circus stripes of orange and deep green bore dancing letters of bright yellow, spelling out the name of the business.

Pierce and I crossed the sidewalk and climbed the several steps of cracked concrete that led to the door. A fat, gray tabby dozed on a black rubber welcome mat, soaking up the midmorning sun and blocking the door—not very professional. With a chuckle, Pierce bent down and patted the cat's furry haunch. Grudgingly, the tom stood and stretched, flipping us his tail, displaying his wares. When he strutted off the mat, Pierce opened the door.

Our entrance was announced by a rusty bell on a tired spring, a functional device that had endured years of use, but had not rung much of late, I gathered. The wide, bare floorboards creaked under our feet as we approached the counter in the front office. A buxom, pewter-haired woman looked up from a desk spread with paperwork, taken unawares by our presence—was she deaf? "May I help you?" she mewed, peering over the eyeglasses chained to her collar. Their lenses came to sharp points at the sides, making her look distinctly feline—like a plump, blue-furred mate for the tom on the porch.

Pierce introduced himself, saying, "I think Dale is expecting us. Is he in?"

She didn't answer, but slid her chair back, scraping the floor loudly. She disappeared into the rear of the building for a moment, then reappeared, followed by Dale Turner. As she sat again at her desk, hunching over her papers, Dale strode forward, extending his hand over the counter. "Morning, Doug. Thanks for stopping by."

Pierce returned the greeting, telling Dale, "You've met Mark Manning, of course. I thought he might be able to help us piece this together. Three heads are better than two."

"Any day, any day," agreed Dale, shaking my hand. (Again I noted how comforting I found the feel of his firm, callused handshake.) "Welcome, Mark. Come on in, gentlemen. Let's talk in my office."

Pierce and I rounded the counter and followed Dale toward the back of the building. He wore clothes similar to those I'd seen at the reception—denim shirt with olive-colored work pants—except that today's outfit was freshly laundered and pressed. Walking behind him, I took a moment to size him up again. He was a few years younger than me, midthirties or so, with a body well toned by physical labor. I recalled finding him a friendly, sociable sort on Saturday, reasonably good-looking too. Today Dale's ruggedness struck me as flat-out handsome. He turned through a doorway, telling us, "Sorry about the mess, guys."

His office was no showplace—*Architectural Record* would not be popping in for a photo shoot anytime soon—but it wasn't that bad either. There was no way to mask the age and ungainliness of the building, which extended into the office, but Dale's work space was neat, clean, and functional, hardly what I'd call a mess. Small, high windows squinted through the outer wall, admitting little light, so a large fluorescent fixture hung from the middle of the ceiling, centered over Dale's gray-green metal desk. Its top was arranged with precisely stacked papers, folders, and mail. To the side, a wall of shelves held files, books, technical literature, a few knickknacks (masculine stuff like horses, race cars, and a dusty taxidermed trout [or whatever]), and bulky sample books containing all manner of canvas swatches. Another wall displayed a few business-related plaques (Rotary, Chamber of Commerce, Goodfellows) and some dozen or twenty dime-store-framed color photos of his tents erected at various events.

"Please, guys, sit down," he offered, gesturing toward a pair of wooden chairs—captain's chairs, the spindly sort with saddle seats, more typically found in homey kitchens a generation earlier. Dale sat behind the desk in his gray metal armchair.

Settling in, Pierce and I both opened our notebooks and readied our pens. Pierce slid his chair forward a few inches so he could use the front edge of the desk. I leaned back, content to prop my pad on my knee, the better to observe and remain in the background.

Pierce said, "First of all, Dale, I do want to thank you for handing over that video on Saturday evening. I found it highly useful."

Dale smiled. "Yeah, that's what you said on the phone. What'd you find?"

"Well, you were right—the camera was aimed at the bar area when you left it running, and before it ran out of tape, it did indeed pick up the scene when Mrs. Ashton was electrocuted. We got a good look at exactly what happened."

"Terrific!" Then Dale's smile fell. "Oh, sorry—I mean, it was terrible, of course." He shrugged an apology for his enthusiasm regarding the tape.

Pierce laughed softly. "That's quite all right. The scene on the tape gave me a sense of direction for launching this investigation."

Dale prompted, "And that direction is . . . ?"

"Let me tell you what we saw." Pierce then detailed the action we'd seen on the tape, the action he'd described less than an hour earlier to Wesley Scott. Then he summarized, "It can't be coincidence that the fuse box had been tampered with and the extension cord had been rigged to fall into the vat of ice water. Either of those factors, considered independently, might be dismissed as happenstance, but taken together, they point to premeditated mischief—deadly mischief. We're dealing with homicide."

Dale had listened to Pierce's narrative with a sober expression, absorbing every word. Weighing Pierce's conclusion, Dale said glumly, "God. First the penny in the fuse box. Now this."

"The cord that ended up in the vat," said Pierce, tapping his notes. "Was it simply a spare that happened to be dangling from the tent rigging?"

"God, no. My setup would never pass the electrical inspection that way."

"Then the cord couldn't have been there late Friday during inspection?"

"I'm sure it wasn't," Dale replied without hesitation. "The cord that fell into the vat was run behind the bar to power the blender."

"Did you plug the blender into the extension cord?"

"No. The caterers didn't bring the blender till Saturday morning— I'm not even sure *if* they brought it."

This, I noted, was consistent with Wes's story and neither heightened nor lessened the possibility that Roxanne had rigged the cord for murder.

Dale shook his head. "It's enough to make you think that someone was trying to sabotage Tip Top." From a mug on his desk he pulled a pencil and twiddled it with his fingers.

Intrigued by this angle, I emerged from my listening mode, asking Dale, "Can you elaborate on that?"

"Well, think about it. It seems as if someone, for some reason, was trying to cast suspicion on *me*. I mean, that's a no-brainer. An old lady is electrocuted under circumstances that point to—who else?— the electrician. Clearly, I could have rigged the fuse box, rigged the extension cord, and predicted the result. I'm not the paranoid sort, but jeez, it sounds as if someone was trying to set me up and ruin my business—not that it'd take much." He poised the pencil upright, with its lead poking the tip of his index finger and its eraser stubbing the desktop, the very picture of tension, a fragile equilibrium that could fail with the next pulse of blood through his veins.

I noticed that the slick yellow surface of the pencil had been perforated by someone's teeth, presumably Dale's; flecks of the paint had been buried beneath the surface of the gnawed wood. Had this been the result of worry, preoccupation, or mere habit?

The condition of his pencil was little more than a distraction, a detail hardly worthy of thought. His contention that he himself had been victimized by the murder was far more heady. He had succinctly proposed a plausible scenario for his own undoing, and my mind spun to connect the dots he had sketched.

Pierce asked, "Who would want to set you up like that? Who would want to make you appear incompetent as an electrician?"

Dale flumped back in his chair, letting the pencil fall to the desk. "Beats me."

I asked, "What about a competitor? Is there someone who would profit if your business failed?"

Dale's eyes searched the ceiling for a moment; then he shook his head. "Tip Top is the only tent service in town. My nearest competitor is in the next county. As for awnings, well, there are several sign companies that supply lettered awnings, but that's just a sideline for them, and they generally subcontract the work to me anyway. It doesn't add up that anyone would resort to murder to steal my business."

Pierce suggested, "If someone set you up but had no interest in your business, the culprit must have been an enemy pure and simple—someone with an ax to grind. Why would someone be out to get you, Dale? Is there something you haven't told me?"

"Sheriff, I swear to God, if I felt that I had an enemy—a killer with an ax to grind—you'd be the *first* to know." With a halfhearted laugh, he added, "I'd come *running* for protection."

I believed him. Dale didn't strike me as the sort of person who might incite either a competitor or an enemy to turn murderous. He was a businessman trying to make a go of it. He had a wallful of plaques attesting to his community involvement. He played by the rules. Still, he sat there voicing concern that someone was plotting against him.

Pierce's brow wrinkled. "If the motive was neither a competitor's greed nor an enemy's revenge, I can't think of any other possibilities."

The room grew quiet for a moment as we thought about this.

"Actually," I said, "I can think of *two* other possibilities."

Dale looked up from his desk. Pierce turned toward me in his chair.

"One: Betty's electrocution may have had nothing whatever to do with Dale, his competitors, or unknown enemies." I paused. "Or two: Dale himself may have been responsible for it."

Dale's eyes bugged as he heard my words. Yup, big brown eyes.

I assured him, "I'm not suggesting that I think you killed Betty, but you yourself acknowledged that the circumstances point in your direction—arguably, you had both the means and the opportunity to commit this crime. Which leaves one, huge, dangling question: Did you have a motive?"

Pierce picked up my train of thought, telling Dale, "I too have no reason to think that you killed Betty, but it is plausible, and the quickest, surest way to confirm your innocence is to place you above suspicion with regard to a possible motive. Earlier this morning, Mark and I questioned another *potential* suspect along these very lines. So I'm asking for your help."

Dale was fully cooperative. Pierce and I ran him through the same questions we'd asked Wesley Scott, eliciting the same answers: Dale had never met Betty Gifford Ashton. He was not related, even distantly, to any member of the Gifford or Ashton families. He was certain that none of his records would reveal even the slightest connection to the Giffords or Ashtons, and he eagerly volunteered complete access to any records Pierce might care to examine. In short, Dale convincingly demonstrated that he'd had no motive to harm Betty, much less to kill her in a manner that would so readily point back to himself.

Concluding that Dale must be held above suspicion, I realized that my emotions were mixed. On the one hand, he seemed likable enough, not the sort of person I'd enjoy exposing as a killer, so I was pleased to confirm my initial judgment of his character. On the other hand, clearing Dale led my scrutiny back to the videotape and to the two individuals who might be seen as controlling the action recorded there—Wesley Scott and the new Mrs. Creighton.

Not an hour earlier, Pierce and I had questioned Wes, who, like Dale, had had the means and opportunity to rig the fuse box and the extension cord. Wes, like Dale, had also demonstrated that he'd had no motive to harm Betty. Logically, then, both Wes and Dale should now be held above suspicion, leading me back to Roxanne, who did indeed have a plausible motive to harm Betty.

Viewing the situation purely from the perspective of logic, I was aware that Roxanne could have committed the crime we sought to solve. From my perspective of *knowing* the woman, however, I found it impossible to consider any prospect of her guilt. Based on what I now knew of the circumstances of the crime, I concluded that my best hope of exonerating Roxanne was to explore Dale's fear that the electrocution was intended to set him up, frame him, or destroy his business.

If that was true, then Betty could not be considered the intended victim of the crime; her electrocution may have been the arbitrary consequence of a plot not specifically targeting her. I liked this angle because it neatly shifted the issue of motive away from Roxanne. Unfortunately, if our task was now to identify an unknown enemy with an unknown motive, our investigation was sinking deeply into a mire of what-ifs.

I asked, "Dale? I wonder if you could give us some background on your working relationship with the Scotts." My intention was to nudge the conversation in a more personal direction. Knowing nothing of Dale Turner's past, I hoped that by getting a better picture of the man, I might be able to glean a theory or two regarding possible enemies.

Dale said, "Wes and Alanna have been good to me, good *for* me. It's worked both ways, I guess."

"How so?"

"Good for business—mine and theirs. The Scotts opened A Moveable Feast some ten years ago; they've worked hard, and now their shop is firmly established. I was an electrician by trade, but during a building slump about four years ago, I opened Tip Top. It's been a struggle, and I still can't say the future of my business is secure."

I recalled, "You mentioned earlier that if someone was trying to ruin your business, it wouldn't take much."

"That's for sure. I meet my payroll week to week—barely—but the other bills don't get paid until I do. Fortunately, September and October are good for weddings, so I'm hoping to get caught up."

Pierce asked, "How do you keep up with the payroll?"

Dale paused. With a sheepish grin, he admitted, "It's only Pat out front. She's the only full-timer—me too, of course. Everyone else is part-time labor, as needed."

"A lot like the catering business," I noted.

"Exactly. That much, I do have in common with the Scotts. Like I was saying, they're in much better shape than I am, but over the past year or two, we've started working a lot of events jointly, offering package deals to customers, and it's been good for both of us. I just wish more catering jobs needed tents." He ran a hand through his hair. "Winters are dead, dead, dead for me."

Okay, I thought, enough about business. "How well do you know the Scotts?"

Dale rose from his chair and planted his hands in his pockets. I watched the lumps of his knuckles burrow beneath the cloth of his pants. He told me, "I've come to know them well enough. I think of both Wes and Alanna as good people, dedicated to their business. Honest too—there's never been the slightest problem in all our dealings together."

"Do you think of them as friends?"

"Well, sure. They're important business associates."

"I mean, *friends*. Do you socialize? Ever go out for an evening together?"

He pushed his hands deeper into his pockets. "God, no," he told me, sounding almost bashful.

The response itself didn't surprise me, as I simply hadn't known whether they were social or not, but the tone of Dale's response struck me as peculiar. He made it sound as if a night out with the Scotts was unthinkable.

Pierce picked up on this as well, asking Dale, "Why not? You guys are all about the same age, involved in similar work, with—"

"Sheriff," Dale interrupted, "you know the old saying: three's a crowd."

Realizing how truly little I knew of Dale, I asked, "You're not married?"

He shook his head. "Divorced."

I decided to push further. "Dating?" I was tempted to add, You'd be a hot catch in the adult-singles pool. Sanely, I refrained.

"Now and then. Nothing serious." He hesitated. "To be honest, I've been pretty much out of circulation for a while, and that's fine by me—lets me focus on the job."

Pierce countered, "You know the old saying: all work and no play . . ."

Dale chuckled. "Yeah, maybe you're right, maybe I should get out more, but even if I did, I don't think I'd be double-dating with the Scotts." He gave a single nod, as if the implications of his statement were self-evident.

Pierce and I glanced at each other. I took the reins, telling Dale, "Even though I've lived in Dumont for nearly three years now, sometimes I still feel like an outsider. Pardon my ignorance, but what are you driving at with regard to the Scotts?"

Dale pulled his hands from his pockets, crossed his arms, then uncrossed them and scratched his neck. "Well"—he laughed awkwardly—"don't get me wrong. I *like* Wes and Alanna, but they're not exactly my idea of a good time. I mean, a night *out* with them? The *tension.*"

Aha. I now understood, but decided to play dumb. "Yeah"—aping Dale, I scratched my neck—"at the reception on Saturday, I got the impression that there might be some trouble between them. It's serious? Their marriage is rocky?"

"Very."

"Is this, uh . . . common knowledge?"

Dale shrugged. "It's common knowledge to anyone who *knows* them."

"What's the gist of it? Their problem."

Again Dale shrugged. "No idea. I don't pry. And they haven't confided in me. Besides, that's none of my business."

I nodded thoughtfully. "You're right, of course." But my thoughts weren't centered on the Scotts' privacy—quite the opposite. I was wondering about a seeming contradiction. I'd just heard that the Scotts had not confided the nature of their marital problems to Dale, who'd been a close business associate, practically a partner, for over a year. Earlier that morning, though, Wesley Scott hadn't hesitated to pour his heart out to the sheriff and me, a virtual stranger, telling us how badly he wanted a baby, how his wife was afraid to conceive and carry it, due to her age.

Clearly, something was off, and I assumed that either Dale or Wes had not given us the straight story. What's more, all my instincts told me that Dale's version was not only plausible, but likely, while Wes's outpouring of such private matters had struck me as odd from the outset.

"Anyway," Dale was saying, "my relationship to the Scotts is strictly business, and that's the way I like it. Let's just say I prefer to keep to myself."

Pierce allowed, "It keeps a man out of trouble."

They bantered on in this vein, weighing the rewards of a life lived alone. I kept out of the conversation, as I simply didn't agree with them. My life before Neil had been focused and productive—nose to the grindstone—but now those bachelor years struck me as empty and deluded, a mere preamble to couplehood and the boundless new dimensions my life would later take on when "I" became "we."

Doug Pierce was another matter, another sort of person. He'd been an enigma to me since we'd first met, shortly after my arrival in town. Back then, I suspected he was gay, and though he readily befriended Neil and me, who'd always been open to the world about our relationship, Pierce took another year to confide that aspect of his life to me. As an elected county official, he was naturally circumspect and discreet, but even after he'd opened up to me, he seemed to show no interest in any particular man or men. He lived alone; he was wed to his law-enforcement career. So it didn't surprise me to hear him seconding Dale Turner's stated preference to keep to himself.

What did surprise me was hearing Dale state this preference in the first place. When I'd met Dale at the reception on Saturday, I was struck by his affable manner, his industriousness, and the pride he took in his work. These notions were reinforced by my current visit to his office, where I sat facing a wall hung with mementos that included engraved encomiums of his involvement with civic and fraternal organizations. My impression of the man was topped off by his attractiveness, which gave him a clear edge in dealing with others—of either sex. Now here he was, having a heart-to-heart with the sheriff, baring aspects of an introverted personality that seemed better suited to a cloistered monk.

Just goes to show you, I thought, how misleading first impressions can be. Dale's outgoing, easy manner on Saturday had been an act, deceiving mainly himself, masking financial anxieties as well as social uneasiness.

Immersed in my inner conversation, I'd failed to notice that Pierce's conversation with Dale was wrapping up. The interview was over. Pierce was pocketing his notebook and rising from his chair. Instinctively, I did likewise.

Dale told Pierce, "I wish I could say that this meeting helped put my mind at ease, but now that we've talked everything through, I'm *really* worried."

"Try to keep a clear head about the situation. At this point, we have no proof that Betty's electrocution was staged to harm you or your business—though I admit, it sounds like a good theory."

Dale led us toward the office doorway. "I hardly need to mention, Doug, that I'm hoping you'll get to the bottom of this and make a quick arrest. The sooner you wrap it up, the sooner we can *all* get back to business as usual."

Glancing in my direction with a wry grin, Pierce told Dale, "It seems *everyone* has an interest in closing this case quickly—the DA in particular."

Dale extended his hand to Pierce. "I know you'll do everything you can. Thanks a million." Then Dale turned to me. "And thank *you*, Mark, for taking such an interest in the case. Never hurts having the press on your side."

I shook his hand. "We appreciate your insights. For your sake, Dale, I hope you're wrong about someone plotting against you." For Roxanne's sake, however, I hoped his paranoia was justified.

Pierce gave assurances that the case was his highest priority, and Dale promised to alert us to any new ideas or developments. "We can find our way out," said Pierce. Then he and I retraced our steps toward the front of the building as Dale turned back toward his desk.

Walking the hall, I said to Pierce, "You mentioned the DA. Has the pressure from Kaiser escalated since yesterday?"

"Afraid so. He managed to nab me this morning—at the gym, if you can believe it. He's gloating, Mark. As far as he's concerned, Roxanne's already arrested, tried, and convicted."

As we walked through the front office and rounded the counter, Pat glanced up from her desk, paused to adjust her cat glasses, then pawed a little carton of milk, sucking it through a straw.

Pierce had commitments at his office that afternoon, so we made tentative plans to return to A Moveable Feast the following morning, hoping to talk to Alanna Scott. Pierce would phone her and try to set up an interview.

Having been away from my desk all morning, I returned to my office at the *Register* for a busy afternoon. Already scheduled was a meeting with Lucille Haring, my managing editor; we needed to plan further treatment of the Betty Gifford Ashton story. It would be a good opportunity to bring Lucy up-to-date on what I'd learned that morning and to recruit her assistance in solving the case as well as reporting the story.

Business first. We decided that our Tuesday edition would carry only a brief page-one follow-up story, as developments today (so far, at least) did not seem to warrant overblown coverage. We'd report that an ongoing police investigation had begun in earnest, and we'd print details of Betty's funeral arrangements, assuming they'd be available by deadline.

We sat in my outer office, around the low conference table, essentially a large, round coffee table. A speakerphone sat within my reach; otherwise the table was clutter-free, save for my notebook and a pile of manila morgue folders that Lucy had brought with her from the *Register*'s archives. She'd gotten busy with her research and was already exploring several angles.

Lucy scratched the bristly red stubble on her temple with the eraser of a half-used pencil; I noted that its painted yellow surface was still pristine, showing none of the teeth marks that Dale Turner had inflicted upon his Ticonderoga number two. "So," said Lucy, "your interviews this morning with Sheriff Pierce proved inconclusive?"

"Afraid so. Interesting, yes; conclusive, no." I ran her through our visit to A Moveable Feast, where Pierce and I had talked to Wesley Scott, but not his wife, Alanna. Then I detailed our visit with Dale Turner at Tip Top. "Pierce and I agree that the upshot, to date, is this: both Wes and Dale had the *means* and the *opportunity* to electrocute Betty, but neither one had an apparent *motive* to do so."

"Roxanne," Lucy countered, "had a plausible *motive* to commit the crime, as well as the *means,* but she lacked the *opportunity.* She was unaware that Betty would be at the wedding until meeting her at the reception. Therefore, Roxanne could have felt no threat from Betty prior to the wedding, which is the only time when she could have rigged the fuse box and extension cord unobserved." Lucy lolled back in her chair with an easy smile, pleased to hold Roxanne so neatly above suspicion, pleased with her certitude that the object of her affection could not be deemed a killer.

I truly hated to dissuade Lucy of this notion, but she needed to know all the facts if she was to be useful in helping me exonerate our friend. I paused before telling the truth. "Lucy, you've nicely summarized the argument used by Carl to convince Doug Pierce that Roxanne couldn't possibly have killed Betty. Unfortunately, Carl was mistaken. And so is Pierce."

Lucy sat forward. Her spine tightened. Her shoulders squared. "*What?*"

Now that I'd opened this difficult door, I found immeasurable relief in hearing the words flow from me: "Carl's logic was flawed because it was based on a mistaken premise. True, Roxanne had not invited Betty to the wedding, but she did indeed know that Betty would be there prior to meeting her at the reception. Early Saturday morning, Roxanne read about the expected guests in Glee's society column. At breakfast, before she was dressed, before she stocked the bar with her bottled water, Roxanne asked Neil and me all about Betty, sounding dismayed that Betty had been invited. Bottom line: Roxanne had motive, means, and an unholy shitload of opportunity to plant the seeds of Betty Gifford Ashton's sizzling demise."

There. I'd finally said it.

Lucy looked spooked. Her spiky hair seemed theatrically erect. Then she shook her head. "I'll *never* believe that Roxanne could be capable of this."

"Good." I smiled. "Neither will I. But the situation is heating up for Roxanne, and she needs our help. Can I count on you?"

139

With half a smile and no hesitation, Lucy replied, "Well, of course."

"Then let's put our heads together." I uncapped my Montblanc and began writing notes.

Lucy had already opened one of her files to a blank sheet of paper. Clicking a ballpoint, she asked, "Who knows about Carl's mistaken logic?"

"Just Roxanne and I—and now you. Roxanne and I have not yet discussed this little wrinkle, but we need to do so, and soon. I don't like it that we're allowing Doug to shape his investigation on a premise that we know to be false. There are ethical and possibly legal aspects to all this that I can't begin to unravel. Sorry, by the way, for putting you in this compromised position."

She wagged a hand, unwilling to accept any form of apology. "I appreciate being included, and I want to help. Period." She flipped a page and continued to write. "Neil doesn't know about this?"

"No," I answered, sounding guilty, feeling it too. "Not yet. He was in the kitchen with us on Saturday morning, but he never heard the details of Carl's argument on Sunday. He's just happy knowing that Doug doesn't consider Roxanne a suspect. I hope it stays that way, but Harley Kaiser has started applying some serious pressure on Doug. As far as our DA is concerned, Roxanne is the prime suspect."

"Kaiser's irrational," Lucy reminded me. "He'd *love* to make trouble for Roxanne. He may *want* to consider her the prime suspect, but he's got nothing to base it on."

I raised a finger. "We *do*, however. Knowing what we know, weighing everything objectively, Roxanne *should* be the prime suspect." A sobering thought.

Lucy understood this as well. Though her crush on Roxanne colored Lucy's thinking with emotion, it could not ultimately cloud her objectivity. A proven researcher and a computer wiz, Lucy saw the world spinning on an axis of needle-sharp, black-or-white logic. She swallowed, as if suppressing her feelings, before telling me, "Roxanne had means, opportunity, and a single, narrow, far-fetched, but plausible motive. If you ask me, the best way to clear Roxanne is to find another motive—one that points away from her."

I nodded. "Well put, Lucy, as always. And we've already got a theory cooking that could supply just such a motive." I went on to explain Dale Turner's fear that the target of the crime was not Betty, but himself. "His business is faltering, and it wouldn't take much to put him under, but he claims there are no competitors with anything to gain from his demise. Similarly, he claims to have no personal enemies who'd be likely to plot his undoing. Which leaves us with little to go on, except"—I circled the word on my pad—"divorce."

Lucy's brows arched with interest.

"Dale mentioned a divorce, and it seems to have left him with some scars of insecurity. Maybe there's an ex-wife with an ax to grind."

Lucy grinned. "An ex with an ax?"

"Think you can track her down?"

"Piece of cake," she told me, noting something in a square she'd drawn. I'd seen this technique often: when puzzling out the various aspects of a sticky story, the sort that too often involved murder, Lucy would draw a grid on her notes and begin filling in the squares, a means of lending graphic tangibility to her logical, but amorphous, thought processes.

"Hey," she said, looking up from her notes, tapping a square on the page, "if Betty was just the arbitrary, hapless victim of this crime and someone else was the actual, ultimate target, we needn't limit our focus to Dale Turner. Sure, it reflects badly on an electrician when someone is electrocuted as the result of his wiring, but there were other folks involved who stood to lose far more than reputation."

I squinted. "Who?"

"The bartender, Wesley Scott, for instance—his professional reputation wasn't on the line, but his *life* was. After all, the vat of ice water was primarily for his use, making him the most likely 'accidental' victim of the rigged wiring. He had his hands in that water all the time."

"God," I recalled, "so did all those kids. *Anyone* could have gotten it."

"Still, odds are, it would have been Wes. If *he* was the target, who had the motive? Who wanted Wesley Scott dead?"

This was, to say the least, an intriguing new possibility. Once again, however, it pointed to an unknown enemy with an unknown motive. "I barely know Wes," I thought aloud, "and I know virtually nothing of his past, *except . . .*"

Lucy poised her pen over an empty square. "Yes?"

"All I know about Wesley Scott's background is that he and Alanna were married about ten years ago, started the catering business shortly after that, and postponed having kids, which Wes still wants. But Alanna doesn't. As I understand it, this has escalated into a serious conflict, and it's now common knowledge that the marriage is shaky." Though I didn't state it, I left hanging in the air the groundless insinuation that Alanna may have tried to electrocute Wes, which I recognized as a preposterous leap of logic.

Lucy caught my unspoken meaning, and she didn't buy it. "Look, Mark, I'm not interested in having kids either, but I wouldn't try to *kill* a man just because he disagreed with me." She laughed at the notion and its melodramatic overtones. Then her smile fell. "Unless . . ."

My turn to poise the pen. "Yes?"

Lucy balled her fists, hissing a sigh through clenched teeth. "I wouldn't try to kill a man for wanting children—unless he'd tried to *force* his way. Whether they're married or not, in my book, that's rape. And it might tempt many a woman to consider deadly revenge."

I paused, not having expected the seedy scenario suggested by Lucy, and I was doubly disconcerted by the passion she vented in suggesting it. What's more, Lucy's speculation made sense. "Good God," I told her, "that *would* be a motive, and the rest adds up. Alanna had ample opportunity to rig the electrocution. The question is, did she have the means, the know-how?"

"First things first," Lucy reminded me. "The *big* question is, did Wes rape Alanna?"

Setting down my pen, I drummed my fingers on my forehead, unsure of which aspect of this new theory to pursue first. Tossing both hands, I concluded, "I need to talk to Alanna. I can't do *anything* with this until I hear her version of the problem she's having with Wes—*if* she's willing to open up and share it."

Lucy suggested, "I could ask her to pay a visit to the newsroom on some pretext." We'd resorted to such tactics on previous stories.

"No need for that. Doug is phoning Alanna this afternoon. We'll try to meet with her tomorrow."

"Be sure to get her alone."

"Good thought. That'll be important." I made a note to talk to Pierce. Then I closed my steno pad. "Thanks, Lucy, for a productive meeting. I've finally got something to work with."

"Not so fast." She pulled another folder and opened it to a fresh page of notes.

"Hmm?"

"Our follow-up story in tomorrow's edition ought to include details of Betty's funeral. The official obituary notice we received from the family said the plans were still pending."

I nodded. "There's bound to be a lot of public interest in the funeral; Betty was a peach. Unless the family is planning a private service for some reason, we should help them get the word out. Who's the Ashtons' local attorney?" Even as I asked the question, I could have predicted the answer.

"Elliot Coop." Lucy pulled a page from her notes and set it before me. It included the lawyer's phone number.

Elliot Coop was a kindly soul, surely in his eighties, an old-school, all-purpose attorney whose long career had been devoted to the various legal needs of Dumont's "better" families, including the Quatrains, my mother's clan. My dealings with the man had been few, but each encounter had been significant. Elliot was the man who'd tracked me down in Chicago, informing me that my uncle Edwin had died and that I'd inherited the magnificent house on Prairie Street. Later, he'd assisted with my buyout of the *Dumont Daily Register*, negotiating the terms with Barret Logan, the paper's founding publisher.

Elliot had also overseen my cousin Suzanne Quatrain's estate planning, naming me guardian of her son, Thad. When Suzanne died unexpectedly, it was Elliot who informed me that I'd inherited not only a teenager, but a substantial amount of money (okay, a windfall, a fortune) to ensure that the boy was brought up properly. Finally, it was Elliot who'd helped fend off a custody battle threatened by a homophobic feminist claiming an interest in Thad's future.

"It seems like ages since I've talked to Elliot," I told Lucy as I reached for the phone. "I'm surprised he hasn't retired." More precisely, he was such a doddering sort, I was surprised he hadn't died.

"Still going strong," Lucy assured me. "I saw him argue a case at the county courthouse just a few weeks ago, and he trounced our DA, who's at least thirty years younger."

"Good for Elliot." I punched his number into the phone and let it ring over the speaker. Lucy and I listened as Elliot's secretary answered. I identified myself, asked if Elliot was available, then waited a moment.

"Good *morning*, Mr. Manning. How very nice to hear from you."

"Good morning, Elliot. It's good to hear your voice as well. I trust you've been keeping busy—and healthy."

"Reasonably so," he allowed, chuckling.

"I understand you're handling the Ashton estate?"

"My, yes, indeed. Such a blow, Betty's passing. The end of an era."

I agreed, and we shared a few thoughts bemoaning the community's loss. "Do you happen to know, Elliot, if the funeral arrangements have been made? We'd like to publish the plans if the family has no objection."

"Quite the opposite—I'm sure they'd appreciate it." Elliot prattled on, telling me that the funeral would be held on Wednesday morning, ten o'clock, at Saint Matthew Episcopal Church, with a burial service to follow at All Saints Cemetery; the public was welcome. As he spoke, Lucy took notes.

Having gotten the information I'd phoned for, I thanked Elliot, and our conversation took on the inflections of wrapping up.

"I am but a humble servant," Elliot bulled, "and my pleasure rests in serving. Do feel free to phone anytime, Mr. Manning—and you needn't wait till someone else *dies*, you know." He tittered.

I had to laugh. "Gosh, it does seem our encounters are limited to the aftermath of death. Sorry, Elliot. I'm decidedly more sociable than *that*."

"As am I, Mr. Manning. As am I. So it must be the nature of my profession that limits our association to wills, trusts, and estates. When a person of means leaves this world, those left behind are faced with the task of tidying up."

I noted, "And Betty Gifford Ashton was a person of means," a profound understatement.

"My, yes, indeed. The terms of her will are particularly complex, as you might imagine. Fortunately, with her nephew here in town, we were able to settle the estate with remarkable efficiency."

"You're referring, I assume, to Blain Gifford?" All this talk of wills and wealth reminded me of something I'd lost sight of. A wealthy person had been killed, and one of the classic motives for murder is greed. I'd been so wrapped up with Roxanne's possible motive of silencing Betty, I'd been sidetracked from the most obvious of questions: Who stood to benefit most from Betty's death?

"Yes, Blain Gifford—a charming, intelligent man. Though he seems rather . . . 'driven,' don't you think?"

"I noticed that, yes." Wondering whether Elliot was trying to tell me something, I decided to help him along. "You mentioned that the terms of Betty's will are complicated. With no children, did she spread her wealth among her various charities, or did she keep it in the family?"

"Both, Mr. Manning. There was plenty to go around."

"Yes, I'm sure. I can't help being curious—nosy me. Can you tell me if there was a principal heir?"

"There was indeed."

"Are you free to identify that person?"

Elliot paused. "Is this for publication?"

"No, strictly off-the-record."

He paused again. "Well, I have finished reviewing the terms of the will with the heir, and the documents will be filed with probate later this afternoon. Since the details will soon be a matter of public record, I have no qualms telling you that Betty's principal heir is none other than her favorite nephew, Blain Gifford."

"Ah," I said nonchalantly, "that comes as no surprise."

"No, I suppose it doesn't." He said something else, but I wasn't listening. Lucy and I exchanged a blank stare before she leaned over her notes and began writing. I uncapped my pen and scrawled a few thoughts of my own. I heard Elliot say, "If there's nothing else, Mr. Manning, I really must ring off. As always, I've enjoyed talking to you."

I expressed similar sentiments, thanked him again, then punched a button to disconnect the call.

Lucy plunked the pen on her paper. "Well, now. The Republican spinmeister has gained a fortune as the result of his aunt's death."

"Uh-huh. Not only that, but from the get-go, Blain has seemed brashly eager to cast suspicion on Roxanne, which struck me as unjustified. I chalked off his indiscretion as an irrational manifestation of grief, but it may have simply been a ploy to cast suspicion away from himself."

Indignantly, Lucy added, "A *transparent* ploy."

"To my way of thinking, Blain Gifford must now be considered a viable suspect—he had a motive worth millions."

At home that evening, before dinner, Neil and I partook of cocktails in the living room with our three houseguests—Roxanne, Carl, and Chick Butterly. This ritual, so festive and adult by nature, had become a favorite time of day for us. Neil had done his typical, meticulous job of preparing and presenting the liquor cart, stocked with bottles, crystal, and ice, while Barb still puttered in the kitchen, filling our home with the appetizing aroma of things to come. I played bartender; Neil served. It didn't take long to get a glass in everyone's hand, as the round of drinks was nothing tricky—Carl and Chick both opted for Scotch, Neil and I had our usual vodka with orange peel, and Roxanne had her requisite mineral water. The hot weather had waned, and the evening was cool, so I flirted with the notion of lighting the season's first fire, but decided against the idea, judging it pure affectation. The friendship, alcohol, and something Puccini, played softly, were sufficient to establish an atmosphere of conviviality.

Except, the tone of our gathering was muted by an underlying anxiety. Try as we might, it proved impossible to set aside for a few minutes the deepening mystery surrounding Betty Gifford Ashton's death—and the deepening predicament surrounding Roxanne.

Chick couldn't relax. He stood, fidgeting with the cell phone in his pocket. He asked me, "Is Sheriff Pierce anywhere near making an arrest? We need to see this matter brought to a speedy close." By *we,* he was referring to the Sagehorn-Creighton gubernatorial campaign.

"Sorry," I answered, "but as far as I know, Doug's investigation is still in the preliminary stages. No arrest is imminent—though the DA is applying pressure."

"Good." Chick took a slug of Scotch.

"Hardly," Roxanne told him. "Harley Kaiser would like nothing better than to haul *me* in on murder charges."

"Jesus." Chick slugged more Scotch.

Carl recounted for his campaign manager the history of bad blood between Roxanne and Kaiser, concluding, "If we hadn't been able to establish that Roxanne had no *opportunity* to rig the electrocution after learning of Betty's presence, I have little doubt that Sheriff Pierce would be compelled to accede to the prosecutor's wishes."

Carl was relying, once more, on defense logic that lacked crucial, contradictory information. Neither Chick nor Neil knew the particulars of Carl's oversight, but Roxanne and I did. In effect, Carl had just told us that there was sufficient circumstantial evidence for his wife to be arrested and booked for murder—*if* it was made known that she had learned at breakfast on Saturday that Betty would be attending the wedding.

I felt it was time to clear the air, to straighten out Carl's misunderstanding of the facts, and to seek his expert counsel on how we should proceed. Granted, there was no "good" time to do this, but I reasoned that sooner was better than later. What's more, the five of us in the room were united in our purpose and our loyalties. There would doubtless be no better, more sympathetic situation in which to expose and evaluate this mortal chink in Roxanne's defense.

"Carl . . . ," I began, then stopped short, noticing Roxanne's eyes. Previously, her look had begged me not to speak of this; now her stern gaze told me flatly, Don't you dare.

"Yes, Mark?" Carl swirled the ice and whiskey in his glass.

I wanted to excuse myself, to grab Roxanne by the arm, march her out of the room, and lecture her about the limits of friendship. Instead, I calmly told Carl, "Our best bet is to let the investigation run its course. Just today, several new angles emerged from the case, any one of which could clear Roxanne. Doug is a highly competent detective. We need to be patient and let him do his job."

"Be *patient?*" blurted Chick, his voice rising a register. "Every day this drags on, the uncertainty grows more threatening to the Sagehorn-Creighton ticket. The *governor's* race is at stake, and if you think the Giffords won't milk this mess for all it's worth, you don't know politics. We need to close this case and close it fast. Timing is everything."

I kept hearing that. "Doug is working on it," I assured Chick, "and so am I. As I said, there are a number of angles we need to explore. For example, first thing tomorrow, we'll visit the catering company again. We've already spoken to Wesley Scott, but now we need to talk to his wife, Alanna."

Neil entered the conversation, echoing my unruffled, rational tone. "That sounds like progress. What did you learn from Wes?"

I didn't want to air the whole business about babies and the rocky marriage; it seemed too emotionally laden for the moment. So I told everyone, "It occurred to us—actually, Lucille Haring raised this point—that the intended victim of the electrocution may not have been Betty, but Wes. He was the person who most frequently had his hands in the ice water, so the rigged wiring may have been intended for him."

Carl raised his glass. "Bravo. Most logical. And if Wes was indeed the intended victim, there's no conceivable motive that could lead back to Roxanne."

"Precisely. We're back at square one in terms of *finding* a motive, so we need to start looking. That's why Doug and I are going to question Alanna tomorrow." My words were meant to appease everyone, to convince them that the situation was not as bleak as it seemed, to give them the confidence that this new direction in the investigation pointed solidly away from Roxanne.

But Chick was hardly pacified. "*Alanna?*" His voice again slid perilously near the falsetto range. "Do you mean to say you suspect

Alanna of attempting to kill her husband? You can't be serious." He plunked his glass on the mantel and began pacing in front of the fireplace.

"It's plausible," I told him. "There's been some trouble in their marriage. We need to ask about it."

Chick stopped pacing and turned to me, hands on hips, looking steamed (attractively butch and feisty as well). "It's preposterous to hound that woman. If she's got trouble at home, that's *her* business. Alanna is obviously a good person, a hard worker, trying to deal with some heavy issues in her life. She was as devastated as anyone by what happened on Saturday. She's clearly above suspicion."

As Chick delivered this defensive testimonial, I recalled watching him ingratiate himself to Alanna at Saturday's reception. Then, on Sunday morning, he'd gone for a run with Neil, who reported back to me that Chick had spoken of Alanna and little else while jogging through the park. Now, Chick's impassioned words not only reinforced the assumption that he'd taken a personal interest in the woman, but they also gave the distinct impression that he and Alanna had recently met and talked.

There was only one conclusion I could draw from all this. It added up: Chick Butterly was a heterosexual male who'd set his lusty sights on a heterosexual female who seemed stuck in an unhappy marriage. This may have had implications for the investigation; I wasn't sure. I was certain, however, that it had implications for my dream, my lingering fantasy that Chick and his Republican counterpart were secret lovers. It was now obvious that I'd been ridiculously off base.

Chick was saying, "This isn't shaping up at all the way we'd hoped. Lowell is getting worried, and I don't blame him. The situation in Dumont could have a negative impact on his campaign in Illinois. Any way you slice it, it's bad PR."

I reminded him, "The purpose of the police investigation is to solve a murder, not to elect Lowell Sagehorn."

"Yeah, yeah." Chick began pacing again. "Christ, what a mess."

Too bad, I thought. You've got your problems; I've got mine. Turning to Neil, I raised my empty glass and suggested, "Another?"

"Sure. I'll get it."

"I'll help." I didn't need another drink so much as I needed to turn my back on Chick's pothering. Stepping away from the fireplace toward the cocktail cart, I felt instantly more sane and in control.

Neil dropped fresh ice into our glasses. Over the clinking, I heard Chick yammer to Carl and Roxanne, "I'm late reporting back to Lowell. He wants regular updates, and I'd hoped, by now, to have something positive to tell him. God, he's not gonna like this . . ."

Carl said, "Lowell is as reasonable and accommodating as they come. These circumstances are beyond anyone's control."

"I'm glad *you* think so." Chick's cell phone blipped and bleeped as he punched in a number.

I tuned out, focusing on Neil, who'd raised his glass to mine. We exchanged a silent toast, then sipped.

Out in the hall, I heard Thad's energetic footfalls bounding down the stairs. A moment later, he crossed past the doorway, toward the front of the house.

Neil called, "Heading out?"

Thad stopped, turned, and poked into the room, greeting everyone with a smile. "Just going over to Kwynn's. Just hanging out."

Neil noted, "Not many evenings left for you two."

I added, "Not many evenings left for us three."

Thad stepped up to me and squeezed my shoulders. There was nothing he could say. I knew he'd miss the home, the family we three had built. I also knew that, in his mind, he was already in California.

Chick was now jabbering to Sagehorn, as evidenced by his deferential, bootlicking cadences.

With a finger snap, I asked Thad, "Are you free for lunch tomorrow—you and Kwynn? Why don't we all meet downtown at the Grill?"

"Great. I'll ask her tonight. I'm sure she'll be up for it. Noon?"

"Sure, noon." I turned to Neil. "You can make it, can't you? All four of us."

Neil heaved a comically exaggerated shrug of disappointment. "Sorry. I've got a meeting with my clients out at the industrial park." He smiled. "You guys go ahead. Maybe I'll show up for dessert."

Thad checked, "You really don't mind?"

"Of course not." Neil truly didn't mind. Peevishness was foreign to him.

Thad gave him a wink. "We can talk later. Bye, guys." And he was gone.

Neil and I chorused a wistful sigh.

Turning back toward the fireplace, I was about to offer refills to the others, but noted that Chick's telephone conversation had become agitated.

"All right, hold on," he said into the phone. Then he thrust it toward Carl. "Lowell wants to talk to you."

Carl nodded, taking the phone. "Good evening, Lowell. I hope you're well. . . . Yes, thank you, I suppose it was time to 'tie the knot.'" Har-har.

We listened openly as Carl bantered away with his party's Illinois standard-bearer.

I asked Chick, "Does Lowell check in with Carl every night?"

"No." Chick said no more, letting insinuation hang in the air— whatever was happening on the phone now was anything but routine.

Roxanne told us blithely, "Lowell is such a sweetheart. I've rarely met such a charming, soft-spoken gentleman—at seventy-two, he's an absolute pussycat. I'm sure he asked for Carl so he could extend congratulations on the wedding."

Ominously, Chick asked her, "You think so?"

"What's that, Lowell?" asked Carl. "Yes, it was a regrettable incident. Yes, I understand that it carries some disheartening overtones. Yes, I'm quite certain that the local officials here are fully capable of—" Then Carl was cut off by Sagehorn, who apparently had something to say. Carl listened, offering occasional grunts of assent. With the phone stuck to his ear, he began pacing, just as Chick had done.

This went on for fully two or three minutes, with nary a clue from Carl as to what was being said. He pinched his brow; we strained to hear. He tugged his lip; we craned our necks. Finally, Carl said, "Yes, Lowell, I understand completely. Yes, thank you. Good night." Flipping the phone shut, he handed it back to Chick. Then he crossed to the end table where he'd set down his glass. Picking up the drink, he downed the remaining Scotch in one swallow.

The rest of us waited with an impatient, collective gaze that asked, Well . . . ?

"For God's sake," blurted Roxanne, "what'd the old gasbag have to say?"

Carl set down his glass and cleared his throat. "Well, it was not what I'd classify as pleasant or idle chitchat." Carl checked his watch, tapping its face. "In forty-eight hours, on Wednesday evening, Lowell will begin his all-important televised debate with Raymond Gifford, who's already reaped a measure of popular sympathy from the loss of his cousin Betty. We've noted a small spike in the polls since the weekend, and it is not in our favor. Lowell feels, with some justification, that the uncertain circumstances in Dumont, coupled with the mounting air of suspicion against his own campaign—meaning Roxie and me—could quash his own chances for victory in November. So he's decided to make an opening statement at Wednesday night's debate. What Lowell wants, of course, is to announce that all questions surrounding the death of his opponent's cousin have been resolved, clearing the Democratic campaign of any complicity. If, however, Lowell is unable to make that announcement, he'll announce instead"—Carl paused—"he'll announce that he's dumped me from the ticket."

"My God," said Roxanne. "I'm so sorry, darling."

"Lowell feels that the only way to keep his hands clean will be to make a 'public sacrifice' of me—those were his words."

"That's so unfair," Neil commiserated.

"I tried to tell you," muttered Chick, "but no one would *listen.*"

"Carl," I said, sounding an ameliorating note, "I presume that Lowell was simply trying to light a fire, so to speak—to speed the investigation along, if at all possible. His tone wasn't actually threatening, was it?"

"In fact, Mark, it was." Standing ramrod stiff, Carl summarized, "The kindly, avuncular Lowell Sagehorn just ripped me a new asshole."

Barb bopped into the room. "Everybody hungry? Dinner's served."

———

It was a quiet meal. Barb joined us at the table, so we were six. We had invited Roxanne's mother, of course, but she had declined, claiming the onset of a bout of migraines. Lauren Creighton had also declined our invitation, offering no excuse. Clearly, the two women had come to detest each other and were taking no chance of being caught together at the same table. Ironically, since both had decided not to join us on Prairie Street, they had only bettered the odds of encountering each other elsewhere—in the hallways of the Manor House, for instance.

As for the *other* wedding guest staying at the Manor House, Blain Gifford, it goes without saying that we had not invited him to sup with us. I had no way of knowing his plans for the evening, but I could well imagine him either measuring his late aunt's house for new draperies (something a little less flowery, perhaps a nice, fresh, nononsense ticking) or simply taking to his room, making an inventory of his new assets, counting the loot.

After dinner, Neil helped Barb with something in the kitchen. Carl and Chick retreated upstairs to weigh Sagehorn's threat and to strategize damage control. Roxanne waffled in the front hall; it was too early for bed.

I asked her, "Could we spend a few minutes talking about something? It's important."

"Sure." She gave me a skeptical, inquisitive glance.

"Just want to check a few points regarding Thad's trust funds. Now that he's leaving for college, I've been pondering the future a lot."

"Sure," she repeated.

"Let's use my den. It's private."

My quest for privacy had nothing to do with trust funds. It was time, at last, for Roxanne and me to confront our lie of omission. Entering the den, I closed the door behind us and suggested that we settle together on the small sofa facing the hearth. Given the awkward topic I meant to broach, I didn't even consider the nicety of lighting the fire to set a cozy mood.

Once we were seated, she asked suspiciously, "And, uh, where are your notes?"

"Notes?"

"Or your files or whatever? And your old fountain pen?" With a lavish roll of the eyes, she added, "You don't quite look prepared to discuss the kid's trusts."

My hip squeaked on the leather cushion as I turned to face her squarely. "I've just about *had* it, Roxanne. You can drop the irony, the cynical tone, the smirking, and the eye-rolling right now."

She flinched as if I'd slapped her.

I'd been tempted. "You're a friend. Neil and I love you. And I'm forever indebted to you for bringing Neil and me together. But—"

"That was never my intention," she reminded me flatly, not daring to toss her head, to grin, or to inflect her words with a sardonic lilt.

"I know that. But that's how it worked out. You brought us together."

She looked toward the ceiling, a pensive gesture, not eye-rolling. "I never *dreamed* you two would connect, and when you did, I felt wounded. Eventually, I managed to pull myself out of my misery, to settle for the friendship you and Neil offered, and finally to find love with a man who could return it—Carl."

I took her hand. "You also managed to kick the bottle."

"Yup. That was the silver lining in my 'mistake' of delivering Neil to you, so we both have our debts of gratitude."

"And that's what makes this so hard."

"What?" she asked, dropping my hand, looking genuinely confused.

"Roxanne, you know very well there's something we need to discuss. And, yes, your perception was correct—it has nothing to do with Thad's trust funds."

"Okay." She nodded with an air of despondency. "Fire away. And be specific—the sooner we're on the same page, the better."

I smiled; she'd reacted exactly as I'd hoped. "I'm talking, of course, about our lie of omission."

She dared a little smirk, a moue. "Our 'lie of omission'? You call that specific? Come on, Mark, you're a writer; you can do better than that."

With a laugh, I conceded, "It seems we could *all* use a refresher in eschewing obfuscation."

"Huh?"

"Never mind." Eschewing obfuscation, I laid out my concerns in detail: "I'm talking about the argument raised by Carl on Sunday morning after Doug showed us the videotape. Thanks to your smart-mouthing at the murder scene about the penny trick, plus the clear link between you and the Perrier bottles, Blain Gifford had already seen you in a suspicious light. The tape reinforced the notion that you'd had the *means* to kill Betty.

"Later that morning, when Blain dug up the history of your fiasco with the Gifford family's SEC filing, we knew you'd had a plausible *motive* to kill Betty—silencing her, burying an ugly story from the past that could raise a whiff of scandal sufficient to influence the outcome of a tight political race.

"With apparent means and possible motive to link you to the crime, your best defense was to demonstrate that you'd had no *opportunity* to murder Betty. Carl hit upon this defense after viewing the tape, when he argued that you'd had no time to rig the electrocution. He reasoned that you'd had no idea that Betty would be at the wedding until you met her at the reception. Because Betty was killed only minutes later, Carl easily convinced Doug Pierce that you could not have been responsible.

"You and I both know, however, that you were fully aware of Betty much earlier that day, at breakfast. Doug arrived in the kitchen after we'd discussed Betty, so he still has no way of knowing that you had *plenty* of opportunity to rig the fuse box and the extension cord—if you were so inclined. As a result, he's shaping a murder investigation based on the logic of Carl's argument, which *we* know to be in error." Pausing for breath, I concluded, "And *that* is our lie of omission. Sufficiently specific?"

Roxanne had listened to all this with a blank expression, withering as I detailed my knowledge that she'd had the motive, means, and opportunity to commit murder. Though she was currently held above suspicion by Sheriff Pierce and her husband, we knew that, by rights, she ought to be considered the top suspect, in search of a new defense.

"Mark," she began lamely, "you don't honestly think that I . . . ," but she couldn't finish the question.

"No," I assured her, "I don't think you plotted to kill Betty—at least I *hope* you didn't. I hope I know you better than *that.*"

She shook her head vigorously, as if to clear her thinking. "Then what's the difference? If Doug and Carl have judged me above suspicion, reaching the right conclusion for the wrong reason, what's the big dif?"

With an exasperated toss of my hands, I explained, "You're a lawyer, for God's sake, and I'm a journalist. We're both bound by professional ethics and by strict principles of clean, aboveboard objectivity. You know very well that the end does *not* justify the means. By remaining silent and not correcting the known facts of this investigation, we're committing, at the very least, a violation of public trust."

She swept an imagined strand of stray hair from her face. "What's the *public* got to do with this? We're harming no one. But I assure you, we'll be harming Carl's chances for election—to say nothing of my own chances of proving my innocence of this crime—if we go running to Doug and tell him that Carl was wrong, that I knew Betty was coming to the wedding before I waltzed outdoors that morning in my bathrobe to stock the bar with my own bottles of Perrier. Christ, Mark, you might as well just lock me up and turn the keys over to Harley Kaiser. No, we just need to let this . . . play out."

"That's nuts, Roxanne. It's not only dishonest, but dangerous. If, by your silence, you stick to Carl's mistaken story, and then the truth later comes to light and you're exposed as having hidden something, you'll appear all the more guilty of the crime."

We were at loggerheads. She said nothing. She knew I was right, but she was simply unwilling to own up to our mistake and live with the consequences.

I reminded her, "This little charade puts *me* in a horribly compromised position. I don't claim to understand the tangled legal ramifications of what we're doing—*you're* the lawyer—but I do understand that if this goes much further, and we're exposed, my credibility goes down the crapper. I've worked hard, for over twenty years, to build my reputation as a journalist, first as a reporter and now as a publisher. My name *means* something. I owe you my loyalty as a friend, Roxanne, but I do *not* owe you the integrity of my career."

She shook her head again. "No, of course you don't. I don't expect that—I wouldn't want that."

"Okay then." I touched her arm. "How are we going to handle this? How are we going to correct the sheriff's misunderstanding of the facts?"

She thought for a moment; I could have sworn I heard gears grinding. "What if," she said tentatively, "what if, sometime soon, the crime gets solved? I mean, if the killer is unmasked—someone other than me, of course—and the case is closed, the issue of my 'opportunity' becomes moot, right?"

I shrugged. "Right."

"So here's the deal: let's keep everything *entre nous* just until Wednesday night. We'll keep our little secret until Lowell Sagehorn's opening remarks at the debate. By then, either the crime will have been solved, and everything's hunky-dory, or the identity of the killer will remain a mystery, and Carl gets unceremoniously booted from the gubernatorial ticket. If *that* happens, God forbid, the worst of my fears will have materialized and I won't really care about the rest. I swear, Mark, throughout this mess, I've cared only about its impact on Carl, not myself. If that broken-down puckfist Lowell Sagehorn dumps Carl, I'll come clean to everyone about the 'opportunity' issue and hope to mount an alternate defense—assuming I'm not disbarred in the process. As for you, I won't drag you into my confession. If it would assuage your own sense of ethics by chorusing a few mea culpas, be my guest; it's your call. Either way, another two days will neither magnify nor diminish our guilt. What's done is done."

I flopped my head back, moaning.

"What's wrong?"

"You, Miss Exner, are far too persuasive for your own good."

"Then you'll keep your mouth shut and get cracking on this case with Doug?"

"We already *are* cracking, and trust me, the puzzle is getting *more* complicated, not less so. Which reminds me"—I sat up straight— "when you went outdoors to stock the bar on Saturday morning, did you happen to notice the orange extension cord? It was meant for the blender, and obviously, it's crucial for us to determine when the cord got moved to the shelf."

"I didn't notice the cord at all. There was too much on my mind that morning. But I'm *certain* it wasn't dangling from the shelf when I stashed my Perrier there—I'm not *that* ditsy."

"You're many things, Roxanne, but hardly a ditz."

"Thanks. I think."

I paused, then exhaled loudly. "Doug and I have our work cut out for us. Untangling this is a tall order."

She sniffed. "Don't be silly. You guys are good at this." With a twisted grin, she added, "Really, Mark—you've *got* two days."

I glanced at my watch. "Not quite. We now have forty-six hours."

She groaned, dropping her head into her hands.

Wrapping an arm around her, I pulled her close to my side. "Oh, well. Now, at least, I'm working against a clear deadline."

Turning her head to look up at me, she asked, "And you *never* miss a deadline, right?"

"Rarely," I allowed.

M y tight deadline shrank overnight from forty-six hours to thirty-six. The debate would begin in Chicago the following evening at eight o'clock, which would place it, inopportunely, smack in the middle of Thad's going-away party.

On Tuesday morning at around eight o'clock, Sheriff Pierce stopped at the house on Prairie Street to join us for breakfast. Neil and I told him about Lowell Sagehorn's threat to dump Carl Creighton from the gubernatorial ticket if the circumstances of Betty Gifford Ashton's death were not clarified prior to the debate.

"Just what I need—more pressure," remarked Pierce with a put-upon but good-natured sigh. "Harley Kaiser has been relentless in needling me to make a quick arrest. He's now threatened to bring the whole matter before the county police-and-fire commission. I'm not sure what he intends to accomplish—other than to publicly question my competence and to openly cast suspicion on Roxanne. It's bad enough that Harley has a vendetta against Roxanne as a liberal, outspoken outsider. Making matters worse, Harley has enjoyed hefty campaign contributions from the Ashton family, so I'm sure he's feeling some payback pressure."

Pushing my coffee away (I had no taste for it), I asked, "When's the next meeting of the commission?"

"Thursday. So Lowell Sagehorn's Wednesday-night deadline is as good as any. God knows, we now have plenty of motivation to get this wrapped up." Pierce ticked off on his fingers: "We want to solve a murder and see justice done. We want to clear Roxanne of the unwarranted suspicions that are rising against her, promoted largely by Blain Gifford. We want to prevent Carl's political career from being needlessly, unfairly ended. And a highly personal motivation—I don't want to give Harley Kaiser the satisfaction of grandstanding against me, my department, or my investigation."

I could have added, but did not, a motivation of my own—to preclude the need for Roxanne and me to own up to our lie of omission, which would devastate Carl (possibly threatening his and Roxanne's days-old marriage), would leave Pierce feeling betrayed (probably ending our friendship, certainly destroying his trust), and would irreparably undermine the credibility of the *Register* and its esteemed investigative reporter turned publisher (me).

Neil was telling Pierce, "Roxanne hasn't come out and said it, but I know the situation is really starting to scare her—as well it should. She came up here for a nice, simple wedding, and now, three days later, instead of lolling on a beach, sipping virgin mai tais from a coconut, she's pondering the possibility of murder charges against her and the demise of her husband's career. One thing's for sure: she hasn't been her spunky old self."

"Well," said Pierce, cutting one last slice of kringle (raspberry, my anytime favorite), "let's see if we can fix that. After all, Mark and I have *all day* to figure this out—and most of tomorrow." He was being facetious. The success of our mission seemed chancy at best.

In the pit of my stomach, something acidic was punishing me for harboring facts Pierce deserved to know. Focus, I told myself. Focus on the task at hand, help him solve the riddle, and the rest won't matter.

Soon, we were on our way, returning to A Moveable Feast. Today we took both of our cars, since we each had uncertain plans for the remainder of the morning. As I parked behind Pierce in front of the neat little storefront, I noted that we were right on time. My dashboard clock flashed nine o'clock precisely—and our deadline had tightened to thirty-five hours.

Standing on the curb with Pierce, I asked, "You made sure Alanna would be here, right?"

He nodded. "When I phoned yesterday afternoon, Wesley Scott answered, and I asked if Alanna could find time to talk with us. Wes was sure that this morning would work for Alanna, and he asked if we needed to meet with *him* again. I answered, nonchalantly, of course, 'No, I suppose not, if you have other things to do.' "

"Great. Let's hope he takes the hint and makes himself scarce. It'll be much better if we can get Alanna alone."

We stepped inside. As on the previous morning, we were greeted by a jumbled potpourri of food smells, which seemed both disjointed and curiously appealing. There's something so primal and *nurturing* about kitchens and cooking and the preparation of real food that has never touched plastic. The bank of glass-doored refrigerators continued to drone. Someone puttered in the back room, quietly clattering metal, perhaps sorting cutlery that had just been washed. No radio played today; no one spoke on the phone.

Pierce closed the front door behind us with a thud.

"Coming," said a woman's voice from the back. The clattering stopped; footsteps approached the front room. "Morning, Sheriff," said Alanna Scott as she appeared in the doorway, striding toward us, wiping her hands on a long, white apron stitched in green with the logo of A Moveable Feast. "Hello, Mr. Manning." She extended her hand, reddened from hot water, still damp.

We greeted her in turn. Pierce thanked her for making time for us. I thanked her for the splendid job she'd done, catering the reception.

"It was a *joy* working with Neil," she told me. "He knows exactly what he wants, he's clear in his instructions, and he's so well organized. In short, he knows how to entertain. Most clients haven't a clue. With many big parties, especially weddings, it's a constant struggle for me to overcome the feeling that there's a disaster in the making." She laughed.

Then we all realized the unintended but underlying irony of her words.

"Sorry," she muttered, "didn't mean to make light of what happened."

Pierce smiled. "No problem, Alanna. We understand. Besides, you've hit upon the very topic we came to discuss." He gestured toward the conference table. "Let's sit down."

We stepped to the table, and I helped Alanna with her chair. Pierce readied his notebook and pen; so did I.

Pierce said, "I'm sure Wes told you that Mark and I met with him here yesterday morning. He was most cooperative, and we appreciated his candor."

She seemed puzzled. "Candor?" A wrinkle creased her brow, a momentary distortion of her strong, handsome features. It was easy to see that with a touch of makeup and a bit of primping, she would be very pretty indeed, but given the nature of her work, she had refrained from dolling up. I recalled Wes telling us that he was forty-three, Alanna was thirty-nine. Though she looked her age, she wore her years well.

Pierce hesitated, not ready to broach the topic of the shaky marriage. He simply explained, "Wes was very open with us."

Her brow wrinkled again, deeper. "You don't think *Wes* was responsible for what happened, do you?"

"No, certainly not. The circumstances of Betty's electrocution might be seen as pointing to Wes, but I'm satisfied that he had no motive to harm her."

"In fact," I added, "we've been working on a theory that perhaps Wes was the intended *target* of this crime. It's possible that the whole setup was directed not at Betty, but at him."

Alanna sat back in her chair. "I don't know whether to be relieved or alarmed by that, Mr. Manning."

"I admit, it *is* cause for concern."

Pierce continued, "And that's one of the reasons we wanted to spend this time with you, Alanna. If you don't mind, let me run you through some very routine questions." He glanced down at his notes.

"I'll help any way I can, Sheriff. What would you like to know?"

"First, since you were present during much of the setup for the reception, I'm wondering whether you saw, heard, or noticed anything unusual—anything suspicious—especially with regard to the wiring of the tents."

She thought for a moment, appearing at a loss. "Sorry, Sheriff. I don't recall seeing anything the least bit suspicious, but then, I'm a total dummy when it comes to electrical stuff, so I doubt that I'd have recognized anything sinister even if I saw it. Besides, I was frazzled with my own . . . uh, 'issues' that day."

Pierce and I glanced at each other. I asked Alanna, "What sort of issues?"

With a half laugh, she explained, "*Food* issues, naturally. For starters, my béarnaise bombed. Then Wes started carping that the bar was understaffed, and with the heat, it was—"

"I get the picture." I tried calming her with a placid grin.

She smiled. "Anyway, I wasn't paying attention to the wiring. That was someone *else's* problem, thank God."

Pierce asked, "You're referring to Dale Turner?"

"Sure, essentially. He had some help from that theater guy setting up the sound system, but otherwise, Dale was in charge."

I said, "That 'theater guy' is Whitney Greer. When he was working on the amplification for the bandstand, did you notice anything peculiar about his behavior?"

She eyed me askance. "He's sort of peculiar to begin with."

Pierce laughed.

"No," Alanna continued, "I didn't notice anything strange about the way he wired the sound equipment—not that I'd be able to."

Pierce said, "We've learned that the fatal extension cord was originally intended to power the bar blender. Did you happen to notice the orange cord behind the bar? More precisely, did you at any point notice the cord *missing* behind the bar?"

"That's Wes's domain. Sorry, Sheriff. I was dealing with my own problems."

"Okay"—Pierce struck something from his notes—"you observed nothing suspicious. Next, I'd like to move along to the theory Mark mentioned, regarding your husband. Alanna, this is where I could use some real candor: Can you think of any reason why anyone would want to harm Wes?"

"No," she said at once, shaking her head. "If you're asking whether Wes has enemies, no, that's ridiculous, not Wes."

Pierce studied her for a moment. "You seemed awfully quick with that response—and certain of it too. How come?"

She shrugged. "I know Wes. Look, Sheriff, he may not be the backslapping type—in fact, a lot of people think he's sort of distant or just plain contrary—but that's his nature, and it's harmless. Underneath, he's true to his friends and he's honest in business. I can't imagine there'd be sufficient reason for someone to bear any ill will against him, much less a life-threatening grudge."

She seemed fully confident in her assertion that no business associates or erstwhile friends had plotted against her husband. My best theory, however, was that if someone had plotted against Wes, it would likely have been Alanna herself. It was time to raise the issue of the Scotts' problematic marriage.

I glanced at Pierce, a visual nudge for him to proceed with the next item on his list, but something in his return glance told me that I should do it.

"Alanna," I began uncertainly, "when we spoke to Wes yesterday, he was candid in relating to us that you've experienced some difficulties in your relationship of late." Hearing my own words, I chided myself for obfuscating. I clarified, "Wes told us outright that your marriage is shaky, and the issue, as I understand it, is children."

She gave me a blank look, surprised by this turn in the discussion.

"I do apologize for raising such a personal matter; neither Sheriff Pierce nor I intend to pry. However, the rift in your marriage seems significant in the context of understanding Wes—what makes him tick—and understanding what may have motivated someone to plot deadly mischief against him." Was I obfuscating again? Perhaps, but I couldn't bring myself to ask Alanna, Did *you* try to kill him?

She listened, then tossed her head, shaking it slowly with evident melancholy. "There's no need to apologize. Our problems are hardly a secret. Anyone who sees us together should be able to figure out that things aren't exactly rosy."

"Was it ever rosy?"

"Oh, sure, at first. We married out of love, and we enjoyed our mutual goal, to build, from nothing, a thriving business. Now that we've done that, something seems lacking."

"Wes said that it's *kids* that are lacking."

She nodded. "That seems to be the point of contention, yes."

Pierce checked his notes, asking, "Wes wants children, but you don't, correct?"

"Correct." Alanna elaborated, recounting the same story that her husband had told us the morning before: they had agreed to put off having children until the business was firmly established, but now that they'd become financially secure, Alanna feared that pregnancy would be dangerous for her or the baby, and Wes felt cheated out of parenthood.

In the somber silence that followed her narrative, I recalled Lucille Haring's speculation that Wes may have tried forcing a pregnancy, that Alanna may have felt raped, giving her a strong motive to wrest revenge while putting a permanent end to his demands.

I asked, "Wes feels pretty strongly about all this, doesn't he?"

"You bet. I honestly don't know if we'll survive it—I mean 'us,' together."

"Has he ever tried to, uh . . . take matters into his own hands?"

She squinted. "Sorry? I don't know what you mean."

Eschewing obfuscation, I asked, "Has Wes ever tried to forcibly impregnate you?" If I didn't blush, I should have.

Alanna's reaction was unexpected, to say the least. She fell back in her chair, laughing, hand over mouth. "Oh, Lord . . . ," she sputtered. "God, you can't be serious." Composing herself, she put her elbows on the table, saying, "I'm so sorry, Mr. Manning. I don't mean to be rude, but clearly, you don't know Wes very well. Forcible? In the bedroom? No, *not Wes*." She suppressed another laugh.

Deadpan, Pierce told her, "We appreciate your candor." He added something to his notes.

I was inclined to believe Alanna, to accept her assertion that Wes was a mild-mannered lover at best, and to conclude that Wes had neither raped Alanna nor incited her hell-bent revenge. So much for

Lucy's feminist-lesbian perspective on justifiable homicide.

Pierce had reached the same conclusion, closing his notebook, judging the interview a wash. We were nowhere nearer naming Betty's killer.

"If there's nothing else . . . ?" asked Alanna, sliding her chair back from the table and rising.

Pierce rose. "No, Alanna. Thanks so much for your time and assistance."

I also stood. "Again, I apologize—sorry the discussion turned so personal." Pierce and I began moving toward the door.

"That's okay. I understand. Everyone's just trying to figure out what happened to Mrs. Ashton—like that nice Mr. Butterly. He's staying at your house, right? Say hi to him for me, will you?"

I flinched. "Chick Butterly? Yes, he's staying with us. I'll be happy to extend your greetings." I couldn't resist asking, "Did you, uh, get acquainted Saturday at the reception."

"A little." The trace of a smile crossed her face. "But then he stopped by the shop yesterday afternoon, and we had a chance to talk some."

"Oh? What'd he want?"

Alanna laughed. "You know, I'm really not sure. He just stopped in to say hi, said the party was nice—that kind of thing."

"Did Wes happen to be here?"

"Don't think so." She paused to recollect, then answered definitely, "No, Wes was out."

Walking along First Avenue with Pierce, I told him, "So it wasn't just my imagination—Chick Butterly has a personal, active interest in Alanna Scott."

It was a few minutes before noon. After meeting at A Moveable Feast, Pierce and I had returned to our offices, agreeing to compare notes later that morning. We now strolled along Dumont's main street from the *Register* building toward First Avenue Grill, where Thad and his friend Kwynn would join us for lunch.

"What's a 'personal, active interest'?" asked Pierce.

With a chortle, I realized that I was obfuscating again. "Chick's got the hots for Alanna."

"*She* didn't seem aware of it. She said he'd merely dropped by to say hi."

I looked askance at Pierce while crossing a side street. "She's married. She's a cateress living four hours from Chicago. Why would she think for a minute that Chick's on the make?"

"Why do *you?*"

Stepping to the far curb and continuing toward the restaurant, I filled Pierce in regarding the dynamics I'd noted at the reception, as well as Chick's interrogation of Neil during their run. "So something's up. Sure, it could be physical attraction, pure and simple. Or maybe something else is going on."

Pierce laughed. "God, you *are* a suspicious sort, aren't you?"

I reminded him, "*You're* the detective. Sometimes, nosiness pays off."

Without comment, he stepped under the awning of the restaurant and opened the door, gesturing for me to pass. We were greeted by another pastiche of food smells, only the current assortment of aromas had focus and cohesion—meals were being prepared to be served and eaten, not merely the random parts and ingredients we'd sniffed that morning at the catering shop.

The restaurant occupied a converted storefront looking out to the bustle of traffic on the street (not that traffic in Dumont ever truly "bustles," but at noon, that description could plausibly be stretched). The interior was handsome, clean, and spare, passing for "urban" in our remote, homey little burg. The black-and-white tile floor lent a note of clatter to the room, while white linen tablecloths softened the noise and hinted at serious cuisine.

Indeed, First Avenue Grill was easily the best restaurant in town, which I'd discovered several years earlier during a trip north from Chicago to discuss buying the newspaper. The *Register's* founding publisher, Barret Logan, had taken me to the Grill for lunch, as was his habit. The habit, as well as the *Register,* was now mine. I had a standing reservation at "my" table, which occupied a prime spot between the fireplace and a corner window.

The Grill's reputation was due solely to the culinary vision and guidance of its owner, Nancy Sanderson, a skilled amateur cook who had been widowed in her late forties and then had established the restaurant out of necessity for her livelihood. Fortunately for Dumont, as well as for Nancy, her efforts had flourished, and with the passing of a few years, her talents had matured and broadened, putting her on a par with many pedigreed executive chefs.

"Good afternoon, Mr. Manning," she greeted me with a bob of her head. "Good day, Sheriff Pierce"—the same deferential bob. Her smile was restrained but genuine. I'd come to understand that her proper bearing and reserved manner were signs of respect, not emotional distance. She dressed smartly, as always, in a suit of matching skirt and jacket, tweedy autumn colors today, never flashy. Her hair had turned a steely, stately gray, which she wore "up" in a tight, conventional style, always perfectly in place. She reminded me of a maiden aunt, likable and caring, but seemingly from another planet.

She said, "Your usual table is ready. Is Mr. Waite to join you?"

"No, Neil has another commitment today, but my nephew and a friend are coming, so we'll be four."

"Ah." She picked up four menus and, motioning this-way-please, began leading us across the room, heels pecking the hard floor.

As it was not quite noon, few other patrons were in the room, so after Pierce and I were seated, I spent a minute or two chatting with Nancy, going over details of the next night's dinner party for Thad. "I think it might be better," I told her, "if we begin a bit earlier than originally planned."

"Whatever you wish"—again the bob. "The entire dining room is reserved for your use all evening."

"Then I'd like to ask people to arrive for cocktails around six, with dinner at six-thirty, to finish by seven-thirty."

"Of course, sir." My wish was her command, but her face couldn't hide her surprise. Though Midwesterners do generally dine early, this was pushing it.

I explained, "The adults can linger, drink, and talk, but I suspect the kids will prefer running off to alternate amusements." This was true enough, but my underlying rationale for the speed-feeding was to finish the festivities before the start of the eight-o'clock debate in Chicago. With Carl Creighton's political future on precariously thin ice, to say nothing of the deadline Roxanne and I had imposed on ourselves for fessing up (a deadline now thirty-two hours away), there was no telling what the evening might bring—emotionally or otherwise. We'd all be there in the dining room when the debate began and Lowell Sagehorn made his opening announcement. I didn't want the kids to be around if and when our lives started falling apart.

Worst-case scenario: Sagehorn would dump Carl. Roxanne would confess her lie of omission and would then be arrested by Pierce. Pierce would disavow our friendship. Neil would feel betrayed for having been left in the dark. And I would lose all credibility in the only career I'd ever known or cared about.

Nancy reviewed the menu with me, concluding, "I've hired some extra help to make sure everything runs smoothly. Fortunately, the Scotts weren't booked for the evening, so Alanna will help with the kitchen, Wesley with the bar."

"Excellent." I didn't know whether Chick Butterly would be back in Chicago by then or would still be here with Carl, at Thad's party. If he stayed, tomorrow night's uncertainties would be intriguingly amplified.

Nancy offered to get us drinks while we waited. Pierce asked for iced tea; he never drank alcohol during the day. Though I had a taste for a glass of velvety, chilled Lillet, which Nancy kept in stock for me, I decided that Pierce was wise in opting to keep his head clear, so I ordered tea as well. Then Nancy bowed her leave, literally backing a step or two from the table before turning and moving away.

"Interesting." Pierce unfurled his napkin, placing it in his lap. "Wes and Alanna will be here tomorrow night." Pierce would also attend Thad's going-away dinner; he was family by now.

"Exactly what I was thinking. We can observe their dynamics—if we don't have this wrapped up by then." Snapping my own napkin, I exhaled a lame laugh.

"What do you think, Mark? Our meeting with Alanna this morning—did we learn anything?"

I paused, reluctantly concluding, "Not much. Other than this new twist regarding Chick Butterly, we didn't hear anything we didn't already know. To my way of thinking, the most significant point of our discussion was Alanna's confirmation that her marriage is shaky due to the issue of kids. When we first heard it from Wes, it struck me as 'off' somehow. But Alanna has seconded the story, so that's that."

Pierce nodded, thinking. "Okay, Wes wants kids and Alanna doesn't. It's sort of a role reversal, and I'm sorry they're having troubles, but the bottom line is, their discord is hardly a sufficient motive for Alanna to attempt *killing* Wes."

"Agreed. So where does that leave us?" Fingering the rim of my water glass, I answered myself, "It still seems that this crime most logically focuses on Wes. If he was the culprit, what was his motive? But if he was the target, who, if not Alanna, was out to get him?"

Pierce tapped the table. "Don't forget Dale Turner. Yesterday we concluded that *he* seemed the logical target of the crime. If so, who had the motive?"

"Not sure." I smiled. "But Lucy tracked down his ex-wife. Busy after lunch?"

"I am, in fact. Why?"

"The ex–Mrs. Turner is coming to the newsroom at one. Lucy thought she'd have to concoct some pretext to lure her in, but *this* gal, apparently, was more than ready to talk."

"Hngh. Why? Does she sympathize with Dale's predicament, or does she have some beef with him?"

"My impression is, the latter—an ex with an ax to grind. Sure you can't be there?"

Pierce shook his head. "Wish I could, but I offered to update Harley Kaiser in his office, hoping to keep him at bay a while longer. It wouldn't look good to cancel on him. You can cover this. Let me know if you turn up anything promising."

Nancy reappeared with our iced tea, explaining, "Berta's busy with another table, and I didn't want to keep you waiting."

We thanked her. "Nancy," I said, squeezing a wedge of lemon into my glass, "you mentioned that the Scotts will be working at tomorrow night's party. You seem to know them quite well."

"I know Alanna very well, yes. I've come to think of Alanna as my closest confidante, and I daresay the sentiment is mutual. Our shared interest in cooking has grown into genuine friendship. Wesley, however, is more of an acquaintance."

"I've been meaning to thank you for helping Alanna rescue her failed béarnaise at Saturday's reception."

Head bob. "It was my pleasure, naturally. If you'll pardon my immodesty, I've always had a way with the classic sauces." She allowed a tight little smile of pride to stretch her lightly rouged lips.

"On Saturday, I heard Alanna tell Neil that if it weren't for you, she wouldn't even be in the food business."

Nancy's eyes fluttered downward. "That's an overstatement, I'm sure. It is true, though, that I've mentored Alanna in both the culinary and business aspects of A Moveable Feast. She's always had such interest, drive, and talent. She lacked only some direction and experience."

Pierce asked the question I was thinking: "How does that work? I mean, don't you see her as, well . . . *competition?*"

"Not at all. She doesn't run a restaurant, and I don't do offpremises catering. Our two humble enterprises seem to complement one another. What's more . . ." She hesitated, then plunged ahead, "I'm fifty-eight now; Alanna is not yet forty. Retirement is not terribly far off for me, and I see Alanna and Wesley as the likely buyers of First Avenue Grill. It would please me immeasurably to know that the restaurant has passed into able hands."

I asked, "Have you mentioned this to them?"

"To Alanna, yes. We've spoken of it often, and she's highly interested."

"What about Wes?"

With a barely perceptible shrug, Nancy answered, "I *assume* he's interested." Then the trace of a frown crossed her face. "Under the circumstances, I suppose it's hard to tell."

Aha, I thought, an outside perspective on the Scotts' rocky marriage. I asked, "By 'circumstances,' are you referring to Wes and Alanna's personal difficulties."

Nancy lowered her voice. "Yes, of course. It's most distressing. I've tried to warn Alanna, but my words have fallen on deaf ears." She gave a tiny, knowing nod.

Pierce and I exchanged a puzzled glance. Reticently, I asked Nancy to clarify: "You've tried warning Alanna about what—having a baby?"

Nancy now looked more befuddled than we did. "Why would I . . . ?"

I paused, then made explicit the details of my confusion. "Wes and Alanna's marriage is threatened by their disagreement regarding children. Wes wants to have a baby, but Alanna thinks it's too late to start a family. What I can't figure out is what you've warned her about—the dangers of midlife pregnancy?"

Nancy raised both hands in gentle admonishment, shaking her head. "It seems you've gotten some crossed signals, Mr. Manning. It's really not my place to discuss such matters, but I feel it's incumbent upon me, for Alanna's sake, to disabuse you of a highly mistaken notion. Yes, Alanna is acutely aware that her clock, as they say, is ticking, and it's for that very reason that she *wants* to have a baby, badly—before it's too late."

With blank bewilderment, Pierce asked Nancy, "Alanna *told* you that?"

"Plainly. More than once."

Surprised as I was by this contention, I was still stuck on Nancy's previous statement, so again I asked, "Then what did you *warn* Alanna about?"

Nancy flopped a palm to her chest. "I'm sorry, Mr. Manning, but I've already said far too much, and my luncheon patrons have begun to arrive, and I—"

"Nancy," Pierce interrupted. His tone was hushed and soothing. "Mark and I aren't asking for gossip. We're working on something important. Though we're not certain if the Scotts' marriage is relevant to this matter, it would be helpful for us to have a better understanding of the difficulties between Wes and Alanna. We'd truly appreciate any insights you can offer."

She paused to consider this, then pronged her fingertips on our table, leaning closer. "Well," she said with a thin smile, "as long as this isn't 'gossip' . . ."

"Absolutely not." I shook my head—perish the thought.

"Well"—she leaned another inch—"I can tell you with reasonable certainty that the problems between Alanna and Wesley have nothing to do with babies, wanted or otherwise. Alanna won't listen to me, but I've warned her more than once—"

"Hi, Mark. Hi, Sheriff," said Thad, approaching the table with Kwynn. Engrossed as I was in Nancy's nongossip, I hadn't noticed the kids enter the restaurant.

Kwynn also greeted us as Thad helped her with her chair.

Nancy told them, "Welcome, Miss Wyman, Master Quatrain. So then—it's off to college soon?"

"Way soon," they chimed. "This week." Pins and needles. Couldn't wait.

Nancy said, "I'll send Berta right over. I hope you'll all have a splendid lunch."

"Uh, Nancy," I said as she began to step from the table, "you were about to tell us something, I believe?"

"Not *now*, Mr. Manning." Her eyes slid to the kids. "Perhaps later." And she marched away from the table, snapping her heels.

Thad and Kwynn bubbled into conversation, telling Pierce they were glad he could join us, expressing disappointment that Neil couldn't, talking about packing and travel plans and the dinner party tomorrow night and on and on. I kept an ear to the discussion, nodding and smiling where appropriate, but my mind was still locked on Nancy's unfinished narrative.

Both Wes and Alanna had told me earlier that Alanna didn't want children, and now Nancy had claimed otherwise. Was Nancy mistaken? If not, had the Scotts conspired on their story to Pierce and me? If so, why? Suddenly, I couldn't even be certain there was a rift in the Scotts' marriage. If there was, and the wedge between them wasn't the issue of children, what was it? Because Nancy had clammed up in front of Thad and Kwynn, I presumed she'd judged the tenor of her message indelicate. Was one of the Scotts "fooling around"? If so, I suspected Wes, as Nancy had seen fit to warn Alanna about . . . *something*.

"Would you mind, Mr. Manning?"

Snapping out of my thoughts, I looked across the table at Kwynn, who peered back at me with an expectant, pretty smile. "Sorry," I said through a quiet laugh, "must have been daydreaming."

Thad brought me up to speed. "We were just saying that because Kwynn is leaving for college this week, tomorrow's party is really *her* going-away as much as mine. Her parents are already invited, but we were wondering if it'd be all right if she asked a few other people as well."

Kwynn added, "Just a few close friends, really."

"Sure," I told her, "please do. We'll have the whole restaurant to ourselves, so there's plenty of room for your friends and family. Be sure to give the names to Nancy by tomorrow morning. She's keeping track of the numbers."

Kwynn nodded eagerly. "Thanks so much, Mr. Manning."

Berta, my usual waitress—a buxom Wisconsin woman in a white uniform that made her look like a nurse—appeared at the table, bringing drinks for the kids (a Diet Coke for Kwynn and a cup of coffee, of all things, for Thad). Berta then recited a few specials, took our orders, and left.

I don't remember what I chose to eat, having done it vacantly, preoccupied by the sight of Thad sipping coffee. I couldn't recall having *ever* seen him drink it, and there he was, playing grown-up. Except, of course, he wasn't playing; he was as grown as he was apt to get. "Master Quatrain," as Nancy had quaintly addressed him, was now at the threshold of manhood. In two days' time, he'd be off on his own, starting college, pursuing a career that would lead him to God knows where.

"It is just *so* cool," Kwynn was telling Thad, "to think that next week, you'll not only *meet* Claire Gray—you'll be studying with her, working with her every day." Kwynn shook her head dreamily, still amazed that Thad had beaten the competition and had been admitted to the illustrious director's new theater program in California.

Thad gave Kwynn a playful nudge of the elbow. "Not having second thoughts, are you?"

"About what?" she asked defensively.

"Journalism. Northwestern."

"Nah." Kwynn gave me a grateful glance. "Someone helped me make the right decision. But still, *you*, Thad—studying theater with a *superstar*."

I told them both, "Claire is a first-rate talent, granted, but don't forget, she *is* human. Once you get to know her, Thad, I'm sure you'll consider her a friend—as well as a theatrical genius."

From the side of his mouth, Pierce told the kids, "That's Mark's way of reminding us that he and Miss Gray are old chums."

"Hardly," I countered. "We've met. We've talked and laughed." I couldn't resist adding, "We've danced."

"We've heard," said Pierce, feigning boredom.

Kwynn got dreamy-eyed and starstruck again. "I wonder what she's doing—I mean right now, this very minute."

I shrugged. "It's the week before classes begin at a newly built college on the ancient, sweeping sands of the Sonoran Desert. I'm sure she's got her hands full—scheduling, syllabi, and whatnot."

Our banter wove onward in this pleasant manner, and I was able to set aside, if only temporarily, the angst I felt because of Thad's imminent departure, to say nothing of the vexing puzzle of Mrs. Ashton's electrocution. Berta brought salads, followed by the main course. As we ate, our conversation became more sporadic, but no less enjoyable.

While we considered dessert—Nancy had been experimenting with a chocolate-meringue concoction that sounded promising—Pierce reached inside his sport coat and unclipped from his belt a pager that had apparently signaled him. "Ugh," he said, holding it at an angle to read its message, "sorry, guys, I'm needed down at the department."

Tentatively, I asked, "Anything to do with the Ashton case?"

"Afraid not." He smiled. "Just a minor bureaucratic crisis, but it needs my attention." He wiped his mouth, placed his napkin on the table, and slid his chair back. Standing, he told me, "I'll ask Nancy to put this one on my account."

"Don't be nuts. The pleasure was ours."

Kwynn told him, "Be careful, Sheriff."

"Honest—it's a computer crash, not a shoot-out."

Thad asked, "You're coming tomorrow night, aren't you?"

"Wouldn't miss it." Pierce turned to me. "Good luck with your meeting with the ex." With an exaggerated, ominous tone, he added, "The ex with the ax."

Thad and Kwynn exchanged a wide-eyed glance.

I told Pierce, "I'll fill you in later." Then I stood briefly to shake his hand. We all said our good-byes, and he left.

During dessert, Thad, Kwynn, and I gabbed nonstop, agreeing that Nancy had outdone herself with the chocolate meringue. Her creative gallimaufry of tastes and smells included a thin layer of coconut, a drizzle of rum, and a thick disk of sponge cake on the bottom, which sopped up all the flavors, including a hint of orange, perhaps triple sec.

With a rapturous groan, I forked a chunk of the soggy cake and dragged it through a brown puddle near the edge of the plate, telling the others, "Neil would love this. Maybe Nancy could serve it tomorrow night." Thad seconded the idea, but I missed exactly what he said, as my attention had drifted to the door.

Someone familiar had entered the restaurant. There was no mistaking the tight blond curls, the big lavender sunglasses, the flamboyant air—it was Whitney Greer, executive director of the local orchestra and theater groups. He checked in with Nancy at the host's podium near the door, engaging her in some cheery chitchat, in no hurry to be seated. It seemed he was waiting to be joined by someone.

During our meal, the dining room had gotten crowded, just noisy enough to lend a pleasing note of conviviality. Through the minor din and the shifting silhouettes of diners, Whitney didn't notice me at the corner table. I waited till he glanced in our direction. Then I waved discreetly above the crowd—a salute and a smile—acknowledging his presence.

He returned the greeting, nodding, but I got the feeling that he looked suddenly discomfited. He leaned close to the podium, said something to Nancy, then spun on his heel (away from me, I noted) and stepped outside the door, waiting under the awning.

Kwynn and Thad prattled on, and I tried contributing to the conversation, but without much success—my attention was focused on

Whitney. Had I merely imagined that he was bothered by my presence? We'd always been on friendly terms. Why, then, had he stepped outside? Did he perhaps want to smoke while waiting for his lunch partner to arrive? Thrown into this inquisitive mode, I pondered yet another question: Who was meeting him?

From where I sat, the window commanded a broad view of the street, but the angle did not afford me a clear look at the area just outside the door. I could see the top of Whitney's head; he seemed to gaze down the street in the opposite direction. I saw no blue furls of cigarette smoke rising through the still autumn air, so my hypothesis lost its punch.

Finishing my dessert, listening to Thad and Kwynn, interjecting a comment now and then, I kept an eye on the window, toward the door. Whitney remained standing there, watching.

Then he moved.

Stepping out to the sidewalk, he met another man, and they paused together in greeting. I now had a clear view of Whitney's back, but he blocked the other figure. Perhaps because I could not identify the other man, perhaps because my curiosity had been piqued, perhaps because it was impossible to hear what they were saying, I readily imagined that their purpose was laced with stealth, their words colored with collusion.

Chiding myself for entertaining these melodramatic notions, I cleared my head and focused on the kids, asking their plans for the afternoon. I had all but set aside my stewing over Whitney's secret rendezvous when the two men on the sidewalk turned, stepped off the curb, and crossed the street together. As they did this, I got a passing but unobstructed view of the other man's face.

"What's the matter, Mr. Manning?" asked Kwynn, dismayed.

I had dropped my fork. "Uh, nothing," I said with a quiet laugh, using my napkin to dab a smear of chocolate from the tablecloth, making it worse. "Sorry, Kwynn. You were saying?"

She continued, but her words escaped me. I was watching Blain Gifford—the Republican campaign manager, Betty Gifford Ashton's principal heir—as he crossed the street with Whitney Greer and disappeared on the next block.

When our lunch was finished, I apologized to the kids for having tuned out, but they'd barely noticed, preoccupied with their visions of the next four years.

Berta brought the check, and while signing it to my account, I noticed that Nancy was no longer stationed near the door. Hoping to spend a minute or two with her, wanting to hear her theory regarding the root of Wesley and Alanna's marital problems, I asked Berta, "Is Nancy in the kitchen? There's something I'd like to discuss with her."

"I'm sorry, Mr. Manning, but she needed to step out. She should be back soon, if you'd care to wait."

I checked my watch. Dale Turner's ex-wife was due any minute at the *Register*'s offices. "Thanks," I told Berta, "but I need to run."

"Can I give her a message?"

I shook my head, then reconsidered. "Yes, Berta. Do tell Nancy that her chocolate meringue was a big hit. If it's possible to serve it tomorrow night, that would be wonderful."

"Of course, sir. I'm sure that can be arranged."

And Berta waddled off.

Arriving back at the *Register* building, I entered the lobby through the street door and paused at the receptionist's window to ask Connie, "Has a Mrs. Turner arrived yet?"

"Mrs. . . . ?" Connie glanced at the log sheet in front of her, adjusting her glasses. "Oh! Yes, Mr. Manning. Fawnah Zapp-Turner is already here. She's upstairs with Lucille." An odd smile bent Connie's mouth.

With a curious laugh, I asked, "What's wrong?"

"Wrong? Nothing, sir." But Connie's grin didn't fade.

With wary curiosity, I crossed the lobby and climbed the stairs to the second-floor newsroom.

Lucy was at the far end of the room, hovering near the city desk, and spotted me at once. She beelined through the maze of desks, meeting me halfway. "You're *not* gonna believe this"—she brandished a yard's worth of computer printout.

"Try me."

"It's a wire story, a press release issued by the Republican gubernatorial campaign in Illinois."

I raised a palm to my forehead, as if staving off something painful. "Don't tell me—they're getting vocal about the death of their candidate's benevolent Wisconsin cousin. They're demanding an immediate arrest."

"No, no. Off by a mile."

Well, at least *that* was good news. At least that's what I thought.

Lucy informed me, "Raymond Gifford's headquarters has announced that the candidate is 'studying' the issue of same-sex parenting in Illinois. He's considering whether to include in his platform a call for state legislation banning adoption by gays or lesbians, which he terms 'an affront to the sanctity of the family.' This is clearly a trial balloon, but if it flies, he plans to launch his new platform issue during tomorrow night's debate."

I felt myself wither from within, sapped by the audacity of this expedient nod to homophobia. All the more sickening was the obvious assumption that Blain Gifford had found inspiration for this hateful tactic in the discussion we'd had on Saturday regarding Thad's relationship to Neil and me. "This is Blain's doing," I told Lucy. "I'll bet Raymond Gifford doesn't even *care*. He's a businessman. I'll bet he doesn't give a shit about same-sex unions, gay adoption, or the organized bigotry of the religious right."

Lucy shrugged. "I doubt it. But he's in a squeaky-tight governor's race, separated from his opponent by a slim but fluctuating margin in the polls. He's grasping for an issue—anything emotional—that can throw a few votes his way. That's all he needs."

"The ploy is so *transparent*," I ranted. "And the worst part is, it generally works. A candidate—almost always a Republican in a tight race—needs only to invoke the defense of marriage or the sanctity of family, and people seem to go nuts, rallying around motherhood, the flag, and the cross."

Lucy shuddered.

"When marriage-and-family measures end up on a ballot, through referendum or initiative, they tend to pass, often by a lopsided margin. So if a candidate like Gifford actually *campaigns* on this issue, then wins, it's a shoo-in with the legislature. Even moderates, who don't in their hearts believe in the equity of antigay measures, feel compelled, for the sake of their political lives, to hop on the bandwagon. And it doesn't take much to get the wagon rolling."

Lucy waved the press release. "It looks as if Gifford plans to get it rolling tomorrow night."

I took the printout from her hand and skimmed it, muttering, "A sanctity-of-family debate is like an evil genie—once you let it out of the bottle, it's hard to stuff it back."

"Meanwhile," Lucy reminded me, "Dale Turner's ex awaits."

"Oh, jeez," I said, tossing the printout onto the nearest desk. "Where is she?"

"In your outer office." Lucy began leading me toward the glass-walled conference room across the aisle from the newsroom. Over her shoulder, she told me, "This gal's a piece of work. When I phoned and told her we had a few questions regarding her ex-husband, she couldn't *wait* to come in and talk. In fact"—Lucy checked her watch—"she arrived twenty minutes early."

I could see a figure sitting at the low, round conference table in my office suite. Even from a distance, even through the jumbled reflections on the window, I could tell that she wore an astonishingly big hairdo. She was hunched over, apparently reading something.

Lucy opened the door. I followed her inside, closing the door after us.

Our interviewee turned in her chair, looking up. "Hi," she said through glossy, hot-pink lips, outlined black, chewing a wad of gum that snapped in the silence of the small room. All that would have been needed to complete the picture was a nail file, idly stroking her talons. Instead, her hands held a copy of *Soap Opera Update*. Close enough.

Lucy stepped to her place at the table, where she'd already set her notes, a tape recorder, and a stack of research folders. "Mark," she said, sitting, "this is Fawnah Zapp-Turner, Dale's ex-wife. Fawnah, I'd like to introduce Mark Manning, editor and publisher of the *Register*."

"Pleased t'meetcha," she said, dropping the magazine and lifting a hand to me like royalty. Was I supposed to kiss it?

I shook it, noticing that her nails, enameled a liverish shade of maroon, appeared to be inlaid with exotic, perhaps Tibetan, gold calligraphy. Incongruously, one of the nails, that of her middle finger, sported a cartoonish decal of a bad-boy figure pissing on a Ford logo. I reasoned, therefore, that Fawnah drove a Chevy pickup with a measure of defensive pride. Fear this, baby.

Sitting across from her, I said, "It was good of you to make time for us." I pulled a steno pad from the inside pocket of my jacket.

"I told the other girls at the *salon*"—she said the word with exaggerated, breathy elegance, a ridiculous stab at a French accent—"I told them they'd just have to rearrange a few appointments. I mean, this is *important*." The snap of her gum put a period on the statement.

With remarkable composure, Lucy informed me, as if I couldn't guess, "Fawnah is a beautician."

"Ah." Before uncapping my Montblanc, I rolled it in my fingers like a cigar for a moment, studying Fawnah. She'd had installed a pair of big boobs to match her big hair and big attitude. Her skirt was six inches too short for the fashion of the day, and her flouncy pink blouse looked like the top of a nightgown from some dated Doris Day movie. Her black patent stiletto heels were so steep and so sharp, I don't know how she wore them, let alone walked in them.

Fawnah was a living, breathing cliché of glammed-up hyperfemininity. In stark contrast, not two feet from her, sat lesbian Lucy in her short-cropped hair and mannish, military pantsuit, the one that reminded me of a Texaco uniform. Lucy and Fawnah appeared to be about the same height, perhaps the same weight, but otherwise, they were the spawn of two different species. In fact, due to Lucy's style of dress, and despite her chromosomes, she resembled Dale Turner more than she resembled Dale's ex-wife.

Lucy was telling Fawnah, "The police are working on several theories regarding what happened at the wedding reception on Saturday."

"It was *awful*, wasn't it?" Fawnah flicked both hands, rattling two armloads of brassy bracelets.

"It was," I agreed, scratching the nib of my pen on my pad. "I was standing right there when it happened. Poor Mrs. Ashton."

Fawnah sat back in her chair, asking through a squint, "And what about Dale?"

Confused, I asked, "Poor Dale?"

"Naaah"—she leaned forward, elbow to knee—"I *meant*, was Dale right there when it happened? Musta been quite a jolt." She arched her penciled brows.

Still confused, I asked, "A jolt for Dale or for Betty Gifford Ashton?"

Fawnah laughed wildly. "You're a stitch, Mark! I *know* the old lady got jolted. I mean, did it knock Dale on his ass?"

"Not in the literal sense, but he was greatly upset. Although he didn't witness the mishap, he came running as soon as the power failed."

"Okay"—Fawnah nodded—"I got the picture." She paused, running her tongue across her teeth, first the uppers, then the lowers. Where was her gum? Had she swallowed it? "So then. What'd yawanna talk to me about?"

Glad to bring some focus to the interview, I said, "I wonder if you could give us some background on your relationship with Dale. The marriage, the divorce, the timing . . ."

"Not a problem." Getting relaxed, she planted one elbow behind her on the top of the chair back, which caused her opposite shoulder—and one of her breasts—to jut toward me, looming huge in a freakishly foreshortened optical perspective. "Me and Dale got married six years ago. It was a *beauty*-ful ceremony; you shoulda seen the dresses. Then, two years ago, we split." She waggled the fingers of her left hand. A diamond still perched near the knuckle of her ring finger, but the wedding band had been ditched.

"So you were married for four years."

She paused, doing some mental math. "Yeah."

Lucy asked, "Did you have children?"

"No. Thank Gawd."

"Why?" I asked. "You don't like kids?"

Fawnah shook her head; her coif teetered. "It's not like that. It's like, we just never got around to it, and now that we're split, it's just as well." She blinked. "Right?"

With a shrug, Lucy obliged, "Right."

I said, "When you and Dale got married, I assume you loved each other—it's not as if you were pregnant and felt you *had* to marry."

"Oh, sure, we loved each other, I guess. At least I *thought* that's what it was. I never felt that way before—but I was kinda young then."

"May I ask your age?"

She primped. "Twenty-eight." Her gum must have been stowed in a cheek, because she was chewing again while she did some more ciphering. "So I was twenty-two when we did the church thing."

Lucy said, "That's not so terribly young."

"Tell me. My mom was sixteen when *she* got married. But I was kinda young compared to Dale."

I recalled pegging Dale in his midthirties or so. I asked Fawnah, "How much older was Dale?"

"He was nine years older than me." She put a finger to her temple, adding, "Except in March and April, for some reason, when he was eight years older. Or was it ten?"

Okay, I thought, that adds up. "Which means he's thirty-seven now."

She smiled awkwardly. "Whatever." She'd run out of fingers.

Making a note of their ages, I asked, "So what went wrong? Why did your marriage go sour?"

"Lotsa reasons. Money—what else is new? But mostly the age thing."

"Your age difference drove you apart?"

"Yeah. Really. It did." Fawnah nodded, looking enlightened, as if this were a revelation to her, as if she'd never thought about it. She summarized, "I married too young, and Dale was too old for me. Don't get me wrong—the sex was good, it was great—he could *never* get enough. But our minds were like a million miles apart. I guess you'd say we were just, uh . . . uh . . . ." She whirled a hand, groping for a missing word.

Lucy supplied it: "Incompatible?"

Fawnah's shoulders slumped. "And *how*. When we'd fight, we'd always—"

"You fought?" asked Lucy. "Physically?"

"Nah, no rough stuff. I mean, like, words. We argued a lot. And I always ended up calling him an old fart or something, and he always ended up saying he was nuts to marry a child or a bimbo or whatever." Fawnah shook her head, muttering, "Cripes, a 'bimbo'—can you imagine?"

Thank God she'd asked the question rhetorically, as the answer would have been difficult to fudge with a straight face. Glancing at my notes, I said, "You mentioned money problems, Fawnah. What was that about?"

She grinned. "There wasn't *enough*."

I laughed. "So I figured. Can you be more specific?"

She heaved a big sigh. Her rubbery bosom rose and fell like a tsunami in her blouse, leaving a wake of quivering flounces. "Dale was an electrician, a pretty good one, I guess. But shortly after we got married, the construction business sorta went south on him."

I recalled, "He told me there was a serious slump in Dumont back then."

"Yeah, a slump, that's what they called it. So anyway, about"—a quick pause for another round of mental math—"about four years ago, he got into the tent-and-awning biz. From the start, anyone could see that it was going, like, *nowhere,* but it seemed to take up more and more of his time. Thank Gawd I'd started cosmetology college. Before long, I had a nice job at the *salon*—my own chair and everything— and I was bringing home more money than he was."

Lucy asked, "Did that bother Dale?"

Fawnah shrugged. "I dunno. I suppose he figured at least *one* of us was gettin' some cash. You know, I don't think it did bother him. But it sure bothered *me.*"

Lucy had begun drawing the familiar grid on her notes. "Why?"

"Because it's not supposed to *be* that way. He's supposed to take care of *me*, not the other way around. So"—she flipped her hands—"I dumped him."

"Just like that?"

"Just like that. Oh, sure, I had to get a lawyer in on it, and you don't get divorced overnight, but finally, two years ago, it was over.

And I'm glad I got out when I did. After putting up with that lunk for four years, I wasn't awarded a fuckin' nickel in alimony." She spewed a bitter laugh, adding, "My lawyer told me I was lucky not to be paying *him.*"

Listening to her speak, I concluded that it was Dale, not she, who was lucky to be rid of the other. Filling a silent void, I asked, "Do you ever see each other anymore?"

"Never. I mean, we see each other 'around'—it's a small town. But we don't, like, visit or go out or anything. We sure don't have sex together." She crossed her arms (with difficulty—her breasts were so large, the fingers of each hand barely reached the opposite elbow). "Which suits me just fine. But him, he could never get enough."

"Yes, I believe you mentioned that."

"Fawnah," said Lucy, turning to a fresh page of notes, "despite your feelings toward Dale, I hope you can help us help him."

Fawnah fixed Lucy in a steely gaze. "How?"

"The police have a theory that Dale may have been set up, framed. Someone may have been trying to get Dale into trouble."

"It'd serve him right." Sniff.

I recounted to Fawnah, as simplistically as possible, the logic behind our hypothesis that Betty Gifford Ashton had been a random victim of the electrocution. "And if that's the case, the intended target of the crime may have been either the bartender, Wesley Scott, or your ex-husband. So this next question is important, Fawnah: Does Dale have any enemies who might be behind this?"

"*Plenty,*" she answered without hesitation. "That tent business of his is pathetic. He has more creditors than customers—at least he did when we were still together—and some of those guys struck me as kinda shady, to say the least."

I flipped back through my notes. "Are you sure about that? Dale admitted that he's behind with some of his bills, but he told us that he couldn't think of a soul who'd want to ruin him by implicating him in a crime."

Fawnah wobbled her head knowingly. "He *would* say that."

Lucy began drawing a new grid. "Then who, Fawnah, are these shady business associates you've referred to?"

"*I* don't know." She sat bolt upright in the chair. "Just guys, just creeps. That was years ago—it's not like I was making *lists* or something."

I was getting frustrated, so I dropped all circumspection and asked her point-blank, "What about *you*, Fawnah? Do you still have an ax to grind with Dale?"

She paused as the implication of my words sank in. "Mr. Manning," she said haughtily, puffing herself up (she now looked so top-heavy, I thought she'd tumble from the chair), "I resent that insinuation."

Huh?

"And I'll thank you, please, *not* to insult my intelligence."

With that, she rose from the chair, spun on her daggerlike heels (I feared for the carpeting), and marched toward the door.

Reaching for the knob, though, she turned back, looking suddenly composed. "Lucille, honey, give me a call when you decide to do something about that hair. Just let it grow some, okay? *Then* I'll fix you up."

Fawnah Zapp-Turner winked at Lucy, ignored me, and left.

By now, there was plenty on my mind. By telling us that Dale Turner had many potential enemies, shady ones at that, his ex-wife had bolstered my theory that he may have been the actual target of the crime. But Fawnah was dense as a brick, with no recollection of names, so I was still in search of an unknown someone with an unknown motive, not against Betty, but against Dale.

At lunch, confoundingly, Nancy Sanderson had disputed the contention that Alanna Scott did not want a baby (what was that all about?), and Whitney Greer had seemed reluctant to let me know that he was meeting Blain Gifford (what was *that* all about?). What's more, the pressure to unravel the mystery prior to Wednesday's debate had been complicated by the announcement from Raymond Gifford's campaign that the candidate might start stirring the divisive, turbulent waters of an emotional and, from my perspective, irrational sanctity-of-family debate. Worst of all, I'd become consumed by the gnawing guilt of my lie of omission. Though Roxanne seemed able to justify this silent deception with ease, I could not. In my heart, I knew that I had betrayed principles I held sacred and people I loved—notably, Neil.

Most of it, I could handle; compromise and disappointment are elements of life. But Neil was the one that really, ultimately mattered, and now I'd deceived him. Granted, my lie of omission allowed him to believe what he wanted to believe. True, if I'd confided my lie to him, I'd have forced him to choose either conspiring with Roxanne and me or blowing the whistle, a painful decision. Still, in spite of these justifications, I could not escape the conclusion that I'd erected a wall between us, and I couldn't stand it.

So I took the rest of the afternoon off. I needed a run in the park.

This may seem a frivolous distraction, the untimely avoidance of a deepening dilemma. I have found in the past, however, when puzzles have grown hopelessly complex and drop-dead deadlines have loomed perilously near, that I can often gain a clearer perspective of my predicament by stepping back from it and clearing my head, giving me room to think and space to breathe. What better place to breathe than in the bouldered, verdant park near the house on Prairie Street? With Neil as a sounding board, all the better.

On that Tuesday afternoon, after meeting with Fawnah Zapp-Turner, after reviewing my notes with Lucy and phoning a report to Doug Pierce, I landed back at my desk and called Neil at his office down the street. Waiting for him to answer, I checked my watch. It was just before three o'clock—twenty-nine hours till deadline.

We greeted each other like lovesick teens. He inquired about my lunch at the Grill; I asked about his meeting at the furniture factory. I started to fill him in regarding the day's developments on the Ashton case, then stopped midsentence.

"Look," I said, "here's an idea. Here's why I called. Let's go home and take some time for ourselves. We can go for a run together, and—"

"Say no more," he told me. Before we'd hung up, I could hear him shutting down his computer and switching off the office lights.

Within minutes, ten max, we were both back at home, upstairs in our bedroom, changing out of our street clothes and into basic running gear—shoes and shorts, no shirts that warm afternoon. We gabbed like kids out of school; there'd be ample opportunity to discuss heavier matters while we pounded off a few miles in the park. And by the time we returned, I resolved, we'd have dealt with my lie of omission.

I had reached what I considered a satisfactory plan. My intention was not to tell Neil the whole story outright, but rather to explain to him, in abstract terms, that I had needed to keep something from him. I would further explain that my motive had been not deception, but a desire not to place him in a conflicted position. In effect, I planned to ask his permission for me to keep him in the dark a little while longer.

We headed out of the bedroom together and began bounding down the stairs, only to find Chick Butterly bounding up from the front hall.

"Hey!" he greeted us, pausing on the landing, blinking up at us with those big brown beauts. "Looks like it's time for a workout. I can spare a few minutes—mind if I join you?"

I was disappointed; I'm sure Neil was too. But what could we say? I told Chick, "Make it fast—we're hot to trot." And he tore up to his room to get out of his business clothes.

Waiting outside on the front porch, Neil gave me a sly nudge with his elbow. "I know this little getaway was supposed to be 'just us,' but in case you forgot, Chick's not bad in a pair of shorts. We'll have some extra scenery today."

Hmm. He had a point. My features brightened.

"Remember though: it's look, but don't touch."

Moments later, the subject of Neil's discourse, the Democratic spinmeister himself, appeared in the doorway. He'd taken his cue from Neil and me, nixing the need for a shirt. Stepping out to the porch, Chick small-talked with Neil while dropping to the floor to do a few quick stretches. I tried to join the conversation and to break my indiscreet stare, but without success. My eyes savored each of Chick's sensual contortions as he stretched, pulled, and repeated, grunting in self-imposed agony.

"There!" he said, hopping to his feet. "Ready?"

"You bet!" My tone was far too enthusiastic.

Neil caught my eye and broke into laughter as the three of us took off at a trot, heading from the house to the street, then turning down the block that led to the perimeter of the park.

Chick knew the way, having run with Neil on Sunday, so he now took the lead, guiding us along the path that crossed the grassy embankment, descended the woody slopes of a ravine, then leveled off on the expansive field of turf that formed the floor of the park's hushed interior. Ahead lay a glassy-surfaced lagoon and its fanciful, jigsawed pavilion, freshly painted white, dazzling in the slant of afternoon sunlight. Beyond and all around, craggy, tree-topped, blue-green hills—the remnants of a glacier that had formed these moraines—jutted skyward, smelling of pine, bark, moss, musk, and earth.

And directly in front of me ran Chick Butterly. His shoes kissed the gravel pathway, sending up puffs of dust, which I inhaled through my open mouth and tasted on my teeth. His calves bulged handsomely with the long, taut muscles within. His back trickled sweat into the swaying crack of his shorts. His thick hair bobbed in rhythm with his stride. Neil and I drank it all in, uttering not a word, as if mesmerized by the spectacle of him. But Chick didn't get it—or didn't care. In his mind, alas, he undressed and cavorted with Alanna Scott.

Having completely circled the field, Chick twisted his head, asking over his shoulder, "Walk awhile?"

"Sure," we said. "Why not?" And the three of us simultaneously slowed our pace till we were walking side by side. Instinctively, Neil and I jockeyed to place Chick in the middle.

When our breathing had eased enough to allow casual conversation, I asked Chick, "What's the word from headquarters today?"

Chick flicked sweat from his brow with an index finger. A drop spattered on my arm, stinging cold-hot in the charged atmosphere that seemed to radiate from his body. He answered, "Lowell's still on the warpath, scared shitless that the mess up here is going to cost him the election."

"I was hoping he'd softened since tearing into Carl on the phone last night."

"Sorry, he's all the more resolved to sacrifice Carl if it means the difference between winning and losing."

Neil said, "But that sounds so desperate. Will voters buy it?"

Chick reminded him, "If Lowell dumps Carl, it's my job to convince voters that the decision signals strength, not desperation."

Under my breath, I told Chick, "Good luck."

"I like Carl. Roxanne too. So I hope it doesn't come to that. I hope everything's sorted out by tomorrow. But if the ax does fall, at least it gives us a dramatic edge at the debate. Otherwise, it'll be tough stealing the thunder from Raymond Gifford."

Reluctantly, I asked, "You're referring to his antigay gambit?"

Chick nodded.

Neil froze in his tracks. "What are you talking about?"

Chick and I stopped and faced Neil. I told him about the press release.

"Why, that . . ." Words momentarily failed him. "How in hell did Raymond Gifford get wound up with that religious-right nonsense?"

Chick arched a brow knowingly. "I'm sure this wasn't Ray's brainstorm. He's a moneyman; he wouldn't know a social issue if it bit him. A ploy like this is pure spin. Who thought it up? *That's* no mystery, at least to me."

Neil asked, *"Blain?"*

"Who else? It's not enough that he's reaped from his aunt's death a sympathy-goosing in the polls for Raymond. And it's not enough that he's inherited a fortune from the old gal. He still wants to cinch this election—and he's turning to an issue that always stirs up raw emotions." Muttering, Chick added, "If I didn't find it so reprehensible, I'd try it myself."

I reminded Chick that Blain had questioned me on Saturday about Thad's status in our household. "I'm sure that's what triggered this. How could he be so . . . so hypocritical?"

Chick gave me a blank look. Then, through a low laugh, he said, "It's not very *nice*, I admit, but what's hypocritical about it?"

My reasoning was that if Blain Gifford was homosexual and was using homophobic tactics to win an election, he was the very embodiment of hypocrisy. The gaping flaw in my reasoning was the assumption that Blain was gay, a notion that had come to me first as an inkling, then in a dream. I'd had the same inkling about Chick, after all, and I'd been dead wrong. Still, my suspicions about Blain continued to be fueled, albeit flimsily: on Sunday, I'd seen him wearing clothes like mine, and today, I'd seen him meet Whitney Greer for lunch, a man I assumed to be gay. I now realized how moronic I'd sound voicing these suspicions, even to Chick, who instinctively viewed Blain with disrelish.

Scratching my neck, I echoed Chick's laugh, telling him, "Wrong word. I must've meant 'hypercritical.'"

Chick and Neil exchanged a puzzled glance.

"It's just that when anyone starts talking 'sanctity of family,' my blood boils. I even hate the terminology."

Neil seconded, "You and me both."

"Hey, guys," said Chick, "calm down. I know you don't *like* this stuff, but what's the big deal? We're talking about Illinois, and you're up here in Wisconsin."

Neil and I looked at each other. It was a sensible question—from a sympathetic but pragmatic heterosexual who felt neither threatened by the issue nor particularly interested in it. I nodded to Neil, telling him, in effect, You make the speech.

"Chick," he began, "I guess it's impossible to feel, from your side of the fence, the underlying hatred of these debates—from 'defense of marriage' to 'sanctity of family' to the 'anti-pro-gay' initiatives that attempt to monitor and censor what's taught in public schools. From *this* side of the fence, I assure you, these legal maneuvers are recognized as pure bigotry, seeking to relegate us—*me*, this is personal—to second-class citizenship through a codified double standard. It's arrogant, it's ignorant, and it's wrong. Mark and I will fight this crap with everything we've got, not only here in Wisconsin, but anywhere it bubbles up."

"Especially in Illinois," I added. "I'm *from* there, remember, and I know that its people are not, by and large, an intolerant lot. It's the most populous state in the Midwest, a region traditionally known for its equanimity and fair-mindedness. It's the 'Land of Lincoln,' which still ought to mean something. And few outsiders realize it, but both

Illinois and Wisconsin blazed landmark trails toward tolerance: Illinois was the first state to ditch its sodomy laws, and Wisconsin was first in the union with statewide gay-rights legislation."

"But Illinois," Neil jumped in, "moved a step backward a few years ago, when social conservatives managed to pass state legislation preemptively barring same-sex marriage. The next logical step on the right-wing agenda would be to bar gays from adopting, or even serving as foster parents. That issue has lain dormant in Illinois—till now. Mark and I truly care about this, Chick. We simply can't afford to let such outworn attitudes gain momentum—not in *our* backyard."

I smiled at Neil. He'd summed it up nicely. I had nothing to add.

Chick had listened with sober attention.

I asked him, "Sorry you asked?"

"Not at all." With a grin, Chick added, "At least I know where you stand."

"As if you couldn't have guessed." Neil began walking along the path again.

Chick and I followed. I asked, "If worse comes to worst—if Lowell dumps Carl from the ticket and Raymond Gifford starts beating the drum in defense of traditional 'family values'—where would Lowell stand on the issue?"

"Depends on the polls. Sorry, but Lowell doesn't care about gay rights; he cares about getting elected. Carl, on the other hand, is the most principled politician I've ever met—he's a rare breed—and it goes without saying that he's solidly in your camp. If you're serious about quashing Gifford's threatened campaign of homophobia, your best bet is to keep Carl in the race."

Neil gave me a sly look. "And the only way to keep Carl in the race is to prove, by eight o'clock tomorrow, that Rox had nothing to do with Betty Gifford Ashton's death." Blithely, Neil reminded Chick, "Mark's working on that," as if it were all but wrapped up.

Right.

Chick's pace slowed. Looking straight ahead, watching a duck waddle into the distant lagoon, he asked me, "How, by the way, is it going?"

Watching the duck glide toward a tiny island that supported a single willow, I answered honestly, "Not well. Doug Pierce and I are exploring several promising theories, but the possibilities keep expanding, and that's the problem. I'm just not sure we can sort it out in a day."

"Wish I could help. Unfortunately, detection isn't exactly my thing."

"Yeah," said Neil, chortling, "spin and innuendo are more your style."

"I'll take that as a compliment." Chick broke into an easy trot.

We'd ambled long enough. Neil and I picked up Chick's gait and were soon running with him. I ended up in the middle, enjoying being sandwiched by the two younger men. If I played it just right, I could alternate brushing elbows with each of them—cheap thrills.

This pleasant diversion was overshadowed, of course, by the perplexing riddle that had sprouted all those promising theories, one of which, I now realized, related to Chick. Glancing over at him, I said, "Maybe you *could* help."

"Oh?" With a look of surprise, he asked, "How?"

"I don't mean to pry, but I'm wondering about your interest in Alanna Scott."

He hesitated. "You noticed, huh?"

Neil blurted, "You were anything but subtle."

I told Chick, "Alanna said you visited her at the shop on Monday afternoon."

"I did, in fact. I admit it—she's my type, but without all that city jadedness. She's, well . . . she's a good person."

Neil reminded him, "She's also a *married* person."

"Yeah, I'm not sure what to make of that. Don't get me wrong— I have no interest in breaking up a happy little home. Point is, anyone can just *tell* that she and that bartender are on the outs."

"You're right," I said. "They're having problems. Did she tell you what the rift was about?"

"God, no. We didn't get anywhere *near* that. I was just . . . testing the waters." Then Chick turned the tables. "Do *you* know what's wrong between them?"

"I thought I did, but now I'm not so sure." Then I detailed for

193

both Chick and Neil the story told by Wes and later confirmed by Alanna: he wants a baby, and she doesn't. "Today at lunch, though, I heard a dissenting view from Nancy Sanderson, who has mentored Alanna in the food business and claims a close friendship. Nancy says that Alanna *does* want a baby and that the problem in the marriage stems from something else." I paused to consider this discrepancy.

"We're all ears," Neil prompted me.

"Yeah," said Chick. "What's the bottom line?"

"I don't *know*. Nancy wouldn't come out and say it, but she left the impression that Wes was involved with another woman. She said she'd tried to 'warn' Alanna, but Alanna wouldn't listen."

"Hmm," said Chick. "Quite promising, at least from *my* selfish perspective."

"Not so fast," Neil told him. "Something doesn't add up. If Alanna wants a baby, and Wes is cheating on her, why would she corroborate his story that *he* wants the baby and she doesn't?"

"Exactly," I said. "That's what I can't sort out."

We ran quietly together, mulling all this, approaching the hill that would lead us out of the park. Before we began the climb, Chick stopped on the trail and said, "For some reason, Mark, *you're* not getting the straight story. Either Nancy was mistaken, or Alanna lied to you. If Alanna lied to you, there's little point in your questioning her again. Meanwhile, I've been looking for an excuse to pay another visit. Would you like *me* to take a crack at her?"

Panting, I smiled. "In a manner of speaking, yes, I would. By all means, do 'take a crack at her.'"

Chick nodded. "Purely in the interest of your investigation, of course."

"Of course."

And the three of us headed home.

My lie of omission never got addressed that afternoon. I'd fully intended to do some soul-baring to Neil, but not in the presence of Chick Butterly, who was a direct conduit to Carl Creighton as well as the aging and ever crankier Lowell Sagehorn. What's more, my mind was now diverted from my mission. Unwittingly, I'd inspired the Gifford campaign's threat of a homophobic assault. This contemptible ploy had originated not with the candidate, but with the campaign manager—Blain Gifford, who happened to be staying right here in Dumont, who had profited handsomely from his aunt's death, and whom I increasingly suspected of being a closeted gay Republican. Equally intriguing was Chick's open declaration of a romantic interest in the local caterer, a married woman with a mysterious problem that might—or might not—have had some bearing on Mrs. Ashton's electrocution.

Far from clearing my head as intended, our run in the park had given me all the more to ponder. So when Neil and I returned home with Chick, left him in the hall, and retired to our bedroom to shower and dress for the evening, I'd lost the will to broach with Neil the thorny topic of Roxanne's opportunity to commit (at least in theory) murder. In fact, as we spiffed up in our bathroom, our discussion barely touched on Roxanne. Instead, we spoke of our plans to entertain her mother, Gale Exner, at home that night.

"With everything that's been going on," said Neil over the howl of his hair dryer, "we haven't been able to spend much 'quality time' with Gale. Hope she doesn't think we've been neglecting her."

"I'm sure she doesn't think that." (She probably did.)

Neil switched off the dryer. "I'm going to give Barb a hand in the kitchen—want to do some experimenting with that new soufflé recipe—so maybe you could drive Rox over to the Manor House and pick up Gale together."

"With pleasure."

Sometime after six-thirty, closer to seven (twenty-five hours till deadline), Roxanne and I drove the several blocks to the converted mansion that had served as overflow housing for our wedding guests. In recent weeks, the days had grown shorter, and though summer would not officially depart for another ten days or so, the evening carried an unmistakable hint of autumn. The fresh, dry air seemed to cool by the minute. Venus and Mars flirted with a gibbous yellow moon in a cloudless purple sky. Quiet driveways were littered with abandoned skateboards and flashy aluminum scooters as kids hunkered indoors with their homework. My Bavarian V-8 coasted noiselessly to the curb and settled under the giant red maple, looming black against the twilight.

Walking from the street to the door, Roxanne told me, "I'm truly sorry about everything—the houseguests, the out-of-towners, the extra nights, the lack of privacy." She paused, then added wryly, "Not to mention the murder in your backyard and the investigation that landed in your lap."

Slinging an arm around her, I dismissed her apology. "It'll make a great story—once it's over. And one way or the other, everything is starting to converge." That was an understatement. Wednesday would bring Betty's funeral, Thad's going-away party, the gubernatorial debate in Chicago, and in all likelihood, momentous events that would affect Roxanne and Carl for the rest of their lives. I had no idea whether those events would be tragic or triumphant, but, yes, come hell or high water, everything was starting to converge.

Roxanne asked, "You mean, you've got it figured out?"

"Hardly. Sorry."

"Maybe if we all put our heads together at dinner . . ." We'd spoken of little else for three days, but it was worth another try.

Stepping up the limestone stairs to the porch, we approached the heavy door, closed to the impending night. I rang the bell. Seconds later, the door swung open and we were greeted by Milton Tallent, gnomish banker turned innkeeper. Admitting us to the front hall, which glowed in the warm light of several oversize wrought-iron sconces, Milton told Roxanne, "I believe your mother is waiting in the parlor." With a sweep of his hand, he showed us the way.

We didn't need direction. Mere steps down the hall, the parlor had been the scene of our acrimonious run-in with Lauren Creighton and Blain Gifford on Sunday morning. As we stepped inside the walnut-paneled room this evening, only Gale was present. She stood to greet us, dressed for a night out, rising from the Victorian sofa—the tasseled love nest that had crash-landed in my dream. "Roxie," she burbled, outstretching her arms. "How's my baby?"

"Fine, Mom. We're all holding up." Roxanne hugged her mother. They kissed.

"And Mark"—Gale turned to me, inviting a hug—"are we playing chauffeur tonight? Congenial host? Or intrepid sleuth?"

"A bit of all three," I acknowledged, giving her a full embrace.

"Mmm. Yum!" she said, hanging on for a few extra seconds.

"Down, Gale," her daughter scolded. "Bad girl."

Gale whimpered like a puppy.

Through a laugh, I told her, "I'm glad we're able to spend some time together tonight. You've come all this way, and I've barely had a chance to talk to you."

"You've been busy."

"Even so, we're overdue for a quiet family dinner." It would be an odd sort of family gathered at our table that night—Gale, Roxanne, and Carl; me, my architect lover, and our Jewish housekeeper; and just for good measure, a Democratic spinmeister nursing his hots for a married woman on the other side of town. My nephew Thad had taken the hint, readily deciding to spend the evening with friends.

Gale struck a pose, hand in the air. "It's now or never, my dears."

Roxanne and I exchanged a quizzical glance. She asked her mother, "Huh?"

"I'm *leaving* tomorrow morning. Dumont is quite lovely, but I've been here since Friday, and it's time for me to get back to Minneapolis."

Roxanne moaned. "God, the time got away from me."

"That's a shame," I told Gale. "We all assumed you'd join us at Thad's dinner."

Roxanne explained, "Thad is leaving for college on Thursday, and there's a going-away party tomorrow night. Everyone will be there. Can't you stay?"

Pleasantly addled, Gale told us, "Well, I'm flattered you'd ask, but I don't know. I suppose the flight could be rebooked, but—*ah!*" She waved toward the hallway. "Mr. Tallent, do you have a moment?"

Roxanne and I turned to see Milton enter the room.

"Mrs. Exner?"

Gale told him, "I may want to change my plans and extend my visit. Is it possible for me to keep my room until Thursday morning?"

"Of course, Mrs. Exner, we'd be delighted to have you for a sixth night. I don't have new guests arriving until the weekend."

Roxanne asked her mother, "All settled then?"

Gale weighed her options briefly. "Of *course*. What fun. Thank you both for suggesting it."

I wasn't entirely certain the next evening would be "fun" for Gale—the chances that her daughter would be booked for murder were inching upward by the hour, and the political career of her new son-in-law was hurtling toward a humiliating collapse. Even so, she would doubtless prefer to be here with her loved ones than to learn of their woes on the ten-o'clock news. And it *would* be news.

Keeping these thoughts to myself, I suggested, "Let's drive over to the house. It's cocktail time."

"How delicious," said Gale, peeping inside her purse—just checking—then snapping it shut.

Milton told Gale and Roxanne, "Have a lovely evening, ladies," backing out of the parlor as we all stepped into the hall.

We arrived near the front door just as it opened, and in walked Lauren Creighton. We froze. She froze. Trapped.

After several moments of excruciating silence, I greeted her, "What a nice surprise."

With a crooked smile, she said, "You're too kind, Mr. Manning." Eyeing the Exner gals, she added, "Going out?"

The Exner gals would not have responded if their lives had depended on it.

I told Lauren, "We're just going over to the house, just a quiet family dinner." I then realized the embarrassingly obvious—Lauren was "family" too. It hadn't even occurred to us to invite her, as the level of enmity between her and her new stepmoms had advanced from smoldering to combustible. Not knowing what to say, I felt short of breath. A knot rose to my throat, and I feared I might choke. Against all my better judgment, I managed to ask, "Join us?"

Roxanne and Gale looked as if they would drop through the floor.

Lauren watched them squirm before letting me off the hook. "As I've already noted, Mr. Manning, you're far too kind. But I have plans, thank you." And she whisked through us, stomping through the hall in her big black shoes (the trendy type that Neil keeps egging me to wear, that I've laughingly dismissed as a fad for, gosh, several years running). Before reaching the stairs, she stopped near the entrance to the parlor, where Milton still stood. Turning back to us, Lauren said, "If you would, Mr. Manning, please tell my father that I'll pop over to say good-bye tomorrow morning on my way out of town."

"You're heading back to Denver?"

She nodded. "It's time."

"I'll tell Carl to expect you." Then I thought of something. "I don't know what your schedule is, but I suggest you visit early. Mrs. Ashton's funeral is tomorrow at ten, and everyone's going—I'm sure your father plans to attend."

"Ah. Thank you. I *will* come over early. I need to be on the road by ten."

I'd have sworn that I heard, behind me, a chorus of relieved sighs from the Exner ladies, but they were surely not so indiscreet as I imagined. I myself felt a healthy measure of relief, simply knowing that a considerable distance would soon separate these fractious female forces. Having heard Lauren's departure plans and feeling confident they were firm, I ventured airily, "What a shame you need to return so soon. My nephew Thad is leaving for college, and we're having a going-away dinner for him tomorrow night, downtown at First Avenue Grill. Just friends and family, an affable group—your father will be there. Too bad you can't join us." Pushing my luck, I added, "Can't you stay?"

I watched with utter dismay as she raised a finger to her chin, considering logistics. "That's *awfully* kind of you. You know, I might . . ." She turned to Milton Tallent.

The accommodating hotelier chuckled. "Say no more, Miss Creighton. A sixth night for you as well—you're more than welcome to extend your visit."

Stupid, stupid, magnanimous me. "How nice," I told Lauren, plucking the Exners' daggers from my back. "Everything's settled then. Please join us at the restaurant for cocktails at six."

"It's a date," she said. Then she gave her stepmoms a steely smile, turned, and clomped upstairs. Her big black shoes disappeared beyond the landing.

Under my breath, I told the gals, "Let's just go, okay? One day we'll laugh about this."

We filed out. I closed the door behind us, and the three of us descended the porch stairs, headed for my car. Roxanne said, "I've never met Carl's first wife, Beryl, but she must have been a fright." Meow.

Gale assured her daughter, "Carl's well rid of her."

I had no intention of entering their discussion. Besides, I was distracted by a car that was pulling to the curb, parking a few yards behind mine. There was enough light in the sky for me to discern two figures in the car, probably male, but not enough to identify them. Instinctively, I slowed my pace toward the street. The ladies did likewise, nipping their catty chatter.

As the passenger door swung open, a light went on inside the car, and I instantly recognized the driver as Whitney Greer—there could be no mistaking his lavish crop of curly blond hair. As the two men talked in parting, a leg protruded from the car to the curb, clad in starched, neatly creased khaki. Before the entire figure emerged from the car, I understood that Whitney's passenger was Blain Gifford, who'd been staying at the Manor House since Saturday's wedding. Because I'd seen Blain and Whitney meet outside the Grill at lunch that day, I could only conclude that the two had been together the entire afternoon.

Blain thunked the door shut, and Whitney pulled away from the curb, disappearing down the street. As Blain turned to approach the Manor House, he stopped with a gasp, having not expected to encounter a gang of three nearing him on the sidewalk.

I found it laughable to imagine that Gale, Roxanne, and I appeared menacing, even when backlit by the dying dusk. "Hi, Blain," I greeted him with a friendly cadence, "it's just us."

He squinted. "Ah! Manning, hello." Then he nodded to the women. "Ladies."

With a twisted smile, Roxanne asked, "Jumpy, Mr. Gifford?"

"No," he said, pinching the knot of his tie, straightening the lapels of his blazer, "just a bit preoccupied today."

Roxanne nodded. "We've all been busy with our thoughts."

"Indeed."

I had no idea why Blain had been skulking around with Whitney Greer, but I wanted him to know that I was aware of it. Not only, I reasoned, might he find this disconcerting, but better yet, he might feel compelled to offer an explanation for their meeting. So I asked, "Did Whitney mention tomorrow night's dinner?"

Blain looked at me as if I'd queried him in Hindi.

I elaborated, "Whitney Greer dropped you off just now, and I happened to see you meet earlier downtown. Did he mention tomorrow's get-together at First Avenue Grill? It's a going-away dinner for my nephew. Whitney will be there."

"Oh?" asked Roxanne matter-of-factly, wondering what I was up to.

"Yes. You see, Whitney has come to know my nephew through his work with the community theater, and our housekeeper is close to Whitney because of their involvement with the local orchestra. So Whitney is practically family." Turning to Blain, I added, "If you'd care to join Whitney at the party, you're more than welcome." I smiled.

The Republican seemed dazed by my unexpected invitation. I couldn't tell whether he suspected I was up to something or if he merely found my hospitality off-the-wall. In any event, he offered no explanation for the time he'd spent with Whitney. "That's, uh, most gracious of you, Mark. Thank you, but I won't be here tomorrow night; I'll be in Chicago. Have you forgotten? Raymond Gifford debates Lowell Sagehorn at eight o'clock."

"Ah. Guess it slipped my mind." Like ducks.

"The timing *is* unfortunate—with regard to my aunt's funeral, that is. Raymond will be driving up early in the morning so he can attend the services, then we'll both ride back together for the telecast."

I commiserated, "That's a lot of time in the car tomorrow . . ."

"It is. But I'm looking forward to spending those hours one-on-one with Raymond. It'll be a good opportunity for us to review final preparations for the debate." Blain paused. Smugly, he added, "We also need to brainstorm an important new campaign strategy."

I presumed his point in mentioning this was to determine if I'd seen the Gifford campaign's press release that afternoon. He surely understood that his proposed strategy would gall me, but I refused to give him the satisfaction of hearing me confirm it. Instead, I simply noted, "It's a shame you have to discuss such weighty issues in the car—on the run, so to speak."

"In politics," he reminded all of us, "timing is everything."

Then he nodded to the ladies, turned, and headed up the walk to the Manor House.

His pace was brisk.

He was a man with a plan.

PART THREE

Rites of Passage

DUMONT MOURNS

All welcome to pay last respects at burial services this morning

By CHARLES OAKLAND
Staff Reporter, Dumont Daily Register

Sep. 11, DUMONT WI—Betty Gifford Ashton, Dumont's benevolent matriarch killed under tragic circumstances last Saturday, will be buried this morning from St. Matthew Episcopal Church. The public is invited to attend the 10:00 A.M. funeral, to be followed at 11:00 by interment services at All Saints Cemetery.

Blain Gifford, nephew of the late Mrs. Ashton and principal heir to her estate, said in a statement issued through attorneys, "My aunt loved this community and thought of its people as her family. Her later life was dedicated to raising the quality of life in Dumont, which is the only legacy she sought. All are welcome to join in laying her to rest."

Among the many attending Wednesday's services will be Raymond Gifford, cousin to the deceased, who is currently embroiled in a tight election contest for the governor's seat in Illinois.

Even as Dumont gathers to grieve, an ongoing investigation seeks to clarify the mysterious circumstances under which Mrs. Ashton was electrocuted while attending a Saturday wedding reception. Dumont County sheriff Douglas Pierce and coroner Vernon Formhals are treating the incident as a homicide.

Pierce told the *Register,* "Our investigation has been thwarted by our inability to identify a clear motive for this crime. We are considering several possible suspects. Though no arrest has been made, the case is being treated as my department's top priority."

Further, Pierce explained, "We are exploring the possibility that Mrs. Ashton was not the ultimate target of the crime. Rather, she may have been a random victim of deadly mischief intended for someone else. This theory vastly expands the scope and complexity of our inquiry."

Meanwhile, pressure has been mounting from the Gifford and Ashton families and from Dumont County district attorney Harley Kaiser to bring the investigation to a decisive close. ❏

Wednesday, September 11

Early Wednesday morning, before awaking to a day that would be a race against time, my mind swam with images that had nettled my subconscious since Saturday.

I relived, for example, the moment at the wedding reception when I'd stood waiting at the bar and turned to see Betty Gifford Ashton with her hand in the vat of ice water, when I'd comprehended her peril and my helplessness to save her. In replaying this horrible scene, my brain took a few liberties with reality—the vat hissed, roiled, and sparked, and Betty's heart exploded through her chest, spattering on-lookers with her lost life.

My sleeping mind also flirted with images of Roxanne. As before, she sported an electrified hairdo, which was now complemented by a flowing lace wedding gown, charred and tattered. I saw her in the kitchen, opening the refrigerator; its door creaked like the lid of a tomb. She withdrew several icy green bottles of Perrier, hitched her burnt skirt, and skulked out of the house, through the backyard to the bar, where she arranged the bottles on a shelf. Wrestling a thick, aggressive extension cord (it spat and glowed hot orange, like a nasty eel), she rigged the cord behind the bottles—just so. Then she plucked a huge copper penny from her bodice and went to work on the fuse box.

I saw myself in this dream, following Roxanne, watching her every move, trying to stop her and to warn others, but my mouth was sealed, wound tight with shiny black electrical tape.

The last of my dreams that morning had a different character altogether, not nightmarish, but erotic.

Once again, the ornate Victorian sofa appears in a room much like the living room on Prairie Street, positioned squarely in front of the fireplace. A freaky pink-and-green fire again burns in the hearth, but the mantel now supports a claw-footed clock, hugely out of proportion. On the tasseled sofa, as before, two men in business suits loll in each other's arms, engaging in some sensuous foreplay.

One of them, I already know, is Blain Gifford. He's all over the other guy, whose identity is still a mystery to me. Blain tells him, "I've never seen eyes so brown. Most handsome." Then he offers his ear to the other man's tongue.

I step into the dream, appearing from the slit of the heavy velvet curtains that have hidden me. "That's rather hypocritical, Blain, don't you think?"

His eye slides in my direction. "What are you talking about?"

"You're a *gay Republican*."

"Don't be ridiculous," Blain snaps. "There's no such thing." Then he nuzzles his ear closer to the other man's mouth. "Oooh, yeah, deeper."

"And to think you have the nerve to promote political measures that would institutionalize homophobia, while—"

"*Look*, mister." Blain turns to me, plenty peeved, while settling on the other man's lap, getting comfortable. "Enough of your bleeding-heart, left-wing indignation. Don't you have better things to do? How about unmasking my dear auntie's killer?" He points to the big clock on the mantel; its face is spinning like a roulette wheel, then screeches to a halt, smoking. "It's six in the morning already—fourteen hours till deadline, dollface." Blain grinds his ass against the other man's pants. "Oooh, yeah, deeper."

He's right, I realize, about the hour. Though I know I'm asleep, though I know I'm dreaming, I'm aware of the time somehow, as if I've kept a dozing eye on my bedside clock.

Blain kicks his shoes off; they land with a thud on the Turkish rug before the sofa, disappearing into the jewel-toned pattern of arabesques. The air is heavy with the spice and tang of incense. Blain twists his torso and seems to levitate a few inches from the sofa. Turning in midair, he descends again, planting his knees in the cushions, straddling his lover's lap, facing him. "Your eyes," he says again. "I've never seen eyes so brown. Most handsome."

Which again leads me to wonder about the identity of the other man. He could be almost anyone—I've encountered brown eyes at every turn since first dreaming about them on Sunday morning. Easily the most handsome of those brown eyes belonged to Chick Butterly, the Democrat, Blain's counterpart, the man I've imagined in this fantasy since the start.

But Chick is straight, I remind myself. The apple of his limpid brown eyes is a hardworking, middle-aged cateress. Chick isn't likely to have his tongue in any man's ear, let alone Blain Gifford's.

"And your hair," Blain continues. "I've never seen hair so golden, so rich with tight blond curls. Most beautiful."

Huh? I watch, riveted, as Blain wriggles out of his clothes and begins to undress the other man as well. At last the Republican moves aside, and I get my first clear look at his brown-eyed, blond-haired lover. It is Whitney Greer, the same man I saw him meet on Tuesday afternoon.

Blain and Whitney get down and dirty, fast, glancing in my direction as if performing for my benefit, intending to shock. But their lusty antics neither shock nor titillate me. Rather, I am intrigued— and puzzled.

What does this *mean?* Aware that I am dreaming, I wonder if Blain and Whitney's pairing on the Victorian sofa is merely a figment of my sleeping mind, inspired by seeing them together the previous afternoon. Or, on the other hand, might I now be witnessing the logical basis for their meeting in reality?

They tangle, groaning in ecstatic agony, then lose their equilibrium, crashing to the floor.

Pink sparks spray from the giddy green fire.

Around seven that morning, after Neil and I had dressed for the day, we came downstairs to join Barb in the kitchen. She'd already made coffee and now fussed with something in a big square baking dish. I could tell from the debris surrounding her on the counter that she'd been beating eggs, grating cheese, and chopping fresh produce—parsley, scallions, spinach, and such.

"Wow," I said, looking over her shoulder. "Quite a production for a weekday."

Folding the whole brew together with a spatula, she told me, "Today isn't just *any* weekday."

Wistfully, I summarized, "Betty's funeral, Thad's going-away dinner . . ."

Neil laughed. "I don't think that's what Barb had in mind, Mark."

"You got *that* right," Barb confirmed, glancing at us as she worked. "This is the last morning we'll be serving a houseful of overnight guests." Deadpan, she added, "Not that it hasn't been fun."

I asked, "What makes you think they've spent their last night here?"

Barb recited, "Tonight's debate could spell the end of Carl's political career—*unless* the mystery of Mrs. Ashton's electrocution is solved by then. Either way, there's no point in the Illinois crew hanging around Dumont any longer." Barb had heard these logistics discussed, ad infinitum, every time the household had gathered for a meal.

Neil reminded her, "Everyone is staying for Thad's party tonight. I'm as eager as anyone to reclaim our home and our privacy, but it's a long drive back to Chicago. I doubt if our friends will be in any mood to hit the road so late, regardless of the evening's outcome."

Barb shook her head, still blending the yellow glop in her baking dish. "I suppose you're right."

I suggested, "Why don't you pop that into the fridge? We can feast on it tomorrow."

"Nah. Better when it's fresh. Tomorrow, we can improvise."

Under his breath, Neil added, "Besides, by tomorrow morning, our guests may have lost their appetite."

Taking the glass pot of coffee from the counter to the table, I told

Neil brightly, "Let's show a little confidence. This isn't over yet." In truth, I had no idea how Pierce and I could possibly bring Betty's killer to justice before eight o'clock that evening.

Barb glanced up at the wall clock. "Less than thirteen hours, Mark."

"I'm well aware of my deadline." Sitting, I poured coffee for Neil and me. The slosh in the cups, the bracing aroma, lent a comforting note of normalcy to the start of a difficult day.

Neil joined me at the table. "I know you'll do everything you can. What rotten timing that this is coming to a head just when we're trying to focus on Thad. We need to assure him that, wherever his new life leads him, he'll always have a home here—with us."

Barb and I groaned in unison. Not that we found Neil's comment mawkish—to the contrary, he'd stated the very concern that none of us wanted to think about, let alone discuss. Day by day, our emotions with regard to Thad had grown ever more fragile and sentimental.

Needing to change the topic, I asked Barb, "How's that 'little project' going?"

"Hm?" She was playing dumb.

"You know—something to do with Whitney Greer."

"Yeah," chimed Neil. "You told us that Whitney is the kind of guy 'who makes it happen.' Then, having tantalized us, you clammed up. What's the big secret?"

Barb was still standing behind me at the counter. She offered no answer.

After swallowing a hot mouthful of coffee, I lectured, "It's considered rude to tantalize your friends—all the more so when you're in their employ." My tone was facetious, not threatening.

"My God," said Neil, sliding his chair back and rising, "what's wrong, Barb?"

Alarmed by his words, I turned in my chair and saw Barb gripping the edge of the counter with both hands. Her head was bowed and her shoulders heaved spasmodically—Barb was crying.

Rising, I joined Neil, as we stood on either side of her.

"Ugh," she said, swiping a tear from her cheek with the back of her hand, "it's nothing. Really."

Neil held her shoulders. "It's obviously *something.*"

She shook her head, patting one of Neil's hands. "Really, nothing's wrong. It's a *good* thing, honest. Guess I'm just worked up about Thad. God, tomorrow he's . . . *gone.*"

A lump rose to my throat. "I wish you wouldn't put it quite that way, Barb." I mustered a feeble laugh.

"Sorry." She turned between us, facing into the room, tweaking Neil's right cheek, my left (an affectionate gesture that nonetheless annoyed me). "My project with Whitney has nothing to do with Thad. I'm anxious to tell you about it, and I *will*—all in due time."

"Why not right now?"

"Because nothing's . . . nothing's settled yet, okay?" Then her lip quivered and she suppressed another sob.

Neil and I exchanged a bewildered glance as Barb turned and lifted her egg concoction from the counter. Stepping across the kitchen, she managed to get the oven door open without spilling the baking dish, slipped it inside, then closed the door. She twisted a dial and punched a button.

"This takes maybe forty-five minutes, not sure," she told us. "If you don't hear any action upstairs within half an hour, give 'em a yell. Got it?" She moved toward her room, just off the kitchen.

"Uh, sure," said Neil, understanding her directions but not their purpose. "Going out?"

"Yeah," she called from inside her room, then reappeared with her sunglasses, keys, and bulging gold-lamé wallet. "I just need to do some quick shopping. We're running low on a few things, and if the others will be staying again tonight, well, I'd better . . ." And she slipped out the back door with a little wave, without completing her explanation.

Neil and I turned to each other, befuddled. He asked, "What was *that?*"

"Beats me." I moved to the table and sat again.

Neil sat next to me, topping up our coffee. "She sure got goofy when we mentioned Whitney. You don't suppose she was rushing out to meet him, do you?"

"At this hour? She said she was going shopping."

"At *this* hour?" Neil had a point—it did seem strange.

But I told him, "We have to be careful not to let our imaginations get carried away. We've had murder on our minds since the weekend, so it's all too easy to start finding everything—and everyone—suspicious. We've lived under the same roof with Barb for nearly two years. Let's just take her at her word." I slurped some coffee.

So did Neil. "Still, it's kinda funny—isn't it?—that yesterday you saw Whitney sneaking around with Betty's nephew and now, this morning, Barb got ditsy and rushed out the door at the mention of Whitney's name. Was it sheer coincidence?"

With a low laugh, I told him, "If there's one thing I've learned in twenty years of investigative journalism, it's this: there are very few genuine coincidences."

"Fine. Then what about Barb? Do we 'take her at her word' that she slipped out of the house for an urgent bout of early-morning shopping, or do we—"

I completed his thought: "Or do we suspect her of complicity in something sinister?" Laughing softly, I touched my lover's forearm. "No, Neil. She went shopping."

He paused, considering what he'd almost said, then laughed with me.

Leaning back with my coffee, I mused, "Barb has her quirks; that's one of the things we love about her. At her core, she's a good person with a good heart—we *know* that—but we don't know Whitney Greer that well, do we? What *was* he up to yesterday afternoon with Blain Gifford?"

Neil echoed my position, leaning back in his chair. "Not a clue."

"What's more"—I hesitated—"Whitney and Blain's secret assignation didn't end last night when I saw Blain arrive at the Manor House in Whitney's car."

Neil sat upright again, setting his coffee on the table. "Huh?"

I paused to sniff the first cheese-heavy smells of Barb's frothy egg-thing wafting from the oven. "Do you recall that I had an erotic dream on Sunday morning, a dream featuring Blain Gifford and some unknown, brown-eyed man?"

With a laugh, Neil reminded me, "Hard to forget—it knocked you out of bed."

"Indeed it did. Well, this morning before waking, I had essentially the same dream again."

Neil twitched a brow. "You didn't land on the floor this time. I heard no squeals of rapture in your sleep."

"Most perceptive of you."

"What was so different about this morning's version of the dream?"

"It was every bit as erotic as the first dream, but this time, the identity of the other man ceased to be a mystery. I hoped that Blain's juicy-tongued lover might be Chick Butterly, as I had previously fantasized, but no. He wasn't Chick."

Neil frowned skeptically. "Why do I get the feeling we're about to discuss Whitney Greer again?"

"Your perceptive skills are well honed this morning. So tell me: Does Whitney have brown eyes?"

"Can't say I've ever noticed. With those tinted glasses, it's hard to tell."

"Precisely. But I assure you, the other man in my dream was Whitney, and his eyes were most definitely brown. Blain said so."

"I *can't* believe this," Neil said flatly, crossing his arms. "*Now* who's letting his imagination get the best of him? Do you—Mr. Objective—mean to tell me that Blain and Whitney are sexually involved because you saw them cavorting in a *dream?*"

I qualified, "I do need to confirm the color of Whitney's eyes."

"*What?* Even if Whitney does have brown eyes, what does *that* prove?"

Reluctantly, I admitted, "Nothing, I guess."

"Look, Mark, I'm as eager as anyone to wrap up the Ashton case, send our guests home, and get our lives back. But you're *way* out on a limb with this. Even if, by some far-flung chance, Blain and Whitney are secret lovers, what light does that shed on Betty's electrocution?"

"As far as I know, none. But"—I leaned over my elbow toward Neil—"it would put a whole new spin on Blain's latest scheme to elect Raymond Gifford by promoting homophobia."

"Ahhh." Neil sat back in his chair, enlightened. "If Blain is in fact a closeted gay Republican, his antigay ploy could seriously backfire."

"Right in his face."

"It's a tempting thought. But is there anything *to* it? I mean, you're basing this theory on little more than a hunch—and a dream."

I didn't want to explain that I was also basing my theory on Blain's starched khakis, a factor that seemed too nutty to verbalize, so I told Neil, "The dream proves nothing, obviously. I have no idea how Blain ended up in *either* of my dreams, but Whitney's surprise appearance in this morning's rerun is considerably less mysterious. This was doubtless the result of my having seen the two men together twice yesterday, first outside the Grill, then outside the Manor House. While these encounters may explain this morning's dream, what explains the encounters?"

Neil nodded. "Good question."

"Blain and Whitney were apparently together all of yesterday afternoon. What were they up to?"

The back door cracked open. "Any coffee left?"

"Sure, Doug," we answered. "Come on in."

Doug Pierce entered the kitchen, fresh from his shower at the gym, bearing, as usual, a large, wrapped kringle, fresh from the Danish bakery on First Avenue. Neil rose to get an extra cup as Doug placed the pastry in the center of the table, took off his tweedy sport coat, hung it on the back of his chair, and sat next to me. I unwrapped the end of the kringle and slid it out of the bag. Peach—an offbeat choice, not my favorite.

Pierce must have read something in my face. He explained, "I was feeling sort of funky this morning—maybe the funeral."

With a snort, I suggested, "Maybe the deadline."

"That too," he admitted. Picking up a knife, he began slicing several wedges from the curved end of the pastry. Sniffing the air, he asked, "What's cooking? Smells good."

"Barb whipped up an egg-thing for the houseguests. Hang around long enough, and you'll get some."

Neil returned to the table and poured coffee for Pierce, asking him, "You're going to the funeral, aren't you?"

"Well, sure. All of 'official Dumont' will be there, and I've added a few extra men for security, since Raymond Gifford will be rolling up from Illinois with his entourage."

My nose wrinkled. "Hope it doesn't turn into a media circus."

Pierce grinned. "That's an odd sort of comment, coming from *you*."

Neil laughed, passing out paper napkins.

Lamely, I explained, "It's just that *Betty* should be the star this morning, the center of attention—not the Republican candidate for governor of Illinois." Tasting the peach kringle, I found it better than I'd expected, so I took another bite.

"Fair enough," said Pierce. "Still, the funeral is a public event, and it'll be instructive to note exactly who attends, who does not, and the interplay of emotions among those who are there. So even though my primary purpose at the funeral will be to mourn the passing of a respected member of our community, I'll also be on full alert—for any clue as to why Betty died."

"We could *use* a clue or two."

"Uh, Mark," said Neil, tapping my arm, "have you told Doug about this new . . . 'spin' we were discussing this morning?"

Intrigued, Pierce arched his brows.

I had not yet voiced to anyone but Neil my suspicion that Blain Gifford might be gay because it was so conjectural and seemingly irrelevant to his aunt's death. Now, instead of spelling out my evolving theory for Pierce, I decided to backtrack, asking him, "What do you know about Blain Gifford?"

Pierce paused to think. "Not much. He's Betty's nephew and heir. He's from the Illinois side of the family and is serving as campaign manager for Raymond Gifford in the governor's race there. Is there anything *else* I should know?"

"Not sure." I fingered the rim of my coffee cup. "You're forty-seven, right?"

"Yeah. Why?"

"Blain, I recall, is forty-nine, only two years older than you."

"And you're forty-four, three years younger than me. So?"

With a quiet laugh, I explained, "I don't fit into this equation, but Blain might. Betty described him as her 'favorite nephew,' which she proved in her will, so I was wondering if you have any direct knowl-edge—or recollection—of Blain's background."

"I wish I could help you, Mark, but I grew up right here in Dumont, and as you know, Blain's family hails from Illinois. Sure, there was a link by marriage, but—" Pierce stopped short, as if something had clicked.

"What?" I asked.

Pierce's eyes popped, and he flumped back in his chair. "God," he said, combing his fingers through his still-damp hair, "was that . . . ? It *had* to be."

"*What?*" asked Neil.

"Now that you mention it, I think I *do* recall Blain as a boy. Betty had a nephew who used to come up for long summer visits—it *must* have been Blain. Since he was older and didn't go to school here, I never really got to know the kid, but sure, I remember him."

"Why?" I asked. "In what context?"

"There was a Y day camp that a lot of us went to back then—swimming, hiking, basic scouting skills, that sort of thing—good, clean fun with an emphasis on the outdoors. Betty used to send her visiting nephew to the camp on weekdays. I found out who he was because I didn't recognize him from school and I asked around. I was probably ten or so, which made him twelve, a big difference at that age, so we never hung out together; he was with the older kids. There was one in particular, I remember, who Blain spent a lot of time with. He had blond hair and glasses, seemed nice enough, but the poor guy had a reputation as a sissy—you know how rough adolescence can be."

"Do I ever," agreed Neil. Glancing at me, he added, "Doug, this blond kid, did he happen to have curly hair?"

Pierce stared at Neil, amazed by his seeming clairvoyance. "He *did*—tight, golden curls. Someone called him Shirley once, meaning Shirley Temple, and the name stuck. How on *earth* did you know about the curls?"

Neil swirled the coffee in his cup. "It's entirely possible that Blain's friend was Whitney Greer. I've gotten to know him pretty well through the Dumont Players Guild, and I recall that he celebrated his fiftieth birthday a few months ago. That makes him about Blain's age, a year older. And Whitney grew up here."

Pierce slowly shook his head, astonished. "Sure, that makes sense— Blain's friend was a local kid, and I remember that he had a girlish name. Whitney would have been in junior high then, so I wouldn't have known him *or* Blain. Wow. *Tempus fugit.*"

I could barely conceal my eagerness in asking, "Did they seem to be, uh . . . *close* friends?"

Pierce chortled a low, meaningful laugh. "Uh-huh. In fact, something 'happened.' No one ever said what it was—everything was so hush-hush back then—but as a result of this mysterious incident, Whitney never attended the camp again and Blain never came north for another summer visit."

"What do you *think* happened?"

Pierce hesitated, but not long, before answering, "I was too young to understand it at the time, but I assume that Blain and Whitney must have been discovered in some sort of sexual encounter."

Neil and I gaped at each other.

Pierce continued, "Must have been a phase, at least for Blain. Whitney—who knows? He's long been presumed gay, and given his involvement with the arts, well, who cares?"

I noted, "But Blain's situation is altogether different."

Our openly gay sheriff said, "And how. The gay card is a tough sell in politics, and in *some* political circles it's a death knell."

"Meaning," suggested Neil, "Republican circles."

"By and large." Pierce shrugged. "It's virtually unthinkable that a Republican campaign manager, working for a candidate for high office, could be actively gay and remain within his party's good graces. If Blain and Whitney had a boyhood fling, I'll bet it's so repressed by now that Blain doesn't even remember it."

"Don't be so sure," I ventured. "On Saturday at the reception, I was with Betty and Blain when Whitney appeared on the scene. Betty reintroduced them, asking her nephew, 'You remember Whitney, don't you?' They greeted each other tersely. Blain soon excused himself, looking perplexed."

"But the corker," added Neil, "was yesterday. It seems Blain and Whitney spent the entire afternoon together."

I explained to Pierce, "When you and I had lunch yesterday with Thad and Kwynn at First Avenue Grill, you were called away. After you left, I saw Whitney meet Blain outside on the street, and they rushed off together. That evening, I was at the Manor House when Whitney dropped Blain off in his car." I was tempted to add some supporting evidence from my dreams, but decided against that tack.

"Meanwhile," said Neil, "Mark got a press release from Raymond Gifford's campaign headquarters announcing that the candidate may introduce a right-wing plank in his platform, prohibiting adoption by gays in Illinois."

"It's Blain's doing," I assured Pierce. "He practically crowed about it when I ran into him last night."

"Christ," muttered Pierce, shaking his head. "Anything for a few votes."

Neil reminded him, "It's a perilously tight election."

A voice from the hall called brightly, "What's this I hear—campaign strategy at the crack of dawn? That's *my* kind of breakfast chat." Chick Butterly appeared in the doorway, dressed for a day of business. "Morning, all."

"Hi, Chick," we said. "Good morning." "Join us."

He grabbed a cup from the counter. "Is it just my imagination, or is there something wonderful in that oven?"

"Gosh," said Neil, getting up, "I'd better check on that." He rattled about, opening the oven, getting a fork from a drawer, poking Barb's concoction, sliding it back on the rack. "Are Rox and Carl up and about?"

Chick told him, "They'll be down any minute."

By the time Chick had settled at the table with his coffee and Neil had set out a stack of plates and cutlery in anticipation of the cheesy egg-thing, Roxanne and Carl did appear, as predicted, entering the kitchen, greeting us, commenting on the delicious smells. Roxanne wore a stylish but simple gray dress, perfect for that morning's main event, the funeral. Carl looked every inch the politician in a dark blue suit, muted red tie, and starched white shirt. We crowded some extra chairs around the table—a familiar routine in recent days—and the six of us gabbed over coffee and kringle while waiting for the fluffy egg dish to finish baking.

I saw Roxanne steal a glance at her watch; it was nearly eight o'clock.

"I was just thinking the same thing," I told her. "Twelve hours till deadline." Everyone in the room understood the significance of that night's debate in Chicago, but only Roxanne and I grasped the additional meaning of the deadline, the baring of our lie of omission.

She flicked a crumb of icing from her lips. "Mark, Doug, tell me honestly—what are our chances of wrapping this up before the shit hits the fan?" She could be achingly blunt when the situation called for it.

I didn't know how to answer.

Doug jumped in. "It'll be a tall order to find definitive answers within twelve hours, but it's not hopeless. Even though this morning's funeral and burial robs us of some precious investigative hours, I'm planning to use that time to stand back, weighing the situation and the personalities with fresh eyes. With any luck, we may notice someone or something that's been overlooked."

I added, "We keep finding more pieces to the puzzle. Now it's time to put them together and make sense of them."

"Just this morning," said Neil, offering a point of encouragement, "Doug and Mark pieced together the damnedest new angle. I'm not sure what to make of this, but you're *not* gonna believe it."

Roxanne smirked. "Try me."

Neil, Pierce, and I savored the moment—which of us would be the one to drop this minor but tantalizing bombshell? I gestured to Neil, as if to say, Be my guest.

"What would you say," he asked Roxanne, "if I were to tell you that Blain Gifford may be gay?"

Roxanne's lips sputtered with laughter. "Don't be ridiculous."

"He's a Republican," Carl completed Roxanne's thought, sipping his coffee.

Chick didn't comment, but listened to Neil's words with wide-eyed attention, as if to hear them better. He already grasped the political implications.

I elaborated on Neil's theory, explaining to the others that I'd gotten vibes from Blain since meeting him, that I'd seen him rendezvous with the effeminate Whitney Greer for some unknown purpose the previous afternoon, and that Pierce recalled circumstances suggesting a sexual relationship between Blain and Whitney during their adolescent years.

"And to *think*," added Neil, indignant, "that this is the man promoting institutionalized homophobia on behalf of Raymond Gifford's gubernatorial campaign." Harrumph.

"*What?*" asked Roxanne, midchew. Flaky kringle crust fluttered from her mouth. Though Carl and Chick were well aware by now of the opposing camp's latest strategy, they had not burdened Roxanne with it, who already had plenty to fret over—most notably, the growing possibility of murder charges.

Neil filled her in.

"Well, for Christ's sake," she said with a burst of relieved, jubilant laughter, "let's *out* the bastard! What are we waiting for?"

"She's right." Chick nodded eagerly. "This is exactly the break we needed."

"Uh-uh-uh"—Carl rapped the table—"hold on now. This whole business sounds rather speculative to me. You have no proof of this, Mark, do you?"

I affirmed, "We do not. It's sheer conjecture. But speaking as a journalist, I find it highly compelling."

"The point is," said Carl with measured, lawyerly diction, "we are unable to substantiate any claims with regard to Blain Gifford's sexual preferences, past or present." He pinched the knot of his tie. "The Gifford campaign would be quick to brand any such allegations both libelous and politically motivated."

Chick admitted, "Carl's got a point. This could spin the wrong way."

"*Plus*," I said, sounding a frustrated note, standing, "there are some serious ethical considerations at stake here."

"Ethics?" someone asked.

"Gay ethics. Outing, by its nature, seeks to *punish* a person for being gay. Outing, by its nature, reinforces the notion that there's something *wrong* with being gay, that it's something worth hiding in the first place."

Pierce sat back in his chair, looking demoralized—recalling, no doubt, his own outing during a reelection campaign not two years past.

"Mark," said Neil, "I couldn't agree more with you—normally. If the purpose of outing is merely to disgrace and humiliate, it's wrong, it's vicious. But if the purpose behind the outing is to expose hypocrisy and protect gay interests, that's another matter entirely."

Pierce rose from his momentary slump. "I agree. A person's sexual identity is nobody's business—it's private—*unless* that person 'turns on his own' in an attempt to reinforce the image that he is what he is not. If Blain is indeed gay, I can't fathom what would motivate him to lash out against gays on the issue of adoption. You'd think *any* conservative would support the efforts of some homosexuals to 'mainstream' both their family lives and their role in society. Maybe Blain can justify any reprehensible tactic for the sake of the election. Maybe he's been confused by religion and has learned to hate and fear his true self. Maybe he's just plain sick or evil—I don't know. But I do know that he deserves to be stopped."

Neil smiled. "Well said, Doug."

Pierce had surprised me with his verbal fervor. As a rule, he was taciturn, more inclined to deep thinking than to expressive speaking. Clearly, the issues surrounding outing had become both personal and emotional for him, but no less logical, and I found myself inclined to agree with his every word. Stepping next to Pierce, I hugged him by the shoulders before sitting again at the table.

Chick politely applauded Pierce's speech.

Roxanne snarled, "Let's get that two-faced fucker by the balls." She wasn't acting or exaggerating; she had a taste for blood. She gripped her coffee so fiercely, I feared the cup would implode in her hand.

Carl, the voice of moderation, reminded us, "We don't know if it's true about Blain. We have no firm basis for what you're proposing."

"Then I suggest," said Chick, stern and determined, "that we concentrate on *finding* that basis. The Gifford campaign is *handing* us the seeds of its own undoing—if we can prove that Blain is gay."

Carl shook his head. "That's a mighty big 'if.' Outing Blain is a risky gambit at best. It could backfire, and even if it doesn't, I have no taste for such tactics."

"But Lowell Sagehorn might." Chick didn't need to add that, within twelve hours, Carl's views might well be irrelevant to the Sagehorn ticket. "I need to inform Lowell of these developments. It's his decision where we'll go with this."

"For God's sake, Chick, think about what you're saying. How do you plan to 'prove' that Blain Gifford is gay—by asking him outright if he sleeps with men?"

Chick didn't answer, but he looked steamed by his candidate's lack of enthusiasm for a maneuver that he felt could win the election.

"Obviously," I said, "it makes no sense to ask Blain about his bedtime proclivities. But I can think of someone *else* who might be willing to talk."

Neil's eyes widened. "Whitney!"

"So *call* him," said Roxanne. "Right now. Grill him."

I tisked. "Under the circumstances, and given the general realm of inquiry, I think we'll be better served by a more subtle approach."

"Maybe," she allowed. Then she tapped her watch. "But not *too* subtle."

Neil laughed, pushing back his chair and rising. "Don't worry, Rox." He crossed to the oven, turned it off, and opened the door. "Mark's on top of the situation—he's a master of timing."

"And timing," Chick reminded us, "is everything."

Even though that morning would be dominated by Betty Gifford Ashton's funeral, other matters needed our attention as well, so we reviewed our logistics while devouring Barb's cheesy egg dish.

I would go down to my office at the *Register* and try to get in an hour or two of work. I needed to skim overnight wire stories, deal with any in-house crises, and review with Lucille Haring our anticipated treatment of that day's big story, the funeral. I hoped, of course, that the day might bring a bigger headline still—the unmasking of Betty's killer—so Lucy needed to be prepared for an alternative makeup of page one.

Chick, as planned the previous afternoon, would pay another visit to Alanna Scott, a mission that would serve dual purposes. From his romantic perspective, Chick simply wanted to see the woman again. From the broader perspective of the murder investigation, we hoped to straighten out the conflicting reports of whether Alanna did or did not want to have children, and why.

Because Chick would have his hands full with Alanna (so to speak), Carl would phone Lowell Sagehorn, inform him of our suspicions regarding Blain Gifford's duplicity on the gay-adoption issue, seek Sagehorn's counsel with regard to outing Blain, and generally try to mollify the old gasbag and stave off his threat to dump Carl from the ticket that night.

Pierce would be busy downtown at the public-safety building, overseeing last-minute arrangements for security at Betty's funeral. He also planned to corner Harley Kaiser, our pugnacious DA, bringing him up-to-date on the investigation and laying out the argument, once more, that Betty's killer was anyone but Roxanne.

Roxanne's best bet was to lie low, keeping well clear of the investigation in general and Kaiser in particular. So she decided to accompany Neil, who would attempt to track down Whitney Greer prior to the funeral and engage him in some banter that might, with any luck, shed light on Whitney's presumed relationship with Blain Gifford.

Our plans were set.

By the time we all left the house—it was after eight—I noted that Barb had not yet returned from her hastily announced shopping excursion.

What in hell, I wondered, was she up to?

Churches and I share a rocky past.

My mother's family, the Quatrains, were of French Catholic descent, and I was raised within the Church, schooled by nuns through eighth grade in the quiet suburbs north of Chicago. An apt pupil and a disciplined child, I readily bought into the doctrines I was taught and came to appreciate the caparison and rituals of the religion itself.

With maturity, however, came skepticism. I managed to set my doubts aside, dismissing them as honest inquiry, keeping the faith till my twenty-ninth birthday, when even the lure of Catholicism's theatrics (candles! vestments! incense!) proved insufficient to convince me that God exists, that Christ, his son, is my personal savior, or that Peter's successor in Rome is the anointed know-it-all of faith and morals. Though soul-wrenching, the decision to chuck religion, in toto, was the bravest and most honest act of my life. On that day, some fifteen years ago, I was born again.

Yes, the nonsense of religion has left some psychological scars—and a chip on my shoulder. I do not actively promote enmity with god-folk, but they seem to go out of their way to vent hostility toward me and others like me who have dared to pooh-pooh their beliefs. So it's difficult for me to resist the opportunity to indulge in a bit of faith-bashing, particularly when the faith is of the Roman variety.

It can be argued, I suppose, that Catholicism has been the most harmful of organized Western religions (it's the oldest, so it's had the most time to inflict the most damage), but I've made no particular study of this issue, which would only add to the mental energy I've already wasted over a god that's not there. Bottom line: when the occasion calls for apostasy, Catholicism is my favored target because Catholicism is the target I know best.

Oddly, Episcopalianism doesn't raise my hackles in the least. It has often been noted that Episcopalians are "more Catholic than Catholics," an assertion rooted not in doctrine, but in trappings. No doubt about it—when it comes to refined architecture, genteel rituals, silver-tongued sermonizing, gold-garbed clergy, stately music, and hymns well sung, Episcopalians take the prize for pomp. A point in their favor.

Bonus points: in days of yore, their Anglican forebears defied Rome, and in modern times, they have been inordinately friendly to their gay members. Though I take issue with their core beliefs (God, an afterlife, and such), I find Episcopalians a benign lot who have sufficient class to limit the practice of their religion to the confines of their churches and sufficient flair to paint the doors of their churches a bloody scarlet—a touch of liturgical verve, gutsy yet tasteful.

So as I knelt beneath the varnished rafters on that Wednesday morning, I felt an easy reverence for my surroundings and for the communal purpose of the believers who had gathered to celebrate Betty Gifford Ashton's goodness, mourn her death, and commit her remains to the earth. The service bore an uncanny resemblance to the requiem masses of my youth, except the words were not in Latin, but in English—exceptionally lofty English at that. The church was packed; it had surely not held such a crowd since Christmas, if then. I stood, sat, and knelt at the appropriate times, going through the motions, joining in a hymn or two, focusing my thoughts on Betty, putting at bay for an hour the vexing puzzle of her death and my deadline for solving it, which had crept perilously near.

At eleven o'clock—nine hours till deadline—the throng left Saint Matthew's and formed a long, slow motorcade to All Saints Cemetery, a tranquil, hilly expanse of green occupying several square blocks of old Dumont. Surrounded by a high stone wall, the parklike setting was shaded by ancient, native oaks that had served as Indian landmarks along a trail to forgotten hunting grounds. Headstones peppered the manicured turf. Here and there stood actual tombs—little marble mausoleums that looked like storybook banks—with the names of Dumont's "better" families inscribed in gold above their locked, gated doors. One was engraved ASHTON. Its open doorway gaped black within, framing the priest, who now wore a simple cassock and long, lacy surplice.

The spotless white hearse and several limousines, first to arrive, waited in a gravel-paved clearing while the rest of us gathered on a knoll facing the door of the tomb. When we had settled in the late-morning silence, broken only by birdsong and the occasional sputter of distant traffic, the family emerged from their limousines and the undertakers removed Betty's bronze casket from the hearse. As this small procession crunched the gravel, moving a few yards from the cars to the priest, strobes flashed and two or three television cameras were hoisted onto shoulders—the appearance of Betty's cousin, Raymond Gifford, the Republican gubernatorial candidate from Illinois, had generated a measure of media hoopla, adding the lone distasteful note to that morning's services.

While the priest read his prayers, the assembled mourners bowed their heads. Someone near the front sobbed openly. Others sniffled. Most stood sedately in respectful silence. I surveyed the crowd.

At my side was Neil, exactly where I hoped he would always be. There was nothing remarkable in his presence at Betty's services; he shared in the loss felt by our entire community. Thad and Kwynn were present as well, which I found touching. Neither had known Betty, and both were preparing to leave town, but they'd set aside this time and had shown the maturity to observe a somber occasion that had no connection to their past or future lives.

As my attention drifted to others, though, it seemed that each had played some tangential role in the circumstances that had led to this morning's funeral. Sheriff Pierce knew this as well, and I saw him standing at a distance with a few of his deputies. Earlier, at breakfast, he'd spoken of his hope to notice someone or something that had been overlooked. Was Betty's killer standing there, right now, among us?

Roxanne and Carl stood nearby. Gale Exner and Lauren Creighton were with them, presenting a strained tableau of the newly merged families. Of this fragile foursome, Roxanne had most to gain or lose from the outcome of Betty's murder investigation. In the eyes of some, Roxanne was the prime suspect. Although I could still not bring myself to consider seriously the possibility of her guilt, I understood the DA's contention that the circumstantial evidence against Roxanne was compelling—in fact, there were as yet no other active suspects in the case.

Watching Lauren Creighton, I was struck by her body language as she stood at her father's side, opposite Roxanne. The younger woman's stance, her slouch, her sagging shoulder, managed to telegraph combined messages of defiance and boredom. She had made no secret of her hostility to Roxanne, and for this I instinctively disliked her. It now occurred to me that Lauren had had a plausible motive to want Betty dead—simply to implicate Roxanne, her mother's usurper, whom she despised. I reminded myself, however, that Lauren had had no opportunity to commit the crime, having arrived in town late, appearing at the reception after missing the ceremony altogether. Ah, well, it was a promising notion, but I couldn't very well convict the woman on the flimsy basis of a bad attitude. And for once, I mused, her urban-black attire seemed suited to her surroundings.

Someone else with a highly plausible motive for Betty's death was her favorite nephew, her principal heir, Blain Gifford, who stood near the front—with the priest and the candidate and the coffin—making a show of his dignified grief, a grief beyond price, even the millions that were suddenly his. I didn't resent his fortune (I'd similarly benefited from deaths in my own family), but I did resent his religious-right politics, specifically, his homophobia and apparent hypocrisy. I would, therefore, reap immense satisfaction if I could prove that Blain's deepest, most hidden sin was not a taste for men but a boundless, murderous greed. Unfortunately, from my perspective, there was nothing to suggest, let alone prove, that he'd had the means or the opportunity to electrocute his aunt.

Blain's Democratic counterpart, Chick Butterly, watched all this from the top of the knoll, as if to maximize the distance between himself and his rival. Which struck me as odd. Chick was not, by nature, a retiring sort, not the type to remain in the background and allow an adversary, Blain, to hog the limelight. Then I noticed that the hand near Chick's face held a cell phone; he was doubtless reporting to Lowell Sagehorn and had kept at a distance to avoid being heard. Perhaps because this gave him an air of secrecy, I pondered a new question: How far would Chick go to assure the election of the Sagehorn ticket? It had been no secret that Betty had been virtually bankrolling the opposing camp. Chick was still an enigma to me. He was smart, aggressive, and driven. Was he also conniving and diabolical? And what were the undertones of his interest in Alanna Scott?

A few stragglers were still arriving at the cemetery, parking on the street and milling just inside the stone wall. No sooner had I thought of Alanna Scott than I noticed her arrival. She, husband Wesley, and

Dale Turner walked from the street together and climbed the rear of the knoll, where they settled as a threesome in the shade of an oak (the warm morning was turning hot), engaged in quiet conversation while watching the end of the service. Chick saw them, pocketed his phone, and I wondered if he had managed to meet with Alanna earlier that day as planned. She showed no sign of recognizing him.

My attention shifted to Alanna's husband, Wesley Scott, the bartender. I could not dismiss the crucial detail that it was he who had moved the bottle of Perrier, allowing the live extension cord to slip into the ice water only moments before Betty dipped her hankie. Wes may have rigged it, or Wes may have been set up. I also wondered if Wes was fooling around with someone, as I'd inferred from Nancy Sanderson's comments. And what about his story that he yearned for children not wanted by his wife? Alanna had seconded the story, but Nancy had refuted it.

Dale Turner, the good-looking tent guy, leaned to tell Wes something, laughing softly. Wes shook his head, grinning. On Monday morning in Dale's office, I'd come to understand that his convivial manner was something of an act, blanketing his insecurities and anxieties. The greatest of Dale's worries—now—was the fear that he himself had been the ultimate target of the electrocution, staged for his ruin. This scenario had become all the more plausible on Tuesday, when I'd met with his ex-wife, the ditsy Fawnah, who portrayed Dale as a hapless loser, hopelessly indebted to nameless thugs. My instincts were beginning to focus on this angle, which, if correct, would give me the double satisfaction of helping Dale as well as Roxanne. Unfortunately, I had yet to scratch the surface in terms of naming Dale's unknown enemy.

Mulling this, I nearly missed the arrival of Whitney Greer, the orchestra manager. In truth, I don't know if he arrived just then or if I simply hadn't noticed him earlier. He was down near the limousines, near the family, standing next to Elliot Coop, the old attorney. Prim, proper, and balding, Elliot *always* looked as if he'd dressed for a funeral—he'd seen his share of them, God knows. Whitney's attire, on the other hand, was more flamboyant, but even he had toned it down today, wearing a dark, conventional business suit. I might not

227

have spotted him in the crowd at all had it not been for the oversize lavender sunglasses and curly crop of brassy blond hair. He stood not twenty feet from Blain Gifford, who now bent to pull a rose from the lavish spray atop his aunt's casket.

What was the connection between Whitney and Blain? At the moment, there was no interaction between them, not even a nod of recognition. Was Pierce correct in surmising they'd been boyhood sex pals? If so, what had been the purpose of their meeting the prior afternoon? Even though I had vividly witnessed their pairing in my dream that morning, my mind now reeled at the thought of their possible conjugation in reality. It wasn't just that they struck me as inordinately odd bedfellows (there's no accounting for mutual attraction); more engrossing by far was the notion that Blain's secret proclivity would be so contrary to the morals espoused by the fundamentalist element within his own party. Is that why he was gearing up for a hatchet job on gay adoption? Did he need to "prove" something?

And a new thought: if Blain had a motive to kill his aunt, it may not have been so obvious as greed for her cash. If Blain had a sexual past with Whitney, Betty had surely known about it. Had Blain grown desperate to silence his aunt's harmful memories, to close the book on them—precisely as he had accused Roxanne of needing to silence harmful memories of her alcoholic past?

". . . through Christ, our Lord," the priest concluded.

"Amen" rippled through the crowd around me.

The priest closed his book and stepped aside, clearing the dark doorway to the mausoleum. A well-drilled group of husky pallbearers stepped forward to lift Betty's bronze coffin, then with slow, synchronized steps carried her remains into the tomb, where now, after so many years, she would again lie next to Archibald Ashton, the legendary paper-mill baron.

Outside, in full sunlight, we mourners tried to peer within the stalwart little building of marble and granite, but the final, funereal duties performed there were invisible to us. We heard a shuffle and scuffing of shoes on the stone floor, a clank of metal, a few echoed words spoken by subdued voices, unintelligible. Then the pallbearers reappeared—empty-handed—marching back to the daylight. Someone closed and locked the door, the priest read a few more words from the gilt-edged pages of his black leather book, and with that, Betty's burial was complete.

Pierce nodded to his deputies, who went to their various posts, preparing to escort the limousines from the cemetery, direct traffic, and generally be of service to the family and townspeople. The television crews were first to scamper off and disappear. I saw Blain Gifford shake the priest's hand; he then introduced Raymond Gifford, the candidate. Within the minute, Blain and Raymond had ducked into their limousine, which rolled silently through the gate and onto the street, then roared away, heading south. Behind tinted windows, the Giffords were already hard at it, preparing for that evening's debate.

"Well," said Neil quietly, touching my hand, "that's that."

I nodded. "She led a good life." The comment had the sappy ring of platitude, but the situation seemed to demand it. Bridging from the pensive mood of the funeral to the vexing business of the day would take a moment.

Roxanne and Carl approached us. "Act two," announced Roxanne. "Curtain going up." So much for subtle transitions.

Carl looked despondent—who'd blame him? At a loss for words, he suggested, "Can I take everyone to lunch?"

I glanced at my watch; it was pushing noon. "Thanks for offering, but I'd better get down to my office. There's a lot going on today."

Roxanne rolled her eyes. "That's putting it mildly."

I encouraged them to have a good meal, suggesting that Neil join them. Everyone's mood seemed lackadaisical, but they agreed they'd better eat, and after a bit of hawing, they'd worked out their logistics. To my surprise, both Roxanne's mother and Carl's daughter agreed to join the group—either their mutual hostility had thawed some, or they were hungry. Thad and Kwynn, on the other hand, declined the invitation—they had people to see, things to do, plans to make—and besides, they'd be spending the evening with all of us at the going-away dinner.

229

As the crowd began to disperse, we joined the flow toward the street.

Thad happened to fall in next to Lauren Creighton. He told her, "I hear you've extended your visit in order to attend the party. That was nice of you."

Lauren smiled. "It was nice to be invited. I wouldn't miss it."

The reason she had decided to stay, I knew, was to be with her father on a night that would be difficult for him. But I appreciated that she had stretched the truth for Thad's benefit.

Roxanne told Thad, "My mother's staying too."

Kwynn gushed, "Everyone's been so *thoughtful*, changing plans and all."

Gale Exner echoed Lauren's comment, "We wouldn't miss it." Then, under her breath, she added, "Besides, a sixth night at the Manor House is hardly what I'd call 'roughing it.' "

We all laughed our agreement.

Nearing the top of the knoll, the kids broke away from us, as they'd parked down the block. Chick Butterly was walking in that direction as well, and I noticed that they all seemed to be heading toward the oak tree, where Alanna and Wesley Scott still stood conversing with Dale Turner.

I kept an ear on the conversation with my companions, but kept an eye on the oak. Still curious as to whether Chick had met with Alanna that morning, I wondered if he'd been able to clarify whether she wanted children or not—a touchy subject at best. If in fact they'd met and talked, what sort of interplay would now transpire between them?

As Chick approached the group under the tree, everyone turned to acknowledge him with a nod, but no display of recognition. After all, Wes and Dale had probably seen Chick at Saturday's reception, but I had no reason to assume they'd met. I knew otherwise regarding Alanna, of course, and sure enough, once Chick had passed the group, he paused, looking back. Alanna glanced over her shoulder just then and, catching Chick's eye, ambled the few yards to where he stood. They leaned together, exchanging words. Though both took pains to appear discreet in this encounter, there was no mistaking the girlish smile that lit Alanna's face, a face that I'd previously seen colored only by stress.

Clearly, they'd met again since Chick's first visit to the catering shop, which Alanna had reported to me as being without apparent purpose. Clearly, Chick's purpose was now more than apparent to her, and just as clearly, she was interested in his overture. I had originally fantasized that Chick was gay; I'd been proven seriously off base. Was I equally off base in assuming that the problem with Wes and Alanna's marriage was Wes's interest in another woman?

Intrigued as I was by this encounter, I almost failed to notice another. As Chick left Alanna and moved away from the oak, Thad and Kwynn drew nearer. My group was moving toward the street, far too distant to hear anything said at the tree, but I saw Dale Turner greet the kids, who stepped up to him and stopped. Thad shook his hand, the three of them gabbed briefly, then Thad and Kwynn moved onward, toward the street.

What, I wondered, was that all about? I was stumped. How did the kids even know Dale? Everywhere I turned, it seemed, I witnessed puzzling encounters that added questions to a long mental list. Were any of these questions relevant to the mystery I was trying to solve, or had the frustrations of a fruitless investigation merely shifted my suspicions into overdrive?

Within moments, my catalog of suspicions grew all the thicker. As Neil and I descended the back side of the knoll with Roxanne, Carl, Gale, and Lauren, I spotted in the cemetery driveway, near the gate in the stone wall, Whitney Greer. He was no longer with the old attorney, Elliot Coop, but with our housekeeper, Barb Bilsten. They huddled together in animated conversation, oblivious to the passersby who streamed around them toward the street. Whitney had broken into a sweat, due, no doubt, to the dark suit he'd worn that day instead of his usual jaunty seersucker. Barb, with her back to me, was talking with her hands, and from the look of it, the discussion was intense.

Stepping up to them, I asked with a laugh, "Plotting something?"

Barb froze. Then, turning to me, looking guilty as a kid caught with his dad's *Playboy*, she bulled, "Mark! There you are. I've been, uh, looking all over for you."

"Well," I stated the obvious, "here I am."

"So I see." Nervous laughter.

Neil said, "Hi, Whitney. You're planning to be at Thad's dinner tonight, aren't you? I don't think we got your reply."

Suddenly at ease, Barb told us, "That's *just* what we were talking about." This seemed unlikely.

With a weak smile, Whitney pulled a fresh linen handkerchief from his breast pocket and dabbed sweat from the underside of his chin. "Certainly, Neil. Of *course* I'll attend. Sorry for the lapse—it's been a hectic few days."

Roxanne muttered, "*I'll* tell the world."

Whitney continued to dab sweat, telling Barb, "If there's nothing else, I really ought to run." He paused to remove his purple-lensed glasses and blot his eyelids.

"No, Whit, nothing else. Thanks."

Whitney then shook his golden locks, fluttered his lashes, and peered—*with big brown eyes*—directly at me. "There's something I *really* must tend to." With an apologetic sigh, he plopped the Jackie-style glasses back on his face.

"Of course," we told him. "See you tonight." By the time Roxanne had added, "Keep cool," he'd already turned, left the cemetery, and skittered down the street toward his parked car.

"Barb," I asked, "uh . . . ?"

"Sorry, Mark. Not now, okay?" And she too was gone.

The rest of us stood in silence for a moment, sharing a round of confused glances before walking through the gate to the street.

As Neil had ridden to the funeral with me, and Lauren had driven alone, Neil decided to ride with her to lunch, where they'd meet Roxanne, Gale, and Carl. I would drive alone to the office, where I'd scavenge whatever I could from the vending machines. Roxanne and Carl's car was parked near mine, but Lauren had parked on the next block, so she and Neil took their leave, heading down the street, away from us.

Walking toward our cars, Roxanne yakked with her mother, masking her dejection with the sort of grim humor that only a funeral can inspire. Carl and I spoke quietly, weighing our chances of clearing Roxanne and saving his career before the start of that evening's debate in Chicago. With only eight hours remaining, the prognosis was less than rosy.

Roxanne's tone turned sincere as she told her mom, "It seems you and Lauren have reached a state of fragile détente. I'm glad."

Gale breathed a soft laugh. "The sparring was pointless. It was time for a truce. After all, this'll be our sixth night under the same roof. There will surely be more."

As they pattered on in this philosophical vein, the reference to a sixth night finally broke through their small talk and registered in my consciousness. Gale had mentioned it earlier, at the cemetery. And I now recalled the previous evening, when Lauren had asked Milton Tallent, the Manor House proprietor, about extending her visit. He'd told her, "Say no more, Miss Creighton. A sixth night for you as well."

I stopped in my tracks. "Gale?"

The others stopped and turned to me. "Yes, Mark?" said Gale.

"When did you arrive at the Manor House?"

"On Friday." She shrugged. "The day before the wedding. This is Wednesday, and I'm leaving tomorrow—that makes six nights in Dumont."

I paused, rubbing the back of my neck. "I'm confused. Yesterday, Milton said something to Lauren about 'a sixth night for you as well.' "

Gale shrugged again. "So?"

Roxanne and Carl turned to each other with a look of dismay.

I explained to Gale, "But Lauren arrived in town late—on Saturday."

"No, she didn't. She arrived Friday night. I saw her."

Looking stricken, Carl asked through a feeble laugh, "Are you *quite* sure about that, Gale?"

"Yes. Why?"

Carl didn't want to say it, but he was crestfallen to learn that his daughter had been in Dumont in time for the wedding and had failed to attend.

I didn't want to say it, but I suddenly found his daughter to be a highly viable murder suspect.

Back at the *Register*, I greeted Connie in the lobby, climbed the stairs to the newsroom, caught Lucille Haring's eye, and gestured for her to come to my office.

My desk was piled with proofs for my okay and correspondence for my signature; the phone was flashing, bloated with voice mail. As Lucy crossed my outer office, entered, and settled in the chair opposite my desk, I flipped through the paperwork, deciding that nothing was urgent. The voice mail would have to wait; maybe it would just go away, vanishing in an electronic limbo.

Lucy carried, as usual, a stack of research folders under one arm. In her other hand was a freshly opened orange-cellophane bag of Chee-Zee Corn Curleez. "Have some?" she offered.

I was hungry. And there was no point in pretending anymore that I found junk food contemptible. Doug Pierce had started this kick— an afternoon snack as predictable as his morning kringle—and now we were *all* hooked. "Sure, Lucy. Thanks." I grabbed a handful as deftly as any twelve-year-old.

Lucy asked, "How was the funeral?"

I popped the first few Chee-Zees into my mouth. They reminded me of dyed pellets of Styrofoam, chemically altered to mimic cheddar. Pure rapture. I swallowed, then answered, "Nice—as funerals go."

She placed her folders on my desk, staining the top one with an orange thumbprint. "Can I assume there were no dramatic breakthroughs on the case? No one went to pieces in church, wailing an emotional confession?"

I tisked. "Episcopalians don't do that."

"Tut-tut," she quipped, "stiff upper lip." Her upper lip, I noted, was now as orange as her hair.

Downing more Curleez, I sat back. "I'm not sure if this qualifies as a breakthrough, but I discovered an enticing nugget of information just as we were leaving the cemetery." And I told Lucy about Lauren

Creighton's Friday arrival in Dumont, her story that she'd arrived too late for Saturday's ceremony, and the obvious contempt she'd shown for Roxanne upon meeting her at the reception.

Lucy opened a folder and began taking notes. "So the daughter of the groom lied about her whereabouts at the time when her 'evil stepmother' was being set up to take the fall for a murder case."

"It's plausible."

"Want a background check?"

I nodded. "Lauren is an attorney in Denver."

Lucy made note of it. "That'll be easy. I'll get right on it. Anyone else?"

I thought for a moment. My mind was awash with vague, unfounded suspicions regarding just about everyone—from Alanna Scott and Chick Butterly to Barb Bilsten and Whitney Greer—those strange encounters at the cemetery. But there was only so much Lucy could handle at once. "No," I told her, "no one else, not right now."

"Afternoon, boss." There in the doorway was our features editor, Glee Savage, looking perky and fashionable as ever—even in her funeral garb (she'd covered the services, hoping to get a society column out of it).

"Come on in, Glee. Have a chair." There was one remaining in my cramped inner office.

"Chee-Zees!" she said, eyeing the cellophane bag as she sat.

With a grin, Lucy turned the bag toward her.

Glee dipped into the bag, plucking a single Curlee. With her other hand, she waved a fax—"This just in"—then handed it to me over the desk.

I assumed it was not political news or a police development; such items would not have been directed to Glee. I was correct. This was publicity related to the arts, and at first, I couldn't imagine why Glee had seen fit to rush in with it. Skimming the press release, though, I realized with a start that it was possibly relevant, and highly so, to the Ashton case. "Good Lord," I muttered.

"Huh?" asked Lucy, caught with a mouthful of munchies.

"It's an announcement, for immediate release, faxed on the shared letterhead of the Dumont Symphony Orchestra and the Dumont

Players Guild. The contact person listed for more information is, of course, Whitney Greer, executive director of both groups. The upshot is that both the orchestra and the theater have received major endowments, left in trust by the late Betty Gifford Ashton. It concludes, 'Lump-sum disbursements will allow instant, lavish renovation of both the concert hall and the theater building, while generous annuities will assure long-term financial security for both organizations, which have perpetually struggled to meet expenses.' "

"I *thought* you'd be interested." Glee popped a Chee-Zee into her mouth and crunched away.

"God, I saw Whitney as we were leaving the cemetery, and he told me, 'There's something I *really* must tend to.' He practically skipped down the street."

Lucy noted, with heavy understatement, "He didn't waste much time getting the word out."

My fingers drummed the desk. Thinking aloud, I told my editors, "I doubt if Whitney just now learned about this. Presumably, the announcement was already prepared, and he waited till after the funeral to send it."

"Just barely," said Lucy. "The fax machine must have been warmed up and waiting."

Glee reminded us, "It's *wonderful* news for the community."

"It is," I agreed. "No argument with that. But was it 'news' to Whitney?"

"Good question," said Lucy. "I'll bet Elliot would know."

I recalled, "Elliot Coop was standing with Whitney at the service. I wonder if he's back at his office now."

Glee retrieved the press release from my desktop and, adjusting her reading glasses, squinted at the tiny line of type in its header. "This fax was *sent* from Elliot's office."

I stood. "Let's get him on the speakerphone."

And we filed out to the conference table, settling in chairs clustered near the phone. Lucy read the number from her notes, and I dialed.

Elliot's secretary answered, saying I'd just caught him; he was stepping out to lunch. A moment later, the old attorney was on the phone.

After exchanging a few words of greeting and another lament or two for Betty, I got to the point: "Elliot, a fax just arrived in the newsroom regarding the endowments for the theater group and the orchestra. It was sent from your office, so I assume you played some role in setting up the trusts in the Ashton estate."

He chuckled. "Guilty as charged."

"This is fantastic news, obviously, and we'll play it up big in the *Register*, but I just want to make sure I've got the facts straight."

"Admirable, Mr. Manning. How can I be of service?"

"I was curious about the timing of the announcement. I mean, there was nothing about this in the probate report filed on Monday. Were these gifts only recently discovered?"

"Not at all, Mr. Manning. Sorry for the confusion. The endowments, you see, were set up as trusts, which, by their legal nature, are not subject to probate and are not, therefore, a matter of public record. Well"—he chortled—"they're a matter of public record *now*, since Mr. Greer has seen fit to notify the press."

Elliot prattled on, lecturing on the distinction between trusts and other legal instruments. Lucy took copious notes. Glee sneaked back to my desk, snatched the snacks, and returned to the conference table. Slitting the cellophane bag wide open, she plopped the cheesy cornucopia next to the phone. We all grabbed. Elliot cleared his throat. "Does that answer your question, Mr. Manning?"

"Completely. Thank you, Elliot. These trusts, then, came as no surprise to Whitney Greer—they were set up long ago, I take it."

"In fact"—Elliot tittered—"they were not. Well, in a broader sense, I suppose they were. You see, Mr. Greer had curried Mrs. Ashton's goodwill for *years* in an attempt to secure a major endowment for the arts. She had always expressed interest in making such a gift, but it was only recently that she asked me to begin drafting the trusts. Finally, the documents were executed here in my office—not two weeks ago." Lowering his voice, he added, as if confiding a distasteful secret, "The ink was barely dry, Mr. Manning."

Glee stopped chewing; weighing Elliot's words, she licked orange, greasy crumbs from her fingers. Lucy's pen stopped; her eyes slid toward mine. Had Elliot just told us that Whitney Greer may have had a motive for murder?

Meanwhile, something else was beginning to make sense. "Elliot," I asked, "did Blain Gifford know about these trusts?"

"Since Monday, yes. Mr. Gifford is not only Mrs. Ashton's principal heir; he was also named executor of the estate. So he's been responsible for settling all of its finances, including the trusts."

"Can I assume, then, that Blain and Whitney have met with regard to this?"

"Indeed you can. In fact, they spent much of yesterday afternoon at my office, discussing terms of the trust and finalizing details of its disbursement."

I now understood that Blain and Whitney's Tuesday rendezvous had been strictly business, not a lusty assignation. Further, it now seemed that Blain and Whitney's boyhood sexual relationship (if, in fact, there was one) was irrelevant to Betty's death. Still, Blain had had a vested interest in Betty's death (the inheritance), as had Whitney (the arts endowment).

Then I had another thought. "My God," I gasped.

"What's that, Mr. Manning?" rasped the elderly lawyer's voice over the phone.

"Nothing, Elliot. Thanks so much for the information." And we rang off.

The ladies gave me a curious look.

I explained, "I just remembered something. Whitney Greer was not only *at* the wedding reception when Betty was killed; he helped *set it up*. He wired the sound amplification for Barb's woodwind quintet. Both Wesley and Alanna Scott mentioned having seen him 'fiddle with cords,' or words to that effect."

Glee shook her head. "I think you're reading this wrong, Mark. Whitney had a legitimate purpose behind the scenes at the reception. He knows music, he knows staging, and he knows acoustics. There's no one in town with a more passionate love of the performing arts."

Lucy countered, "But that's just the point, isn't it? He loves the arts with a *passion*, and his own press release whined that both the orchestra and the theater 'have perpetually struggled to meet expenses.' He may have seen a quick solution to their financial dilemma."

I hated to say it: "If you ask me, we now must consider Whitney Greer a highly motivated suspect."

Lucy pulled a list from one of her files. "Background check?"

"Sure."

As the afternoon wore on and the eight-o'clock deadline drew nearer, Lucy's list expanded. She subjected not only Lauren Creighton and Whitney Greer, but also Wesley and Alanna Scott, Dale Turner, and his ex-wife, Fawnah Zapp-Turner, to extensive computer checks that included police reports, credit histories, tax rolls, and court records.

We were looking for anything that might suggest some connection to Betty Gifford Ashton or past trouble with the law or with finances. Aside from Dale's difficulties with his faltering business, which he'd been up-front about, we came up blank. So we reviewed these records a second time for any light they might shed on unknown parties who might attempt to scapegoat Dale, Wes, or Roxanne. Finding nothing remarkable—certainly no glaring motive for murder—we even ran checks on the two opposing campaign managers, Blain Gifford and Chick Butterly. But all of this research proved futile, and by mid-afternoon, we were no closer to naming Betty's killer.

At some point, while Lucy was typing away at her terminal, I managed to reach Chick on the phone, and I learned that he had indeed met with Alanna that day—not once, but twice—early, before the funeral, then again that afternoon. To my dismay, he'd lost sight of his mission. I reminded him that my point in suggesting their meeting was to determine whether Alanna wanted children or not.

Chick laughed. "We didn't get *that* far, Mark. We barely broke the ice, but, hey, I think she likes me."

Aarghh. "I don't give a damn if she likes you—what does she think of *Wes*? And does she or doesn't she want to have kids? She claims to fear pregnancy."

"Oh. Gosh. Sorry, it didn't come up. I'll try again tonight." Chick had learned that Alanna and Wes would be working at the going-away party that night, so he'd phoned Lowell Sagehorn, suggesting there might be some late-breaking developments on the Ashton case. Hearing this, the candidate had instructed his campaign manager to stay on top of things, to remain in Dumont for the evening rather than return to Chicago for the debate.

Around three-thirty, Sheriff Pierce visited my office to review where we stood. His investigation had made no more headway than mine had, and we were forced to discuss the possibility of failure.

I asked, "If it came down to it, would you *arrest* Roxanne?"

"Not on the basis of the facts of the case, not as I currently understand them. But who knows? Tomorrow, if Harley Kaiser makes good on his promise to stir the waters at the police-and-fire commission, he could raise an outcry for action. If he feels justified in issuing a warrant, I'll *have* to execute it."

I breathed a sigh of exasperation. "What have we missed, Doug? We must be overlooking something."

With twisted brow, Pierce thought for a moment. "Let's drop in on Vernon. Maybe a refresher in the pathology of the case will ring a new bell."

"Let's go."

So around four o'clock—four hours till deadline—we drove over to the public-safety building for an impromptu visit with the coroner. Fortunately, we caught him in his office and he had time to review his findings with us. Unfortunately, his graphic recapitulation of how Betty had died by electrocution was far more disturbing than enlightening. The torturous details of her final moments didn't begin to hint at why someone had wanted her dead—or who that someone might be.

Shortly after four-thirty, Pierce and I parted ways. He retreated to his office to pore over his files once more, and I left the public-safety building, driving through downtown. Swinging onto First Avenue, I weighed whether to stop at the *Register* again before going home to get ready for Thad's dinner. It would be an early evening, I reminded myself—cocktails at six.

Nearing First Avenue Grill, I recalled our lunch there the day before, when Nancy Sanderson had disputed my claim that Alanna Scott feared pregnancy. Her explanation had been interrupted, and I had yet to hear her version of the story. Since Chick had failed in his mission to clarify Alanna's true feelings, I was now struck that this issue represented a loose end. Whether it had any bearing on the Ashton case, I hadn't a clue, but since I'd run out of other angles to explore, I pulled the car to the curb outside the restaurant and parked.

Stepping inside, I spotted Berta among several other workers arranging the dining room for the party. On the pretext of checking last-minute preparations, I asked to speak to Nancy.

Berta said, "Everything's set for the chocolate meringue, Mr. Manning. Nancy was delighted you enjoyed it so."

"Ah. How nice. But I'd still like to discuss a few other details with her."

"Certainly." Berta waddled away.

Moments later, Nancy appeared from the kitchen, looking not quite frazzled, but busy. "Yes, Mr. Manning? May I help you?"

Not wanting to waste her time, I stepped her over to a quiet corner of the dining room. "Yesterday at lunch, Nancy, we were discussing your friendship with Alanna Scott, and you described yourselves as confidantes."

With a thin smile of studied patience (she had better things to do), she said, "Yes . . . ?"

"We were discussing whether Alanna did or did not want to have a baby at her age. There seemed to be some confusion on this point, but you assured me that Wes and Alanna's marital problems 'have nothing to do with babies, wanted or otherwise.' "

"Mr. Manning"—Nancy raised a finger—"I was entirely out of line yesterday. I should not have spoken of this."

"But I was hoping you could shed some light—"

"My remarks were totally inappropriate. I regret having made them."

"You said that you'd 'warned' Alanna. Has Wesley been—"

"Mr. Manning"—she was firm—"I would truly appreciate dropping this. It's pointless for me to elaborate on a matter that's none of my business. I'm doubtless confused on the particulars anyway."

I opened my mouth to persist, but realized I had already pushed the bounds of polite cajoling. Besides, it was time for me to focus on Thad for a change. This was to be his evening, his party—and it seemed unwise to antagonize the chef.

"Thank you, Nancy." I nodded a farewell. "We'll see you at six."

A few minutes before six o'clock, Neil and I arrived at First Avenue Grill to make sure that all was in order before our guests began to arrive. We had offered a ride to Barb Bilsten, our housekeeper, but she was puttering with something and decided to drive her own car; Chick Butterly would ride with her. Roxanne and Carl would come in their car, stopping at the Manor House to pick up Gale Exner and Lauren Creighton. Thad, our perfect gentleman, would swing by the Wymans' house to pick up Kwynn and her parents, Lee and Lisa.

The restaurant's dining room had been rearranged and decorated for us, as we would be the only patrons that night, some thirty of us. The tables sported flowers and a few balloons, and a wheeled bar had been positioned at one end of the room to supplement the service bar in the kitchen. Wesley Scott was already present, clanging bottles and polishing glasses, prepared for the onslaught. Alanna Scott scurried in and out of the kitchen with Berta and the rest of the staff, spiffing the tables, checking the settings, lighting candles, and placing printed menu cards near the top of each dinner plate. Nancy Sanderson, the proprietor/chef, had devised a simple but elegant three-course meal that offered limited choices for the main dish—tenderloin, swordfish, or a mushroom-and-vegetable lasagna (some of the kids had gone green). We would finish with Nancy's spectacular chocolate meringue.

Nancy stepped up to us. "Is all to your liking?"

"Everything's lovely," Neil told her.

Quiet pride colored her grin.

I added, "You've given us the makings of a memorable evening."

Neil glanced at me with a wan smile—"memorable" indeed. This would be the last night when Thad would sleep under our roof as our child. Sure, he'd be back, there'd be school vacations, but he'd return as a man, a visitor, with a life of his own. Though we intended to give him a festive send-off, there was no mistaking the bittersweet overtones that this evening would carry.

Not to mention the overtones of a murder unsolved. Within two hours (I'd have sworn I heard the ticking of a clock), Lowell Sagehorn would make his opening statement at the televised gubernatorial debate in Chicago. If the identity of Betty Gifford Ashton's killer was still a mystery, which seemed ever more likely, Carl would be dumped from the ticket, bringing an abrupt, ignominious close to his promising political career. Roxanne would confess her lie of omission, in which I had colluded. She would suddenly be seen as the only viable suspect who'd had motive, means, *and opportunity* to commit the crime; our vindictive, hot-dog DA would have her on the fast track to prosecution. As for me, I would lose my journalistic integrity, Doug Pierce's trust and friendship, and just possibly, Neil's respect and affection. Frosting this hellish cake, Raymond Gifford would move forward with Blain's hateful, hypocritical campaign strategy, vilifying and stigmatizing would-be gay parents in Illinois.

Which is why I'd called the party so early, why dinner would have to be ridiculously rushed. By the time the clock struck eight, I wanted the kids somewhere else, with only pleasant memories of this night. I reminded Nancy, "Everyone should be seated by six-thirty. Begin serving at once."

Though she doubtless thought I was nuts, she gave a polite nod.

Neil flashed her a sympathetic glance.

"As you requested," she explained, "I've arranged two round tables seating eight; the others are smaller."

"Perfect." I asked Neil, "Did you bring the place cards?" We'd decided to assign places for guests at the two main tables; others could seat themselves.

Neil pulled the stack of cards from a pocket. "Let's each take a table."

And we went to work. The eight at the head table would be Thad and Kwynn, guests of honor; Neil and I; Kwynn's parents; and Barb and Pierce, whom we considered family. The second table for eight

would include Roxanne, her mother, Carl, his daughter, Chick Butterly, Whitney Greer, and my two editors, Lucille Haring and Glee
Savage.

Nancy surveyed the unassigned tables, checking the available seating against names on a list: the *Register*'s receptionist, Connie; Thad
and Kwynn's school-play director, Mrs. Osborne; three or four other
teachers; six or eight classmates; and several members of Kwynn's
extended family. Nancy did a final count—we'd be thirty-two.

Many of whom had begun to arrive. I'd stressed promptness, as our
cocktail "hour" would be brief. Our guests had taken me at my word,
filing through the door and beelining toward Wes at the bar. I knew
everyone, with the exception of a few of Thad's teachers and Kwynn's
relatives, so Neil and I began to mingle and play host, greeting by
name those we knew, introducing ourselves to those we didn't. Berta
spotted us working the crowd and, realizing we were too busy to fend
for ourselves at the bar, offered to bring us drinks from the kitchen,
which we gratefully accepted.

We had glasses in hand by the time Thad arrived with Kwynn and
her parents, so we were able to join in an impromptu toast, greeting
the soon-to-be collegians, followed by a warm round of applause.
Nancy had switched on some jazzy cocktail music, and the gathering
now felt like a party. It was almost enough to make me forget that
the evening was headed toward a regrettable climax.

Pierce stepped over from the bar and shook my hand.

I eyed the tumbler of clear liquid in his left hand. "Water?"

"Thought I'd better keep a clear head tonight."

"Ah." I downed a goodly slurp of Japanese vodka, bracing myself
for whatever lay ahead.

Roxanne had her usual mineral water (I'd made sure Nancy had
some Perrier on hand), but Carl, like me, needed fortitude, so he'd
opted for Scotch. They both stood with Thad and Kwynn, smiling
and gabbing good wishes.

Chick had arrived with Barb, and both now stood at the bar, ordering drinks, clustered in conversation with Whitney Greer. I noted
that Barb kept leaning close, speaking into Whitney's ear about something. I also noted that Chick's cell phone was conspicuously dis-

played in a holster on his belt. He would doubtless be in touch with Lowell Sagehorn in Chicago from time to time during the evening. Though the debate would be broadcast only in Illinois, the moment Lowell dumped Carl from his ticket, we'd know about it. Right now, though, Chick seemed to have little interest in the election; his glance kept following Alanna about the room. They exchanged goo-goo-eyed grins whenever they confidently, but mistakenly, felt unobserved.

"Hey," said Neil under his breath, nudging me with an elbow, "he dresses up pretty hot."

Following his glance, I saw that Dale Turner, the tent guy, had just entered the restaurant, wearing a nice summer suit of navy-blue poplin. "I've noticed," I told Neil with a laugh. "Did you see him at the funeral today? Not bad."

"Clothes make the man." Neil sipped his vodka through a lecherous grin.

"Not to sound ungracious, but why is he here?"

Neil shrugged. "I assume Kwynn invited him. Dale's her uncle."

"Duh. Of course. She asked me if she could invite a few people." I now recalled Kwynn encountering Dale at Saturday's wedding reception. She'd said, "Hi, Uncle Dale. Everything looks great." The comment had reminded me that I was still something of an outsider in small-town Dumont, where everyone seemed to be related. I'd forgotten this detail due to the general commotion of the lawn party and the particular diversion of Betty's electrocution. This explained not only why Dale was at tonight's party, but also why Kwynn and Thad had paused to greet him at that morning's burial service—two minor mysteries solved.

What's more, Dale's presence reminded me that Roxanne, Carl, and I weren't the only people with a vested interest in a speedy resolution to Betty's murder. Dale feared that the whole atrocity had been staged to precipitate his professional and financial ruin, a theory that still made sense to me. It was not only plausible, but appealing— because it pointed so convincingly away from Roxanne, who had no connection whatever to the handsome electrician. Hoping to help him, I felt all the more motivated to unmask Betty's killer, but even as I formed these thoughts, precious minutes were slipping away.

"It's nearly six-thirty, Mr. Manning." Nancy's words yanked me back to the moment. "Shall I begin asking your guests to be seated?"

I glanced at my watch. "Yes, please."

Within five or ten minutes, everyone had settled at table; then the staff began serving salads, also pouring wine for the adults. It had to happen—someone clanked a glass, one of Thad's classmates—and a chorus of "Speech, speech" rippled briefly through the room.

Neil laughed softly. I smiled at Thad. He stood.

"Gosh. I wasn't prepared for this." His theatrical training had paid off—he spoke with perfect composure and confidence, making every word heard and understood. And I had a hunch he had indeed prepared for this. "I want to thank all of you for coming tonight, but most important, I want to thank Mark and Neil, my two dads, for hosting this dinner and making the evening so special for Kwynn and me."

Kwynn applauded us, quickly joined by the others.

Thad continued, "Growing up in Dumont . . . ," and he told everyone some history of his childhood, grateful for his privileged upbringing, but he kept coming back to Neil and me, "who helped me finally 'find myself' and who built a family for me, in spite of my protests, just when I needed it most . . ."

Oh, how I wished Blain Gifford could have been there. Though Neil and I had not adopted Thad, we could have—perhaps we should have—and the legality of that relationship, recognized by the state, would be a clear reflection of the bond that now existed between us and our child. Or rather, our adult son.

Neil felt for my hand, and as our fingers locked, we listened to Thad's stirring testimonial to his past, his dreamy yet reasoned vision of a future that would always find its roots back in Dumont, back in the house on Prairie Street. Someone at another table had begun sniffling happy little tears, and sure, I was getting a bit misty myself. Barb looked so choked up, I thought she might collapse, blubbering, in her salad.

Thad's speech was truly a rite of passage. Before our very eyes, it seemed, he shed the cocoon of boyhood and donned the mantle of maturity, stepping into the world at large. This, on the same day when we had witnessed another rite of passage, that of Betty Gifford Ashton, who had left this world behind.

When Thad finished, we all stood, clapping—not boisterously, but warmly—it was one of those moments. I needed to touch him. He surely sensed this, for he stepped around the table to hug me, then Neil, and we all got sort of soppy. Holding both guys in my arms, I lifted my left wrist to check my watch—ten minutes had passed. "I think we'd better eat."

Then the meal began in earnest. There were a few toasts; Kwynn stood and spoke; Mrs. Osborne paid a brief tribute to her two favorite students. But people kept eating, and I kept catching Nancy's eye, making sure the service moved along.

During dessert (the chocolate meringue prompted an ovation for Nancy, who accepted our adulation with genteel modesty), Neil and I rose and began circulating from table to table, wedding-style, briefly visiting each of our guests. At Roxanne and Carl's table, I sensed a spirit of easy conviviality and was pleased to note that even the in-laws, Gale and Lauren, were now conversing, not sniping.

"How are the winters in Denver?" Gale asked Lauren.

Carl's daughter answered, "If you like snow, they're fabulous."

"We know all about *snow*," said the mom from Minneapolis.

Roxanne said to her stepdaughter, "Carl tells me you're rehabbing an old house. Sounds like quite a project."

"Yup—and I've got the scars to prove it." Lauren displayed a few slow-healing abrasions on her hands and forearms.

Carl shook his head. "I still can't believe it—little Lauren, wielding a hammer."

"I'm a tad amazed myself, but it seems I've blossomed into a jack-of-all-trades—carpenter, plumber, electrician, *and* lawyer."

Carl wagged a finger in good-natured admonition. "I suggest you concentrate on your lawyering, young lady."

"Yes, Daddy. I'll remember that."

During this conversation, Chick Butterly turned away from us in his chair, as if to excuse himself while placing a call on his cell phone. As a rule, I don't approve of phones at the table, but in this instance,

I was glad Chick didn't leave the room. Assuming he was speaking to Lowell Sagehorn, I wondered what was being said. To my disappointment, I couldn't hear a thing.

Though Chick did not leave the table, Whitney Greer did. He slipped over to the head table to hobnob with Barb, whose manner again turned secretive.

Coffee was being poured, so Neil and I returned to our seats to finish dessert before it was cleared. It was well past seven now, little more than half an hour till deadline. Forking the last of the meringue and delivering it to my mouth, I paused, letting my tongue loll in the rum and the chocolate.

For a moment, it felt as if time were suspended, and sitting there, I observed the patter and interaction of our thirty-some guests, hearing snatches of things that had been said throughout the evening, growing more convinced that the answer to the riddle of Betty's death was right there in the room with me. I ticked through my most recent list of active suspects: Wesley and Alanna Scott, Lauren Creighton, Whitney Greer, and a long shot, Chick Butterly, all present. Also suspected, but not present, were Blain Gifford and another long shot, some unknown enemy of Dale Turner's. Mulling all this, I dabbed my lips, set my napkin on the table—and suddenly choked.

"Mark?" said Neil with a wary smile. "Are you all right?"

"Sorry." I laughed. "Must've been a fleck of coconut."

The others at the table returned to their conversations.

But it wasn't coconut that had choked me. It was the answer to the riddle—at least I *thought* it was. Something had clicked, something that had been said that night. To be certain, though, I needed just one other kernel of information: What had Nancy tried to tell me at lunch yesterday? Seeing her pouring coffee at the next table, I excused myself, stepped over to her, and asked if we could talk.

"Is something wrong, Mr. Manning?"

"Nothing at all. Everything has been wonderful, Nancy. But I need to have a word with you."

We stepped to the far side of the dining room, which was not occupied, away from the din and clatter of the crowd. Sternly, Nancy said, "I hope this isn't about—"

I nodded. "Wes and Alanna."

"Mr. Manning, I've already told you: I'll have no part in spreading gossip."

"I appreciate that. I have reason to believe, though, that this is somehow related to Mrs. Ashton's death."

"You can't be serious."

"I am. And I'll explain completely—soon enough. But first, I need a simple yes-or-no answer from you."

"Do you think this is a game, Mr. Manning? I will *not* play twenty questions with you."

"I don't have twenty questions, Nancy. I have just one. And I need the answer. It's important."

With strained patience, she told me, "I can't promise I'll answer, but you're welcome to ask."

Leaning near, I asked a brief, direct question, concluding, "Yes or no?"

She paused, then arched her brows, looking instantly at ease. "Well. Since you already seem to know—yes, Mr. Manning, you're quite right."

I surprised her with a quick kiss. "Thanks, Nancy." And I rushed back to the table.

Neil had been watching me. "What was *that* all about?"

Coyly, I told him, "Just paying our compliments to the chef."

"Uh-huh."

"Gosh," I said to the table, tapping my watch, "it's seven-thirty already." I pushed my empty coffee cup away, signaling the meal's end.

Kwynn's parents glanced at each other, wondering what was wrong with me.

Barb cracked, "Ready for bed, Gramps? The night is *young*, Mark."

"I know, I know. Everyone's welcome to stay for more coffee or drinks, but I just thought the kids might want to go out on their own tonight." I fished a wad of bills from my pocket. "Maybe they'd like to go bowling."

From the next table, Roxanne blurted, *"Bowling?"*

Over my shoulder, I told her, "They do it under black light now."

Thad explained, "They call it 'midnight bowling,' Roxanne. One of the alleys in town has been converted to a teen bar. Pretty cool—everything *glows*." Thad and his contemporaries had never seen black light before, having missed the disco era entirely, not to mention the psychedelic era before that. Now, a rather frumpy old pastime had reinvented itself and was all the rage again—at least in Dumont.

Roxanne allowed, "Whatever turns you on—I guess."

Thad asked, "Really, Mark? You don't mind if we leave? I mean, I don't want you guys feeling *ditched* or anything."

I laughed, handing him some twenties. "Have fun. Not too late though. Big day tomorrow."

And within two minutes, Thad, Kwynn, and their pals had gotten up, said their good-byes, and rushed out to spend a last night together before parting ways and leaving town for college.

"The bar's open," I told the remaining adults, some two dozen of us. "If you'd care to relax with an after-dinner drink and enjoy some conversation, by all means, be my guest."

Instantly, chairs scraped the tile floor as several people rose to visit Wes at the bar. Nancy and her crew began circulating with coffee again, refilling cups.

Sitting at the table, Neil leaned over his elbow toward me. "Why the big rush to get rid of the kids?"

Obliquely, I answered, "I'm afraid the evening may soon get a little dicey, and there's no point in upsetting them."

Neil looked at his watch, then nodded knowingly. "Ah. The eight-o'clock deadline." With a sigh of defeat, he added, "Less than thirty minutes remaining."

Chick, I noticed, was on the phone again with his party's standard-bearer, reporting, I presumed, that things looked bleak in Dumont. It seemed all but certain that Carl was to be dumped from the ticket. Neil was correct in assuming that I wanted to spare the kids the emotional aftermath that would descend upon the dining room if and when Carl got the ax. What Neil didn't realize, however, was that I had no intention of witnessing the dissolution of Carl's career. I intended to unmask a killer within the next few minutes, and *that's* why I'd been so eager to get rid of the kids. (Most of them would doubtless have enjoyed the coming spectacle beyond measure, but still, the more responsible plan was to let them read of these developments in Thursday morning's *Register*.)

The others were getting settled with their drinks and coffee, engaged in conversation at their tables. There was wistful talk, naturally, of kids and college and empty nests, but invariably, each of the tables turned to the topic on everyone's mind—the unsolved murder that had hung over the collective conscience of Dumont for the past five days. Before long, guests began mingling from table to table, trading ideas and floating hypotheses. Everyone's fragmented chitchat then seemed to congeal, and the entire dining room was now engaged in a single, focused group discussion.

"So tell us, Sheriff," one of the teachers asked Pierce, "when do you think we'll have some final answers regarding Mrs. Ashton?"

Sitting across the table from me, Pierce had been fingering the teaspoon next to his cup; he set it aside. "When? Not soon enough, I'm afraid." Glancing over to the Creightons' table, he added, "Sorry, Roxanne."

Roxanne and Carl exchanged a blank, dour glance.

Pierce said, "My department has given this case our every effort—and Mark and the *Register*'s staff have pitched in too—but so far, the solution to Betty's murder remains a mystery."

"Actually," I announced, checking my watch—twenty minutes remaining—"the mystery is now solved."

Predictably, the room erupted with astonished babble, skeptical comments, and a flurry of questions. "Uh, Mark," said Pierce through a cautious laugh, "is there something you haven't told me?"

"There is, Doug. Sorry. I didn't mean to keep you out of the loop, but I just now figured it out. Something was said tonight. Shortly after that, everything started to make sense."

The room grew dead silent. He asked, "You're sure?"

"I am." Needless to say, all heads were turned to me. The restaurant staff, sensing the drama of the moment, had abandoned their tasks and gathered near the kitchen and the bar. It seemed appropriate for me to stand, so I did.

Doug sat back, arms crossed comfortably, ready for anything. Lucille Haring, I noticed, already had a steno pad and tape recorder in front of her on the table—she correctly sniffed a page-one story in the making. Chick was punching a number into his cell phone, trying to reach Sagehorn again. Neil turned his chair for a more comfortable view of me, grinning proudly. Roxanne eyed me with a look of wary amazement, tapping her watch as if to say, Well? Get the hell *on* with it.

"Murder," I began on a philosophical note, "is the most heinous of crimes, one that demands detection and exposure as a matter of simple justice."

Roxanne rolled her eyes.

"In the case of Mrs. Ashton's death, however, the need to name her killer is especially urgent. The victim was a cherished and benevolent member of the community, whose loss is felt by all. What's more, the circumstances of her death threaten to have a profound impact on friends of mine, who need a speedy resolution to the crime. Timing, as they say, is everything."

Roxanne now rolled her hands in a cartwheel gesture, urging me along—I'd wasted a full minute.

"As all of you know, Mrs. Ashton died by electrocution at my home on Saturday, while attending a wedding reception for Roxanne and Carl Creighton, whom Neil and I consider among our closest friends. As you may also know, suspicions arose at once that the motive for Mrs. Ashton's death traced back to Carl's political campaign. There are some who now consider Roxanne herself the prime suspect in this case. As a friend, I found it impossible to imagine that she would—or could—stoop to murder under any circumstances. As an investigative journalist, I'm happy to report that my trust in her was justified. Roxanne had no complicity in Betty Gifford Ashton's death."

Carl cleared his throat. Speaking to me but eyeing his watch, he said, "Uh, Mark—we've known all along who *didn't* do it." He, of course, was still laboring under the assumption that Roxanne had had no opportunity to commit the crime, an assumption bolstered by Roxanne's lie of omission—and mine. Now, thank God, there was no need to dissuade him of his theory.

I told Carl, "I appreciate the stress you've felt in the past few days, knowing that the fallout from this crime threatened both your career and your new wife."

He exhaled a weary breath. "It's been terrible. It *has* hit awfully close to home."

"Ironically, it turns out, the key to unraveling Mrs. Ashton's murder does indeed hit close to home. It's something of a family matter."

"Meaning"—Carl nodded, thinking—"the motive was the inheritance?"

"No. Let's back up." I paused to ask Nancy, "Could I have some water, please?" My throat had gotten dry.

As the room swirled with whispers, Nancy poured the water, brought it to me, and stepped aside. I drank some, then set down the glass.

"Lauren," I said, "when your father announced his plans to marry Roxanne, to bring her into your family, what did you think?"

The young lady in black looked stunned. Straightening her back, she answered, "Really, Mark, that's awfully personal. I'd rather not say."

"Truth is, you resented having Roxanne in your father's life. You saw it as an affront to your mother."

Roxanne and Carl glanced at each other, incredulous. Gale Exner eyed the younger woman with a steely gaze.

I continued, "In your mind, Lauren, you had vilified Roxanne to such an extent that you skipped the wedding. At the reception, you apologized, saying you'd just then arrived late in town. But that was a lie. You arrived on Friday, the night before, checking in at the Manor House sometime after Roxanne's mother did. As we all know, Betty Gifford Ashton died on Saturday afternoon at the reception; she was electrocuted when she dipped her handkerchief into a vat of ice water. A live extension cord had been rigged to fall into the water, and the fuse on that circuit had been rigged not to blow, requiring a measure of electrical savvy on the part of the culprit—"

"Mr. Manning," Lauren interrupted coldly, "what in hell are you driving at?"

"It's arguable, Lauren, that you had a *motive* for committing this crime—framing or possibly killing your reviled new stepmother. You had the *means* to rig the electrocution—you told us tonight you've become a jack-of-all-trades, an electrician, while rehabbing your house in Denver. Most important, you had the *opportunity* to set up the crime—during the wedding, when you were supposedly still on the road but actually here in town, with your exact whereabouts unaccounted for."

Lauren rose from the table. I expected a defensive outburst, but instead, Lauren sighed deeply. "I'm sorry," she said to no one in particular. "I suppose I've brought this on myself—these suspicions. I should have been more willing to give Roxanne a chance. Obviously, I should not have lied about my 'late arrival.' " She turned to Carl. "Sorry, Pops, but the honest-to-God truth is that I just couldn't bring myself to attend the wedding. Yes, I was already here in Dumont, but I couldn't face the reality of your second marriage. I hope I was wrong about Roxanne. I hope you'll be good for each other. And I hope you'll believe me when I assure you that I never plotted against her— or anyone. I had nothing to do with what happened to Mrs. Ashton."

Carl stood next to his daughter. "Of course, honey. I believe you." They shared a teary embrace.

I told Lauren, "I believe you too. And I apologize for seeming to accuse you." I turned, telling everyone else in the room, "Lauren's circumstances may seem incriminating, and in fact, throughout the day, my suspicions rose against her. But I was mistaken."

Carl and his daughter sat again. Roxanne leaned to whisper supporting words.

At the same table, Whitney Greer turned in his chair to face me. "After all this buildup, Mark, do you mean to tell us that you have *not* unraveled the mystery of Betty's death?"

"No, Whitney, I merely mean to demonstrate the danger in jumping to conclusions, especially when the stakes are so high, as they always are with murder."

As these words sank in, I paused to sip my water. I then continued, "For instance, just today you announced, with considerable fanfare, that the local theater group and orchestra, which you manage, had received enormous financial trusts from the Ashton estate. I later found out that you'd been attempting for years to secure these trusts, and 'the ink was barely dry' on them when Betty was killed. What's more, last Saturday, you helped set up the wind quintet's amplification for the wedding reception, and your backstage theatrical experience would give you sufficient know-how to rig the fuse box, with predictable results. In other words, Whitney, one might say that you had the motive, means, and opportunity to electrocute Betty Gifford Ashton."

Amid the stir of whispers that rose from the room, Whitney rose from his chair, bracing himself with one hand on the table. With his other hand, he removed his big tinted glasses and wiped his brow. "I'm mortified," he told me, "to think that my actions could suggest that I'd played a role in Betty's death. I hadn't realized that the timing of my press release might give the impression of gloating or opportunism, and I apologize most sincerely for this lack of insight."

Replacing his glasses, he told the whole room, "I always thought of Betty as a dear friend, not just a benefactor. She had a rare passion for the arts, a passion that I daresay is matched by my own. She took great delight in knowing she had the special means to support the arts in Dumont, and thanks to her final gesture of philanthropy, live theater and live orchestral music will continue to thrive in our community. As a friend and as a fellow arts enthusiast, I loved Betty. Please believe me: I would never think of harming her." Whitney sat again. In the silence, he turned to look at me.

"I believe you, Whitney, and I apologize for seeming to accuse you." To the rest of the room, I said, "Whitney's circumstances, like Lauren's, may seem incriminating. For a while, I had my suspicions, but I was mistaken."

Chick Butterly lowered the cell phone from his face, covering its mouthpiece with his hand. "If greed wasn't the motive behind Betty's death, what was?"

"Nothing." I paused for effect. "Nothing at all."

"Huh?"

"When a wealthy person dies under suspicious circumstances, we naturally ask, 'Who had the most to gain?' It might have been Betty's heirs; it might have been the beneficiaries of her philanthropy. Or, in this case, it *might* have been political interests in a squeaky-tight governor's race that she was funding. This was an especially perplexing angle, because it seemed to point in both directions; conceivably, her death could be seen as a boon to either the Republican or the Democratic campaign. Which led me to entertain suspicions of both Blain Gifford and—sorry, Chick—you too."

Alarmed, Chick said into his phone, "I'll get right back to you," and flipped it shut.

I laughed. "But I was way off base. Betty didn't die as the result of political treachery. It turns out, there was *no* motive to kill Betty. She was a random victim."

"Good heavens!"

I turned to see Connie, the *Register*'s receptionist, sitting bug-eyed with a hand to her mouth. She asked, "Are you saying there's a *madman* on the loose in Dumont? Do you mean that Mrs. Ashton was killed for no reason at all?"

"No, Connie. The killer had a purpose, all right, but Mrs. Ashton wasn't the true target of the crime. This was a scenario that got more and more attractive as the investigation progressed. In the end, it seemed that an unknown enemy had plotted against one of three possible targets—Roxanne, Wesley Scott, or Dale Turner." I pointed out these people as I spoke, explaining to the crowd, "Wes was the bartender at Saturday's reception, and Dale had installed the tents and the wiring. Because of the sequence of events leading up to Betty's electrocution, as captured on a home videotape, I reasoned that either someone had tried to frame Roxanne or someone had tried to frame Wes—or murder him. Later, we realized that the tragedy could also have been staged to victimize Dale, the electrician. My instincts told me all along that Roxanne was not a part of this equation, which left me wondering who would plot lethal mischief against Wes or Dale."

"Hold on," said Roxanne, perplexed. "This all makes sense, but you said earlier that the key to Mrs. Ashton's murder could be found in a 'family matter.' "

"Exactly. But the family matter has nothing to do with the Ashton family."

Roxanne (I saw it coming) rolled her eyes, then slumped back in her chair.

"We're getting there," I assured her—and everyone. Checking my watch, I noted that I had some ten scant minutes to prompt an arrest.

From the bar, Wes said, "I follow your logic, Mr. Manning, and I admit, after the tragedy, I was scared senseless to think what might have happened to *me*. I've been losing sleep over this, turning it every which way, but the truth is, I can't think of a soul who'd be plotting to harm me, let alone kill me."

I nodded. "Good point. And that's where this gets sort of . . . sticky. I'm sorry, Wes; sorry, Alanna. It seems everyone's aware of your marital problems, and I don't mean to make them worse. I'm reluctant to discuss such private matters publicly, but a murder has been committed, and there's plenty more at stake."

Alanna moved from the kitchen doorway toward the bar, where she and Wes stood looking into each other's eyes, wondering where I was headed.

I told the room, "Wesley and Alanna Scott own A Moveable Feast, the company that catered the wedding reception. Both Wes and Alanna had complete access behind the scenes during the party and earlier, during setup. What's more, it was Wes who actually moved the bottle that released the extension cord, letting it slip into the vat of ice water, killing Mrs. Ashton. Sadly, Wes and Alanna have been having difficulty in their marriage of late, but there's some disagreement as to the root of the problem. At first, it seemed to be the issue of children—to have them or not. Then I began to suspect that Wes was involved with another woman, but I was wrong. No, neither of the Scotts was responsible for Mrs. Ashton's death. Dale Turner was."

The handsome man in the blue poplin suit sat back in his chair, staring at me in disbelief as the room buzzed with conversation. Sheriff Pierce tensed, on full alert. Lucy drew a new grid on her notepad. Glee Savage was scribing shorthand. And behind me at the head table, Kwynn's mother, Dale's sister, Lisa Turner Wyman, mumbled, "No, Mark—what are you saying?"

I raised a hand, seeking quiet. When the noise ebbed, I explained, "Dale and Alanna have been having an affair, and *this*, of course, is the root of the problem in the Scotts' marriage. Nancy Sanderson tried to set me straight on this point when I lunched here at the Grill yesterday, but she hadn't quite made her point when Thad and Kwynn arrived at the table. She then refused to say more, which not only frustrated me, but mystified me. Just tonight, though, I was reminded that Dale is Kwynn's uncle, a crucial point I had entirely forgotten. Suddenly, Nancy's odd behavior made sense to me; she was reluctant to make unseemly remarks about Dale in front of his own niece. But once I had established the connection between Dale and Kwynn—the 'family matter' I spoke of earlier—the pieces of the puzzle quickly fell together."

"*First*," said Dale, rising, angry, "you're out of your mind. Alanna and I have *never* engaged in even the slightest impropriety."

"Absolutely not," affirmed Alanna, hanging on to Wesley's arm.

"*Second*," Dale continued, "if—"

"Wait," I stopped him. "Save your denials till you've heard me out." I told everyone, "Not only has Dale been having an affair with Alanna"—this I knew from Nancy's answer to my single yes-or-no question—"but also, he's tried coaxing her, unsuccessfully, to divorce Wes, marry Dale, and merge her thriving catering business with his floundering tent business"—this was my own conjecture.

Dale, Alanna, and Wes each blurted something, but I kept going: "I'd become convinced that Dale was the intended *victim* of this crime, perpetrated by some unknown enemy, but inconsistencies in his story, coupled with information from his ex-wife, now make it apparent that Dale himself was the perpetrator."

I quickly ran through these additional points: "When Doug Pierce and I met with Dale on Monday, he portrayed himself as something of an introvert, a divorced man without friends who felt uncomfortable socializing, even with the Scotts. On Tuesday, though, Fawnah Zapp-Turner portrayed her ex-husband in an altogether different light, an extrovert who 'could never get enough' sex and who chided himself for marrying a younger woman. Alanna is two years *older* than Dale, smart too, which he doubtless finds attractive after his failed marriage to Fawnah. This morning, Dale attended Betty's burial with the Scotts as a threesome, looking like the best of friends, countering his earlier statement that they never socialized. Fawnah also made apparent the full extent of Dale's financial troubles, while Dale himself had noted the enviable success of the Scotts' business."

One more sip of water. Then I posited, "Dale, therefore, rigged the fuse box and the extension cord—it was baby simple for an electrician to plot and execute this. Then he conveniently left his camcorder running to capture the 'accident' on tape—not at all the lucky coincidence that it first seemed to be. Dale figured there were two possible outcomes: either Wes would electrocute himself, or Wes would be implicated by the tape as causing the electrocution of someone else. Either outcome would presumably get Wes out of the way so Dale could move in on the unsuspecting Alanna. And the plan might have worked—if the random victim had not been one of the community's most prominent citizens and if the tape had not implicated Roxanne more strongly than Wes, triggering an extensive investigation into what should have passed as a cut-and-dried accident."

I checked my watch: five minutes till deadline. Clearing my throat, I concluded, "Dale Turner, I accuse you of the murder of Betty Gifford Ashton."

Pierce stood. "Well, Dale?"

With a frustrated toss of his hands, Dale told him, "This is preposterous." He tried to reason, "This is *hearsay*, Sheriff. It all hinges on the outrageous accusation that Alanna and I have been . . . *involved* somehow. That's nonsense. I've already denied it, and so has she. There's no way you can possibly prove—"

"You *snake!*" shouted Alanna, moving one step forward from the bar. "I *loved* you. But I *told* you—I'll never divorce Wes—certainly not for the sake of some *business* merger."

"*Please*, Alanna . . ." Dale made a shushing gesture with both hands.

"So you tried to *kill* him? Is that how you planned to 'win' me? Why, you—"

"I didn't think he'd *die*. I just meant to get him into trouble. It was a spur-of-the-moment idea. On Saturday afternoon, right before the party started, I noticed that there was no blender at the bar. I thought I'd better get the unneeded extension cord out of harm's way, but then the plan just sort of fell together. It had nothing to do with Mrs. Ashton . . . ," Dale rambled on.

But Pierce had already heard enough. Moving to Dale's table, he recited the rights and readied the handcuffs.

Alanna spat a robust expletive. (Where had she picked *that* up?)

"No, Dale," sobbed his sister, Kwynn's mom. "This can't be happening . . ."

A bucket of ice crashed to the floor, spattering like broken glass, as Wes rushed from the bar to yell at his wife, "So you were 'afraid' to get pregnant, huh?"

(Nancy had been correct. Alanna did indeed want a baby, but not Wesley's. She had pined to carry Dale's child.)

"It's too *late*," Alanna pleaded.

"It sure as hell is *now*," Wes agreed, struggling to remove his apron, slapping it on the floor, then bolting toward the door.

In the doorway, Pierce backed off, letting Wes pass and thunder out to the street. Then, turning first to give me a nod of thanks, Pierce hauled Dale out to a waiting cruiser he'd already called.

Pierce wasn't the only one busy on his phone. It was three minutes before eight, and Chick was trying to get through to Lowell Sagehorn.

By now, Alanna had collapsed in tears, and Nancy stepped over to comfort her. "I tried to *warn* you," she reminded the younger woman, escorting her to the privacy of the kitchen.

"*Lowell*," said Chick into his phone, breathless, "thank God I caught you . . ."

While Chick told the candidate the good news, I told everyone else, "I must apologize for the unusual turn this evening has taken. It's a shame you had to witness the airing of so much dirty laundry." Whom did I think I was kidding? With the exception of Dale's sister, those remaining in the room hadn't minded in the least—they'd lapped up every delicious detail, enjoying every dramatic moment. "Unfortunately," I explained, "we had no control over the timing, as Mr. Creighton's political career was at stake."

Chick was saying into the phone, "That's right, Lowell. The killer has been arrested, and there was no connection whatever to your campaign. Your running mate—and his new wife—have unequivocally been cleared of any complicity in the death of Betty Gifford Ashton."

I told the room, "You're welcome to stay as long as you like. Please, try to put these disturbing events behind you. Do relax, and have another drink."

Chick checked his watch: one minute till eight. "Lowell, is Blain Gifford nearby? Yes, I'm sure he's very busy, but this is urgent. Tell that little prick I need to talk to him—right now. Tell him I need to ask him about summer camp."

Berta swept up the spilled ice.

Another waitress took over bar duty.

And the rest of us kept her damned busy.

EPILOGUE

Farewells

UNTIMELY DEPARTURES

Bidding farewell to dual tragedies, our community begins to heal

By MARK MANNING
Publisher, Dumont Daily Register

Sep. 12, DUMONT WI—Our community said farewell yesterday to a woman who not only called Dumont her home, but assured that our quality of life would continue to thrive long after her passing. Betty Gifford Ashton, more than anyone else in our town's history, gave life to the arts and still makes them accessible to all.

The sting of calamity that marked Mrs. Ashton's death last Saturday has now been softened some. As reported on page 1 of today's *Register*, her alleged killer was exposed and arrested in dramatic developments last night, assuring the Ashton family and the community at large that justice will indeed be served.

Ironically, the man who now stands accused of murder was himself a contributing member of the community, an active booster of many civic and fraternal causes. Dale Turner had struggled to establish the success of a specialized tent and awning business, but circumstances conspired against him.

Sadly, Mr. Turner resorted to a desperate scheme meant to reap not only financial security, but a romantic conquest as well. His folly—and failure—has made his own situation immeasurably worse. What's more, Dumont's grief is only heightened by the knowledge that Mrs. Ashton died so needlessly and arbitrarily.

Mrs. Ashton has now left Dumont, and Mr. Turner's days here are surely numbered. Can we draw any meaning, perhaps inspiration, from the different circumstances of their untimely departures?

Murder has its price—not only for the victim and perpetrator, but for those whose lives have been touched by both. Though Mrs. Ashton and Mr. Turner came from different social circles, they shared common roots in the town we call home. Let us bid our farewells with a respectful measure of regret, but strive to move forward, healing the collective wound of this dual tragedy. ❏

Thursday, September 12

For the town of Dumont, Wednesday had been a day of painful farewells. For the household on Prairie Street, Thursday would be a day filled with farewells of its own—none of them quite painful, but all of them tinged by bittersweet emotion.

I awoke that morning rested and fresh from a night not dogged by dreams. Proven groundless was my suspicion that clues had lurked within my dreams since Sunday, tantalizing clues that I'd hoped might help me solve the riddle of Betty Gifford Ashton's electrocution. So much for the insights of my sleeping mind. Roxanne was not, after all, a murderous harridan. Chick Butterly's beautiful brown eyes betrayed no secret desire to bed Blain Gifford. And even though I was now all but certain that Blain was indeed a closeted gay Republican, I knew he'd had nothing to do with his aunt's death.

The morning dawned with a clear sky and a cool breeze that whispered of autumn's arrival. By seven o'clock, the entire household was up and about—it was the start of a busy day that would mark big transitions in our lives. As usual, the focus of activity was downstairs in the kitchen.

Barb fussed near the sink, re-creating the eggy farewell casserole that had been enjoyed prematurely the day before. She worked quietly, intently, without joining the conversation, not even contributing a crack or two. She'd been preoccupied for days, but this morning, it seemed, she had transcended to another plane altogether. I assumed she was having a tough time adjusting to the reality of Thad's imminent departure—we all were.

Thad himself was up and dressed (a rarity for that hour), wired with excitement and a measure of trepidation. While smearing peanut butter on a bagel, he sat with Roxanne and Carl, gabbing about his move West. "The flight takes four hours, but because of the time difference, I get there two hours after I leave—pretty cool."

Roxanne smiled, enjoying his enthusiasm. "I assume your housing arrangements are all set."

"Sure, all set. But I won't have a car at first." One of his legs was pumping, tapping his heel on the floor, burning off nervous energy.

I explained, "I'll drive it out in a few weeks, after he's gotten settled."

Neil, who'd been having an earnest discussion with Chick Butterly, turned to ask, "What about *me?*"

"You can go. We'll just have to coordinate our schedules."

Thad got up from the table with a second bagel, telling the others, "I'll see you before you leave—we need to say good-bye." Then he tore from the kitchen and bounded upstairs to do the last of his packing.

"Speaking of schedules," said Carl to Roxanne, "does your mother need a ride to the airport?"

"She's got one. Before we left the Grill last night, Lauren offered to drive her. They both have flights home this morning."

I asked, only half joking, "Do you trust them alone together in the car? Are you sure they won't be at each other's throat?"

Roxanne smirked. "They'll deal with it."

Chick said to Roxanne and Carl, "I'm nearly packed. How about you? We need to head south and hit the campaign trail." Then he added to Barb, "*After* the egg-thing, of course."

Barb turned around with a look that said, You'd *better* eat it.

Neil mused, "Who'd have thought? Rox stumping."

She amplified, "Yoked and stumping."

Chick assured everyone, "And she's a credit to the ticket."

Carl chortled. "I'm just grateful I'm still *on* the ticket. Last night, around seven-thirty, my hopes were sinking fast."

I pooh-poohed him. "It was all wrapped up by then."

Neil told me, "It was good of you to let the *rest* of us in on it." The others laughed in agreement.

"You know," Chick said pensively, "the close timing worked out great. Making his opening statement at the debate, Lowell was able to steal the show with his good news. He not only saved face with his own campaign, but he one-upped the Republicans and even the news media in announcing that the Ashton case had been solved. Raymond Gifford was left playing catch-up all night—*without* resorting to the gay-adoption strategy."

I was circling the table, filling coffee mugs. "Thanks, Chick"—I paused behind him, resting a hand on his shoulder.

He shrugged. "That's what I'm here for—to defuse the opposing camp. It was close though. And sort of a gambit."

"When you got Blain on the phone last night," asked Neil, practically licking his lips, "what'd he say when you mentioned 'summer camp'?"

"Nothing—he was speechless. So I bluffed my way through, explaining that any antigay tactics on his part would look supremely hypocritical. I alluded to outing, but I didn't openly threaten him. And it worked—not a peep out of Raymond about the adoption issue."

"Thank God," said Carl, more and more the statesman. "Let's keep it a clean, honest, focused campaign, without trumped-up emotion or hysteria. That's how Lowell wants it, and I do too."

Chick allowed, "The squeaky-clean approach seems to be working. We got a nice goosing in the polls overnight."

Neil sighed. "I can see it coming, Rox. You're Springfield-bound. Somehow, I get the icky feeling we'll be seeing less and less of you."

She insisted, "That's nuts. You're my best friends."

But I knew Neil was right—Springfield was too distant to allow the frequent, impromptu visits we'd all come to enjoy. Now that Roxanne was married and Carl's political future looked promising, she'd be drifting out of our lives.

Chick must have sensed the melancholy Neil and I shared, so he threw us a bone: "*I'll* be back—often, I hope."

I grinned. "Alanna?"

"Well, I'll want to see *you* guys, of course. But yeah, once things calm down with the campaign—and Alanna gets her life back in order—I *shall* return. There's something there, between us. I feel it."

Wryly, Roxanne noted, "Your timing is impeccable, Chick. Her lover's in the slammer, and her husband's through with her."

Chick answered flatly, "Even on the rebound, I'm interested."

The back door cracked open. "Any coffee left?"

"Sure, Doug." "Morning, Sheriff." "Come on in."

Pierce strolled in, set a wrapped kringle on the table, and took the seat warmed by Thad. As I poured him some coffee, he reached to tear the waxed paper from the pastry, noting, "*That* one was just a little too close for comfort." He didn't need to explain that he was referring to the murder case, not the kringle.

"I'll second that." Carl blew steam from the top of his coffee.

Roxanne turned philosophical. "Did he really think he'd get away with it—winning the hand of his reluctant mistress by staging a deadly 'accident'?"

"Apparently," I said. "But don't forget, Dale's deeper motive was financial."

Neil reminded us, "The two classic murder motives—passion and greed."

"All wrapped up in one tidy package." Pierce began slicing wedges of the kringle. Inside the frosted pastry was a layer of glistening red—most promising. Everyone helped himself.

Roxanne looked over her shoulder to ask Barb, "Do I have time to slip upstairs and do some final packing before you serve that *fabulous* casserole?"

"Yup. I was just going to slide it into the oven. You've got a good half hour or so." The oven door opened with a creak.

Taking their cue from Roxanne, both Carl and Chick rose, deciding that they too would make use of this time to prepare for their departure.

As the three Illinoisans left the kitchen, each with a napkin and pastry in hand, the front doorbell rang. "I'll get it," Roxanne called from the hall, and a moment later, we heard voices raised in greeting. "They're in the kitchen," Roxanne told the visitor as she headed upstairs to the guest room.

Neil, Barb, Pierce, and I turned toward the doorway, listening to the approaching steps.

And in walked Whitney Greer, looking stylish in a camel-hair blazer; with the arrival of fall weather, he'd packed away the seersucker. "Good *morning*," he said with a bounce in his voice to match that in his step. "Hope I'm not intruding."

"Not at all, Whitney," said Neil.

"Have a chair," I offered.

Barb seemed suddenly agitated, fumbling with the coffeepot. "Let me find you a cup," she said, discombobulated, as if she'd forgotten which cupboard the cups were in.

"Thanks," said Whitney, "but I can't stay. Just thought I'd pop over." Lowering his voice, he told Barb, meaningfully, with a wink, "I have some news."

She froze, setting down the coffeepot. "Yes . . . ?"

His eyes shifted about the room. "Here?" he asked, unsure if he should speak in front of the rest of us.

Barb laughed. "*Yes*, Whit. What'd you find out?"

He paused, then blurted, "You're *in!*"

Barb trembled for a moment, hand to chest, before letting out an ecstatic, full-voiced whoop that could have doubled as a bloody-murder shriek of horror.

"*Hey*," yelled Chick from upstairs. "Anything wrong?"

Neil called back, "Don't think so. Just Barb." Enough said.

I asked, "Okay—now tell us—what in *hell* have you two been up to?"

Whitney opened his mouth to speak, but Barb took over: "You know, guys, that my first love has always been music, and when I finally picked up the clarinet again last year, I decided to get serious about it. Whitney's been a wonderful help, setting me up with a teacher, getting me into the orchestra—"

He interrupted, telling us, "Barb won the first chair by blind audition. I had nothing to do with it."

"Yeah, well," rejoined Barb, "he had *plenty* to do with the Peabody."

Neil and I looked at each other. Sensing what was coming, I asked, *"What?"*

Whitney nodded. "It's marvelous, isn't it? Yes, Barb has been admitted to the clarinet program at the Peabody Conservatory in Baltimore. I just got the inside word."

"My God." Neil rose, stepping to Barb, offering a hug.

She explained over his shoulder, "Whitney is a Peabody graduate, and he still has contacts there. He helped nudge along my application and audition tapes. His recommendation carried a lot of weight, apparently."

Whitney assured us, "Barb was admitted on her own merits. She's a highly skilled musician. If she decides to pursue a professional career, I have a hunch she'll know great success."

Neil held her at arm's length. "Barb will succeed at anything she sets her mind to. After all, she made it as a money manager working in Wall Street securities."

"Oh, please, gag me"—she stuck a finger down her throat. "Don't remind me." (It sounded like "doh-wee-*my*-mee.")

Pierce set aside his coffee, beaming. "Congratulations, Barb."

I rose, offering her a hug to match Neil's.

She looked into my eyes. "I'm not deserting you. Not really."

I smiled. "I know you're not. This housekeeping gig was never intended as a career. The deal was, you'd stay on till Thad left for college." I checked my watch, noting, "So we'll need you till noon."

She tweaked my cheek. "You've got me till *Christmas*, goofball. I won't enroll till second semester."

"Thank God," said Neil.

My sentiments exactly.

Pierce rose. "Sorry to break this up, but I've got a busy day downtown."

"Aww," whined Barb, "can't you stay for the egg-thing?"

"Sorry. Sounds great, but I need to run."

"Me too," said Whitney. "Just wanted to relieve the suspense."

After a round of farewells, repeated congratulations, and some dancing at the door, the sheriff and the orchestra manager were gone.

"Gosh," said Barb, getting hyper, "I've got a few *phone* calls to make. Can you guys watch the oven?" She was already through the doorway to her room.

"Sure," we told her. "Spread the news."

And her door thumped shut.

Neil and I turned to each other. The kitchen seemed eerily quiet. Suddenly, it was "just us." He gave a weak smile, as if he might cry.

I stepped to him, took him in my arms, and patted his back. It was all too much to deal with: Thad was moving to the West Coast, where he would study theater with the illustrious Claire Gray. Barb would soon be moving to the East Coast, "starting over," studying music at the prestigious Peabody Conservatory. Roxanne was heading back to Chicago, a married woman with farsighted ambitions for her new husband, the would-be lieutenant governor. And there stood Neil and I in the kitchen on Prairie Street—alone together.

I reminded him, "This is where we started, kiddo. You and me." And I held him all the tighter.

I felt as if we had reached the end of a long entrada.

It had begun five years earlier, in Chicago, when I was at the brink of forty and recurring flight dreams signaled a need for profound change in my life. I discovered it with Neil and have never once looked back. Some two years after we met, our love was tested when a hunky young intern at the *Chicago Journal* made eye contact with me, lingered in my fantasies, and ended up assisting me on that summer's biggest story. That same winter, our love was tested again when professional wanderlust brought me north to Wisconsin as publisher of the *Dumont Daily Register*. Before my first day on the job, though, the familiar body language of someone from my past triggered a chain of events that brought Thad into our lives and cast us in the unlikely role of parents. It was a struggle, but we managed to build a family— Thad, Neil, and I—getting beyond the name games that had vexed me with regard to our roles in this offbeat household. Nurturing Thad through his last two years of high school came to feel fulfilling and natural—to the three of us, but not to everyone. A particularly ugly incident occurred just a year ago, when Thad was involved in a summer-theater production and a fellow actor accused him of being our boy toy, precipitating a serious emotional slip. But we pulled together and pulled through it, and now, within hours, Thad would fly our nest, leaving behind his quiet hometown. Well—maybe not so quiet. Who'd have thought that sleepy, remote Dumont, Wisconsin, of all places, would become a political hot spot, the scene of events that could determine the next governor of Illinois?

Though my shared expedition with Neil—the courtship, the fledgling stages of commitment, and our whirlwind exercise in child rearing—had ended, the journey had not. After five years, our life together had barely begun.

As if reading my mind, Neil said simply, "We're home, Mark."

Stepping out of our embrace, I took his hands, just looking at him. "Never in my wildest dreams—and I've had a few—could I have imagined that we'd end up happily settled in a small town in central Wisconsin."

Neil shrugged. "Even city mice can adapt."

"God, we've even tried our hand at parenting."

He crossed his arms with mock defensiveness. "And I think we've been *reasonably* successful. Let's face it: Thad was a bit of a mess when we 'inherited' him. Now he's stepping into his own life, with stars in his eyes."

"Someday—who knows?—maybe you and I will step into the role of doting granddads, spoiling Thad's kids rotten."

"Doting granddads? Or Auntie Mames?" He sniffed something. "I think Barb's egg-thing is about ready."

Yes, there was cheese in the air. I asked, "Should I call everyone—one last, big breakfast on Prairie Street?"

"Give it a minute." Then Neil stepped near, folded an arm around me, and drew my face to his for a long, coffee-scented kiss.

I knew that morning that it would take us a while to adjust to an empty house, to the loss of the unconventional family we had so carefully constructed for Thad's benefit, as well as our own. Like Thad, like Barb, we'd be starting over, entering a new phase of our shared life. I was powerless to predict what uncertainties might lie ahead, but our love had been tested, and I knew that it would endure. We would always have each other.

And with each other, Neil and I were complete. ❑